I0693066

ALL THOUGHTS LAID BARE

Book 1 of the
Stellar Fragment Trilogy
A Rykolien Immigrants novel

By Warren Dunn

Published by Barry B. Connors

Cover art by Warren Dunn, with royalty-free elements from Shutterstock

Map of Rykol created with Inkarnate, used in accordance with their EULA, 2021

ISBN: 978-1-990275-31-9

for Joanne
my love

Acknowledgements

I read a lot, and my two favorite authors had a huge influence on me, especially when I was young.

This trilogy of books was greatly inspired by J.R.R. Tolkien's <u>Book of Lost Tales</u>, which sent me down a path creating a history of the vekorna for thousands of years before the RIs arrived. And so the memory globes were born.

In my teen years, I read everything Isaac Asimov that I could find, from short stories to novels and some non-fiction as well. The subtle use of telepathy for the art of control left a huge impact on me, and subconsciously led to Aderen and Kirina.

As always, I need to thank everyone who has supported my efforts at writing these stories. The people I interact with are genuinely interested and positive toward my books.

In particular, I thank Bob Dunn and Sandy Dunn, my two readers, for going through every page with an eye to detail (both the story and the words).

This is the first time I sent out a manuscript for impressions before publishing it, and I have beta reader

Khaiyah from The Spun Yarn and B. B. Garin from an Uncharted Magazine contest to thank for their impressions, which led to important changes in the story.

Special thanks go out to Joanne, André and Jacob for giving me the time to write, and the inspiration to do it well. I couldn't accomplish this without you.

And finally, another consistency through these books, as I start a new trilogy, a huge thanks to Barry Connors, who continues to give me the opportunity for publication.

Warren Dunn
November, 2025

Table of Contents

Terms and Characters

Unusual terms

extar vekornan exploratory spaceships

tigal-en a being who can speak mentally over long distances

prin-el second-in-command

lobomai fighting style developed by Kezim on Rykol

vend'ok octagonal hovering ground vehicle

The Races of Rykol

soraen the ancestral race of the vekorna and kolbs

vekorna blue-shell soraen variant

kolbs yellow-shell soraen variant

siims mutant offshoot of the vekorna (black shell)

rokels mutant offshoot of the kolbs (grey shell)

folems flower-like caretakers of ancient technology

loboms spiked ball caretakers of ancient technology

goses the original intelligent race of Rykol

Point of view characters in **bold**.

Humans

Arais

Doj	(M)	*Avenger*
Penagel	(M)	*Kamsar*
Wandel	(F)	*Kamsar*
Pinoa	(F)	*Alnevar*

Arai Descendants

Aderen	(M)	Jairon & Kym's son
Ret	(M)	Kezim & Yenine's grandson
Sarenie	(F)	Doj's granddaughter
Ketaris	(F)	Kezim, Yenine, Rametin & Javiam's granddaughter
Étar	(M)	Penagel's grandson
Akinuf	(F)	Wandel's granddaughter
Illian	(F)	5th generation from Vensimt & Jagarintal
Xeffeya	(F)	5th generation from Krefer & Jagarintal

Rykol

Egalinsor	(M)	First human born on Rykol
Nalimai	(F)	*Avenger*
Lusava	(F)	Firstborn Egalsan
Aneya	(F)	Second-born Egalsan
Nekken	(M)	Fourth-born Egalsan
Rogo	(M)	1st grandchild Egalsan
Orem	(M)	23rd grandchild Egalsan
Kuyi	(F)	24th grandchild Egalsan
Jye-Tan	(M)	1st great-grandchild Egalsan
Mai	(F)	2nd great-grandchild Egalsan

Vekorna

Tararnifal winged, tigal-en, Terran vekornan leader
Samlar   winged, tigal-en, extar commander
Kular   winged
Paknef   winged, shuttle pilot
Sebenet   winged, tigal-en, leader of first raider fleet
Dairnehy winged vekornan leader.
Punad   winged, tigal-en, prin-el
Danosh   winged
Ontral   wingless vekornan leader
Treklay   wingless human supervisor
Talmer   wingless human supervisor
Mlurat   wingless, old Rykol

Others

Arnatak   winged, kolb human liaison
Djaxtal   winged, kolb emissary
Thirp'inc winged, kolb emissary
Alirv (M) folem leader, white and purple
Persinjali siim from old Rykol
Flaorniti siim from old Rykol
Nirk (F) goses from old Rykol
Thof (M) goses from old Rykol

Arai Timeline

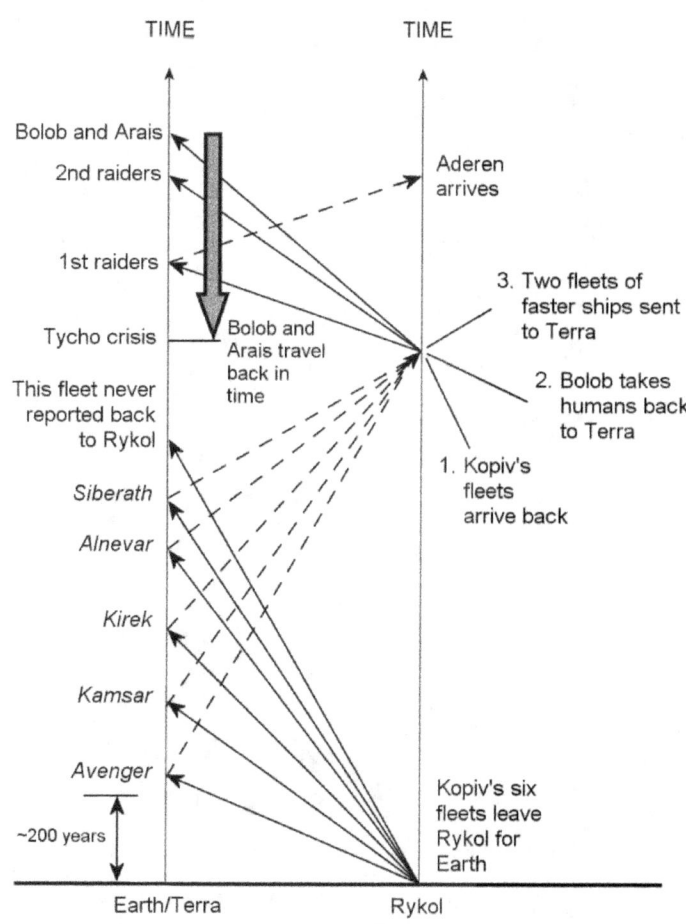

TIME

TIME

Bolob and Arais

2nd raiders

Aderen arrives

1st raiders

3. Two fleets of faster ships sent to Terra

Tycho crisis

Bolob and Arais travel back in time

2. Bolob takes humans back to Terra

This fleet never reported back to Rykol

1. Kopiv's fleets arrive back

Siberath

Alnevar

Kirek

Kamsar

Avenger

~200 years

Kopiv's six fleets leave Rykol for Earth

Earth/Terra

Rykol

Map of Rykol

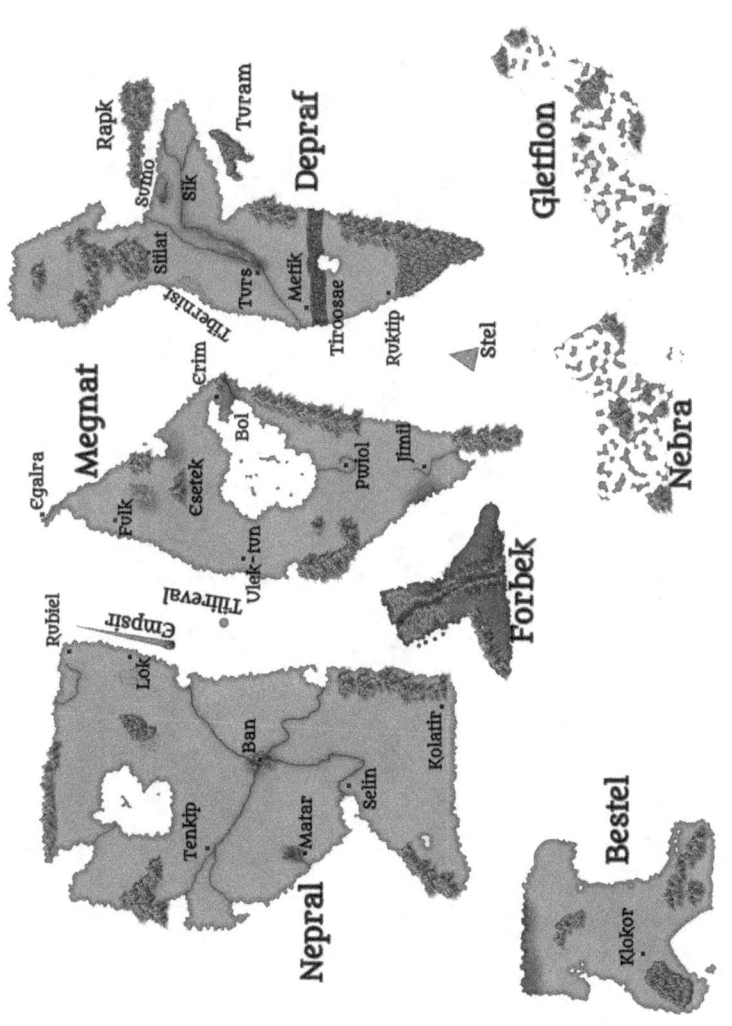

Nalimai's Personal Journal

We should have left with the others when we had the chance. We could be safe on Terra with Jairon and Kym, their fledgling telepathic son Aderen, and the rest of my friends. Instead, I stayed on Rykol with my husband and his mentor while the rest of the human crews were sent back.

My husband, who can influence people with a touch, wanted to stay so he could help the native vekorna reshape their planet.

At first they ignored us, as we built our floating science stations, studied the deadly oceans, the hidden deserts, and even the wrecked kolb islands in the south. We helped them create genetically enhanced grasses to seed this dying world, and engrossed ourselves in other promising experiments.

When Kopiv brought humans to Rykol four hundred years ago, five small ships kidnapped from Terra in different eras, it was to destroy his enemies, the kolbs. We did exactly that, but I know the real reason he wanted us.

The latest vekornan leader already knows my secret, for it's his, too. But when Dairnehy found the stellar fragment, he telepathically connected all minds on Rykol, and I thought it would be revealed. Thankfully, with everyone else's thoughts flowing at the same time, mine was hidden in the noise.

Through the fragment, I learned that Dairnehy sent two fleets to kidnap more humans from Terra. If successful, they should arrive back soon. He expects the new humans to be more pliable, and it's unlikely we will get a chance to influence them. They will be put to work destroying Dairnehy's new enemies, the wingless vekorna.

In the time since the wingless learned they were being slowly exterminated, war has descended again on Rykol, and we are once more caught in the middle. Science has stopped, genetics research is carefully controlled, and the world has grown much more dangerous.

Despite our best efforts, my family is drawn beyond the safety of the shield that envelopes our home, and to the stellar fragment. One of my sons died because of it, and a grandchild is obsessed.

I'm afraid it will tear the rest of us apart.

I should have left with the others when I had the chance.

Part I: The Raider Threat

1. Exercising Control

Heart beating with exertion and anticipation of what was inevitably to come, Aderen stopped at the door to the control sphere, legs floating out behind him as he held onto the handle, installed purely for human use.

The door was closed, and there were no guards. Why would there be, at a friendly meeting between allied vekorna? Sebenet had been invited to explain why he was at Terra, and while both sides were suspicious, there was never any thought of violence.

He had to go in before the others arrived. He'd left them at the shuttlebay so they didn't have to watch, so they would still trust him after what they saw him do.

It had been sixty years since he'd last tried this, to disastrous consequences. He already missed his cabin home in the middle of nowhere, sequestered from the thoughts of the world.

Ret and Sarenie had followed him. Their minds were clear as they navigated the corridors, only a couple of minutes behind. They were both too young to have last seen him in action, and he didn't want to shatter their naiveté. Sarenie was here to negotiate, while Ret thought he could protect them.

Neither had encountered hostile vekorna before.

Taking a breath, Aderen touched the control, also installed purely for human use. Vekorna opened these doors with a telepathic command that he couldn't duplicate.

The control sphere was silent, but Aderen's mind was suddenly on fire as the doors slid open, revealing the opposing forces inside. He froze on the threshold, unconsciously planting his feet on the transparent walkway where gravity held him. It had been a long time since he'd opened himself to this many minds, and he shuddered at the memory of that disaster.

He sensed Ret and Sarenie entering the hallway he'd just vacated. He couldn't be responsible if they got hurt.

The alien vekorna were not confined to the gravitational walkways, which were left over from a time when the wingless used to control these starships. Tararnifal hung in the air facing Sebenet, wings outstretched from his massive armored body, legs bent at both knees, upper and lower arms stretched out in front of him.

Sebenet matched his pose, his long vekornan wings also extended and twitching, meters apart from Tararnifal, but to all other appearances ready to pounce. The intense buzzing that Aderen felt in his mind confirmed that they were engaged in a telepathic contest. Tararnifal wouldn't have summoned him if he didn't feel threatened.

Before opening his mind to the struggle in the center of the starship's control sphere, Aderen glanced around at the other vekorna. Ten of Tararnifal's soldiers hung in the air near their control consoles. Aliens that he'd known for two hundred years were matched one for one with the newly arrived vekornan invaders.

Peaceful explanations had given way to accusations, and the threat of battle. All vekorna wore their full armor, a mottled pale blue that increased their already imposing bulk. The dominant triangular faceplates were created to keep out the heat and dryness of their homeworld, but also protected their sensor heads in battle. Nobody used heavy blasters in a starship, but the smaller wrist lasers strapped to their middle arms, just as deadly to a vekornan, were each pointed at the other side.

"Have you arrived?" Jairon's voice came into his head, the kennis implant in his brain much less efficient than telepathy, but all humanity could create to mimic it.

"Yes, I'm here," Aderen responded to his father, and put a block on further communications, directing them to Ret and Sarenie, just outside the door. He couldn't be distracted, and Jairon would understand.

Beyond the vekorna, blue-green Terra shone through the screens that lined the interior surface of the giant control sphere. Everyone he loved was down there. To the other side, Moon was only a crescent.

Sebenet's eight starships, extars newly arrived from Rykol, were marked with vekornan symbols. They were locked in their own frozen struggle with Tararnifal's three extars, which had been protecting Terra for the last two centuries.

Smaller human spaceships, fighters and merchant vessels, were outlined by squares, unidentified. Aderen expanded his awareness but the minds behind the symbols were too far away to resolve. All would be threatened if he failed.

Aderen took a deep breath and opened his mind. The buzzing intensified, and he readied for the onslaught of vekornan voices and emotions, forced himself to hold fast, to remain open for the first time in decades. Seclusion hadn't readied him for this moment, but he remembered how.

Must leave – fulfill our mission – Bolob dead – wrong – the plan – Rykol needs them – solve our own problems – winged – stick to the plan – the winged know – humans will not solve this – must complete the mission – no!

The thoughts of the two vekorna were jumbled, chaotic, and moving too fast for Aderen to comprehend. He closed himself off again and fell to his knees, holding up a hand to prevent Ret and Sarenie from coming to his aid. He had some context to the ongoing vekornan argument, but needed a moment to regain his composure. He drew on lessons from the past.

He scanned the minds of the other vekorna in the control sphere. Both sides radiated determination. They would fight to the death to complete their respective –contradictory– missions. Not a shot had been fired, but discussions had gone downhill quickly since Sebenet's fleet arrived at Terra.

Entering Tararnifal's mind, he sensed the Terran vekornan leader countering Sebenet's mental thrusts, defending the orders that Bolob had impressed on him before his sacrifice: to keep humanity safe and away from Rykol.

I have done all I can to dissuade Sebenet, Tararnifal mentally responded to Aderen's probing. **The situation is about to turn violent, and we are too few vekorna to defend you. Can you do it?**

I need to know how you failed, Aderen said telepathically. He'd been very young the first time he'd taken control of a person's mind, and hadn't understood the cost. Two centuries later, having withdrawn from society to restore his confidence after the telepathic disaster, he was now called to defend humanity.

Tararnifal's alien thoughts poured into Aderen's mind, and he swung his legs around to cross them, sitting on the transparent walkway, tempering the flow. Vekorna had dozens of senses on their five-sided sensor heads, far more than humans could interpret, even with a kennis implant. It took a lot of effort to dismiss the ones he didn't understand, and filter those he could.

The two vekorna had been locked in this mental battle for the better part of a Terran day. No wonder Terra's military couldn't get any information.

Tararnifal understood Sebenet's mission too well. It was similar to the missions that had kidnapped Aderen's parents, and a total of five human crews, over a millennium. Soon after Bolob left Rykol to return them to Terra, the new vekornan leader sent a fleet of faster extars to arrive before him. They were here to kidnap more humans for their wars, betraying Bolob.

The new vekorna refused to accept time travel, which was how Bolob and Tararnifal came to be on Terra two hundred years before Sebenet's faster extars arrived. Aderen dismissed the debate, involving senses he didn't have. He sensed that the obstinate Sebenet wouldn't back down.

Closing himself completely to Tararnifal, Aderen stood and turned to Sebenet, leader of the expedition to kidnap more humans for Rykol's wars. Physically identical to the

Terran vekorna, even to the outstretched wings that matched Tararnifal's pose, only his mental signature distinguished him.

Carefully, Aderen probed his thoughts, but he was clumsy despite his preparations. Sebenet's attention was drawn to him, and his mental voice came with the buzz that vekornan telepathy produced.

You have opened humanity's minds. They will be more valuable than in the last war.

"You must leave Terra," Aderen said out loud, and thrust his mental might with the associated thought. "You must not fight your fellow vekorna here." He gestured at Terra, the blue-green orb that dominated the control sphere screens.

Winged fighting against winged –we've never fought such a confrontation before, said Tararnifal.

Yes we have, a long time ago, Sebenet replied.

We are not kolbs, to fight in factions.

No, you are something else, Sebenet said. **You are another kind of divarication, distanced from Rykol. The soraen split was ideological, the one that created siims was technical. You have changed, Terran vekornan. I do not like what I see.**

Still, Aderen hesitated. He didn't want to take control of the vekornan mind, for fear of unintended side effects. He suppressed memories of the time in Legionnaire Dalpah's home with a shake of his head. He wouldn't repeat that mistake.

Dots of light appeared from each of Sebenet's orbiting extars, streaming out in lines.

"You've launched shuttles," Aderen said.

At a mental command, Sebenet's vekorna moved to take control of the nearest consoles in the control sphere. Tararnifal's vekorna moved to intercept. Where they'd been stuck in a mental battle for the past day, they now wrestled in physical contact. Still, no shots were fired, as the stigma against killing another winged remained strong.

The result could be dangerous for Aderen and the other humans behind him. Sebenet's vekorna never reached the command consoles, but now vekornan pairs flailed about.

Aderen reluctantly located each of the vekorna with his own mind, risked opening up again. He connected to all of Sebenet's vekorna simultaneously, taking control of their muscles. He'd refined his technique over the twenty decades since that time in the Legion, where he'd mentally immobilized the entire Terran government as a child.

As Aderen held the invaders immobile with a mental command, Tararnifal's crew extricated themselves from the struggle, pushing their floating adversaries together.

Motion at the entrance to the control sphere momentarily distracted him. Sarenie quietly disapproved, but Ret's thoughts were horrified at what he saw. Barely holding onto the vekornan minds, Aderen went through the mental exercises he'd perfected sixty years earlier, when many more people had had that same look, those same thoughts. While his mind threatened to shut down, he kept it open, forced it to obey, concentrating on the necessity of what he was doing. Maybe there was another way, but Aderen didn't see it, didn't have time to see it.

He shut out the humans behind him, and focused on the

vekorna before they slipped his control. As Tararnifal's vekorna took hold of their immobilized attackers, Aderen entered Sebenet's mind.

The tigal-en on each of my shuttles are ready to take command of your extars, Sebenet said to Tararnifal. Aderen wondered if the tigal-en, who had longer telepathic reach than regular vekorna, could remotely enter mental commands into the control sphere consoles. Had security against this kind of situation ever been expected?

In that moment, Aderen slipped deeper into Sebenet's defenses, blocking his telepathy. It wasn't enough just to hold him prisoner, freezing his muscles; he had to be subdued, unable to give telepathic commands to his soldiers.

For good measure, now that the immediate area was secure, Aderen reached out and blocked telepathic communication from all of Sebenet's vekorna in the control sphere. It was getting easier –maybe too easy, he thought.

Sebenet tried to resist him, but he dove into the spaces between the vekornan's thoughts, looking… searching… He realized that he was stretched too far, and had to hope that the tigal-en in Sebenet's shuttles wouldn't act of their own accord. Memories surfaced.

Rykol was two hundred light-years from Terra, but due to their high velocity, those inside the extars had experienced less than twenty relativistic years of travel. Sebenet had spent only half of that in cryo-sleep.

Further back, Sebenet was leaving Rykol. Before that, he was meeting with Shilan, leader of all vekorna, and Dairnehy, his prin-el, second in command.

The two were at odds. Shilan wanted to keep to Bolob's Plan. Dairnehy, who had opposed human involvement throughout the kolb war, was now advocating that Bolob was wrong to send them away. What had changed? Sebenet didn't know, but Dairnehy won the argument.

Like the missions before them, the two new fleets would arrive at Terra staggered in time to take advantage of human technological advances. Sebenet's extars traveled faster than Pranef's second fleet, which would take another two hundred years to get here. They were both to arrive at Terra before Bolob's slower ships, unaware that Bolob had traveled back in time.

In seconds, Aderen replayed the memory of Sebenet's mission multiple times. This was the key moment. The instructions were not explicit. Bring humans back to Rykol. He softened Sebenet's interpretation of the events, as he'd done with Legionnaire Dalpah and countless others over the centuries.

Compromise, for the stability of Rykol, said Aderen, strengthening his hold, ensuring he didn't repeat old mistakes. **Humans are not slaves.**

Tararnifal understood, looking into Aderen's surface thoughts. **We will bring humans to Rykol,** Tararnifal said. **But it will be of their own volition.**

Volunteers? responded Sebenet, perplexed.

Humanity is spread among many beliefs and desires. Some will want to go to Rykol. We will let them decide.

I must fill eight extars with specialists to help keep Rykol stable. Will there be enough volunteers?

Aderen pushed on his mental pathways, making him

more pliable, open to accepting the suggestion. His mental energy was already fading.

We will find the specialists, and you will return to Rykol with volunteers, Tararnifal said.

Again, Aderen pushed, making the vekornan mental pathways more accepting of Tararnifal's suggestion.

Sebenet was unsure. He was afraid to fail his mission, so Aderen continued to soften his memories until his orders, so certain since leaving Rykol, were now open to interpretation.

Volunteers might be acceptable, said Sebenet hesitantly. **If we can find sufficient numbers. Our primary goal is to make Rykol stable.**

We will find them, said Tararnifal.

Aderen found the mental pathways that would make Sebenet believe it. He was treading into familiar and dangerous territory. Any farther, and Legionnaire Dalpah's tragedy would be repeated.

We will follow Bolob's example, said Sebenet. **The three humans he left on Rykol stayed of their own free will.**

Ensuring Sebenet had genuinely accepted Tararnifal's proposal, Aderen released his hold on the vekornan muscles, giving them back control over their motor functions.

He reached out with his mind to Sebenet's tigal-en, waiting for orders in the shuttles. His reach was limited and fading, but they were also reaching in this direction, and he identified them one by one, softening their resolve. None could argue Sebenet back to his original course.

To Aderen alone, Tararnifal said, **This is only the first of two fleets. We must prepare for the second fleet, but what to do about volunteers?**

Aderen didn't dare to look back at Ret and Sarenie, who were still gaping at him. It was the same look he'd seen a hundred times, as people realized he was different.

The moment he saw their reactions, his decision was made.

I will return to Rykol, and make sure no extars come to Terra ever again.

2. <u>Saying Goodbye</u>

The thin sheet separated them, just the way Monera liked it after they'd made love. She lay on top of him, head resting against his shoulder. Aderen breathed in the scent of her dark hair as he felt her heart beating in time with his own.

He couldn't resist her magic touch, ever since she'd grown into a woman and forced her way into his life. She'd discovered his secret long before anyone outside his small, close-knit group.

"Come with me to Rykol," he whispered, and the rhythm of her heartbeat suddenly went out of synch with his. She lifted her head and shook it, pale blue eyes hollow, hair shifting like a halo.

"Just make love to me," Monera responded.

"Again?"

"Forever," she smiled and lifted her body from his, rolling off him and pulling him on top. The sheet slid out from between them naturally.

Aderen caressed her pale skin and kissed her lips, then they were one again, like they used to be, when protecting their families from human threats was all that mattered. It was impossible to leave her behind as he quelled unrest from the sidelines, and she became his anchor.

He felt guilty, but from the emotions she was pushing onto him, she wasn't. He'd shown up at Monera's doorstep after ensuring Sebenet accepted the altered mission, evading the threat of vekorna raiding Terra for human slaves. The look of horror on Ret's expression was burned into his mind, like the reactions he used to get.

Their communication wasn't verbal, and in the brief moment when he stood at her door, he'd emptied himself into her, emotions, thoughts, and ambitions. When he told her he had to return to Rykol, she'd pulled him in, radiating panic, desperation, and finally love.

Without speaking, she knew he wanted her to come with him, to see the planet where her parents fell in love, and where he was born.

Aderen imagined that this was the way vekorna talked to each other. As far as he knew, he and Monera were the only two humans capable of this. She wasn't telepathic like him, couldn't control minds, but she could sense emotions, and project hers onto him.

Their lovemaking transcended the traditional sense of touch. Aderen could feel Monera's heart beating in his own chest, could feel the effect of his fingertips on her skin.

Entering Monera's mind, he saw her love, but also her hidden anxiety. This was what had distanced them from each other two decades ago. It had scared her then, and still did. But now she had added responsibilities. She needed to stay on Terra.

That dissipated as she projected rising emotion. While their bodies moved in time, their minds danced together. It felt like two stars entangled as one, sharing heat and fire, and exploding –sharing atmospheres, joining coronas. He held her mind and she let go.

For minutes, he didn't know where his body ended and hers began. They were literally one, completely entangled. They would always be one.

They stopped breathing, their hearts beating once, twice, three times, no more. Aderen kept them alive as their bodies were ready to burst, unable to hold onto so much emotion. He held Monera so she didn't split apart, kept blood flowing so her brain didn't starve. Their lungs were full of air, so he pushed the oxygen into her bloodstream, and felt the wave of warmth transfer from his own lungs.

Seeing her determination to stay on Terra, even as he left, tore Aderen apart. He knew what she wanted from this encounter, but he was reluctant to respond. She had a happy family now; how would a child from their union affect them?

Yet how could he deny her, either? She was breaking his heart by staying, but it wasn't the first time. It might be the last.

She wasn't physically ready, but he could change that, manipulate an ovum into position. He didn't ask, simply checked her mind to confirm she really wanted this. She was committed to staying behind, and desperately wanted a part of him to stay with her. Her response was another wave of emotion, of love, and he concentrated on manipulating their inner selves to comply.

Finally, Monera gasped a breath on her own again, and her heart fluttered and resumed its rhythm. Aderen released his control, and she withdrew all but a tendril of emotion from him.

"I love you," she breathed, but her inner self held doubts. He was shocked to note that she believed she was never enough for him. He wanted to respond that she was always enough, but held back, allowing her privacy. It would embarrass her, and ruin the moment they shared.

Instead, he responded, "I love you too. Come with me."

Monera put a hand over his mouth, as if that would stop his insistent question. "Stop asking me," she said, her voice overwrought, tears in her eyes. "I'm not ready to leave my home."

Her home was suspiciously empty today, as if she'd known he was coming to her, and she didn't want complications.

He rolled onto his side, and she followed him. Touching her cheek, he said, "Okay." The determination he'd felt in her mind was still there, and nothing could ever compel him to change it. He'd done all he could, but it wasn't enough.

They kissed, her lips meeting his greedily, tears running from their eyes.

When their passion subsided again, they lay face to face, their breath mixing, close enough that his eyes couldn't focus. Hand on his waist, she asked, "Why are you leaving so quickly? What happened that you finally want to run away?"

"I'm not running away," he said defensively, but the moment he said it, his emotion was reflected back, by the one woman who could ever show him who he was, the only one he could ever love. Her face softened as she saw the realization hit him. "It was the look on their faces," he admitted, and cast his eyes down, cheeks flushing.

Monera touched his face, held it in her palm. She wasn't radiating emotions now. She understood, had helped him when his manipulation of the Legionnaire had gone wrong. She knew it had all come flooding back, and left him to sort it out on his own.

"Rykol won't change that," she finally said.

"But the temptation to alter minds will be less."

"Are you sure?" She looked him in the eyes and added, "You are going there to change the minds of an entire species. It will no longer be temptation –it will be a mandate."

He nodded. She wondered if he was running away from her. How could she think that after spending the afternoon with him, more intimate than any two humans had ever been?

"One more time," he said. "Then never again."

She watched him closely, wearing down his inner strength. "Maybe Rykol will finally help you realize who you are. More than just a manipulator who needs to hide away." She nodded, as if agreeing with her assessment. Changing the subject before he could defend his inner turmoil, she asked, "Who is going with you?"

"We've chosen twelve volunteers. Your parents and

mine are staying here."

Their fathers had been among the first crew kidnapped and taken to Rykol to serve in the vekornan wars. Their mothers had been taken hundreds of years later. By traveling at different speeds, most of the abducted crews had arrived on Rykol at the same critical point in the war with the kolbs.

She nodded. "Old Arais and new?"

He never thought any of the original Rykolien Immigrants, now called Arais, would go back to Rykol, but he was wrong.

"Yes, Doj and Penagel were first to volunteer. Wandel will go, too; I think she still feels lost on Terra. Pinoa will be my prime negotiator, and if she can succeed, I won't need to do anything."

"Ret and Sarenie?" she asked, giving him a skeptical look.

"Of course." He smiled, but it was grim. He could have influenced their younger minds to stay behind, especially after Ret's unspoken condemnation in the control sphere.

"But he would know you changed his mind," Monera said, following his thoughts the way only she could.

Aderen nodded. "Yes."

"And this way he would know you *didn't* change his mind."

"Only if he believes he would feel the change."

"Use his negative energy to make yourself stronger." He nodded, not sure he could do that again. "So Sarenie is going with him?" she asked.

Aderen forced himself to look directly into her eyes.

"Yes, as my second negotiator."

Their relationship had been as tumultuous as Aderen and Monera's, though neither of them had any extraordinary senses. It could be the opening Monera was looking for. He allowed himself just a little hope.

Except that she wasn't waiting for an opening to join him at Rykol. She looked away, shaking her head.

Her inner voice was saying "no", over and over again. Monera wiped a tear from her eye.

"They'll have to be open to sharing if you set up a viable human community on Rykol."

He frowned, not wanting to broach that subject. If it came to genetic diversity, he would also have to contribute, the same way he'd just tried to contribute to Monera's legacy.

She touched his nose. "Don't be like that. I'm sure plenty of girls on the mission will want you." She said it playfully, but it ruined the romance of the moment.

"I'm not sure we'll stay," he answered.

Raising her eyebrows, Monera said, "Don't be silly. You'll go all that way just to change Shilan's mind, and then come back again? I'll be a very old woman by the time you return –much older than you are now, if I have enough Rykol-water in my blood." Her eyes became serious. "I won't wait for you. Don't wait for me."

She rolled on top of him again, and they made love one last time, but the finality of her words haunted him until Monera pulled the sheet up over him, the way he liked it. They fell asleep in each other's arms, and when he left, it was with a smile that, if not happy, was content.

He knew he'd never see her again, but they held contact for a long time after he left.

3. Running Away

The solar system was receding, a bunch of brighter stars among much fainter stars. Terra's sun was still by far the brightest in the extar's control sphere as the starship moved away, but in Aderen's mind, one was brighter.

Monera had opened herself fully to him again, her way of reluctantly saying goodbye. He thought her uncertainty would fall toward coming along, but she remained steadfast. It broke both their hearts, but there was nothing more they could do. They'd made their decisions. No human ship could catch up with Sebenet's extars now; they'd left their escort far behind.

Sebenet hovered over the transparent walkway in the center of the control sphere, motionless and once again face-to-face with Tararnifal. The conversation was not civil, but there was no longer any threat of violence. Tararnifal faced a long voyage back to Rykol, deflecting Sebenet's blame.

Several eyestalks peeked through the slits in Sebenet's triangular faceplate toward Aderen. He knew the danger Aderen presented, and that the sparsity of humans was Aderen's fault.

The control sphere was quiet except for Ret and Sarenie's murmuring. The rest of the humans had left for their quarters, but Ret made no secret that he was watching Aderen, daring him to manipulate the mind that found his ability revolting. He didn't realize that Aderen would never force anybody to like him. He tried to put the man out of his mind, allow him to find his own way.

Thankfully, Aderen was distracted by the bright star that lay in the direction of Terra, but he listened in on the silent vekornan conversation, trying to get a sense of this new, hastily planned mission.

We should not be leaving with empty extars, Sebenet said telepathically, keeping three of his eyestalks extended in Aderen's direction. **We could have stayed longer and pressed harder for volunteers. Twelve humans will not satisfy Shilan and Dairnehy's needs.**

Stability will come to Rykol by stopping war, and by ending the desire to use outside help, Tararnifal reminded him. **The volunteers were specially selected to stop vekornan missions to Terra, not to participate in upcoming wars.**

There was a long pause, during which the buzzing in Aderen's mind lessened considerably. Then Sebenet said, **That is counter to my mission. Stability will come by preparing a large number of humans for the upcoming conflict. We should not have left until that goal was satisfied.**

The vekornan's surface thoughts were reeling with confusion toward Aderen's role alongside Tararnifal, accompanied by guilt for succumbing to Tararnifal's suggestions so easily.

Tararnifal's best bet now was to show Sebenet that the original mission was unreasonable.

A large number of volunteers, or abducted humans like those of the five original crews, would make no

difference to Rykol, Tararnifal said.

They helped exterminate the kolbs, Sebenet protested.

The kolbs destroyed their two minor continents without human intervention.

A strategic error because we accelerated our attack, Sebenet said. **We were able to rush in because of human strategies and innovations. If not, the kolbs would have had time to deploy their weapons against us.**

Tararnifal hesitated, moving his sensor head side-to-side, then acknowledged, **We learned haste from humans, perhaps surprising the kolbs, but that is not what destroyed the two minor continents.**

Wings twitching, Tararnifal turned away from Sebenet. **I must contact Mekarifal before our speed is too great for communication.**

They were already out of range of the fleet's telepathy-augmenting crystals, but even normal communications had limitations. Traveling almost at the speed of light, the eight extars would be able to interact with each other, but not the outside universe.

As the new vekornan leader on Terra, Mekarifal now had a mission. It would have been useful to leave most of Sebenet's extars behind to help him confront the second fleet in two hundred years, but Sebenet refused, and Aderen was reluctant to make further changes to his mind.

Intently watching the two vekorna, Aderen ignored Ret's gaze, which was boring into the back of his head. There was a reason why Aderen only made minor mental changes, even beyond the disaster that precipitated his withdrawal from society. At first, when he was very young, he didn't understand why people looked at him strangely. Then he realized that they knew he was responsible for their confusion, even though they were unaware of the change.

Avoiding Ret's surface thoughts, Aderen turned to Sarenie and said, "You are both exhausted, and should get some rest. Cryo-sleep can be tough if you're too tired."

"You first," said Ret, staring back at the solar system.

Aderen sighed and faced the same way. He could barely detect Monera's empathy. Maybe Terra was better this way, left as if Sebenet's raiders had never arrived.

Their attention turned to the hologram of Mekarifal that appeared in the center of the platform between the two vekorna. The new leader of the Terran vekorna stood with wings half unfurled; they served no purpose under Terra's full gravity.

"We are passing beyond communications speed," said Tararnifal. "This is our last chance to speak."

"Our leadership transfer is complete," Mekarifal responded. "The humans are making plans to protect Terra. Before the second fleet arrives, we will train a much stronger military force."

Sebenet was silent, his surface thoughts betraying his disagreement, but he remained pliable to Tararnifal's suggestions.

"The Arais are getting involved?"

"Kezim has always been involved," Mekarifal reminded him. "But he will become even more so."

At the mention of Monera's father, Aderen's attention was drawn back to her emotional beacon. It was almost imperceptible now, as they accelerated close to the speed of light. It was amazing that he could still feel her across this distance, farther than they'd ever tried before.

Not able to use words, Aderen sent a pulse of love across their connection. He hoped she'd receive it. He waited a long time, but even when Mekarifal's hologram faded, he hadn't received a response.

Aderen left the control sphere, nodding to Sarenie, ignoring Ret. Sarenie gave him a worried look, which he understood, but didn't know how to address. It wasn't worth arguing now, when they would just pick it up again after twenty years of cryo-sleep.

Best to leave that to Tararnifal and Sebenet, who would argue and discuss the mission through the night and beyond, maybe for the entire journey to Rykol.

He navigated the corridors until he got back to the human rooms, and thought about the team he'd assembled. It was missing one key element, but he had to forget about Monera now. When they awoke from cryo-sleep, they would be at Rykol. Two hundred years would pass outside the extar, but due to the effects of relativity, those on the ship would only feel twenty.

They would spend all of it in cryo-sleep, yet by the time they arrived, they had to have a plan. He had to have a plan.

Part II: Planetfall

5. The Thinking Room

Vekorna didn't belong on Terra. Bolob had known it when he stayed, sacrificing himself to save the planet from Tycho's terrorist weapon. It was a truth Tararnifal had faced every day as Terran vekornan leader, and except for the fish, he was glad to be gone. He wondered why he'd stayed, even after the governing Legion ordered all vekorna to leave.

Two hundred stellar revolutions later, Sebenet arrived at Terra with a small fleet of extars, his mission to kidnap humans for war against the wingless vekorna. Was that what had inspired Tararnifal to stay on Terra, perhaps a side effect of time travel? Nobody could have predicted that they would go through the wormhole and move so far back in time.

He knew that there was another version of himself out there, traveling the stars between Rykol and Terra, bringing the four remaining human crews back to their homeworld with Bolob. Those vekorna hadn't encountered the wormhole yet. Paradoxically, he'd now left Terra before arriving, though he had lived there for two hundred revolutions. Could there be a resonance between the two of him, allowing him to sense the raider fleets through time?

If I had a choice, I would have brought Mekarifal and all the remaining vekorna back to Rykol with us, Tararnifal said, looking at the red stars in the center of the control sphere's display. Emprok was strong, and provided Rykol with life-giving heat and light. Alpro had been dying for as long as the vekorna could remember.

You *did* have a choice, Sebenet said, fluttering his wings as he settled into the center of the control sphere with Tararnifal. **There was no need to leave your vekorna on Terra to prepare for the second fleet. You forced my mission to fail, but their fate will be worse.**

Tararnifal sensed an undercurrent to Sebenet's mental voice, a continuous searching for Aderen's presence since being awakened from cryo-sleep. His fear of Aderen was stronger, and Tararnifal wondered if cryo-sleep had encouraged it to grow based on memories of being immobilized in this very spot.

It was necessary, Tararnifal said. **The two fleets were sent in secret to undermine Bolob at Terra. The missions to Terra must stop.**

All extar commanders had been replaced by Tararnifal's tigal-en, something else Sebenet resented. The surface thoughts of his vekorna were under constant surveillance, to avoid plots that could doom Aderen's mission.

It was unfortunate that Aderen hadn't manipulated Sebenet to be completely subservient, and fade out of the mission completely. Tararnifal didn't have the energy to watch over him every moment.

Sebenet responded, **I was assured that our missions were necessary, but was not given the reasons.**

The two vekorna connected telepathically, sharing senses other than thought. Sebenet's surface thoughts held no deceit, though a skilled tigal-en could make it seem so. He was convinced that humans were the key to stability on Rykol. Maybe Aderen had overly-strengthened that part of his mission.

Tararnifal didn't move, except for the occasional twitch of his wings to remain centered in the control sphere. The planets of his home solar system and their twin suns moved relative to the background stars as the extar advanced.

We must turn our thoughts to Rykol, he said, not entirely satisfied. It had been easier when Sebenet was in cryo-sleep, leaving Tararnifal alone with his Terran vekorna in the blackness of interstellar space. **Sensors at the Rolm lunar base should soon detect our extars.**

Then I will have to convince Shilan that I have fulfilled my mission, even though we did not fill our extars to capacity.

We will first rendezvous with Rykol's patrols, said Tararnifal, wearying of Sebenet's complaints. **It is those vekorna we will need to convince.**

It would have been easier if you had not dumped the crystals, Sebenet said.

You would have been tempted to use them in secret, Tararnifal responded. The telepathy-enhancing crystals were floating in the vastness of space beyond Terra's solar system. He wondered if their resonance would cause Bolob to stop on the way to Terra, delaying their arrival by a Terran century. **I will control our initial contact.**

Tararnifal guided his senses to the other vekorna in the control sphere and queried Samlar, commander of this extar.

No threats detected, Samlar reported. **The solar system remains clear of zonguan grids**. The warlike zonguans had not been seen for more than a generation, but he kept the extars ready in case of attack.

On the immersive walls of the control sphere, the bright suns faded, allowing the visible planets to brighten. One flashed, almost side-by-side with Rykol, though the zonguan planet was much closer to the suns than their destination.

I am not aware of any grid attacks from TenSik between your departure and my own, said Sebenet.

Bolob and I found the planet abandoned when we went to make peace, just before leaving for Terra, Tararnifal said. **We left patrols there.**

I cannot detect vekornan patrols anywhere in the solar system, Samlar responded.

Curious, Sebenet flicked his wings and dove to a lower console. Suspicious, Tararnifal turned in slow circles, opening his senses to the control sphere's information.

He was tired of always being on alert for danger, longing instead for space exploration, as he'd done before humans arrived. He wanted a place to be free on his own extar, and extended one eyestalk curiously toward TenSik, the planet apparently abandoned by the zonguans.

Returning to the central platform, Sebenet said, **We cannot detect any artificial objects in interplanetary space.**

Where were the vekornan patrols?

*   *   *

The last leg of their journey provided Tararnifal with one last chance to reinforce their updated mission to Sebenet. In the privacy of the extar's thinking room, they shared senses, communicating far faster than possible with verbal or even telepathic speech. Such communication was superfluous, but provided a catalyst for their other senses.

I will not interfere, though it is my duty, said Sebenet, weightless, his outstretched wings barely twitching to keep him on the edge of the sixth platform. **You interfered with Shilan's mission; he will punish you.**

I will do what is necessary to give Pinoa and Sarenie time to negotiate, Tararnifal said.

While Aderen controls their bodies, responded Sebenet, jumping up to the seventh platform. **The human plan is flawed. I saw his limits.**

Yes, it is flawed, but they have options, Tararnifal said, gaging the other's reaction. He didn't seem to realize that Aderen had made him more susceptible to Tararnifal's authority. He jumped down to the fourth level, wings fluttering to propel him through the central shaft. **Humans prefer to negotiate first, knowing that a defeated enemy is still an enemy. Through negotiation, there is less chance of later retaliation.**

Immediately pushing off to the highest of the nine platforms, Tararnifal relished the feeling of weightlessness, wondering why he'd never built a thinking room on Terra. As on Rykol, his wings would have been of little use, but the movement circulated blood to their brains, protected deep inside their chest cavity, and stimulated thoughts.

Shilan is not your enemy, Sebenet said, dropping one platform. **You aligned with humans, and you chose to further their agenda. I don't think the specialists we brought will be enough for the stability we need.**

I aligned with Bolob's mission, Tararnifal corrected him. **As prin-el, Shilan was second to both Bolob and**

Kopiv, both exceptional leaders. He will listen to the humans.

He is unduly influenced by his own prin-el. Dairnehy has already decided their fate, Sebenet replied.

Sebenet wasn't wrong. It would be difficult to convince Dairnehy to listen without the threat of force, when he only thought of them as slaves for the upcoming war. It was interesting that Sebenet felt otherwise.

Shilan and Dairnehy's experience with humans is limited.

Dairnehy worked with Doj's macrobots to seek out and destroy kolbs, Sebenet countered, jumping across to the next level.

Among others, Tararnifal thought. It was not generally known, but Bolob had believed that Dairnehy modified the macrobots to target wingless vekorna, too, including Kopiv, the vekornan leader at the time.

We were not instructed to search out military strategists at Terra, Sebenet continued. **Shilan wanted a cross-section of humanity, like Kopiv before him.**

It was not those with military backgrounds that helped most, Tararnifal agreed, receiving context through other senses. **All contributed to the war.**

Metelek fighter-craft came from human analysis of our fighting techniques, said Sebenet. **Macrobots covered a reconnaissance need, while humans used the exploding armor you described to take over an extar.**

To its demise, Tararnifal reminded him.

Only because they were short-sighted. Humans created many innovations during their short stay on

Rykol. That is undoubtedly what prompted our mission to Terra.

Bolob had planned a silent transition from mixed to a winged-only vekornan species, Tararnifal said. **There was no need for new strategy or innovations. All was set.**

Then something went wrong. Shilan must have discovered a flaw in Bolob's Plan, and prepared for war.

Yet he sent you and Pranef to Terra in secret, to arrive before Bolob. That indicates our leader had something to hide, not a flaw in Bolob's Plan. Only our time travel at Terra exposed this.

Tararnifal extended his wings to their full span, and spiraled down to the second level. It took just as little effort to move down as up in the absence of gravity.

We'll know soon, Sebenet said. **We enter orbit in days, though we have no escort, and no way to communicate such vast distances.**

Tararnifal agreed, but every moment closer to Rykol increased their chances of success.

That is highly unusual. Something else is wrong.

6. Getting Away

Every extar had a sweet spot, a location where a person could sit and be at peace, without the sensation of movement, attenuating the buzz that vekornan mental speech produced in the human mind.

Ironically, on this extar it was in the corner of a busy shuttlebay ceiling. Weightless, Aderen sat in the air, cross-legged in the corner, watching vekorna prepare their shuttles and fighters for what might come next.

The six human metelek fighter-craft were easy to identify, smaller to snugly fit a human, and painted pitch black with four yellow stripes. Unlike the blue vekornan vehicles, these didn't require a telepathic interface. The physical controls had been ripped out, though, so they didn't interfere with the virtual ones accessed through the human kennis implant.

Aderen didn't know why the mental buzz of the vekorna didn't reach him here, when he could feel it only a few meters away. The corner, in a ship where most rooms were round, was a mental blind spot.

It gave him limited peace, like his refuge back on Terra. The noise of reentering society was sometimes too much.

The blind spot couldn't relieve him of anxiety, though. He'd been in cryo-sleep for twenty subjective years, but in reality, the extar had been traveling for two centuries near the speed of light. Now that they were approaching Rykol, the second raider fleet was due to arrive at Terra. Sebenet's defeat had been difficult for Aderen, but it occurred with neither bloodshed nor destruction. Diplomacy had failed, yet Aderen managed to turn the tide single-handedly. There was nobody with his power left at Terra to counter the second fleet. As far as he knew, only Monera had any kind of abnormal abilities, and hers would not be enough, assuming she still lived. Aderen couldn't bear to think otherwise.

A human presence intruded on Aderen's thoughts. He identified Pinoa before he saw her. She floated through the shuttlebay to meet him.

"How's Étar?" Aderen asked, though he knew the answer. Awakened from cryo-sleep soon after Sarenie and Ret, Étar was sick. He might have even died if it wasn't for his kennis' ability to shore up the immune system.

He knew of three people who had died in cryo-sleep on the first crews brought to Rykol. Two others had awakened with serious mental imbalances. Tari, from *Avenger*'s crew, had self-corrected, though not to her original self. Traneel, from *Siberath*, had died not long after awakening.

He wondered if kennis technology could have helped them survive.

"He's recovering, but it'll be a few days before he has strength to join us." She placed herself in the corner with him and looked down at the preparations in the shuttlebay. "Are you still considering options?"

Nodding, Aderen said, "Yes, but mostly I was thinking about the second vekornan fleet."

"Kezim and Rametin will have things well in hand at Terra by now," she responded. "The two raider fleets are an annoyance. This is where the real work will be done. The Legion knows the threat posed by the vekorna, and will be ready to meet them with a new Defense Fleet, larger and stronger than the old navy, and trained by the vekorna."

"I hope so." He looked at her and added, "Monera will be part of that navy."

Pinoa nodded. "Undoubtedly. She's a great pilot." Pinoa put a hand to his cheek, caressing it. "I wish she was here, too."

That might be true, but not in the same way as Aderen. He never realized how much he'd needed Monera's

37

stabilizing effect. Even when they were no longer lovers, she was always there for him, in a way that no other could be. She'd spent years with him in exile, before he convinced her to get another life. Now he was here, and she wasn't.

"I wonder what she's doing on Terra, two hundred years after we left? She's second generation, and wasn't born on Rykol. Does she have enough Rykol-water in her genes to live this long?"

To her credit, Pinoa nodded curtly, refusing to consider any other possibility. "The vekorna created Rykol-water to extend their lives, and they can live a thousand years."

"It has extended our lives considerably, but nobody can say how long we will actually live."

"None of us has died from old age yet," she said reassuringly. "Monera knows how long it takes to get to Rykol. She's probably thinking of us, the way we're thinking of her."

"I don't know if I can pull this off without her." Aderen stared into Pinoa's eyes. "When you came to Rykol, you were with your family, the ones who sustained you through the Information War. My father was with his best friends, and my mother was a professional on a crew full of professionals."

Pinoa nodded. "You've always had trouble making friends. You spent your entire life with us, all ageless, but much older than you."

He grabbed both her hands, and she didn't flinch. "Monera helped reopen my mind after the experience with Legionnaire Dalpah. I sometimes wonder if I could only control Sebenet because I knew Monera was nearby. Now I know she isn't."

He let his hands float out of hers.

"Dalpah was more than sixty years ago," Pinoa said, her voice calm but stern. "I understand why you quit being adjunct to the Legion Council, given what happened."

"People died, and the Arais were exposed, however briefly, because I missed something." Aderen moved so that his body turned partly away from Pinoa.

"You felt that you couldn't trust yourself again," she said. "I understand that feeling. For a long time I questioned myself about my role in the destruction of the kolbs, when I thought I was doing the right thing at the time. Even now, I wonder if it's right to come back to where it all started."

"It seemed clear for the brief moment on that extar, when I helped dissuade Sebenet from his mission. Now, I'm not so sure."

"The first job will be mine and Sarenie's, through negotiation. You will make them more susceptible to our tactics, as you used to do for Kezim and Rametin. Then we'll never have to use those fighters down there." She inclined her head toward the shuttlebay.

Aderen sighed. The fighters were there for a reason, and not because they trusted negotiation or his skills.

Pinoa drew a rectangle in the air between them, activating her kennis-controlled palette. A holographic map of Rykol sprang to life. The red Rykol-water ocean dominated, broken up by the four huge main continents, all of which ran north-south in wide brown bands.

"It looks lifeless compared to Terra," he said.

She nodded. "It is. When I was on Rykol, only a few places were suitable for human habitation. Most of those barely fit the criteria." She expanded the map to show the inland sea of Bol, land of the folems and lobems.

"The most Terra-like," Aderen said. Their shield kept life intact, including the lush forests and grasslands, lakes and the river that flowed out to the dangerous oceans.

To the north, she lit up Egalra, the triangular island where Egalinsor had made his home. Joem, Egalinsor and Nalimai had insisted on being left behind on Rykol, one who wanted to die there, one who had the power to make it happen, and another who wouldn't leave her love. They would be unintentional reminders to the vekorna that they could return to Terra any time for more.

"I'm looking forward to seeing Nalimai," Aderen said, assuming she was still alive, exposed to traces of Rykol-water for the last four hundred years. "She was one of my father's best friends."

"And maybe the closest thing to family?"

Aderen nodded.

Egalra was also forested, though trees didn't grow the way they did on Terra. As far as Aderen knew, it never rained on Rykol, and forests got their water from aquifers that naturally filtered out Rykol-water's deadly liquid form.

Along the equator, one continent to the east, lay Tiroosae, land of the mirkonel insects. Aderen touched the location, and Pinoa said, "Yes, your parents were captured there, but the mirkonel tried to protect them."

Another continent farther east, also near the equator, lay

40

Ban, the military complex where the metelek fighter-craft had been designed by humans.

"Tari kept a garden here," Pinoa reminded him. "She had a special waterfall where she would go to get away from the stress of war."

"It didn't help her in the end."

Pinoa pursed her lips. "No, but it gave her some solace."

She moved the map to Rykol's capital city, on the north-eastern tip of the same continent. "Tari had a more extensive garden in Rubiel, where we grew most of our food."

"That's where I will do most of my work. Shilan and Dairnehy will be at Rubiel."

"I have been giving our strategy more thought," Pinoa said, wiping her palette away with the wave of a hand. "I might have a way to ensure the vekorna of future generations avoid Terra. Doj and Penagel networked vekornan computers through birth chambers. We know that Bolob had been manipulating birth chambers so that only winged vekorna would mature. We could do the same to introduce a fear of going to Terra."

"It's a good idea." Aderen nodded. The asexual vekorna used technology to grow their next generation from the almond-shaped seed pods that ringed their necks. The birth chambers were connected in a way that matured vekorna were not, without the crystals that enhanced telepathy. "It could work, at least in cities."

"It doesn't matter where the birth chambers are," Pinoa reminded him. "Eventually, they will all be synchronized."

"If we can gain access to them," Aderen said.

"We will, but you still doubt yourself."

He nodded, but reluctantly. "I thought it would be a good idea to bring Ret with us, but now I'm not so sure. He reminded me of the others when Legionnaire Dalpah changed so suddenly."

Pinoa brushed off his worries. "You know what to look for now, and I trust you will avoid that mistake again."

He grunted. She didn't understand how different vekornan minds were. What if he missed something because he didn't know their minds well enough? "I'll do what I can, and bear the cost, even if it's only my emotional isolation."

Squeezing his shoulder again, Pinoa said, "You are not alone. Myself, Doj, Penagel and Wandel have all known you since you were a baby. We are with you."

"We have four days," Aderen said. "Then we dock at the Rolm lunar base, and we'll see who is capable of what."

He unfolded his body and pushed off the wall, heading for the door. "Let's get out of here and find some food," he said, and she smiled back at him, nodding.

7. Angry Outburst

The corridor leading to the extar control sphere was the same blue metal as the rest of the ship and the vekornan armor. It wound from two directions to meet at the entrance.

Aderen paused, hand on the wall for stability, as he saw two people around the corner ahead of him. Sarenie's hair was still blonde, unchanged from the color she'd awakened with, tied up behind her so it would stay in place. Ret was

42

kissing her, pressed up against one wall, implying they hadn't seen him.

Cryo-sleep hadn't given Ret the time he needed to come to terms with Aderen's ability to manipulate minds and bodies. According to Sarenie, he was still upset, and intent on watching Aderen's every move.

Fortunately, Aderen had nothing to hide, except his indecision. Manipulating Sebenet had been difficult, but he'd fallen back into the ability easily enough. Unfortunately, his anxieties had returned with Ret's blatant shock at seeing him do it. Sixty years of isolation after Legionnaire Dalpah hadn't helped, just hidden them. This time he was unable to draw on Monera to bring him confidence.

Monera wanted him to use Ret's anger as an anchor for strength, but he wasn't ready to dive into those negative emotions. Instead, Sarenie was helping him with mental exercises, and he much preferred using her positivity. It was closer to what he was used to seeing in Monera. He needed to be solid before they met with Shilan and Dairnehy.

Aderen floated against the wall, holding still, avoiding his habitual small touch of their surface thoughts. Sarenie and Ret deserved to be alone for the moment. Everybody else was gathering in the briefing room. They could wait a few more minutes.

Withdrawing from the kiss, Sarenie pushed strands of long blonde hair away from her face, retying it. Her voice drifted down the corridor, excited. "Before we go in, remember why we're here! Ketaris and Illian want to study

Rykol's plants, but we'll see folems and loboms! You and I are a team. This was our dream –to interact with other species."

Ret nodded wordlessly and kissed her again.

Sarenie let go of his hands and preceded him through the open control sphere door. Aderen counted seconds before continuing, stopping at the threshold. He heard Sarenie call "Doj!", and confirmed through a light touch on their minds that both had left the entryway.

He ignored the vekornan guard as he entered, except to note that several eyestalks were extended, watching them.

Gravity reasserted itself as he placed one foot carefully on the transparent walkway, looking all the way down to the edge of space. Rykol's twin suns were visible to his left, dimmed so they could see the rest of the solar system. Vekornan symbols marked Rykol's large disk and other lights.

Another vekornan approached Aderen from the left as he watched Sarenie leap from the hold of her transparent walkway to the next one up, easily rolling to her feet and launching into the air again, finally coming to rest near Doj and Penagel. Ret followed, bypassing the second level in the weightlessness between platforms.

The door must remain closed this far from Rykol, Samlar said. He was talking to the guard, but had opened his thoughts to Aderen as well. The extar commander could have relayed this command from anywhere in the control sphere, so his intent was to guide Aderen, or to talk privately.

If we need to seal the control sphere and eject, we

cannot afford the possibility of a failed door lock, Samlar continued. It was something the guard would already know, which meant the comment was addressed to Aderen.

I hope you would give us enough notice before ejecting, if it became necessary, Aderen said, taking advantage of the vekornan's telepathic nature to practice his own.

You might have time to get to a shuttlebay and make your escape, Samlar told him. Changing topics, the vekornan said, **Our lack of escorts bothers me, though Tararnifal is not worried.**

He's worried, Aderen corrected him. **But he won't show it to you or me.**

You must not read his mind without notice, Samlar admonished.

Vekornan surface thoughts are open to everyone, for those who are able, Aderen responded. **Tararnifal is your leader. Don't be afraid to question him, scan his surface thoughts. How else will you function as a team?**

Samlar's surface thoughts were in turmoil, but he was incensed to be lectured about telepathy by a human. **Is this how you function with your team?** the vekornan asked.

Humans are different, but I do what I can for efficiency. They've had enough time for reunions. Let's join them. Aderen pointed two levels up, where the discussion seemed to have turned serious.

He leaped from the platform, using compressed air at his hips for guidance, allowing him to seamlessly glide onto the gravity of the transparent walkway. Samlar used his considerable wings to arrive first, but hovered to the side, twitching them slightly to maintain orientation.

Aderen approached with a big smile. "The others are ready for briefing," he said. Doj and Penagel nodded and started to move, but Ret glared at him.

"You've been lucky so far," Ret said, and Sarenie put a warning hand on his shoulder.

Aderen cocked his head to the side. Was this how his anger was going to come to a head? "How so?"

Ret rolled his eyes, body language showing that he didn't believe Aderen wasn't reading his thoughts. "No ships have come to investigate us. Nobody to control, to test your limits."

Aderen frowned and ran a hand over his hairless head. "I know you hold that against me. I've seen it many times before." He'd had this argument, too, sixty subjective years earlier. Even though he knew what he was doing, the arguments, silencing people, had been too much for him, and forced him to retire into obscurity. Until Sebenet arrived.

Glancing briefly at Tararnifal, he spread his arms and said, "We think this is the only way to keep the vekorna away from Terra for good, but are open to other ideas."

It was easy to see the anger flare inside Ret as he shook off Sarenie's hand. "What happens when we land and Sebenet speaks to the vekorna on Rykol? He's always watching for you, wondering when you'll take control of his body again. He'll betray us."

Four eyestalks peered out of Tararnifal's triangular mask, two pointing at Aderen, the others at Ret.

46

Better argue about it now than later, when it could be critical, Aderen told the vekornan. He thought back to Monera's words before they left Terra. How could he use the uneasy energy directed at him? **Let him have his say.**

Two more eyestalks poked through Tararnifal's mask to look at Ret.

"Sixty years ago, something went wrong with one of your manipulations, but there's no record of it. There are consequences to your manipulations!"

"I know what happened, which is why I retired," said Aderen, closing his eyes. He had been part of the cover-up afterward, which was why there were no records. It was not his proudest moment, but had been necessary. "Why did you come to Rykol, Ret?" The others were silent, though Sarenie stayed nearby, intent on not fidgeting. Aderen held back, resisting the almost overwhelming temptation to dive into Ret's mind.

The light of revelation appeared in Ret's eyes, easy to see even without looking into his surface thoughts. "I have to keep an eye on you."

Aderen turned, his face flushed. "Fine, if that's all you want, then follow me." He was disappointed in Ret. For a strategic analyst, he hadn't sifted through his own thoughts, as Aderen had when awakening from cryo-sleep. Monera's advice was to let Ret deal with his emotions himself, but he had better be quick about it.

"If you have anything constructive to add," Aderen finally said, "or if you think of alternatives, feel free to voice them at the briefing."

"That was harsh," Doj buzzed through their kennis, as

they jumped down the next two platforms.

"He needs time to figure out how he feels, then put it to good use," Aderen buzzed back.

"Unfortunately, we don't have time."

Aderen nodded, wiping at the top of his head.

Down the corridor, the door to the briefing room was open, and Aderen entered, Doj and Penagel on his heels, Ret and Sarenie behind them. They all touched the floor as the room's gravity drew them down.

The door closed behind Tararnifal as Aderen registered Ret's surprise at seeing Sebenet on the side of the room. Tararnifal wanted to keep him close, and so far the vekornan hadn't caused trouble, though his surface thoughts were decidedly unfriendly toward Aderen.

"Étar –finally!" Ret yelled, and went to hug his friend. The other man, a pilot like Ret, barely smiled, but put his arms up to return the hug. He was still weak, but upright. Ret glared at Aderen, obviously upset that Étar had been dragged out of the medical ward.

"He'll be alright, now," Aderen responded.

"You're looking better than when you came out of cryo-sleep," Sarenie added. Of the twelve humans, Étar was the only one to have suffered ill effects from the hibernation. Unfortunately, he was one of their few military pilots, and might be needed at a moment's notice. His kennis was working hard to restore his equilibrium.

Sarenie took Ret's hand and pulled him to his seat.

Tararnifal and Sebenet removed their silver faceplates, revealing the blue five-sided sensor heads beneath. Their lower legs were folded at both knees, and their middle arms were touching the floor for balance. Even in this pose, they towered over humans.

Sebenet had extended all of his eyestalks to look at them, three watching Aderen. A scan of his surface thoughts showed that the vekornan remained loyal to Tararnifal, but wanted to be far away from Aderen.

The four other sides of his face were a dizzying mosaic of black dots, difficult to look at, but they gave the vekorna more than just telepathy, including the unique mental buzz for those humans who could detect it in their minds.

"In the absence of communication from Rykol, we will dock at the Rolm moon base," Tararnifal said. Without the faceplate, his voice had lost the metallic twang.

"*Avenger*, *Kamsar*, *Kirek*, *Alnevar* and *Siberath* all docked there when they arrived," said Aderen. "It's a good transition point."

Ret looked around the room, eyeing Sebenet suspiciously. "Are we ready to split the human contingent across the eight extars?" he asked. It was a strategy that had been used in the past, to ensure some of them reached Rykol in case they were attacked.

No, the vekornan leader said. **I want all of you on my extar.**

"Why?" Aderen was taken aback. Tararnifal hadn't discussed this with him. He must have made the decision recently, as it hadn't been in his surface thoughts in the control sphere. Sebenet didn't seem surprised.

The sensor head on top of Tararnifal's body twitched, and one eyestalk pointed toward Sebenet. "Landing on Rolm presents less chance of attack than descending to

Rykol. The absence of escorts suggests that something unexpected has happened. Keeping you together allows me to designate the four other extars to our protection."

"Why?" Ret asked again, watching Sebenet. "Are you expecting an ambush?"

Without warning, the two vekorna whipped their wings out, spinning around toward the door. They grabbed their faceplates, donning them as they leapt out of the room, and away from the force that held them to the ground.

Aderen touched Tararnifal's mind as he and Sebenet gave an extra push with their wings, accelerating them down the zero-gravity corridor.

"We've entered Rykol's orbit, approaching the Rolm moon base," Aderen said, locking eyes with Ret, whose comment seemed almost prescient. "We seem to have triggered an ambush."

8. Obstruction

The hologram in the center of the control sphere looked exactly the same as the mental image Samlar had sent them: a ring of extars, weapons active, threatening their small fleet.

As Tararnifal and Sebenet burst into the spherical command center, they both extended their wings to full, and with three great pushes, they were centered. Tararnifal turned all the way around, taking in readings from instruments attuned to the five sides of his sensor head. Sebenet did the same.

Our extars are ready for battle, said Samlar, relinquishing control. **Shuttlebays are open and pilots are**

in position.

Launch from two, said Tararnifal. It was a tactic that allowed them to assess enemy behavior without revealing all of their capabilities. Were these enemies? he wondered. Despite Sebenet's defiance, Tararnifal didn't suspect him of arranging the ambush.

Their extar lurched as it took a hit from one of the ambushing starships, answering his question. How had Ret known?

Get Ret, Wandel, and Étar to their fighters, Tararnifal said. The humans didn't know how vekorna fought, but they understood tactics. **They've shown ingenuity in simulations, and may be of help.**

Move our extars into a defensive position, ordered Sebenet as they joined in a strategic pairing.

Immediately, the extars shifted. Rykol was behind them, the red moon Rolm ahead. One of Sebenet's extars came side-by-side with their own, facing the opposite direction, while three moved above them, and three below.

The net of extars that had ambushed them was loose but effective. There was no way Sebenet's eight ships could get away without a fight.

Twenty-six extars to capture our small fleet? Sebenet wondered. **What has happened since I left Rykol?**

The bulk of the attacking ships sat closer to the Rolm base, but they couldn't ignore the others above, below and around them on all sides. Was this what it felt like to be inside a zonguan grid?

The control spheres of the twenty six extars were most visually prominent on his screens, giant spheres attached to the bodies by twined arms. Tararnifal noted extra shielding compared with Sebenet's eight ships. Behind the control sphere stretched the long fuselage, extending in a gentle curve to form wing-like structures that tapered sharply back to the main body.

The rest of the fuselage was rectangular, to the engines that pushed it through space. As he watched, the screens splintered into details of each potential enemy, showing weapon emplacements and defensive armaments.

They are heavily damaged, Tararnifal said. **They have been in battle, and not maintained.** He magnified an image to show scarring from multiple laser hits.

Even as they drifted closer, three extars struck at them, the shots absorbed by their defensive cover.

Speak to them, Tararnifal said, taking a chance. He watched shuttles still streaming out of his extars. The others would wait for negotiations before joining in.

"I am Sebenet, returning from an interstellar mission, and am required to stop at Rolm. We are not your enemies."

"You have broken the treaty by using extars in Rykolien orbit," a voice said. It did not have the metallic twang that came from the use of protective faceplates. It could be a good sign that the other commander was not ready for battle, despite the brief exchange of laser fire. "You must land on Rykol and destroy your extars, or transfer them to us now."

"Who are you?" Sebenet asked. "I am here on the authority of Shilan."

"Shilan is dead," said the unidentified voice.

While Sebenet was shocked to silence, Tararnifal reached out to touch the other commander, who rebuffed him strangely. "I left Rykol with Bolob, and bring many of his vekorna home. Would you deny my return?"

"Bolob did not foresee this," the voice said. A hologram appeared in the center of the control sphere, shifting to make it seem like the other commander was hovering over the same platform as them, wings extended. The yellow sensor head could only be kolb, cracked and dry as if by the rugged Rykolien surface. Tararnifal and Sebenet backed away, eyestalks retracting suddenly.

Kolbs were destroyed in the war, Sebenet said, two eyestalks extending tentatively. Tararnifal silenced him. Bolob had hidden the surviving winged kolbs in stasis on Rykol's Black Moon, known to very few. Tararnifal hadn't thought about them since Bolob's death.

"Kolbs have never taken to space," Tararnifal finally said, knowing he should feign more surprise at this appearance. "How did you come to be in control of a fleet of extars?"

"The vekorna on Rykol are to blame. Bolob's Plan is now void," the kolb replied. "We await transfer of your extars to our control, as per the treaty." The hologram disappeared.

Tararnifal didn't understand this turn of events. Why had the winged kolbs revealed themselves?

"We will land on Rykol," said Tararnifal, but it was too late. In his moment of hesitation, his extar commanders leapt against their ancient enemies. The vekornan shuttles went on the attack, and he saw that the formidable kolb shuttles were ready for them.

*   *   *

"We can't fight," argued Ret, standing firm against Aderen's insistence. "We've only been out of cryo-sleep for a few days." He pointed at Étar. "He can't fly."

Aderen shook his head. "He's recovered enough. We instructed Étar's kennis to pump him with the proper balance of hormones and drugs to complete the healing." He pointed to the side of his head. "The fight has already started. I have to get to the control sphere and see if I can salvage this. You need to get to the shuttlebay –now!"

Ret looked to Étar. It wasn't normal to use the kennis in this way, but they had no other choice.

Sarenie touched Ret's shoulder to calm him, buzzing to Aderen, "I'll get them there."

As Aderen was leaving, Wandel stopped him with a hand to his arm. "Why me?" she asked. "It's been years since I fought."

"You're the only one here who has flown a metelek fighter in battle," he answered. "Pull on those memories."

She nodded, acknowledging the fact. Aderen left the room, floating off the floor. He stopped and used his hip thrusters to turn toward Pinoa. "Those aren't vekorna out there –they're kolbs."

"How is that possible?" asked Pinoa.

"I don't know if they'll answer when I ask them."

"I'll prepare our modified meteleks," said Wandel, as she left with Doj, floating in the other direction. She'd helped design the fighters, back when humanity had been deeply involved in the vekornan war to wipe out the kolbs.

She'd never joined the Terran navy, but still flew the fighters on short sorties.

Xeffeya drew a rectangle between her and Étar, opening her kennis. Their only doctor tapped commands into the air in front of her. Ketaris, on the other side, tied her long brown hair behind her head and did the same. They would be giving Étar one last scan.

"Come to the control sphere when you're ready," Aderen told Sarenie. "I'll need you there."

Pinoa floated beside him as they made their way to the front of the extar, the corridor bucking around them each time it was struck by a laser blast.

9. Search and Rescue

The vekornan guard at the entrance to the control sphere let Aderen and Pinoa through without a thought of protest, closing the door behind them.

The images that filled the entirety of the sphere had changed, strategic maps showing each of the twenty-six extars that surrounded their little fleet.

They gently pushed off the transparent platforms and glided into the center to join Tararnifal and Sebenet. Samlar was at a higher vantage, supported by his wings. Aderen and Pinoa used their hip thrusters to stop without getting too close to the vekorna.

Tararnifal's sensor head twitched side-to-side as he gaged the different instruments within the control sphere. Aderen gleaned what he needed from the vekornan leader's surface thoughts.

Sebenet was ready for battle, too, and he didn't shy

away from Aderen, though his surface thoughts conveyed distrust.

"The kolbs fired warning shots, but our extars initiated full combat," he buzzed Pinoa. "There is some sort of treaty between them and the vekorna on Rykol. They want us to give up our extars."

"No chance of that," Pinoa responded, and he agreed.

"I need to find out what happened. This reversal of power is unexpected."

"Not to mention dangerous. Get Tararnifal to open contact, and I'll negotiate."

Pinoa drew a rectangle in front of her chest, activating her palette. She pulled up a hologram of the space around them, showing an image more suited to human eyes. Other frames on her palette showed their three pilots.

"I'm ready," Étar's voice came out of one frame. Ret acknowledged him, then Wandel led them out into space.

The kolbs had let loose their shuttle defense, which were taking the brunt of the attacks from Tararnifal's extars. Tararnifal was reigning in his forces, but it was a difficult task, retreating under fire.

Aderen reached out, searching for the long-range telepathy of tigal-en, the extar commanders, and one who commanded all the kolb forces.

"Terebar shuttles," said Pinoa, drawing Aderen's attention. "Ret and Étar haven't simulated against those."

Vekornan metelek fighters, similar to the ones Ret, Étar and Wandel flew, were darting around the bulky kolb attack shuttles. Both sides had launched the older rolp-class shuttles, most holding back near the extars.

"You take point," Wandel said, comms open to Tararnifal's battle frequency. "We'll be on your wings."

Tararnifal's vekorna would be linked directly to his tigal-en mind, to a distance of several hundred kilometers, but some commands still came by way of comms signals.

Although Wandel had fought in the kolb war, she'd been self-trained, unlike the other two human pilots. She'd loved testing her designs in battle, but refrained from joining another military venture after returning to Terra.

Ret shifted into position, acknowledging her request.

"The kolbs are hiding something on the other side of their net," Aderen buzzed Pinoa and Sarenie. "The tigal-en on Rykol's side have instructions to widen the net, while those on the Rolm side are tightening it."

"What for?" Pinoa asked.

"I don't know. Their minds are slippery, more than vekornan minds. Get our pilots through, and find out what they're hiding."

"Why?" Sarenie asked as she entered the control sphere. "They need to cover our retreat."

"The vekorna can cover the retreat. Do you really think Tararnifal sent them out for such a mundane task?"

"He sent them because we think differently than vekorna and kolbs," Pinoa buzzed. "They have a better chance of threading through the net."

Aderen nodded as Sarenie went silent, relaying his recommendation. He wasn't a battle commander, so didn't give orders. He expected them to follow him, nonetheless.

Before Sarenie could ask again, Aderen interrupted her, shaking his head. "I may have found one, but am not sure yet." It was a difficult admission.

Sarenie looked exasperated. "They found a hole, and are going through," she said. He understood. Her lover was out there, and waiting helplessly was the hardest part.

"Got him," Aderen said out loud. A kolb hologram appeared in front of them. "It's up to you now." Most other kolbs were beyond the limit of his telepathic range, and impossible to influence.

He fell back on his old ways, making this one more compliant, while his team negotiated. There was still room for error, as his experience with Dalpah had shown, so he kept his manipulation to a minimum.

"I am Arnatak," the kolb said, hovering body level with Tararnifal. "Are you ready to relinquish your extars according to the treaty?"

Sarenie pushed forward, between Arnatak and Tararnifal. Aderen's pliancy dulled any shock the kolb might have had at human interference.

"I am Sarenie of Terra," she said, adjusting her height so her face was even with Arnatak's sensor head, and she could look into his eyeslits. He wore no faceplate, and the hologram was so detailed he could have been there with them. The sensor head was yellow and chapped, unlike the moist blue of the vekorna. In some places it looked ready to crack. Several eyestalks were extended from the pair of stacked rows that harbored them. Nothing else moved.

"We will comply with your treaty, but not until we have landed with our cargo –humans. When we arrived, you offered Tararnifal the choice to give up the extars now or to land on Rykol and destroy them."

"The choice was taken from us when your extars attacked," said Arnatak.

"We were as surprised to find kolbs with extars as you were to see humans on board ours," Sarenie said. Aderen slipped her some information, which he picked from Arnatak's mind. "We helped in the war against the wingless, and Bolob used the war as a distraction so you could survive. Allow us the same chance."

As Arnatak hesitated, Aderen gave his mind a slight push, hopefully in the right direction.

"Withdraw your fighters, and you may land on Rykol, but we will watch that your extars do not take to space again."

Recalling all fighters, said Tararnifal. **We are overwhelmed and cannot win this fight.**

Aderen reached out to the human fighters, who had gone dark. They were out there somewhere.

He found Ret's distant mind, and dove in. **Come back to the fleet. Sarenie has given us a quick window.** Then he recoiled as Ret's mind rejected him. In all his long experience, that had never happened before. It was like an electric shock, worse for its unexpectedness.

"Help me," he buzzed to Sarenie and Pinoa, drawing on their mental strength. This was something he'd been practicing with them since awakening from cryo-sleep. He didn't dare touch other minds like this.

Wandel was almost out of reach. They should have deployed a kennis node into the solar system before entering orbit. The three pilots were out of the limited range of normal kennis implants, but they couldn't launch a node in the middle of battle.

He found Étar, and relayed the same message. Étar, at least, was open, and tried to respond telepathically. His words were jumbled, but the meaning was clear.

"They're near Rolm, and are on the way back," he buzzed. To Tararnifal, he said out loud, "Retreat slowly. We can't leave them behind."

The net of kolb extars retreated with them, a loose spherical shell, padded toward Rolm, moving in the direction of Rykol.

Visual confirmation of thruster firings on the other side of the kolb net appeared on the control sphere's interior display. It automatically enlarged, and Aderen saw three ships. They were being chased.

"It's a terebar attack shuttle," whispered Pinoa, enlarging the same area on her palette. "More have gone to investigate."

"Are they going to make it?" Sarenie asked, hands stroking her hair, anxiety in her surface thoughts. Aderen withdrew from her mind.

"Negotiation while slipping reconnaissance beyond our lines nullifies the agreement," said Arnatak, and his hologram disappeared.

"I'll get him back," said Aderen as Sarenie glared at him.

Suddenly comms came active, and Ret's voice said, "We're faster than they are. Let's get back to the safety of Tararnifal's extars." A moment later, he asked, "Where's Wandel?"

Her light had disappeared from Pinoa's palette. Aderen

reached out and found her mind.

"She's still stuck near the extar," Étar responded. "One of my lasers is damaged."

"We have to help her," Ret said.

Arnatak's hologram reappeared in the center of the control sphere. Sarenie tore her gaze away from Pinoa's palette to speak. "Three humans have drifted across your lines, and we want them back. It was not reconnaissance, but accidental," she lied. Vekorna had not shown the ability to communicate telepathically with human minds at extar-to-extar distances, but just to be sure, Aderen distracted him, tugging on a wary part of his mind.

Aderen watched as two fighters, Ret and Étar, sped away from their attackers toward the much larger kolb extar. Ret's damage indicator lit up and he swore. "We can't do this by ourselves!" he shouted.

"We need to send help," Aderen said.

To Arnatak, Sarenie said, "Allow us to rescue our pilots, then we will be away."

"Falling back," Ret said as he came under attack again.

"Direct hit!" Étar whooped, in synch with a small explosion.

"Great job!" Ret answered. "Get to Wandel."

Sarenie addressed Arnatak, his hologram still hovering in front of them. "If you won't allow them to escape, we'll take them back by force."

Tararnifal had directed an extar into close proximity with the kolb ship near the three human pilots. Three more were engaging other ships, drawing away enemy fire.

"Time to go," Ret said. "We have company."

The shuttlebay is open, Samlar said. **Direct them inside.**

They watched as kolb and vekornan extars each fired.

"Hold your fire, and we will allow them to leave," said Arnatak.

"Stop firing and we'll retreat with them," Sarenie replied, her voice firm despite the panic in her thoughts.

As the meteleks approached the extar's shuttlebay, four terebars came around for another pass.

"Stop them!" cried Sarenie, and Aderen pushed on Arnatak's mind. He switched his focus to the distant kolb pilots as Wandel said, "I'm going into the shuttlebay."

"I'm helping Ret," Étar responded.

"No, get inside!" Ret countered, his fighter drifting away.

Aderen gripped the minds of the kolb pilots, but hesitated, searching for a way to inhibit their ability to fire.

Then Ret's fighter exploded, and Sarenie cried out.

Acting on shock and impulse, Aderen realized he'd suddenly killed the four kolb pilots. He withdrew from the space around them, from Arnatak and the others, horrified at what he'd done.

"Wandel and Étar are inside," Pinoa reported.

"Find Ret!" Sarenie called. In that instant, he reached out into space again, but it was so large, and he'd lost track of where Ret was supposed to be.

He closed his eyes as he realized he couldn't sense another human out there.

10. A Response

The kolbs are opening a lane, said Tararnifal, watching the screens closely, taking in all the details his extar's sensors could offer. **They are letting us go.**

Not all of us.

With the two human pilots rescued, the net of kolb extars was shifting closer to Rolm, leaving a path to Rykol clear. Unfortunately, three of his extars were caught in the net.

Arnatak's hologram disappeared, strangely silent, and inaccessible even as a tigal-en. He made a quick strategic assessment; the kolbs would not be releasing the captured extars, and they risked their own freedom if they went up against that many enemy ships. It was time to go home.

Nine humans stood on the mid-level of the control sphere, arguing.

"You have to get his body back," Sarenie said, tears in her eyes. Her hair was now black where it covered her skull, blonde beyond that, hanging free.

I do not know where his body is, Tararnifal responded. **The kolbs will not permit us to search the area.**

The debris from Ret's fighter had already dissipated, and there was no sign of human life.

The damaged extar holding Étar and Wandel retreated, somehow not caught in the kolb net. A few terebar attack shuttles harassed them, but none seriously.

Sebenet said privately to Tararnifal, **The humans should not be here. We sacrificed three extars for three humans – not worth the trade. Aderen was useless, but you are complacent about his threat. He does not trust**

me or my crew.

Tararnifal didn't respond, watching the humans. The kolbs would be winged, and if they still followed Bolob's plan, would not mistreat winged vekorna. But he agreed that it had not been worth the sacrifice.

"Ret could have survived," said Doj, cradling Sarenie's head to his shoulder. "His heat signature could be masked by debris or the bulk of the extars themselves."

Aderen hung his head, shaking it slowly. "I can't sense him either, but he closed his mind to me."

It is true that they can provide us little insight in their grief, Tararnifal told Sebenet, steering the conversation away from Aderen.

They are weak in their grief, Sebenet said.

Tararnifal disagreed, but refrained from saying more. He had seen grief make humans very strong.

"We will scan as long as we can," Tararnifal replied aloud. "Doj and Penagel, take the rest of your team back to the conference room. Aderen, stay with us." Sebenet extended an eyestalk in concern.

At that moment, another hologram appeared in the center of the control sphere. Étar and Wandel looked ragged, their hair matted with sweat.

"Did you find him? Is he okay?" Étar asked.

"No," Aderen responded. "We can't find any trace of his body or mind."

"You have to find him," Wandel said. "We caught a brief kennis burst after the explosion. It means he must still be alive."

"Or he was for a few seconds," Aderen said. Sarenie,

retreating, gave him a look of horror. Doj continued guiding them down two levels, and the door to the control sphere closed behind them.

"We are retreating to Rykol," Tararnifal said. He interrupted the human protests by saying, "We have no choice. Ret sacrificed himself so that you both could escape. We must do so or risk being overwhelmed."

"We should drop a kennis node in Rykol's orbit," said Aderen.

Étar nodded, regaining some of his composure. "If he connects to the node, he can signal us."

"Is there anything we should know beyond their net?" Aderen asked.

"The Rolm base has been destroyed, but Ret found something," said Étar, standing tall, though it was clear his health was deteriorating quickly. He needed rest after his ordeal in the cryo-sleep tanks. "The kolbs are excavating, digging deep. I don't know what they are searching for."

"Something they don't want us to know about," Wandel added. "Maybe analysis of our data will show something."

Aderen pursed his lips. "Get cleaned up and we'll meet you at Rubiel. Stay in contact."

Étar and Wandel both nodded, and their holograms disappeared. Aderen advanced toward Tararnifal.

Instead of concentrating on Rolm, which seems lost to us, we shall land on Rykol, Tararnifal said. The images of Rolm's devastation were being transferred to this extar as they spoke. To Aderen's unasked question, he answered, **We have to assume kolbs destroyed the base. Perhaps those at Rubiel will be more willing to enlighten us.**

Changing his target audience, Tararnifal said, **Find one of Rykol's artificial satellites, so that we may tap into their communications.**

We have yet to find a satellite, said Samlar, flapping his wings to join Tararnifal and Sebenet in the center of his control sphere.

Surprise emanated from Aderen.

They were likely destroyed long ago; there is no debris, Samlar replied. **Sensors have turned to Rykol. Shuttles are flying between cities, much as when we left long ago. We have accounted for all known cities in the areas that we scanned, and have added new ones to our database.**

"Life goes on, even though kolbs watch from above?"

It would seem so. There was an old hatred in Samlar's words, but Tararnifal said nothing to counter it, even though the kolbs were winged.

The net of extars protecting the remains of the Rolm base were now points of light in the distance. Tararnifal wondered if the kolbs inhabited the complex under the surface. How far had they expanded from the Black Moon?

With space-based capability, especially if the vekorna were restricted to Rykol's surface, kolbs could sweep in and do irreparable damage any time they wanted.

The red of Rykol's oceans contrasted with its brown continents. The giant inland sea on Megnat was a hazy grey-blue compared to the Rykol-water oceans, the folem lands protected by their giant shield.

The same poison that had killed all life in Rykol's oceans also permeated the atmosphere. Devised to extend vekornan lives, it had done the same to humans.

They deployed two kennis nodes. Much smaller than the missing satellites, the kennis nodes would find their way to opposite sides of the planet, and adjust their orbits to blanket the entire surface. Humans would communicate through the nodes as they did on Terra. In the unlikely event that Ret had survived, he would be able to contact them through his kennis.

Unfortunately, if he was breathing, his air would soon be depleted, and they had no way to retrieve him. If he wasn't breathing, his air would last an indefinite amount of time, but he would not be connecting to the kennis node.

Finally, Tararnifal ordered the five remaining extars to descend to Rubiel, in the far north of the planet, on the eastern edge of the largest continent.

Can we believe the kolb claim that Shilan is dead? Sebenet asked. His thoughts indicated he was uncertain of his role.

If so, Tararnifal said, **Dairnehy is now the vekornan leader. Bolob made him Shilan's prin-el to learn patience and respect, as a second-in-command should. We can only hope he learned those lessons.**

He seems to honor the apparent extar treaty with the kolbs, Sebenet responded. They would see.

The extars moved deeper into the atmosphere, but aside from a slight blurring of the view ahead, there was little sense of motion. Compared to human craft on Terra, extars neutralized almost all vibrations as they descended.

Still above the ocean, they leveled out and began their approach to the vekornan capital city.

The protective shield is within range, Sebenet said. His thoughts kept drifting uncomfortably to Aderen.

Broadcast your hologram, instructed Tararnifal. Aderen looked from one vekornan to the other, ready to respond if necessary, but there was no betrayal in Sebenet's surface thoughts.

"I am Sebenet, returning from my mission to deep space." After a few seconds with no answer, Sebenet continued, "I was sent on this mission long ago, and return with humans, in fulfillment of my goals." This was not the time to reveal that he'd failed his mission.

The hologram is not getting through, said Samlar.

An audio response filled the air throughout the control sphere. "You are in violation of the extar treaty. Leave now, or you will be destroyed."

What's going on? Sebenet asked.

"They think we're kolbs," Aderen said. "The kolbs also thought we were in violation of their treaty."

As tigal-en, Tararnifal should be able to touch any mind in Rubiel. He searched for Dairnehy, but the vekornan leader flinched away. Other vekorna in the city closed their minds to him as well.

If they could see the hologram, they would note my vekornan shell, said Sebenet, removing his faceplate. His thoughts had focused, intent to get through the shield.

The five extars continued across the red ocean, dropping in altitude as they approached the outer edge of the shield protecting Rubiel.

"I am Sebenet, returning from deep space. I am unaware of the treaty. Allow me to land and deliver my cargo."

Tararnifal brushed Sebenet's mind again. His thoughts betrayed a desire to deliver his version of events first, including a warning about Aderen. The mission to Terra had been ordered by Shilan, but Dairnehy had pushed for it. Would the new vekornan leader still care? Frustrated, Tararnifal found no open minds in the city.

Laser fire streamed out from emplacements just beyond the edge of the continent. Their aim was poor, but the extars would be forced away from the shield to avoid getting hit.

"We will not renegotiate the treaty unless your leaders return their part of the stellar fragment. Until then, kolbs must remain on the three moons, while the planet belongs to vekorna. This is your last warning."

"Get me in closer," said Aderen. "I can't reach their minds from here." Sebenet watched him in concern with two eyestalks.

Do you think you'll be able to control them across the shield? Tararnifal asked, speaking privately to Aderen.

"I've done it through Terran shields." Distance had always been Aderen's telepathic weakness.

Sebenet signaled another extar to follow them closely, while the rest stayed out of range. Laser fire increased in intensity, peppering the air around them.

Once again, Sebenet tried to contact the vekorna inside Rubiel. "I am not kolb. I have come from a long journey through deep space to Terra and back."

Suddenly, the barrage grew heavier. The laser beams, which had been slender and focused, became large cylinders of light that flew alarmingly close.

Have you connected? Tararnifal asked.

"Not yet." Aderen's face was twisted in concentration.

Their ship dove suddenly as Samlar detected what he had not, lurching slightly as it scraped a hardened pocket of air. The extar to their left stopped suddenly, suspended helpless in the air as lasers ripped a huge gash through one of the wing-like protrusions, all the way back to the rear engines.

It started tumbling, and Tararnifal said, **All ships retreat.**

We are not welcome in orbit or on land, Sebenet said.

The body of the damaged extar sagged, folding in half where it had been hit by the blast. The control sphere detached from the body, but couldn't get away. Hit by the fuselage, they both went crashing into the red ocean. The Rykol-water ravished the skin of the extar before it sank.

Rubiel's has powerful defenses, Tararnifal said.

We should land in the desert to the south, Sebenet suggested. **There is space for us to regroup. We are too few, now.**

"They didn't believe you," Aderen said, speaking to Sebenet below him. "Could they have forgotten about your missions?"

It has not been long enough to forget about a mission of this importance, said Sebenet, fighting gravity to rise to the next level, putting Tararnifal between them.

"Unless Dairnehy is dead, too, and the details of the mission died with him."

Maybe they know of what you can do, Sebenet countered.

Dairnehy is not dead, but he is not willing to share thoughts, said Tararnifal.

Sebenet approached Tararnifal. **They don't believe our extars are friendly; we must approach Rubiel another way.**

"We should make another stop before going to Rubiel," Aderen suggested, walking to where the two vekorna had moved along the platform. "If Egalinsor, Nalimai and Joem are still alive, they'll welcome us."

If they are still alive, Sebenet stressed.

Seeing the hesitation in Tararnifal's mind, Aderen said, "Egalra isn't far from here, and we could gain valuable information."

Egalra cannot hold an extar. We must land and return by shuttle.

Tararnifal diverted the remains of the fleet eastward, to land in the deserts of Megnat south of the island that had been given to the oldest humans. He wondered, in this strange new political landscape, if it had remained unspoiled.

11. Memories of Rykol 1

Aderen stopped quietly as he stepped onto the reddish sand of Rykol for the first time in two hundred years. The others walked around him while the vekorna hid their extars in the ruins of the ancient city. It gave them a moment to regroup, though they were eager to see old friends, left behind when he was a child. Aderen and Pinoa agreed that a smaller party should go to Egalra.

Wandel and Étar, looking fully recovered, were

reuniting with Sarenie, speaking animatedly, likely about an attempt to rescue Ret. Aderen had failed. It was already too late; if he'd survived, Ret's air would have run out by now. Wandel was particularly disturbed. Her older memories from living on Rykol were probably resurfacing. She'd lost friends during the war with the kolbs, and now she'd lost Ret, who died protecting her. How had the kolbs survived? Arnatak's thoughts indicated that Bolob had something to do with it.

He should say something, but hesitated, his awareness dissipating, his vision clouded as he entered a different world.

*   *   *

We have been waiting for your arrival, a voice said into his mind. It was deep and heavy, weighing him down. The voice was old and in pain. It slipped from his mind as it faded away, and a new landscape appeared outside the window, far below.

Though it had been so long, Aderen recognized Rubiel as if in a dream. It was strangely silent, without any buzzing to identify the vekorna in the top of the tower.

He had time to wonder what was going on, about to reach for the others through his kennis, when one of the vekorna spoke. He heard it in his mind, a very different voice from the heavy one that had just spoken. He was certain that first voice hadn't been vekornan.

It is coming in very fast. I don't think we can stop it.

Can we launch an extar to divert it? another vekornan asked.

No. Our entire fleet couldn't change its direction

sufficiently to keep it from hitting Rykol.

Aderen observed the interaction from an external perspective, as if he was a ghost. Had the vekorna noticed their extars coming in to land? It didn't seem right.

How did the asteroid avoid detection? the first vekornan asked.

Unknown.

The holographic display in front of them showed an asteroid falling through space near Rykol. Aderen wondered if they were in danger. He looked up, but only saw Rykol's purple-blue sky through whatever vision he was having.

Calculations in alien text hovered over the console as extars rose from the moon base to observe.

From its speed and angle, a land hit will create a crater more than a hundred kilometers wide, which would shatter the lands around it. The impact could also create tremors rebounding through the entire planet. A hit into Rykol-water could cause untold contamination.

They watched as the asteroid came closer, and time seemed to speed up for Aderen.

The vekornan had donned its triangular face shield, as if that could protect it from the falling asteroid. He placed his four hands inside the hologram and renewed his calculations.

It will hit north of Rykol's equator, the vekornan said.

Are we in danger here at Rubiel?

Any of the northern cities could be in danger.

The vekorna called to evacuate Rubiel and the other

northern cities. Within hours, all vekornan shuttles and extars were in the air, but it wouldn't be enough to hold their entire population. Aderen wondered if they would be able to stay out of the path of the asteroid. The moment felt old, offset like history, but he couldn't think why it would be transmitted this way. Was he the only one seeing it?

The two remaining vekorna in the top room of the tower could have been the only ones left in the city, for all Aderen knew. It was impossible to tell if these were the same ones that had sounded the alarm.

They watched the holographic screens, until a great blue and yellow streak passed above them from west to the east, angling southward.

I have the projected impact point. A map of Rykol grew into the hologram, expanding until the marker was visible. **The eastern coast of Depraf has a very low vekornan presence. Shuttles from cities on other continents may land.**

Extars and shuttles near the trajectory of the asteroid transmitted videos of the fiery streak as it sped toward the surface. Explosions ripped parts away, but it continued diving. Finally, a massive explosion signaled the asteroid impact. Dust from the desert rose a hundred kilometers into the air. The impact scars spread concentrically, breaking the edge of the continental shelf and creating a small new bay of the dangerous Rykol-water from the ocean. Aderen wondered if there was a risk of tsunami.

The hologram registered the shock of the impact, moving from the impact point across and through the planet. Aderen watched the counter hit forty minutes over just a few seconds and saw vibrations in the tower as the ground shook unnaturally.

A voice came over a speaker almost immediately, metallic as spoken through the triangular vekornan faceplates.

"Vacuum control of the birth chambers has malfunctioned. Send help, or all vekornan embryos will die."

With the evacuation of the city, there were few vekorna to help. Aderen seemed to float along the corridors as a vekornan raced to the elevator shafts. At the lowest level of the tower, the vekornan grabbed a pressure suit and pressed it to the top of his head. It expanded to quickly cover his entire body, providing his skin with oxygen.

The airlock doors to the birth chambers opened without cycling. This would be a problem, Aderen knew. The birth chambers needed a complete vacuum.

Another vekornan extended eyestalks toward one of the giant vertical cylinders. The liquid inside was turning from blue to green, and was reverberating in time to the small shocks that were still shaking the tower.

That is no longer a vekornan embryo, the vekornan said.

The color was wrong, as were the proportions of the body. What had happened?

The shocks have caused a mutation. Should I destroy them?

Destroy an entire generation of vekorna? No. We shall wait until reports arrive from more birth chambers. Other cities may not have been affected.

What has been created here?

I will get the vacuum chamber working again, and we shall see what happens when these embryos mature. This mutation looks strong enough to be a new species.

Aderen's eyes widened. A new species? He knew of only one mutation severe enough to become a new species. If he was correct, a similar mutation had occurred in the southern birth chambers of the kolbs.

The vision dissipated, and Aderen found himself on his knees. Doj came to put a hand on his shoulder, asking if he was all right.

Aderen nodded, and without saying a word, went to join the others.

12. Island of the Hidden

Brushing branches out of her face, Kuyikal put the tracker down and looked for telltale signs that would lead to her nephew's latest hiding spot. It happened every time, but nobody listened when she recommended leaving him behind when they came to the island.

So when Jye-Tan disappeared, Kuyi was, as always, sent to retrieve him. Never mind that they were now missing a second pair of hands while she did. She was happy to duck out of harvesting anti-pollen, but she felt like a puppet, with no control over her own strings, and no appreciation.

She hiked past a tree with a well-worn trunk. Many of the small branches on nearby bushes were bent or broken, Jye-Tan being careless.

"I found his trail," she whispered into her communicator.

"Bring him back; I'll meet you at the cabins," Rogo responded. She nodded, though he couldn't see her, and shut the device off. She didn't want anything to spook Jye-Tan.

As she navigated the path, Kuyi thought of her aunt and uncle, who were free to do what they wanted, instead of taking care of the wayward generation. Sometimes they showed up at the cabins, with tales of Rykol's history and their own narrow escapes. They were absent this time, and the cabins showed no sign of occupation since her last visit.

Stopping at a fork in the path, Kuyi listened. She heard rustling in both directions, so she continued to wait and watch. The canopy of dark leaves let in a lot of light, and the shadows could play tricks on her eyes.

A fat wigone waddled toward her from the left path, its three rows of teeth shining brightly in the mid-day sun. Kuyi watched its sideways gait, two legs so far apart that it couldn't walk forward in a straight line. The small creature didn't seem perturbed, so she guessed Jye-Tan had gone the other way.

Sure enough, about twenty paces in, she saw more bent branches. Further on, a pile of small sticks and yellow flower petals half-covered the path. Jye-Tan must have stopped here. What entertained him about broken sticks and torn-up flowers was beyond her.

"Don't touch it," called a voice from the forest behind her. Kuyi stood slowly and turned. She raised her head until she saw Jye-Tan low in a nearby tree. He was kneeling on three crossed branches. She'd been so concentrated on the sticks that she'd walked right by him.

Smoothly, he raised himself from a kneeling posture to stand on one long leg, holding the tree trunk for balance. He rested his other foot on the crook of his knee.

She knew better than to tell him to come down. Staring up instead, Kuyi asked, "Why not?"

"Look," he said, pointing down the path. A white rabbit, a rare pure-breed from the look of it, was sitting in a patch of white flowers, almost hidden to the side.

"It likes the flowers, but not without a bed of sticks."

Kuyi knelt down, watching. Rabbits had been brought to Rykol with her great-grandparents, geneticists who had bred varieties that could mate with local animals. Kuyi hadn't realized any purebred rabbits remained.

She became suspicious. Turning back to Jye-Tan, she asked, "What are you planning to do with it?"

He looked offended, but at least he didn't get that hurt look, which meant he could have a normal discussion.

"I'll make notes when I get back to the cabins."

He was trying, but Kuyi thought of the others, sweating in Rykol's heat harvesting anti-pollen. She took a deep breath, trying hard to dampen her anger and frustration.

He wasn't much younger than her, but acted like a child sometimes. Her grandmother often said he was nineteen going on nine, but she couldn't remember what that meant. Then Nalimai would soften and remind them of the defects in the last human birth chambers.

Quietly, Kuyi asked, "Were you trying to catch the rabbit? Maybe bring it back to the cabins?"

Jye-Tan's face brightened, but he didn't answer. He should be able to explain himself, Kuyi thought, fists clenching.

"You know that if it's survived this long, then it probably has a pure-bred family, and will continue to survive on its own. Bringing it back to the cabins will stress it, and will introduce it to hybrids that could contaminate its bloodline."

"I know," Jye-Tan said. "But the folems don't have samples from a pureblood rabbit. They should have one for their genetic zoo."

Kuyi thought about the things the folems had conjured from their ancient genetic zoo, and shivered. They kept a record of not just every Rykolien species, but also alien monsters they brought to life to punish the vekorna and kolbs over their long history. A rabbit was such a benign thing to add to that menagerie.

"Do you think it's tame?" she asked, wondering if the folems still had access to those databases.

Jye-Tan shrugged. "It's been sitting there for an hour. I hope it's not hurt."

He'd been here an hour, while she collected anti-pollen? Her face flushed again, and she realized it was not due to chasing after him. Jye-Tan found time for all his explorations, as incomplete and unformulated as they always were. Why couldn't she find that kind of time?

"Maybe you should take a chance, and go see for yourself," Kuyi suggested over the thudding of her heart. Jye-Tan stood in the tree for a long moment before deciding she had offered good advice.

He descended and walked quietly down the path toward the rabbit. It twitched, and turned as if to hop into the underbrush, but halted as Jye-Tan stopped.

Startled by something, the rabbit hopped a few more paces. Jye-Tan moved quickly to scoop it into his shirt, covering its eyes. It folded its long ears back, but didn't try to escape. It cringed and twitched when they heard thunder.

The hot dry air above the island could sometimes cause thunder, following the crackling of dry lightning. Whenever her grandmother heard thunder, she would animatedly describe water falling from the Terran sky. The kinds of deluges Nalimai recounted seemed unrealistic and improbable.

But air didn't cause the kind of thunder they'd just heard.

"Back to the cabins," she said, face going pale.

Jye-Tan stood still, shocked by her terror. He'd never heard that sound; he was too young.

"It's an extar, and that can only mean one thing. Kolb attack."

Jye-Tan's eyes widened, and they turned up the path together, suddenly too breathless to talk. He took a moment too long to let the rabbit go in a small thicket, but it would be safer here. They left the northern forest behind, entering the copse of bushier trees that surrounded the cabins.

With his longer legs, Jye-Tan was far ahead of her, but he stopped up the path, waiting for her to catch up. She heard a whine in the sky, and Jye-Tan cocked his head, listening.

"Keep going. They can't land here; there's not enough space. They'll be after the vekorna, anyway."

"Do you think the winged will respond?" Her nephew's

eyes lit up, concern quickly dissipating in hope.

They reached the small clearing where six log cabins sat, the two wide cylindrical silos almost hidden by trees to their left. She hadn't grown up here, so to her they represented the freedom of being away from home.

Wondering what to do next, Kuyi started for the door to the main cabin.

"Rogo, Lusava!" Jye-Tan called, and Kuyi looked around, seeing two of her family's eldest running out of the forest on the opposite side. Rogo and Lusava scanned the clearing, both their gazes resting reprovingly on Jye-Tan.

Quickly, Rogo went to Kuyi. "I'm glad you were able to find him, Kuyikal," he said. "I assume you heard the extars?"

"And the whine of a shuttle," Kuyi said. "I think they're coming here."

"There's no reason for them to come to Egalra, but I think you're right," said Lusava. "They're coming for us."

"Why do kolbs want us?" Jye-Tan asked.

"I don't plan to find out."

Orem and Mai came out of the forest carrying cases of anti-pollen. Mai gave Jye-Tan and Kuyi a dirty look, which she ignored.

"Get to the meeting point," Rogo said, seeing them assembled. He looked to the rappel lines in the trees, blowing a long strand of curls from his eyes. "The wingless will get you out of here. Lusava and I will stay to observe."

"No; you'll be captured," Kuyi said.

He gave her a hardened look. "It's not time to be stubborn. They can't detect us in the trees. Get the others out of here. The wingless shuttle will be at the eastern bay."

"Unless they also detected the kolbs," Kuyi argued.

His wary look meeting Lusava, Rogo nodded.

"You're right," Lusava said, green eyes hard and penetrating, and Kuyi beamed at the praise. "The vekornan shuttle will become a prime target. Stay with us in the trees, but make no movement, no sound. Shut off all electronics. We've practiced this."

It had been practice to escape from vekorna, but kolbs would be no better. The fact was there was nowhere else for the small human family to go.

Everyone shut off their communicators, while Kuyi gave the tracker back to Rogo.

They climbed the trees, and, adept at maneuvering around this part of the island, they formed a rough hexagon around the clearing. They were camouflaged so well that Kuyi could barely make out Rogo to her left, and Jye-Tan to her right.

*   *   *

They were quiet as a shuttle descended. Rogo and Lusava both held lasers. Kuyi didn't have a weapon, but she wondered if it would make much difference. The shuttle would contain enough kolbs to quickly overwhelm them.

The ramp lowered, and she held her breath. She almost exclaimed in surprise as two vekorna descended from the shuttle, wrist lasers ready in their upper arms. Where were the kolbs? Was the shuttle unrelated to the extars that had passed over the island? Their mental buzz was unknown to her; she wondered if anybody recognized them.

One of the vekorna looked around, took in the log cabins, noting the silos, and scanned the forest. His infrared vision should not be able to pick them out against these trees, and all of her family was trained in keeping the vekorna out of their minds.

Maybe it would be better if you showed yourselves, the vekornan said, and Kuyi's heart nearly stopped. Had they been spotted? She was certain they were well hidden, especially from vekorna. **You've been here before**, the vekornan added. She frowned, thinking she misunderstood.

To Kuyi's surprise, two human males stepped out of the shuttle, looking toward the cabins, then the forest. They must have been as old as her grandparents. Kuyi turned to Rogo for confirmation, only to find his staring eyes among the branches. Who were they? Sweating hands tightened around her rope.

The bald man looked straight at her, then at Rogo. It was impossible, but Kuyi didn't dare move. She and her family often spied on the vekorna, and it was clear that the vekorna couldn't see their thoughts. Only Kirina could detect them at that range.

After a moment, the bald man strode forward and said, "They've added buildings, but the main cabin looks the same. Egalinsor lived in the largest." He glanced at the trees again, shook his head as if confused, then walked to the stairs on the side of the gallery. The blond man followed him, but the vekorna remained at the shuttle.

The bald man hesitated, then knocked on the front door. When nobody answered, he shouted, "Egalinsor! Nalimai! It's Aderen. We're back from Terra and need your help."

Kuyi looked back at Rogo. Her grandmother told stories of a baby named Aderen, who left with the others long ago.

When nobody answered, the two men went to the other cabins, banging on doors without opening them.

Another whine turned their attention back to the clearing, a single shuttle landing, crowding the open space. It was their escort, the wingless vekorna who ferried them to Egalra's forests for the harvest.

Kuyi held her breath again as the ramp lowered and disgorged their three vekornan escorts, whose familiar mental buzz permeated her mind.

Treklay stepped up to the lead unknown vekornan. **Who are you and why have you come to this place?** Treklay was broadcasting his inner voice for all to hear, probably expecting the Egalsan to be nearby.

I am Tararnifal, leader of an expedition to Terra.

You came on extars. Remove your faceplate.

Why? Can you not sense me through my thoughts?

Remove your faceplate or be destroyed, said Treklay. He raised his wrist laser to back up the threat. Aderen and the blond man were near the main door to the cabin, watching the exchange, faces unreadable.

Kuyi's heart leapt into her throat as she realized Treklay thought these were kolbs disguised as vekorna.

Tararnifal didn't move, but his companion shifted his wrist laser toward Treklay. Two more unknown vekorna came into view at the top of the shuttle ramp. They were holding heavy blasters, weapons that could cause physical damage. Why would they risk damage to trees and equipment, rather than use wrist lasers?

She hadn't seen vekorna use heavy blasters in a long time. Wrist lasers were more civilized, lethal to vekorna as the beam stopped the skin-to-brain oxygen transfer, leaving everything else intact. Nalimai said they were usually non-fatal to humans, though often caused strange sicknesses.

Carefully, Tararnifal removed his faceplate, holding it in his middle hands. His blue sensor head –five-sided, moist, as it should be– was not kolb. The forward face held three rows of eyestalks, and his external vocabulator.

Is this sufficient? Tararnifal asked. Treklay quickly stepped closer, inspecting the sensor head, extending six eyestalks beyond his own silver faceplate. Then he stepped back, descended to four legs, and his mind buzz became more intense as he inspected Tararnifal with other senses.

You are vekornan, Treklay finally said.

I am. Were you expecting something different?

Four extars were sighted flying over this land.

They are ours.

The kolbs did not take them from you?

No, the kolbs that stopped us in orbit told us to land.

That will be confirmed, said Treklay. **I must check the rest of your people.**

Why do kolbs possess extars, when vekorna used to control the space around Rykol, and kolbs were extinct? Why did Rubiel fire on us when we tried to contact Shilan or Dairnehy?

Kuyi held her breath. Why would they go to Rubiel?

Treklay stepped back, and asked, **You would deliver the extars to Dairnehy? Are you winged?**

His wrist lasers were raised again, along with those of

the two other wingless. This could get out of hand quickly.

Vekorna do not have wings, Tararnifal said, a little too carefully, and Kuyi wondered why he would say that. **Why do you ask this question?**

We are wingless, but you are winged! Treklay stepped back again and fired his wrist-laser, but Tararnifal had already stepped out of the way. The laser was absorbed harmlessly by the shuttle.

The new vekorna retreated, while the three wingless took shelter behind or inside their shuttle. Shots rang out from both sides, small beams from wrist lasers, more energized ones from the heavy blasters. One of the trees nearby was shredded, and Kuyi almost screamed before forcing herself to stay hidden. Maybe staying to watch had been a mistake.

A wingless vekornan fell to heavy blaster discharge. One of the new vekorna extended his wings, a huge span that Kuyi had only seen a few times in her life, and jumped from the top of the shuttle's ramp. He landed on four legs next to their wingless escort, and was hit by the beam from a wrist laser before everything suddenly stopped. He toppled over, crashing loudly into the unnatural quiet.

The fight had lasted only seconds. The vekorna were now eerily silent, unmoving. Waiting for something?

Aderen strode, almost glided, between the two sides, unafraid of their lasers. Kuyi's eyes widened. Tararnifal's vekorna shifted, coming out into the open, wrist lasers ready. Treklay and Talmer remained still, as if frozen.

"What do I do with them?" Aderen asked. "I can't control them forever."

Keep your mind away from me, said one of Tararnifal's vekorna, pointing his weapon at Aderen. **You should not control them at all.**

Control? Kuyi shivered at the implication.

Jye-Tan suddenly rappelled down his rope out of the trees, motion among the stillness. The new vekorna turned as one toward him, but Aderen shook his head, raising a hand.

"I knew somebody was there," he said.

"You're like Kirina," said Jye-Tan, echoing Kuyi's thoughts. He looked to Tararnifal and added, "If you're winged, you can get inside Rubiel."

Aderen grimaced, as did Kuyi. She thought Jye-Tan's obsession with the Rubiel fragment had faded. "Winged fighting wingless –so the winged wars have begun?"

"A long time ago," said Jye-Tan.

The second vekornan returned from his shuttle and said, **If the war has already started, these will be two additional casualties.** This time, he pointed wrist lasers at the live, though immobile, wingless.

Rogo dropped to the ground and shouted, "You will bring the winged down on our island!"

"Sebenet –wait," said Aderen.

Incredibly, the vekornan paused, his wrist lasers still pointed at the wingless. **I know you can do more than immobilization. How can you save them?** He wasn't talking to Rogo.

On a whim, Kuyi slowly slid down the rope out of her tree. Rogo didn't seem to notice, or was so distraught he didn't care. Kuyi walked up to Jye-Tan, standing at his shoulder. She was so close to the newcomers, and all the active weapons made her tremble. But if Jye-Tan could do it, so could she.

She felt a change in the air; something was suddenly different, as if a decision had been made just beyond her reach –she was shocked when the vekorna, winged and wingless both, lowered their weapons together. Aderen visibly relaxed, though he seemed angry, even ashamed.

"Let's find out what happened here," he said, and stalked over to sit on the shuttle's ramp, hands trembling.

13. Egalsan

The threat has passed, said Treklay, extending two eyestalks toward the dead winged and wingless before him. Amazingly, he wasn't perturbed by the live winged nearby. Pointing his weapon at the wingless, what had Sebenet asked? How could *Aderen* save them? Then they were different. It was like watching the effect her grandfather had when he was forceful.

A vekornan presence on Egalra will draw Dairnehy's forces, Treklay continued. **We will retreat to the eastern bay.**

"Isn't it a little late for that?" asked Kuyi, daring to speak. Rogo glared at her, but said nothing. Kuyi took a chance and added quietly, "The winged have surely noted the shuttle landing here, and Treklay's response."

Rogo nodded after a second's pause. "Kuyi is right. The shuttles must leave without us." Without waiting for Treklay's objection, he said, "Pick us up at sunsdown. By then, we'll have completed the anti-pollen harvest, and can return to Bol."

Kuyi's back straightened and she couldn't help but smile. Rogo never asked for her opinion, much less accepted it. Maybe this was a chance to become something more than a puppet, shadowing the youngest generation, clipping one of her strings.

From the shuttle ramp, Aderen said, "Don't leave yet. We have questions."

"Ask quickly," Rogo responded. "The longer those shuttles remain in the clearing, the more danger we are in."

Jye-Tan looked longingly at Aderen. Two human women emerged from the shuttle, looking around. Finally, a small weapon poked out, followed by a young man with dark hair and a close-cropped beard. His eyes took in Jye-Tan and Rogo, the two dead vekorna, and the positions of the live ones. He caught her gaze briefly and frowned, then scanned the trees, tapping the air strangely at irregular intervals.

"They should take the bodies when they leave," the bearded man said.

You will not take wingless dead from us, said Treklay.

We will take our own, though I would dispose of both respectfully, Tararnifal responded. Kuyi wondered if Treklay thought the winged would desecrate the body.

Cautiously, on a signal from Rogo, the rest of her family descended to the ground. By habit, they were spaced far apart so they could escape in different directions.

The blond man approached Rogo and Lusava, undoubtedly recognizing them as the oldest of the group, and in no particular hurry despite Rogo's urgent plea. "I'm

Doj," he said, as Aderen watched from the ramp. "Are you Nalimai's children?"

"We are descended from Egalinsor and Nalimai. I am Rogo, first grand-adult, and this is Lusava, firstborn. The vekorna must leave, so ask your urgent questions."

Genealogy was important to her family, but Kuyi had never heard anybody speak about their place in the family tree before. Did Rogo have some formal training in greeting outsiders? Were her grandparents expecting these visitors?

"You said the winged wars have started." Doj said, glancing at Jye-Tan. "How were the winged exposed? Why are there kolbs in space, while the vekorna fight amongst themselves? I don't know which questions are the most important."

We must be brief, though I have questions of my own, said Treklay. Talmer knelt at the dead wingless, retrieving the almond-shaped seeds that would become the next generation of vekorna. Sebenet did the same to his fallen winged companion.

Dairnehy started a new winged war, said Treklay, **but the discovery of the giant stellar fragment alerted him to the kolbs' survival on the Black Moon. The Fragment War armistice resulted in kolbs claiming all extars and the three moons, while vekorna retained Rykol.**

What of Shilan, our leader? Tararnifal asked. **Bolob tasked him with guiding the vekorna to peace.**

Shilan was murdered by Dairnehy, Treklay said. Doj's face recoiled, and Aderen frowned from his position on the shuttle ramp. **The winged monitor this region, and are**

content to allow the Egalsan here, but they will come for us if we linger longer.

He moved away from the group and toward the wingless shuttle. Tararnifal followed. The dead bodies had already been removed.

Bring your shuttle, Treklay said, pointing an extended eyestalk at Sebenet. **The Egalsan will answer human questions.**

"I will return for you at sunsdown," Tararnifal said, his metallic voice booming into the clearing, startling Kuyi. "I require other answers." He donned his faceplate and boarded Treklay's shuttle, probably the first time in history that a winged had joined a wingless voluntarily and alone.

Sebenet and the other winged retreated to their own shuttle, as Aderen rose to join the rest of the humans.

*   *   *

Feeling exposed, Kuyi watched the two shuttles depart.

Aderen asked, "Are we safe here, without a way to escape the island?"

Rogo shrugged. "We're safer with them gone. If Dairnehy comes, we'll scatter, but I don't think that's likely."

"Your family is Egalsan?" asked Aderen. "Named after Egalinsor, like this island?"

Rogo nodded, arms crossed, and said, "I ask again: who are you? When and why did you come here?"

Kuyi was bursting with different questions, and she held Jye-Tan's wrist, undoubtedly ready to ask his own. Rogo's were more important.

"Some of us have been to Rykol before, and returned to

Terra with Bolob," Doj said. Looking to the sky, he added, "Sebenet was sent to Terra in secret to gather more humans for the war."

The shock that must have been obvious on Kuyi's face was mirrored on those of her family, though she didn't fully understand his meaning.

Lusava was first to recover. She grabbed one of her long dark braids and asked, "Why would Dairnehy send extars to bring you back when you'd just left?"

"Presumably to help in the winged wars the same as we helped in the kolb war," answered Doj.

Shaking her head, Lusava said, "I'm not so sure."

Wondering what Lusava meant, Kuyi didn't notice that Jye-Tan had escaped her grip until he rushed forward, unable to contain his excitement.

"Aderen, you were born on Rykol like me. I'm Jye-Tan, first great-grandadult. I've heard about you. You're like Kirina, aren't you? You changed the wingless so they wouldn't be a threat –that's why they were so informative."

Aderen winced.

"He doesn't know Kirina, and you're talking like a lobom," Kuyi said, putting a hand on Jye-Tan's shoulder. "I'm Kuyikal, but my family calls me Kuyi." Then she added, because it seemed important, "Twenty-fourth grand-adult."

As Jye-Tan said, the events of the last few minutes only made sense if Aderen had controlled the winged, puppets far more than she was.

Aderen raised his eyebrows. "You're right, I don't know Kirina, but I think I should meet her. I'm second generation

92

from Rykol," he said, continuing to identify order of birth.

Doj said, "I was part of Nalimai's crew when we were first brought to Rykol. I was looking forward to seeing her again, but it seems she isn't here." He gestured toward the bearded man who had caught her eye earlier. "This is Étar, third generation."

While Doj introduced Sarenie and Ketaris, Kuyi's gaze was stuck on Étar, who was still frowning and looking around as if expecting an attack.

"You've already met Rogo, Kuyi and Jye-Tan," said Lusava. "This is Orem, twenty-third grand-adult."

"I'm Mai," said the shortest of the Egalsan. "*I'm* actually the first great-grandadult" She winked up at Aderen. "But I let Jye-Tan think otherwise." Kuyi was surprised she'd managed to hold her tongue this long.

Lusava took Mai by the arm and said to Kuyi, "Take them to continue harvesting. We can't stay another night, and we don't want to be short anti-pollen."

Kuyi closed her eyes as the usual acid rose in her gut, but did as Lusava said, ushering Mai and Jye-Tan toward the forest. She hung back, though, watching the twins natter at each other, but listening to the others.

"Orem, bring full baskets to the silos for storage until sunsdown," Lusava said, giving motion to the stagnation that had set in amongst her family. To Aderen, she said, "Help us collect anti-pollen, and we'll tell you what we know."

"Penagel spent time on Egalra," said Doj. "He doesn't remember learning about anti-pollen. Is that a counter-agent to folem spy pollen?"

"Yes," Rogo said, guiding him and the others into the forest past Kuyi. "It helps ensure folems aren't spying on us." He tilted his head at Kuyi, indicating she should follow.

Reluctant to return to her caregiving duties, Kuyi stayed hidden in the trees as Lusava pulled Aderen to the side, the two of them ostensibly alone.

"Rykol is dangerous for you, if you are capable of the manipulations I just witnessed. Bol will be doubly dangerous."

"Why?"

"My sister was nearly killed for her ability. The folems will be watching, knowing the stories surrounding you."

"What stories?"

Kuyi couldn't see Aderen's face, but heard confusion in his voice. The others had reentered the forest. Jye-Tan was probably slacking off, mourning his lost rabbit, with Mai complaining loudly about his lack of participation. She sighed, but stayed to hear the rest of the conversation.

"Like how you could get your way as a toddler, no matter what your parents wanted." Jye-Tan was right. "Egalinsor knew you would be like him, but I think it's worse. If the wingless think you have made changes to their minds, they will hunt and kill you. Folems won't be much better."

Lusava paused as Orem walked by, finished storing the full baskets. He pulled on Kuyi's hand as he passed, dragging her unwillingly into the forest. She strained to hear the rest of the conversation, but there was nothing but the chatter of people harvesting anti-pollen.

*   *   *

Beyond the cabins, trees grew with wide trunks, crossed branches, and broad maroon-colored leaves. Kuyi picked her way to Étar, who was inspecting the harvesting and lift equipment at the base of one tree, eyes darting everywhere. He saw her and smiled grimly.

"I don't think the winged will come now that the shuttles have left," she said, trying to lighten his mood. She picked up a basket and placed it on the screw-lift. "Join me –I'll show you how to pick anti-pollen."

She stepped onto the metal collar, and held out her hand to help Étar around the basket. She crouched low, and he did the same. As she pressed the switch, the collar jerked to life, causing Étar's face to grow tense.

"There are no rails," he commented, looking pale as they wound around the tree trunk, rising higher.

Kuyi laughed, and said, "Of course not." She wondered why he thought rails were necessary. Their spiral rise slowed as they came within reach of the lowest leaves.

"Now we stand," she said, rising to her full height, leaning slightly in the direction of the tree trunk. "Can you climb?"

When he nodded, she pulled her feet from the metal collar and hoisted herself onto a wide branch. She scurried to the place where the branches inevitably crossed, careful not to touch the leaves just above her head, and sat there, leaving enough space for him. The basket hovered behind her, following. She settled it onto the natural perch.

"Strong trees," he said, sitting facing her. She could tell he was uncomfortable, but admired his fortitude. "Not quite like picking fruit back home."

She reached up and gently peeled the small black tube from the underside of the broad leaf that hung over them. Testing it between her fingers, she felt six pods within, close to bursting. There was enough unharvested anti-pollen that this part of the island was covered in the fine, black dust.

"This must make it difficult for folems to gather information about what's happening on Egalra," he said.

"That makes it a great place to grow up," Kuyi responded sadly. She'd never had the chance. "Unfortunately, the winged and wingless feel the same. Off the island, anti-pollen decays faster than folem spy pollen, so we all need a continuous supply."

Étar peeled a long tube from the same leaf, felt the pods within, and dropped it into the basket. "There's no automated way to do this?"

"It's easier with our soft hands. Mechanical devices and vekornan fingers damage the pods." She peeled another tube from the leaf and looked around for other stable perches.

She caught movement on other trees, the mechanical lifts rising and falling on their cleared trunks. Aderen was with Lusava. Were they talking about his mission? If only she could hear across that distance.

She kept glancing back at him as she noted Doj standing high among the branches of another tree with Rogo, fingers busy peeling the black tubes. To her right, Mai was solitary as usual. She picked tubes at an incredible rate, filling her basket and sending it down, then filling another one. But

Orem was also alone, running from perch to perch. Somebody was missing.

Mai caught her eye and pointed down at the ground, rolling her eyes. Kuyi shook her head, admonishing the young woman, before noticing Jye-Tan listening at the base of Aderen and Lusava's tree. He had the same idea as she did, but was acting on it. Could he hear anything from down there?

Kuyi leaned across Étar's shoulder to gather another tube, a smile coming to her face. He didn't shift away as she brushed against him, depositing it in their nearly full basket. If she couldn't listen to Aderen, at least she was in a pleasant spot.

A little farther out, Sarenie sat with her back to another tree, hands in her head, crying. Concerned, Kuyi turned to Étar, hesitant to ask.

"We lost one of our crew to the kolbs before landing," he said. "Ret was my best friend, and Sarenie's love."

Embarrassed at intruding, even from this height, Kuyi picked another tube. The last unaccounted person, Ketaris was walking the forest floor with her head down, an illuminated panel hanging in the air ahead of her.

Picking up on her gaze, Étar said, "Ketaris is a xeno-biologist." As if that explained anything. He was doing more watching than picking. She reached up pointedly and picked the last tube before he could, then shifted her weight and scampered to the next perch, basket hovering again to follow her. He adeptly traversed the wide branches, gaining confidence as he came to kneel beside her again.

"Before this mission, Ketaris was on Mars, studying

Terran contamination. She's analyzing the anti-pollen down there, which I imagine is much more interesting."

Ketaris was too far below to be sure, but was acting strange as she manipulated the black dust and shed tubes with both hands.

"She doesn't seem to be holding her screen," Kuyi said, blushing when she realized that she hadn't noticed Étar talking again. She'd already peeled four anti-pollen tubes unconsciously.

Étar drew a rectangle in the air, and a screen appeared between them. Kuyi reached across the short distance and tentatively touched the light. Her fingers went straight through. "It doesn't feel like anything."

Étar laughed. "You need a kennis to interact with it." Pointing to the side of his head, he added, "Our kennis implants allow us to project energy screens. The palettes are linked to our bodies, which frees up our hands." He shifted to grab another tube, peeling it gently from the leaf. The screen moved with him. He placed the tube on his screen, and it stayed there.

"My hands passed right through it!" Kuyi said in surprise. She reached over and demonstrated. Yet the anti-pollen tube sat in the air without support.

"It's all controlled by my mind."

"You're more like vekorna, now," she commented. "Their technology is all telepathically linked." She continued harvesting, but her eyes flicked back to the hovering screen.

Étar shrugged and put the pod in their basket. "I'm sure Ketaris is doing a much better job than I could. We brought extra implants; they weren't meant for you, as we only expected three humans."

Three humans… Egalinsor, Nalimai and who else? Joem? She lost track of what he was saying for a moment.

"Ketaris and Xeffeya should be able to install implants in your family, so you can do this, and much more."

He spoke as if her head was a machine. Their own short-lived brain experiments using folem technology had led to deaths among newborn Egalsan.

She frowned at the unfamiliar name, though. "Who is Xeffeya?"

"She's our doctor. We didn't think it safe to bring the full crew to Egalra. The others are hidden with our extars."

Kuyi was surprised. "How many are you?"

"We were twelve, but now we're eleven."

"Because the kolbs killed Ret."

Étar nodded, pursing his lips. He lifted the tube absently from his palette.

Orem had joined Ketaris at the base of a tree, and they were talking. Kuyi saw him put his hand through her palette, the way she had with Étar's.

Étar waved his hand through the air to make his palette disappear, and they harvested in silence. The questions that were bursting in her earlier seemed less important than getting to know Étar. There would still be time for questions.

"Does this stuff inhibit vekornan telepathy, too?" Étar asked a few minutes later.

"No, it doesn't inhibit telepathy. Nalimai puts it in a drink that helps hide our thoughts from them. Along with mental exercises and the blocks Kirina put in place, we can keep the vekorna out of our minds." She was surprised and proud to be a fountain of information. "Like in the clearing, we can spy on vekorna without detection."

"I don't think Aderen found you either."

"I think he might have." Étar looked toward Aderen as Kuyi thought of Lusava's warning. Would the folems try to kill him, too?

"I'd love to help his mission," she said, shifting to another perch. Their basket returned on its own, empty, having deposited its harvest into one of the crates. "I don't know how I can be useful, though."

Settling on his knees, Étar said, "I'm sure you know more than you realize. What do you do on Rykol when you're not picking anti-pollen?" He held up one of the black tubes, squeezing it a little too hard, and got a handful of the black powder for his efforts. She tried not to laugh, but her smile was overpowering. Étar's face went from shock to amusement, too, lighting up beautifully. He shook off some of the powder, where it disappeared in the air currents. He tried to wipe the rest on his shirt and pants, to little success.

"You'll need more than water to get that off," she said, still laughing. She thought about his question. What did she do here, besides follow Jye-Tan and Mai around? As they grew up and required less shadowing, she spent most of her time relishing solitude. Étar wanted to know more than that, though. He was here for a reason, something Aderen had left unsaid, and she needed to offer him important information.

The rest of her family did work for the wingless, and sometimes folems. On rare occasions, Egalinsor let her look through some of his results. Mostly, she did what others wanted, pulling her puppet strings tight.

"We rotate through the needs of the family," she said, trying to be honest. "These days, we're mostly farmers. Orem usually takes care of the lobom algae crops and food supplements, adapting them to our needs. I've helped with that, but I prefer being with Egalinsor and his genetics research." She was only slightly exaggerating her role to him with pride. "We've made progress with grasses that can grow just outside the shield."

Étar nodded in appreciation. "I've heard about the genetics experiments. Back on Terra, some of our people have experimented with grasses, too. Do you work with Rykol-water?"

Her face fell. "Lusava has, but we don't contribute much anymore. You saw the red oceans?"

"Yes, we're using a variation of Rykol-water on Terra to clear some heavily irradiated land from a war long ago. I think we've made progress. Maybe we could pool our resources, for the sake of both planets."

The dangerous oceans were not something Kuyi thought about fixing. Rykol-water had killed most life on Rykol, and all of it in the ocean. There were legends about huge living sea creatures, but her family had never found them, back when they could do those types of studies. Rykol-water could be used as Étar said. Its original purpose was to protect the vekorna from radiation, and came with the side effect of extending their lives. It also came at a great cost.

"I hope you're careful on Terra, otherwise you could destroy all life, so it ends up like Rykol."

Looking down at the ground, Étar said, "I hope so, too." He cocked his head. "Aderen says it's quitting time?"

Wondering how she'd missed the signal, she saw Aderen and Jye-Tan descending one of the spiral lifts. She'd been so concentrated on Étar that she hadn't noticed him changing spots with Lusava. Had Aderen managed to get Jye-Tan to do work, after all? she wondered incredulously.

Mai had noticed, too, saying for all to hear, "Jye-Tan, did you pick your quota this time?" Lusava glared at her, and Kuyi went quickly to shut her up. "It's not sunsdown, yet," Mai complained.

"You can keep picking if you want, but I think we're going to the gathering fire." Lusava had told Aderen they would answer questions, but Kuyi hadn't given Étar much of use. She hoped he didn't resent that.

She left Mai and brushed against Étar's arm, intent on filling him in on everything about Rykol and the Egalsan. His touch made her feel warm. She smiled over at him and said, "We must have harvested enough for our needs, and for the wingless. We have time before sunsdown to exchange information."

He smiled at her, but held back from the group, hefting his weapon in his other hand, watching the others follow Aderen and her family as they disappeared among the trees. Only when everyone had departed did they leave the cover of the forest.

14. Fireside

It wasn't far from the anti-pollen trees to the Egalsan cabins. Incredibly, the largest cabin stirred memories from when Aderen had been here as a toddler —all images and feelings.

Jye-Tan followed at his heels, asking questions which Aderen answered lightly. Somehow, he'd replaced Lusava in Aderen's tree, harvesting with enthusiasm as he continued to ask about Terra. If Jye-Tan had access to a kennis node, he mused quietly, he might spend his long lifetime immersed in it. Étar's had requested implants for the Egalsan, which Aderen sent on to Xeffeya back at their hiding spot.

The silence of the Egalsan was unnerving. They were holes in his mental vision, unreadable and almost undetectable. What were they hiding, or was it truly a defense against vekornan telepathy? He'd hoped to speak with Nalimai, Egalinsor or Joem, but they were far to the south at Bol. He couldn't make that detour, although he was seriously considering sending the others there. Rubiel would be too dangerous for negotiators like Pinoa and Sarenie.

They rounded the back of the cabins, which would have seemed natural in any forest on Terra, only the surrounding trees marking the location as alien. The next path drew them around two short brown silos into another forest with remarkably different trees. It ended at a depression in the land, with a fire pit at its center.

At Aderen's raised eyebrows, Jye-Tan said, "The fire circle is tradition, even though it's already too hot on

Rykol."

The others were seated around the fire, ringing the lowest level of the bowl on logs or old stumps. Rogo was strumming a stringed instrument similar to a Terran guitar. Jye-Tan took Aderen's arm and drew him to a cushion, sitting cross-legged on the padded stump beside him. Aderen reached for what appeared to be a stringless guitar at his feet, but Jye-Tan took it first, sliding a metal bar up and down its length, producing haunting sounds.

Other instruments gave soft life to the hollow as he glanced around, noting how close Kuyi was to Étar, who absently tapped a wooden drum.

Aderen looked to the sky, reminding himself that they had to be patient. Let Tararnifal gather information from vekornan sources.

"We have a little time before sunsdown," said Lusava, blowing notes on a crude flute. Aderen studied her, falling into old habits as he tried to scan her surface thoughts. She was the first child born on Rykol after him. Egalinsor and Nalimai's firstborn. Did she have any mental abilities? What was it about Rykol that had endowed him with the ability to control people? Like the others, Lusava's mind was closed.

"Can we eat while we wait?" Mai asked. Jye-Tan and Kuyi chuckled, at which she rolled her eyes. "Before you ask me to go get it, I already snuck in and brought food for everyone." She held up small packages, and Rogo gestured with his hand.

Mai grinned, handing them to the five Arais and pointing to the cage he had dismissed near his feet. He hung it over the fire with a long rod. The others did the same, and the area grew quiet as they put aside their instruments.

"It's just a snack," Mai said, sounding bored. "Make sure you don't let it cook for too long."

"Rykol has changed since I was last here," said Doj, staring at the cages over the fire.

Rogo nodded and resumed strumming.

"The Rykol-water in your blood gave you long life," said Lusava, combing fingers through her hair, flute abandoned on her knees. "Interesting that even far from the source, the effect didn't diminish." She looked over at Rogo. "That implies human cells are saturated early after exposure and the genetic changes are stable. I wouldn't have come to that conclusion from our studies here." Turning to Doj, she asked, "Why did you come back?"

"The vekorna sent extars to forcibly take us," Doj answered, handling a palm-sized string instrument. "Bolob brought us back to Terra, but Dairnehy sent two faster fleets to get more humans. We returned with the first ships. The second fleet should be arriving at Terra soon."

"How did Dairnehy think he could achieve this secret mission, if Bolob was already on Terra?" Rogo asked.

Nodding at Doj, Aderen picked up a stick and tossed it into the fire. "You see the contradiction," he said. "Bolob won't arrive at Terra for another hundred and fifty Terran years." Aderen had already learned from Jye-Tan that the Egalsan didn't know the term, so he added, "Revolutions around our star."

Carefully, Aderen looked to the others, wondering how

much to reveal. Finally, he said, "You may find this hard to believe, but after Bolob brought us back to Terra, we slipped through a wormhole that took us back in time, which is why we were there before the first raider fleet."

Rogo plucked the strings of his guitar. "Time travel," he said. "It sounds implausible, but I don't know enough physics to comment."

Doj drew a rectangle in front of him, and the shining light of his kennis-controlled palette appeared. Jye-Tan's eyes lit up, watching intently as all music stopped again. Doj drew horizontal lines in the air with his finger, a scale of time. He placed a red dot on the scale above his palette. "We left Rykol here, and arrived here." He pointed to the highest of the lines in his kennis drawing. Aderen watched the Egalsan, seeing them drawn to Doj's ability to write on air.

"We traveled about five hundred and fifty years into the past." His hand swept down more than five lines, where he drew a wavy curve in blue. "On Terra, they called us Rykolien Immigrants, and we are now known as Arais."

Listening through their kennis link from farther south on the main continent, Pinoa reminisced about Tari, her *Alnevar* crewmate who had a tendency to abbreviate words and create new ones based on those abbreviations. Rykolien Immigrant had been shortened to R.I., which then became Arai. Aderen smiled and acknowledged her.

"With Bolob's help, we stopped an attack that would have destroyed Terra." Doj's hand skipped up two lines on his scale. "But then the first of Dairnehy's fleets arrived."

The others had started pulling food from the fire, so

Aderen did as well. He copied the Egalsan as they put the little cage to the side to cool.

"Let's say we believe you," said Rogo. "You were here once, and knew what the planet was like, the endless wars. Why did you choose to come back?"

"It's complicated," Aderen said, feeling insecure without the additional information he would usually pick up from surface thoughts. Rogo didn't flinch, so Aderen continued, taking a deep breath. "We weren't expecting Egalinsor and Nalimai to have so many children."

"There are twenty of us, mostly grand-adults, but I'm a great-grand-adult," Jye-Tan said, no longer able to contain his excitement. "First great-grand-adult."

Muttering under her breath, Mai said, "Barely," but she was hushed by a harsh note from Lusava's flute.

Unperturbed, Jye-Tan continued in a more somber tone. "There should be more, except for the vekornan attacks on Bol. Four of six firstborns are still alive." He nodded somberly toward Lusava. "Only twelve of twenty-four grand-adults, and two of four great-grand-adults –me and Mai."

Doj's eyes grew wide in alarm. "That leaves only two of Nalimai, Egalinsor and Joem alive."

Lusava's face grew grim and she nodded. "Egalinsor and Nalimai live down south at Bol, but Joem died soon after I was born. He was the oldest of us all, a generation removed from Egalinsor."

"I'm so sorry to hear that," said Doj, plucking some chords on his tiny instrument.

From among the hidden extars, Penagel buzzed, "I

remember his Rykolien lemonade." Doj relayed the message.

"We still drink that!" Jye-Tan said excitedly, lightening the mood somewhat. "I'll get you some before we leave."

There was an awkward pause, then Doj relayed another message from his husband. "You have a much larger family than we expected, given your origins. How do you maintain genetic diversity?"

"We're getting ahead of ourselves," Lusava said smoothly from the other side of the circle. "We were talking about you, not of us." She resumed blowing notes from her flute.

Aderen spread his arms wide and bowed his head, as Doj raised his eyebrows. He glanced quickly at the sky again. "Sorry for the change of topic, but we thought there was room for an exchange of knowledge." They'd already pooled knowledge from their time harvesting, and collectively they still knew very little about what happened on Rykol in the last four hundred years.

"We will talk about Rykol and the Egalsan later," said Lusava. "If Dairnehy sent ships to Terra for an army, why did they only bring eleven humans back, including those you are talking to by silent comms? Our family is larger."

She took her food out of the grilling cage and put it into her mouth, sucking on it.

"Twelve," Sarenie said below her breath. Aderen sent soothing thoughts across their kennis, thinking of the sacrifices they'd all made to be here.

He fiddled with his cage, and held the snack in his hand. "We've come back to guarantee no more ships will be sent to Terra to take humans against our will."

Rogo snorted as he strummed. "That's something you could never enforce, even with your extraordinary abilities."

Nibbling at the food in his hands, Aderen found it surprisingly pleasant. They hadn't mentioned Kirina since his arrival, and he hadn't asked, yet. Did she have some of his skills, or was she more like Monera?

They spoke openly about birth chambers, and he wondered if they could get him inside one, if not at Rubiel, then maybe at Bol.

He was about to argue his plan, but Orem emerged from the path. He hadn't noticed the man leave –or had he been here at all? Aderen wasn't used to being surprised by people, and vowed to be more attentive among the Egalsan. Rykol was dangerous to him, indeed.

"I spoke with Aneya," Orem said. "The communications were scrambled, as usual, so the vekorna should only catch carrier waves, if anything."

"If the vekorna destroy one of the transmitters, it will take time for Kirina to replace it," said Rogo.

"That's why we built satellites for the kolb war," said Doj. "It allowed our tanks and macrobots to communicate around the globe. But now they're gone."

"Destroyed in the Fragment War," said Lusava. "I remember that much. What did Aneya say?"

"Egalinsor and Nalimai want to see them at Bol as soon as possible, of course. They knew about the two fleets sent to Terra. They knew this day would come."

Rogo visibly relaxed. Aderen wondered if he'd truly

doubted their story. Was that why he and Lusava were so reticent about sharing? In the trees, Jye-Tan had talked a lot, but supplied Aderen little useful information.

"First sunset is about a minute away," Orem continued. "The vekornan shuttles are almost back from the eastern bay." Étar's drumming sounded a little louder.

"Let's hope the winged from Rubiel are not looking for a fight," said Rogo, standing to put the fire out, setting his guitar aside. Doj wiped away the scale of years that rose into the air with him as he stood, to the awe of Jye-Tan and Kuyi.

The fireside meeting had been less than informative. What were the Egalsan hiding?

*   *   *

You cannot come to Rubiel, and I cannot go to Bol, Tararnifal said, descending the shuttle ramp. Aderen shook his head, but the vekornan didn't let him speak. **I cannot trust Dairnehy to grant you an audience, especially with Sebenet so eager to describe your actions.**

Aloud, his metallic voice booming across the clearing, he said, "Tell the others to board Treklay's shuttle."

Tararnifal moved to the side for more privacy, where he dropped to his four lower limbs, locked into position by his exo-skeleton. His sensor head shifted, the metallic faceplate tilting a little this way and that to pick up disturbances in the clearing. As tigal-en, he could reach across hundreds of kilometers to connect mind-to-mind with other vekorna.

Aderen's own telepathy was much more limited. There was only one mind he could speak into from that distance. Monera was so far from here, he thought with a pang.

He said, **I have to go with you to Rubiel. I feel like we're wasting our time here, however pleasant.**

"This is not your shuttle," Tararnifal said, and Aderen spun quickly, surprised to find Mai padding up silently beside them. So much for being vigilant.

She was absolutely tiny beside the vekornan. She looked way up at Tararnifal, toying with her three long braids. Her face was tinted, with small dark eyes, much like Nalimai, he knew. To Aderen, she said, "Sorry I startled you. You're like Kirina, but you can't read *our* minds, even if you can alter a wingless so he'll invite a winged onto his shuttle."

Mai's directness made Aderen uncomfortable. His parents had impressed on him the need for privacy, his own and that of others. He rarely dove deep, usually able to glean enough from people's surface thoughts, much like the vekorna. To make a change so visibly in front of so many people had been a mistake, and only ever led to problems.

Fortunately, Mai turned away from him toward Tararnifal. "I've never seen a winged vekornan before. Thank you."

Not having access to her mind, Aderen reveled in the girl's unexpected reaction.

"Jye-Tan wants to go to Rubiel, too, but we've been banned since he tried to steal Dairnehy's crystal."

"The crystals that enhance telepathy?" Aderen asked.

"A piece of the Alpro fragment," she said, and Tararnifal extended two eyestalks from his upper and middle left rows. "If you find where he hid it, maybe you could bring Jye-Tan a small shard, and he could start doing real work."

I can make no promises, Tararnifal said.

111

Mai nodded and turned back to Aderen. "Be quick with your questions. We've stayed too long already; it's almost second sunset." She marched off to the other shuttle, not waiting for Aderen's reaction.

Watching her go, he internalized his words to Tararnifal. **Why can't I go with you? What did you learn?**

Mai's request may have more relevance than you realize. I do not have time to tell you everything about the Fragment War. When the stellar fragment was found, it enhanced Dairnehy's tigal-en abilities so he could see into all the minds on Rykol –human and vekornan, folem and lobom, and even kolbs out on the Black Moon. Much of the fragment was destroyed in the war that followed.

Angry that they had been awakened before the completion of Bolob's Plan, the kolbs attacked Dairnehy's forces on Rolm, and gained control of the fleet. Then they attacked Rykol, so quick and intense that they forced Dairnehy into the treaty.

Aderen nodded. That explained their welcome in space. He also deduced the answer to another mystery. Tararnifal hadn't been surprised to see live kolbs.

How did they survive? he asked. **Was the war a distraction, after all?** All that suffering and guilt had been for nothing. He fought to retain control.

Tararnifal withdrew his eyestalks. **Bolob swore me to secrecy, but you could have undoubtedly found out if you scanned deep into my mind.**

Only when necessary, he reminded himself, and it had never been necessary to look deep into Tararnifal's thoughts.

The effect of the stellar fragment on Rykol was worse, Tararnifal continued, altering the course of the discussion. **The wingless became aware of the winged, and a new winged war broke out.**

Dairnehy wanted that war eventually, which was why he sent the two fleets, said Aderen.

Yes, but it is no longer under his control. He attacked the source of the folem spy pollen when he found out the wingless were using it against him. The wingless defended the folems and loboms, and now control Bol.

That's what you meant when you said you couldn't go there, Aderen said, regretting not for the first time that other vekornan senses were unavailable to him. Tararnifal knew more than what was verbalizing.

Correct, said Tararnifal. **And you cannot go to Rubiel. I am convinced that Dairnehy indeed killed Shilan. Bolob's Plan to secretly and peacefully transition from a wingless to completely winged vekornan species has been lost with this war. He must be stopped.**

I don't think you can stop Dairnehy without me, Aderen argued.

It will be more difficult, but even you cannot control an entire city of vekorna bent against your will. I will convince him to see you, and send messages through the kennis node. You can concentrate on the birth chambers.

Tararnifal had a point. His failure in orbit only highlighted how vulnerable he'd become. Maybe it was better to start with controlling future vekorna.

"Good luck," Aderen said aloud. "I'll see what Egalinsor and Nalimai know, but I'll be waiting to hear from you."

15. The Shield Opens

It was a short hop south from Egalra to the mainland where they had hidden the four remaining extars. Tararnifal watched the green island disappear, replaced by red ocean on their right.

The city of Vamurel had been destroyed long ago in the first war with the alien zonguans. More recently, a group of escaped rokels hid there, attacking vekorna and kolbs alike.

Tararnifal identified himself to Samlar within the ruins, then guided the shuttle under overhanging debris, landing near a single extar. The others would be hidden elsewhere among the ruins.

The extar is ready to leave, and rigged for automatic flight, as you requested, Samlar said, approaching from under the extar's wing. **The humans left in a shuttle just before you arrived. Is the situation that bad?**

Aderen's group will join them at Bol. The situation is worse than we suspected. Tararnifal had not sent his thoughts to Samlar after learning of the stellar fragment from Treklay. The short trip from Egalra had allowed him to process the information, and form a plan with Sebenet. Despite his desire to report Aderen as the source of his failure, Sebenet had agreed to try and convince the vekornan leader that it was best to leave Terra to itself.

The old city's tower was a broken cylinder that stretched back hundreds of meters. Its five long arms had been mostly flattened, some of them buried in underground chambers now open to the sky. The ground was uneven, but Tararnifal's four arms helped keep him stable as he moved among the debris, stopping under the extar.

Shilan is dead, and Dairnehy woke the winged kolbs from their cryo-sleep on the Black Moon. In the short battle that ensued, kolbs took control of the three moons, leaving Rykol to the vekorna.

Non-verbal signals bounced between them, filling some gaps in the details. Like Aderen, Samlar hadn't known that kolbs survived due to Bolob's help.

Using the powerful telepathic crystal, he briefly connected all minds on Rykol, much as we tigal-en do during battle. Samlar showed surprise. **Bolob's Plan to give all vekorna wings has been revealed, leading to a new winged war.**

We cannot approach Rubiel in extars, which Dairnehy believes to be a kolb attack, said Sebenet

We will leave the extar in the desert as a gift for Dairnehy, and approach by shuttle, said Tararnifal, extending his wings to full spread and shaking them. Here, on a planetary surface, they had little effect. He belonged on an extar. **Stay out of sight and communication until we return.**

*   *   *

Tararnifal didn't want to bring Sebenet to Rubiel, but couldn't leave him with the hidden extars. Fortunately, he was still predisposed to Tararnifal's suggestions. However, his obsession with Rykol's stability could lead him to support Dairnehy's mission over the human one, to which he was not entirely sympathetic.

They took two escorts, Kular and Paknef, with them across the open ocean from Megnat to Nepral. Tararnifal had spent most of his life in space, then in Terra's blue oceans. Rykol-water was almost foreign to him, but the way the ocean had eaten away at the fallen extar was a grim reminder that it could easily strip away vekornan armor, too, burning them alive.

The extar landed in the deep desert to the south of Rubiel, not far from the coastal cliffs. Sebenet supervised the shutdown of the control sphere, obviously relieved to be away from Aderen. Tararnifal made his way to the forward-most launch bay, where he retrieved the kennis node Samlar had hidden. While humans could connect and link to a local node with their implants, vekorna needed a special receiver.

He had no doubts that Dairnehy would take the extar as bait. Tararnifal changed the kennis node's hiding spot, so it would get inside the shield. He buried his knowledge of it deep within his mind.

Walking through the extar corridor to the aft shuttlebay took longer than it would have in orbit, where he had floated along the same path using a propulsive flick of his extended wings. Now, his wings could only be used for stability as Rykol's gravity pulled on them.

He'd enjoyed the sensation of floating on Terra –not in air, but in Terran water. The freedom his wings permitted in that environment was completely unexpected.

The shuttlebay was empty save for two rolp-class shuttles. Tararnifal walked up one ramp and interfaced with the shuttle's telepathic controls, helping Kular complete his system checks.

Ready to depart, said Sebenet from the other shuttle with Paknef, lifting into the desert air. He was too eager to meet Dairnehy. Tararnifal followed warily, slowly moving north as the continental cliffs spread eastward.

In the distance, Tararnifal could see the edge of the shield as a line in the desert below, a small berm from the sands that had blown up against it, rising with the shape of the shield.

They broadcast their holograms with faceplates off, to show that they were not kolbs, wings fully extended.

Five kilometers from the shield, Tararnifal and Kular were thrown into the forward viewport as the shuttles were abruptly caught by an invisible net, just as the extar had the previous day. It felt like an impact, and took all six limbs to brace against the sudden deceleration. The day before, the extar had hung helpless in the air as Rubiel's defenses fired on it. Tararnifal waited to see what Dairnehy would do.

They will not let us in, Sebenet said from the other shuttle.

Dairnehy needs time. We are still alive. Replacing his faceplate, Tararnifal folded his wings, waiting.

Hours passed before a section of the shield opened high above them, and six shuttles emerged. Tararnifal watched as three landed in the desert sands, the others hovering almost on top of them. They descended together, as Tararnifal's shuttle was forced to the ground, helpless under their proximity.

*   *   *

Silver faceplates from Rubiel's soldiers reflected the two

bright Rykolien suns outside. Tararnifal and Kular stepped onto the sand, their armor sealed against the heat and dryness that would quickly kill them, unless they employed techniques the kolbs had perfected.

Their weapons are not raised, commented Sebenet, as he and Paknef joined them.

One vekornan approached faceplate to faceplate.

You are Tararnifal and Sebenet, the vekornan said, ignoring Kular and Paknef. Four eyestalks extended to inspect them individually, then withdrew.

You are Punad, prin-el to Dairnehy, Tararnifal said, skimming the vekornan's surface thoughts, as usual.

Punad acknowledged him, then said, **You are back from Terra, with no prize. That is not unexpected from Tararnifal, as you were sent to return humans, but is a surprise from Sebenet, who was to retrieve more.**

I met unexpected resistance, said Sebenet. **However, from what I have seen since my return, the mission is now irrelevant.** He gestured to the sky above, then to the east. **Kolbs control the space around Rykol, while wingless are aware of the winged.**

Humans would have provided talent to end this war, said Punad. **Come with me while we inspect your shuttle.**

He turned on two of his legs and lowered his middle limbs to traverse the sand between shuttles.

A mild electric tingling greeted Tararnifal as he leaped up the ramp to Punad's shuttle, as if he was passing through a weak but penetrating forcefield. There was too much security for this task –what was Punad afraid of?

The shuttle sealed behind them. Empty of benches and

equipment, there was ample room for Tararnifal's vekorna and Punad with four guards.

Remove your faceplates, Punad said, echoing the greeting they had received at Egalra.

This time Tararnifal didn't hesitate, feeling the cool air of the shuttle flow over his sensor head. The others followed his example.

Punad's surface thoughts relaxed slightly as he saw the four blue faces, proving they were vekorna. He came close and removed his own faceplate, extending eyestalks from all three pairs of rows on the front of his sensor head. Spots on the other faces darkened as he probed Tararnifal's surface thoughts; anything truly important was buried so deep Punad would be unable to find it.

We will retrieve your extar from the desert south of here, Punad said. **Tell your crew to submit to inspection and transfer command to my vekorna.**

There is no crew, Tararnifal responded.

Surprised, Punad moved to Sebenet. **Where are your other extars? You left with a fleet of eight. Only one sits in the desert to the south.**

The kolbs captured three, and you destroyed one yesterday, said Sebenet. **The others are hidden until we understand what has happened here.**

It is best that they remain hidden, so kolbs do not retrieve more. Are humans hidden with the extars?

No, they were taken by the wingless at Egalra.

Punad responded with momentary distress, then said, **That is unfortunate.**

He finished his inspection of Sebenet, then went to

119

Kular and Paknef, intent on their blue faces, scanning their surface thoughts.

Returning to Tararnifal, Punad said, **Extend your wings.**

The rest of the vekorna crowded away from him, making room. Questions burning in his mind, Tararnifal released the hold on his wings, which protected them from the dryness of Rykol's atmosphere, and from discovery among the wingless vekorna when that had been necessary.

For most of his life, he had been unaware of his wings, until Bolob awakened them with blue water and revealed his true nature. Instinct had kept them hidden from others, who were either unaware of their own wings, or were themselves wingless. That instinct had been tempered on Terra, where there were only winged.

Punad passed behind him, careful not to touch the tough but sensitive wings. He partially extended his own, a gesture of growing trust.

You may fold them, said Punad, and gestured for Sebenet to move to the front of the shuttle. When he was done, Punad retracted his wings and said, **You are genuine.**

You had doubts? Tararnifal asked, though he already knew the answer.

Kolbs and wingless have infiltrated Rubiel before.

How did the war start? He needed more than what Treklay had given them, and from a winged source.

Dairnehy will reveal how the wingless became aware of us. The real war began when they used folem pollen to track our movements and ambush us.

I am aware, but not why folems allowed it. Tararnifal had been astonished when Treklay admitted that they had ways to interpret the pollen data.

Folems had a remarkable resemblance to Terran flowers, and sent pollen into the high winds so it scattered all over the world. In this way they recorded all of Rykol's history, even many of the most secret conversations. Punad, like Treklay, was accusing folems of leaking their knowledge to the vekorna.

Replace your faceplates, said Punad. **The wingless pushed us back to the brink of extinction, ruining all the progress that Bolob and generations before him had made.**

Outside, Punad's vekorna were spraying mists into the two shuttles. Tararnifal wondered if his kennis relay would remain hidden when they did the same to the extar.

Is that anti-pollen from Egalra? Tararnifal asked.

Punad shook his upper left hand. **Egalra is controlled by the wingless. That is a synthetic variety. The electromagnetic sweep at the shuttle entrance has a similar effect.**

Tararnifal stood near the front of the shuttle as Punad took its telepathic controls, watching the ground fall below, and the shield open ahead. Then they were inside the Rubishield, and beyond Aderen's control.

Sebenet's mental voice came to him privately. **Punad saw in my thoughts what Aderen did at Terra, and has sent the information ahead to Dairnehy.** The warning was unexpected. Maybe Sebenet would be an ally here, after all.

Then we are brought into the trap at last.

The interior of the shield was immense, and went right up to the cliff that overhung the ocean in the north. The poisonous red ocean surrounded the city on two sides. It dominated the eastern horizon.

They flew over a desert more closely resembling the deserts of Terra, where sparse life survived. The city could be seen in the distance. A tall tower, gleaming and sparkling red, five arms reaching out from its base, Rubiel was not the most beautiful of Rykolien cities. But the vekorna had always governed from here, rebuilding after it was destroyed generations ago. When the vekorna went into hiding from their unstable sun, kolbs governed from here for a time.

Like most vekornan cities, the southern-facing arm was longer again by half compared to the other four, which were rayed out from the central tower. They settled between the southern and south-eastern arms. Tararnifal counted another fifty vekorna in the landing area, with one standing apart from the others. Dairnehy.

Feeling the vekornan leader reach out to him, Tararnifal responded by searching for the core of Dairnehy's thoughts. They were confused, paranoid, and suspicious. Anger simmered below the surface, but that had been true before Tararnifal left Rykol.

Punad led them down the shuttle's ramp.

"It has been a long time since you stood in Rubiel," Dairnehy said to Tararnifal, his metallic voice booming across the pad. "I would see your crew."

They are hiding for the moment, Tararnifal responded.

"You attacked Sebenet's fleet at Terra," Dairnehy pressed, taking a step toward Tararnifal. "You are withholding the humans you brought to Rykol."

Remaining still on his four lower limbs, Tararnifal did not deny the accusation. **That is more complicated.**

"The situation is not complicated. You inhibited the actions of Sebenet's fleet, and sent them back to Rykol with nothing. You are a traitor." He pointed his wrist lasers at Tararnifal. Armed vekorna surrounded them, similarly threatening.

Tararnifal extended three eyestalks from the upper slits of his mask to peer at Dairnehy.

When I left Rykol, you were prin-el to Shilan. Bolob's Plan had progressed sufficiently that he could go to Terra and return at its completion, the wingless gone, never aware of our existence. You let Bolob's Plan fall apart. Perhaps you are the traitor.

"Bolob's Plan was flawed. He didn't realize how critical humans are. Kopiv knew, wingless though he was. Humans are the key to our domination of Rykol."

There are more humans on Rykol now than when Kopiv's five fleets had been here, and look what you have let happen –division and strife, more than Rykol has ever seen before.

But look at what they've done! Dairnehy exclaimed, mental voice suddenly private to Tararnifal. He pointed two eyestalks at Sebenet. **They changed *him*. Even now, one has touched the stellar fragment on Rolm. Imagine what we could do with them under our control.**

You cannot control them, Tararnifal said, worried at

this unexpected revelation. Had Ret survived, after all?
Aderen is more powerful than you can imagine.

But I can create more like him –I *have* created more like him!

16.Memories of Rykol 2

They should have been going west, following Tararnifal to Rubiel. Instead, they were flying south, farther from his goal. Tararnifal wanted to deal with Dairnehy, and thought Aderen should lead the team to infiltrate birth chambers at Bol. That would take time, as they didn't know if it was even possible to instill a prohibition against Terra into future vekorna. Bolob had programmed the birth chambers to suppress the wingless, so there was a chance. Would Egalinsor and Nalimai be able to help?

His skills would be better used at Rubiel, directly with Dairnehy. If they couldn't get into a wingless birth chamber, Aderen would leave immediately, retracing his path northward.

He suppressed the instinct to push harder into the Egalsan minds, doubting he would get far without their awareness, which would alienate them. He hoped the unexpected number of Egalsan would increase his chances of succeeding at Rubiel. Dairnehy would be used to dealing with humans.

He'd buzzed Wandel and Pinoa. They'd left the ruined city, headed for Bol along a different route. They'd packed supplies, including kennis implants for the Egalsan.

The desert sped by below, and Aderen drifted into a waking dream state. Recognizing this as another vision, he wondered who was sending them, and why he couldn't block them. He stopped trying, and let it flow into his mind.

*   *   *

The heavy voice once again pounded into his thoughts, fading even as it spoke. **We need your help.** He tried to respond, but it was like speaking into the void, his telepathic voice attenuating into nothingness. Frustrated, he turned his attention to the landing shuttle.

It wasn't Aderen's shuttle. One vekornan descended the ramp and extended eyestalks, opening his senses to the grasslands.

Aderen found that he could see from this vekornan's point of view, and could even connect to some of its senses. This was more than a vision. Tararnifal had given no explanation for his prior vision, and his crew hadn't seen it. He was reluctant to ask the Egalsan, yet.

Exit now for your research, the vekornan said.

A second vekornan joined him, and their automatic connection gave him names.

Mlurat said, **It is time to perfect siim birth chambers, so we can breed them into soldiers.**

He'd been right. Vekornan embryos in Rubiel's birth chamber had mutated into the first siims after the asteroid impact. South of the equator, the kolb mutation would have created rokels.

That may be our desire, but I have watched them at Ban, and think they serve us better as researchers, Tenen responded. **They observe everything with their strange senses, and have pursued knowledge we thought impossible.**

125

Aderen watched in awe as the shiny black-shelled siims descended. They had the same body structure as vekorna, with two legs, two arms and a pair of mid-limbs that could function as either arms or legs as needed. They wore light armor, but no protection for their sensor heads.

While the vekornan sensor head was five-sided, the siims' had so many sides that they were almost round. Two rows of eyes extended across many faces, where the vekorna had three pairs of rows only on the forward face. He saw other physical differences, but Aderen knew the greatest ones would be mental.

The area of Tiroosae and Metik had been scoured for kolb patrols. While the kolbs had announced their mutated species and planned to send them immediately into battle, the vekorna were still trying to keep siims a secret, without a firm plan on how to use them.

Aderen did the calculation from the memory, and found that it had been two hundred Rykolien years since the asteroid impact. The sky was clear, meaning dust kicked up by the asteroid had settled.

Twelve more shuttles landed in the grasslands and disgorged their siims, a wave of black covered by scant light blue armor.

Three hundred siims will be a tempting target. Keep watch for kolbs. The shuttle lifted off and adopted a circular trajectory at higher altitude. If kolbs were watching, they would know the vekorna were up to something, but it was the only way to protect the siims.

They want to study the ocean next, Mlurat said. **If their research is approved, we will need a large**

platform to launch from.

Tenen wiggled his left middle hand in a negative gesture. **We have destroyed too many ships trying to descend through the top layer of the ocean. If anything lies below the Rykol-water surface, we will remain ignorant of it.**

Tiroosae will occupy them for a long time, Mlurat said. The grasslands spanned the continent like a belt, and the siims claimed it had an abundant variety of drought-resistant plants that could be used to repopulate Rykol's deserts. The vekorna had never investigated why it hadn't expanded beyond the narrow east-west band.

The hours folded into each other, so the day passed in the blink of an eye to Aderen. Siims came and went, depositing samples in the shuttle, synthesizing strange mixtures that they used to dissolve plants. Their mobile laboratory looked more permanent as the day wore on.

The different groups of siims didn't mingle. Through Rykol's long night, Aderen watched them gather in a circle and join hands and feet, in a display of touch that Mlurat and Tenen didn't understand. It was eerily similar to the Egalsan fire circle, but without instruments.

The two vekorna watched the sky as they relayed the day's results to nearby Metik, hoping their data would not attract attention from kolb patrols.

Before the suns rose, much faster than they would in real life, the siims were visited by tiny lights.

"Mirkonel," Aderen whispered in awe. These creatures had saved Kezim and Penagel from rokels, and defended Jairon and Kym before they were captured by kolbs.

Laughing despite himself, Aderen watched the siims comically try to take samples of the creatures, but the mirkonel would blink out when they came too close.

Mlurat had to remind the siims of their mission, which was to study plants, not glowing insects. Reluctantly, the siims returned to their work, but Aderen saw how they were easily distracted by the mirkonel.

That night, mirkonel again glowed just out of siim reach, as if daring them to try and capture the tiny creatures.

His gaze was drawn to two siims in particular, who remained immobile as the others tried to trap the mirkonel. Eyestalks extended far in different directions; he wondered if they would get tangled.

Seeing the mirkonel through siim eyes was dizzying, but Aderen was able to do it in this strange vision. He saw the pattern of the mirkonel, and with quick motions of his arms, Aderen had captured two of them in a clear metal container.

Confused, Aderen was conscious of his four arms and two legs, wondering when those had appeared. His vision was fractured, as that of an insect, until he focused through one eyestalk.

The mirkonel became intensely red, moving about the container frantically, warming it through their vibrations. By morning, the glow had faded, and the insects were stationary on the bottom.

Aderen studied the insects, inspecting them through his instruments. The siim's thoughts became one with Aderen, his interest in the insects intense. The body was cylindrical, with four wings and three glassy eyes on one end. A secretion on the bottom of the container fluoresced when touched by a green laser.

The mirkonel hadn't moved by midday, so Aderen concluded they were dead, and opened the container for a more invasive exploration of this interesting species.

The two insects leapt into the air, wings disappearing in a blur of motion, even to siim eyes. They faded into the distance, glowing the fierce red of the night before.

Disappointed to lose his samples, Aderen turned back to the plants he'd been studying.

Moments later, or maybe time had sped up again, a roaring permeated Aderen's auditory organs.

Move! Back to the shuttles! The voices in his head were urgent, and he stood tall to see what was happening. Were kolbs attacking? That would ruin their research, the first time they'd been allowed beyond their prison at Ban.

He yelped as his body was pinched where armor didn't cover his four arms. A great cloud of mirkonel had returned, and they buzzed angrily. The swarm hovered over his sensor head and poked at him, annoying brushes as they couldn't pierce his thick shell. Then one did get through, and he flinched. It wasn't long before others also penetrated his shell, and he was paralyzed with the pain. He felt chunks of his sensor head being eaten away as he ran to the shuttles.

A vekornan came to him, and the mirkonel scattered. Why did they attack siims but not vekorna? Aderen tried to separate himself from the siim, watching the vekornan lead him to the shuttle. As the world went black, his visual sensors failing, Aderen found himself on the shuttle, watching vekorna guiding injured siims onboard, no mirkonel in sight.

Damaged beyond repair, said one vekornan, whom he recognized as Mlurat. Aderen watched Mlurat raise his weapon and place it on the siim's chest. He flinched as the vekornan fired, and the siim's mental signature went dark.

*   *   *

The vision dissolved, and Aderen's focus came back. He found himself staring into Kuyi's penetrating gaze. Did she know what he'd just seen? He wondered what she was thinking, and was once again tempted to push into her mind, just to see if he could. Were these visions normal on Rykol? Who did the voice belong to? There were still too many unknowns, and he wasn't ready to ask.

Part III: Manipulations

17. Southward

Sitting across from Aderen, Kuyi tried not to stare at him. Growing up in Bol, she'd only ever known service to her family, reacting to the strings that they pulled. She'd already cut one string, and vowed to get free of them all. With the arrival of Aderen and Étar, things had changed.

Initially, Étar sat on her left, knee-to-knee, which suited her fine. But as the shuttle lifted off and flew over Egalra's unlit treetops, across the small strait of Rykol-water to the mainland, Étar stood to join Jye-Tan at the front.

Their three hour southward flight to Bol would bisect the continent, turning east before the Esetek mountains. It would be a long ride in this awkward silence.

Unable to start a conversation, she now realized how stagnant her life had been. If she'd studied history like her aunt Kirina, she could tell Aderen about more than farming, harvesting, and caregiving.

Lusava and Rogo had relaxed since getting confirmation that their guests were somehow expected, but they seemed just as lost as her.

Maybe she knew enough to get them talking.

"We weren't always farmers," she said, watching Jye-Tan return from the front of the shuttle to squeeze between Aderen and Sarenie. "Nalimai used to build things on Rykol before the war." She sighed wistfully. "That was long before I was birthed."

"We *were* always farmers," said Lusava, with a smile that took some of the sting out of her contradiction. "We had to be, to survive. Vekorna don't eat the way we do, and the loboms make tasteless algae."

"So Egalinsor started the garden at Rubiel," said Doj.

"The gardens grew large as our family expanded," nodded Lusava. "We dug deep wells and aquifers, using wind traps to catch the sparse water. But they've gone wild, as we don't go to Rubiel anymore."

Jye-Tan blushed in guilt.

"Our main gardens are now at Bol," said Rogo.

"We harvest more than anti-pollen at Egalra," added Orem, pointing to the rear of the shuttle, heavily laden with crates. Most of it was anti-pollen, and for a change Mai didn't point that out. "I can show you spices that grow only there." He gestured animatedly at Ketaris, who smiled back.

Through the window, Kuyi found the faint glow she'd been waiting for, and pointed it out before everybody digressed into details of farming.

Jye-Tan stood again, and strode to the front on his long legs. "It's the old science station." He shrugged and returned, standing in front of Aderen.

"It's close to the sea, in the continental notch," she said. "Before the war, Nalimai led science expeditions over the ocean and into the deep desert. That was a docking port." The abandoned station's glow had been slowly fading as its components wore out and it lost power.

"Nalimai was a structural engineer on Earth before *Avenger* was caught by the vekorna," said Doj. "She had many structural tests on board." He raised his eyebrows in surprise. "I'd forgotten about that."

"We used to take our science labs above the ocean, as Kuyi mentioned," said Lusava. "We collected data about Rykol-water, and why it transforms into regular water over the continents, even into lakes and rivers."

"They're abandoned these days," said Kuyi.

"It's too dangerous to go into the deserts now," Rogo clarified. "A lot of the structures were destroyed in the war."

Jye-Tan sat again, once more squeezing between Aderen and Sarenie, whose face was still pale white in the cabin's faint light, draped by her yellow hair. Aderen looked thoughtful. He would be able to access all their scientific data at Bol, which was something she could help with.

"We were a greater society before the war," Rogo admitted. "But you won't see much of it now. Nalimai always blended her structures to the native landscape, to minimize our footprint."

"Like the hidden silos on Egalra," commented Aderen. Rogo nodded.

That strategy continued to this day. In the desert, the mobile labs were inadvertent targets for winged-wingless battles. But at Bol, they were hidden from sight behind artificial landscapes also designed by Nalimai.

Still, she didn't know how this would help Aderen in his mission to stop Dairnehy. The Egalsan had withdrawn from most of Rykol. They had no resources to get into Rubiel, or to draw Dairnehy out to meet with him. If Tararnifal succeeded, how would she be of use?

Jye-Tan went to stand up again, but Mai reached over to grab him by the leg, and pushed him down. "Stay put!" she growled. "There's nothing to see."

Mai was right; there was nothing to see, even during the day. The deep desert was completely inhospitable to humans. She didn't know how her aunt and uncle stayed alive out there.

"I know that the war has made your mission more difficult," Kuyi said, deciding to confront Aderen's problem head-on. "But I'm sure Egalinsor and Nalimai will be able to help. They still have friends among the vekorna."

All conversation stopped, as eyes turned to her.

The awkward silence had returned, but Doj filled it with a smile. "When we were here last, we learned to network vekornan birth chambers, as there is a synergy between the ones in different cities, allowing the soft vekornan embryos to grow into strong, hard-shelled adults. I'm hoping to use them to further our mission."

Kuyi looked to their two vekornan pilots, and wished Doj had brought this up when they were in the privacy of the Egalra meeting bowl. Ontral would hear of this conversation.

"It's how we were programmed to be healthy, too," said Jye-Tan.

"What do you mean?" Doj asked.

Étar turned from the front of the shuttle to look at Kuyi. He sat beside her, stirring emotions again.

"Our birth chambers were also connected, until they failed," Jye-Tan continued. "Kuyi's was the last one fully functional." Jye-Tan had been lucky to survive. On the verge of failing, he and Mai had been extracted early. According to Nalimai, that's what caused his short attention span, and Mai's undersized stature.

Aderen glanced at her neck, where the seeds of the next generation would be on a vekornan. She laughed, breaking the tension as others joined in.

"It's how we maintain genetic diversity, with foreign strains," Lusava said. "You asked about that at Egalra. It's too dangerous for live births at our age."

"Like Tiralie," Kuyi said, and didn't realize she'd spoken out loud until Mai's eyes widened in shock. "It was a surprise; she died in childbirth when I was very young."

Étar looked at her piercingly, but she didn't shy away from his gaze, instead studying his features, his green eyes, dark hair, and commanding beard. Her breath grew short when he touched her, but she didn't want to let go.

"What do you mean by foreign strains?" Aderen asked, the tone of his voice causing Doj to turn his head sharply, eyes narrowing.

Kuyi frowned. It had to be obvious where foreign human strains came from. They'd scoured Rubiel and Ban for human DNA. That's how birth chambers worked.

Lusava sighed, indicating the answer wasn't going to be as simple as Kuyi thought. Finally she opened her mouth to answer.

Instead, she grunted as the shuttle lurched sharply to one side, throwing them against each other. Kuyi's stomach rose, and she had to swallow to keep it under control. By then, the shuttle had banked the other way, and she fixed her restraints to stay seated.

"We're under attack," Aderen said.

Kuyi recognized the look in his eyes. Her aunt would do this, searching telepathically like a vekornan. Their shuttle dove suddenly before rising again, and her stomach flipped.

Jye-Tan fell from his seat, and Étar unstrapped to help him back up. Kuyi noted Étar's return as his leg brushed hers, but she was watching Aderen intently.

Kuyi felt another jolt, hit by laser fire. The shuttle wouldn't last long if this continued.

"They're winged vekorna," said Aderen. Who else did he think would be attacking the wingless? But Lusava and Rogo seemed just as confused. Normally the winged didn't bother with Egalsan. The Arai arrival had obviously changed that.

She felt the shuttle pitch forward, and imagined the hard ground rising up from the darkness out front. She wasn't ready to die, now that she'd found a purpose for life.

Aderen said grimly, "We need to land."

Her inner ear told her the shuttle leveled out, but then it started weaving, avoiding their pursuers, refusing to release the tension in her stomach. She longed for a proper reference in the darkness, aside from the red streaks in her window. The attacking vekorna were close, forcing them lower.

An explosion sent the roof of their shuttle hurtling away, and everything started shaking. They flipped onto their side before settling back.

"Brace yourselves!" Aderen shouted as the lasers suddenly stopped. She barely heard him over deafening wind.

Étar struggled to see out the front, fingers clasped to hers, as the shuttle hit the ground. She was wrenched sideways against the straps, her neck straining as he held her close, cradling her. The crates of anti-pollen toppled over into the cabin, small beads rolling across the buckled floor.

Kuyi's attention fluttered from person to person in the sudden silence, but eventually her eyes settled back on Aderen. He didn't speak, didn't explain, but she knew he had saved their lives.

18. Diverted

Kuyi was still trying to rid her head of fogginess from the impact when Aderen said, "We're surrounded. Wait here." He stood on the uneven floor, glanced once at the open roof, and made for the exit ramp.

Bring out the stellar fragment, a voice boomed into their heads.

"All we have is anti-pollen," Rogo said, but his voice didn't carry beyond the cabin of the shuttle.

Jye-Tan's eyes perked up as he looked around.

"We don't have a piece of the stellar fragment," Lusava called out as she stood unsteadily.

Dairnehy saw human thoughts in your fragment, came the voice.

"Leave us," Aderen's voice boomed. Kuyi managed to stand and looked out one of the windows. Vekorna lined the desert around their crash site, weapons raised.

Aderen pointed in the faint light, and some of the vekorna lowered their weapons. "Leave!" he shouted again. The line of winged slowly backed away, though most of their weapons still targeted the shuttle.

Red light pierced the night as Treklay and Talmer fired at the winged vekorna. Caught by surprise, they took out several targets before any reacted.

"No!" cried Aderen, but if he had any control over the vekorna, it was now broken. Laser bursts hit their shuttle, eating away at the remains of their protection.

"Get to the back with the anti-pollen," said Rogo, herding them. Kuyi struggled to look out the windows as Jye-Tan hung back. She grabbed him and Mai, practically dragging them to the rear of the shuttle.

She made out three shuttles on the ground, and a faint light flew above them with the characteristic whine, indicating at least one still in the air.

A grinding noise shook their shuttle.

"The wingless are turning the turret manually," Orem

said, huddled close with Ketaris. In confirmation, a red light streaked from their position out across the desert, hitting one of the other shuttles. It was followed by a loud boom, and flames lit the area, almost too bright to see.

Rogo lowered the rear ramp, and urged them out into the desert sands. Kuyi's feet sank to her ankles. This was not the safest place to be walking.

Aderen led Treklay and Talmer down the ramp as the front of their shuttle exploded. Aderen was shaking his head, hands waving through the air as if trying to conjure something.

"Defend us, then," he said finally, and the two wingless faced opposite directions, firing their weapons. Return fire hit the sparse shelter of the remains of their shuttle.

"Can't you freeze them like you did to the vekorna on Egalra?" Jye-Tan asked.

"I have, but only to a limited range," Aderen replied, his voice straining. He managed not to sound annoyed. Kuyi was still shaking, but Étar released her, motioning to stay flat on the sand. He raised his weapon, and started targeting their attackers.

Laser fire grew more sporadic, slowing as Kuyi cowered under the debatable shelter of their shuttle's bones.

"I've got most of them," said Aderen, then looked up. Kuyi followed his gaze, wondering if winged shuttles would target them from above.

She shuddered in surprise as a fireball exploded above them.

"Was that you?" Jye-Tan asked. Kuyi was too petrified to be impressed.

"No, not me," Aderen murmured. One of the shuttles lifted off, firing into the sky. "It's Danosh," he said in awe.

Doj strained his neck toward the sky. "Does he know it's us?"

Aderen didn't answer. Kuyi knew of Danosh, but had never met him. His involvement with the Egalsan always led to trouble, but he was more of an ally than Dairnehy.

The sky lit up with laser bursts, while the ground-based attacks faded away. Kuyi could only think of falling debris, and dragged Jye-Tan and Mai under their dubious shelter.

When the noise died down, Étar returned to her side, and said, "I think Danosh won. His shuttles are landing."

"We can't trust him," Kuyi said. She wiped tears from her eyes.

"We have to trust him more than Dairnehy's forces."

He was right. She stood, shaking. Released from her grasp, Jye-Tan and Mai rubbed their arms and peeked out into the desert night.

Shuttles had landed all around, but the vekorna were not interested in humans, searching for the remains of the force that attacked them. To their left, two more shuttles landed, and vekorna were streaming out into lines.

Aderen walked onto the sand, unprotected. Kuyi and Jye-Tan stepped out of the shelter, but didn't get far. Her quick pulse calmed as Étar stopped at her side.

Six shadows stood closer, just inside the shuttle's flaming light, faceplates glowing with diffuse reflection. She could discern their stances, and knew that their weapons were ready.

Vekorna could stand perfectly still, but the shadows in the darkness were unnaturally rigid –frozen in place, like Treklay back on Egalra. Aderen held their strings.

Aderen stepped in front of one winged, who lowered his weapons and dropped to four limbs, advancing into the reddish light.

You are powerful, little Aderen, said the vekornan, his telepathy manifesting as a unique buzz in her mind.

Kuyi bristled at his words. She was insulted for Aderen —she hated being called little.

"You remember me, Danosh."

I remember you as a child who could manipulate others, but not like this. Another with similar abilities roams the desert these days.

He was talking about her aunt, who could also control vekornan minds. Had he seen Kirina recently?

"I won't let you kill our wingless." Aderen motioned to Treklay and Talmer, who were also silent and rigid.

"I have not come to kill wingless, though that was inevitable. I have come for you." Danosh's metallic voice rang over Kuyi as he waved at the destruction around them. The vekorna didn't often speak with their vocalizers, a piercing metallic tone that echoed in her ears.

"We have to get back to Bol," Lusava said, emerging from the tight cluster of Egalsan. Kuyi admired her bravery so close to the winged. Maybe Aderen's show of power gave her courage.

Danosh turned to Lusava. "I will release you in the city."

"We won't go to Erim," she insisted.

After a short pause, Danosh said, "I understand. Come with me to a more secure location."

Lusava looked uncertain.

"What's wrong with Erim?" Étar asked, putting a gentle hand on Kuyi's shoulder.

"Besides the tower being destroyed in the kolb war," Doj added.

Humans have long memories, like vekorna, Danosh

answered silently. **Two young Egalsan were killed on a mission in the rebuilt city when fighting broke out.**

"You coerced them into joining your mission, but didn't watch out for them," said Lusava, clearly upset.

The result was unfortunate, Danosh agreed. **Unlike then, I now control most of the city. However, Lusava is worried that it is too close to Bol, should the wingless decide to counter-attack.**

"You want us to go to Esetek," said Aderen, looking to the south. How did he know?

My surface thoughts would surely be open to you even if I resisted.

Of course. Kuyi followed Aderen's gaze, and saw only darkness. In daylight, the tops of the mountains would be visible over a hazy horizon.

"We've delayed enough already," Aderen added. "What can you offer me if we go?"

"I was once prin-el to Dairnehy. If you really want to meet him, I can get you inside Rubiel."

"Esetek." Lusava frowned, but Rogo nodded. Surprisingly, she turned to Kuyi, who also nodded, though Esetek scared her as much as Erim. Kuyi held her fear in check at being asked, and she straightened her shoulders.

Danosh extended three eyestalks toward Aderen. **Will the wingless come with us, under your influence?**

"Give us our own shuttle, and we'll fly ourselves," said Aderen. "Étar, can you connect to the shuttle's controls?"

"I had a kennis link to this one as soon as we took off from Egalra," Étar responded, mouth set grimly as he gestured to their destroyed shuttle.

"We need our cargo," said Lusava, voice shaking.

Be quick.

143

They each took armfuls of anti-pollen and spice crates, leaving everything else, and transferred them to one of Danosh's shuttles.

Kuyi stayed close to Étar, the only human with a weapon. She felt safer around him. Although Aderen could control minds, she didn't understand his limits.

Amazingly, Danosh didn't insist on keeping any of his winged on the shuttle.

Treklay and Talmer didn't protest when Aderen directed them to the front of the cargo hold, where they rooted their lower limbs to the floor. She wondered how the wingless at Bol would respond to their compliant behavior. Aderen looked like a child standing between them –little, and obviously controlling their minds. His ability to do so without hesitation was disturbing, and she wondered if they were resisting. She always resisted when Lusava and Rogo tried to control her, force her into something.

Though she wanted to be at the front with Étar, Kuyi took the last seat next to the hold, close to Aderen, watching him.

From the window, she saw Danosh fade into the darkness with the other shadows. Despite her agreement, she didn't like this detour, and wondered what Aderen had seen in Danosh's surface thoughts.

It wasn't as if Danosh ever *tried* to hurt them. It was, like Lusava said, that he didn't keep them safe.

*   *   *

The glow of Étar's palette shone even to the cargo hold.

"He's created holographic linkages to control the shuttle," Sarenie said, startling Kuyi. Her face had softened, the tears gone, beautiful in the faint light. Maybe the attack had cleared her head.

"We need a special helmet to interface with vekornan shuttles," Kuyi responded, controlling her shivers with tight fists. "Kennis implants allow you to do incredible things."

Sarenie nodded, playing with the ends of her blonde hair. "They're part of everyday life on Terra." Sarenie guided her to a seat on the other side of the shuttle.

Kuyi asked, "How will your other shuttle get into Bol, if we're going to Esetek?"

"We're closer to Bol than Pinoa, but they will arrive first," Sarenie responded. "Étar suggested they hide until we leave the mountains."

Kuyi nodded. The wingless would probably leave them be. Then the Egalsan would get everyone inside the shield together. Home would be strange with so many new people.

"Why was your family stalling at Egalra?" Sarenie whispered.

Kuyi's eyes widened, and she glanced at Aderen, then back to Sarenie. The woman had transformed from the grieving person she'd met initially.

"Don't worry, he's listening." Sarenie tapped her temple, indicating her kennis. Were all the Arais listening?

She'd seen the relief in Lusava's face when Orem came to the fire circle after talking with Aneya. Her mind raced. "I think they wanted Egalinsor and Nalimai's confirmation."

Sarenie frowned, but nodded.

"They've lived through so much already. You're the first thing that's happened on Rykol since I was birthed."

"Human birth chambers," Sarenie said, as if the thought had been summoned by Kuyi's words. "I'm sure you know more about them than you think." Kuyi opened her mouth to answer, but Sarenie continued, "We'll have that conversation another time." The topic had made Lusava uncomfortable, and she wondered if that's why they'd been stalling.

"Tararnifal told Aderen that the stellar fragment is more important than your family implied. The winged that attacked us thought we had it," Sarenie continued. "Can you tell us why?"

Kuyi felt uncomfortable as she realized Sarenie had changed seats to get farther from Lusava and Rogo.

"For a short time, it played a major role on Rykol," she answered, trying not to sound guarded. "I don't think there's much left, though. The vekorna and kolbs fought over the fragment until only small pieces remained. Even Jye-Tan was obsessed after touching it at Rubiel." This time, Sarenie's eyes opened wide, though she didn't glance at Jye-Tan, who was ineffectually running his fingers through Étar's virtual shuttle controls.

"He said he could see into minds like Kirina, and hid Dairnehy's piece of the fragment." She lowered her eyes. "Gavet died in the escape, and Aneya was badly hurt."

"They stole it from Dairnehy?" Sarenie asked. Kuyi nodded. She had penetrating eyes, much more so than Aderen. It almost felt like she was boring into Kuyi's thoughts. "How?"

Shrugging, Kuyi said, "I wasn't there, and Jye-Tan won't talk about it. Aneya might tell you when we get to Bol."

"I'm sorry about your uncle," Sarenie said, a bit of her grief returning. "Is there more of the fragment on Rykol, maybe at Egalra?"

"I don't think so," Kuyi answered. "Dairnehy hoarded it. All of that happened before I was birthed."

"Except for Jye-Tan's theft."

Kuyi nodded. "That's why we're banned from Rubiel."

Sarenie opened her mouth, undoubtedly to ask another uncomfortable question, when Jye-Tan's voice echoed loudly through the cabin.

"I can see Esetek from here. Jairon and Nalimai escaped from kolb caves there with Egalinsor."

Doj nodded grimly. "Our friend Tari coordinated that rescue mission."

"The giant obom monster was trapped under the mountain after kolbs attacked the folems generations ago," Jye-Tan continued. "It was released by kolb excavations."

More recently, the folems had released other monsters into Rykol's deserts in a misguided attempt to stop the winged wars. Fortunately, their cloning machines had been severely damaged in later attacks on the Temple, and as far as Kuyi knew, most of the monsters had been destroyed.

She held on tight as the shuttle passed through turbulence over the mountains. Not particularly tall, they still posed a navigational hazard for travel to the southern part of the continent.

The shuttle banked hard, and Kuyi looked anxiously over at Aderen, who easily maintained his balance.

"Here we go," Étar belatedly called from the front.

The red lights from Danosh's shuttle disappeared, and Étar followed it into a cave, landing without a bump.

*　　　*　　　*

Danosh and his wingless were already waiting as the ramp lowered to let them out.

"Weapons stay here," said Aderen, and Étar reluctantly nodded, stowing his.

Talmer and Treklay followed Aderen, extending several

eyestalks through the slits in their faceplates. They were undoubtedly absorbing more details with their other senses.

We have intelligence that will interest you, said Danosh, and guided the two wingless to a hollow in the cave. Kuyi sourly wondered how much was of their own volition.

Aderen said, "You can't hurt them. They leave with us."

They will not be harmed, and you may leave with our shuttle. Danosh activated a giant hologram. **Ontral requires this information.** He left them with two winged, which seemed to satisfy Aderen. How far did his strings reach?

Warily, Kuyi followed them down a long hallway, cut straight through the mountain to a large room. It was probably too early to expect trouble. They had as little choice as the wingless vekorna.

The near-circular room was filled with wide tables and more holograms, all devoid of observers. With so many humans, the room almost felt crowded.

There was movement from behind a large opaque hologram; they weren't alone here, after all. Kuyi gasped and stumbled backward involuntarily. Doj hissed a sharp intake of breath beside her.

What were kolbs doing on Rykol?

19. Esetek

Danosh always meant trouble for her family, and Kuyi had found it. He hadn't even bothered hiding the kolbs.

The pentagonal sensor heads with their peaked tops, identical to the vekorna except in color, were familiar enough. Their yellow faces stood out among the silver faceplates entering the cave, and although they didn't appear to notice the humans, she knew better. Danosh walked by them without comment, heading for another passage.

Sarenie, on the other hand, was livid, her face turning red as her eyes narrowed. Fists clenched, hair flailing, her anger bubbled over.

"You killed Ret! Why are you here? You're all supposed to be dead!" Doj maneuvered to cut her off.

Judging from what she'd already seen, Aderen could have frozen them with a thought, but he didn't pull any strings.

"It seems that kolbs have not held to their part of the treaty," Aderen said, following Danosh. "I wonder if the vekorna have hidden extars on Rykol in exchange?"

One of the kolbs rounded a hologram, looking formidable. But he stopped when he had a clear view, extending two eyestalks toward Sarenie, and two more toward Aderen.

Dairnehy has certainly hidden extars; the treaty is not perfect. However, I am authorized to tell you that your lover survived and is alive on the Black Moon.

"What?" Sarenie's eyes grew wide, and she pushed against Doj. "What have you done with him?"

Aderen stared at the kolb, incredulous. "He's telling the truth. Ret is alive, and recovering." He advanced on them in earnest. "We need to speak with him immediately."

We cannot contact the Black Moon.

Aderen continued staring at him, then Sarenie turned away with tears in her eyes. Doj followed her to the wall, where he sat silently with an arm around her shoulders.

Without a kennis, Kuyi felt blind and deaf to the Arais.

Our leaders are experimenting with him, the kolb

continued. Sarenie's face fell in shock. **He is testing the stellar fragment, with hopes of understanding its effect on humans. He will not return until that task is complete.**

"That's why the winged attacked us," Aderen said. "Dairnehy saw Ret through the fragment." Kuyi thought of Jye-Tan's claim that he could read minds with Dairnehy's fragment, and wondered if Ret was testing telepathy.

"That has to be what the kolbs were hiding at Rolm," Étar said. "I thought you said Jye-Tan hid Dairnehy's fragment."

Kuyi blushed, but it was Jye-Tan who answered, glaring at her. "He has many pieces."

Follow me, Danosh called, startling Kuyi.

"You'll be okay here?" Aderen looked from Sarenie to Doj and Étar, who both nodded. With a kennis, she supposed, like on the shuttle, they would hear everything.

Scowling, Lusava went to the wall and sat on Sarenie's other side, comforting her with a touch. Kuyi felt sympathy for her pain, and wanted to stay with Étar, but had to follow Aderen. She couldn't eavesdrop on kennis conversations.

"Jye-Tan, Mai —over here!" she said in a loud whisper. They were staring at the kolbs with Ketaris, and started guiltily when they heard her. The twins came to the tunnel, but Ketaris remained, her palette glowing in the air, unabashedly taking readings until Orem took her arm.

Danosh had to bend onto four legs, his upper arms scraping the floor to fit through the tunnel. Kuyi hunched over on principle, though the taller Jye-Tan had to reach to run his fingers along its upper surface.

Djaxtal and Thirp'inc will help me restore Bolob's Plan, said Danosh. **I was Dairnehy's envoy to the Black**

Moon when the war against the wingless turned against us. The kolbs refused to help, having already destroyed their wingless.

"What is Bolob's Plan?" Rogo asked. "Bolob has been gone as long as they have." He waved his hand at Aderen.

The pause was perceptible, but brief, and it was Aderen who answered. "The plan to eliminate the wingless through atrophy, manipulating birth chambers to mature only the winged." Kuyi wondered if this was common knowledge on Terra, or if he'd stolen the information from Danosh's mind. Rogo seemed as surprised as she was.

Aderen cocked his head to one side as they emerged into another room, which contained a single large holographic map table. She recognized Egalra and Esetek immediately. "Bolob planned to unite the two winged species," Aderen said in awe. "You never told my parents that there was a larger plan, did you? You knew about the survival of the kolbs," he added, facing Danosh across the table. "You knew they hadn't been wiped out."

Aderen was clearly upset. "Did you know that they would destroy the islands in the south?" Pointing back down the tunnel, he said, "My parents' friends flew in those missions. Wandel was stranded for weeks after the explosions."

Was Wandel's anger coloring Aderen's emotions? The other shuttle would probably be settling into its hiding spot near Bol soon. What was it like to get instant reactions from people so far away?

Bolob and I helped remove winged kolbs to the Black Moon, but we had no contact with the wingless, Danosh replied. **I did not know that the wingless were growing explosive crystals in these caves, which they used to**

destroy their lands.

Kuyi advanced toward the hologram, Rogo following her. It felt strange to be leading the family.

"You used them as pawns," Aderen said, his voice now steady.

Kopiv used your crews as pawns in his war, said Danosh. **Bolob saved almost half the kolb population.**

"My father always felt guilty about wiping out the kolbs. You and Bolob knew they would survive, which makes his guilt meaningless."

They served a greater plan. If Shilan had survived, Rykol would have been unified within a generation.

"But Bolob left Dairnehy as Shilan's prin-el, and Shilan wasn't strong enough to control him," said Aderen, turning to the hologram.

Nobody is strong enough to control Dairnehy, answered Danosh. **It was my fault the Rolm lunar base was destroyed. I did not resist when the kolbs attacked. They had already felt the power of the stellar fragment.**

"Why is the stellar fragment special?" Aderen asked.

Kuyi saw Jye-Tan's eyes bulge, earning an audible sigh and another eye roll from Mai. Kuyi nudged her purposefully, holding Jye-Tan back.

When Dairnehy accessed the stellar fragment to enhance his telepathy, he connected all minds on or near Rykol. For a brief moment, the wingless knew the winged among them, human minds were opened to us, and for those who knew where to look, we could see kolbs on the Black Moon.

"We saw into vekornan minds, too," whispered Rogo, shivering. Thinking back to Sarenie's questions on the shuttle, Kuyi wondered how much more her family knew, and were hiding from Aderen.

Danosh said, **Kolbs also saw into our minds. They didn't need my warning to deny Dairnehy, who would have had them fight the wingless on his behalf. Kolbs seized more than half of the fragment at Rolm, and because of Dairnehy's obsession, traded it for our space-based assets.**

"You botched your attempts at peace," said Aderen. "More than once. We are here to negotiate our own treaty between Rykol and Terra. We could help you start again."

You cannot negotiate with Dairnehy, said Danosh. **I tried, and barely escaped with my life.** He took a step backward, twitching his wings.

"What about the folems?" Aderen asked. "They were supposed to be your protectors."

The folems never knew how to stop the fighting, said Danosh. **They made things worse when the winged war started again. Come with me.**

Uncertain, Aderen looked back toward the tunnel that led to Étar, but moved to follow. How deep would he let Danosh pull them? Kuyi felt uneasy. Danosh had offered to get him into Rubiel, but at what price?

"You need to let us speak with Ret," Aderen said.

Your friend is not a prisoner, Danosh told him. **He will return to Rykol as soon as it is convenient.**

"When is that? He's part of our team, and we need him now."

There is no way to get him.

"We have extars; we can go to the Black Moon, if you tell the kolbs to let us through."

Kuyi had seen Aderen pull the strings holding Treklay and Talmer's minds. Why wasn't he forcing Danosh? Was it because Ret had volunteered to stay with the kolbs?

Aderen closed his eyes. "I could find Monera halfway across the solar system," he muttered, clearly frustrated.

"He's having trouble with telepathy," whispered Jye-Tan.

"I think he's reaching for Ret," Kuyi whispered back.

"Watch your step," Ketaris said, just as Aderen stumbled on the uneven floor, his concentration broken.

In the open space of this new cave, Kuyi gaped at three giant black carcasses, thick tentacles and sharp claws resting on the ground, inert.

She instinctively moved to the side, saying, "Those are obom shells." The wall was rough against her back.

Aderen looked like he wanted to advance, but couldn't. "That's the shell of the creature my father fought –and survived, though it poisoned him almost to death."

"Yes, he almost died under this mountain, fighting the obom with Egalinsor and Nalimai," Danosh responded with his audible voice, the metallic sound reverberating through the large space. "I was there, and helped Bolob defeat it, in a cave far deeper in the mountain."

Just beyond lay two smaller obom shells, black claws sitting on top of their long, coiled arms.

"There were more?" Ketaris asked, drawing her palette in the air again, but keeping her distance.

It was Rogo who answered. "These are new. The folems tried to stop the fighting by sending you a common enemy."

"A flawed plan," Danosh said, eyestalks extended through four of the six rows on his faceplate, all pointed at different people. "Monsters are still out there. The folems cannot help us. I need Ontral's piece of the stellar fragment."

There was silence as Rogo looked to Orem, and Jye-Tan's mouth moved without words, for probably the first time in his life.

Finally, Mai said, "Ontral doesn't have a piece of the stellar fragment. Jye-Tan would have found it in the Temple –like Dairnehy, he's obsessed."

Kuyi felt her face growing red as Jye-Tan put his hands on his hips, about to admonish Mai. Rogo glared at them instead. "You were inside the Temple?" He looked around and closed his mouth, probably realizing this wasn't the time to talk about it.

She was thankful when Aderen said, "You want me to steal it, if it exists. That would make things worse. No."

"In exchange, I will get you inside Rubiel and a fair audience with Dairnehy. It is the only way to stop him, which is your ultimate mission." Danosh led them deeper into the caves.

"Why is Danosh talking with his audible voice?" Jye-Tan asked. "Something is wrong with these vekorna."

The corridor was narrow, but Aderen and Ketaris could stand side-by-side, Kuyi and Jye-Tan following.

Aderen stopped at the threshold. "Why would you do this again?" He was staring at rows of crystals, looking like planted crops. "Kolbs grew these explosive crystals to destroy the southern continents. What are you planning?"

"These are different," Danosh responded.

Aderen looked from Danosh to Ketaris, then his eyes defocused for a moment. "What have you done?"

"They can't use telepathy in here," said Jye-Tan, pointing at the rows. "Those are mirror crystals."

"What are mirror crystals?" Kuyi asked. She'd heard of

the exploding crystals, which had collapsed part of this mountain on top of Egalinsor and Nalimai.

"Buzz the others. We have to go back," Aderen said.

"Distress call from Étar," said Ketaris.

Were the kolbs attacking him? Armed vekorna filed into the room, weapons ready. Danosh had a tendency to put her family in danger, but not directly by his own actions. If Étar was in trouble, then so was Lusava.

Effortlessly brushing Aderen and Jye-Tan out of his way, Danosh grabbed Kuyi. Looking at the sharp clawed fingers of the vekornan's lower arm, she went very still.

"No!" shouted Jye-Tan, but Rogo held him back. Mai stared at the vekornan in horror.

"Let her go! Why are you doing this?" Rogo asked, his voice booming.

"To ensure you do as we require," said Danosh.

"Vekorna don't take hostages," said Rogo, perplexed.

Aderen's face was full of anger, straining, but Danosh said, "You are mentally impotent in here."

"Let me see Doj, Sarenie and Étar," Aderen demanded, his voice full of power, but apparently not backed up by his mind.

"You will not see them until you have delivered Ontral's fragment," said Danosh. "I will keep my word, too."

Mirror crystals inhibit telepathy, Kuyi thought. Danosh must be mentally blind as well, which was why he hadn't spoken into their minds since the first cave. How did Jye-Tan know?

"I won't do anything for you. You were a friend to humans when my parents were here. What happened?"

"I must revive Bolob's Plan, and will take more hostages if necessary. Even you can only defeat Dairnehy with the stellar fragment."

Aderen made a hand signal, and Ketaris wiped her palette away, retreating backward through the tunnel.

"We're leaving," Aderen said, following.

"As you must," Danosh responded, holding Kuyi rigidly.

Aderen locked eyes with her. "I'll be back for you. I'm sorry." Kuyi nodded, trying to look braver than she felt.

Growling, Rogo turned and left the crystal room, almost dragging Jye-Tan and Mai. Aderen followed.

Kuyi watched armed vekorna pick up mirror crystals and advance with Danosh. She had to move with him, or risk cuts to her arm from his sharp hands. She heard Aderen shouting in the other room.

They passed the three obom shells and the empty hologram table. Aderen stood with the two kolbs in the next cavern, and Kuyi was pulled up short by Danosh's tight grip, drawing blood. Étar, Doj, Lusava and Sarenie were limping into the long tunnel, toward the shuttle. Étar caught her eye and paused, but at a touch from Sarenie, moved on.

"Give her up, Danosh," said Aderen. "Your gambit has failed. Though I can't touch your mind, the kolbs are more my ally than yours."

"You are outnumbered," said Danosh. "Leave, but I will keep this human."

His vekorna advanced, bringing the mirror crystals deeper into the circular room. Aderen and the kolbs retreated. They were alone against many more vekorna, and Aderen's mental abilities were clearly muted.

As Danosh's vekorna moved from the tunnel choke point into the more spacious cavern, Djaxtal and Thirp'inc suddenly advanced on them.

Thirp'inc made to grab one of the vekorna, who pushed

him aside. Instead, the kolb shifted his weight and thrust his hand at the mirror crystal in a good imitation of a lobomai punch. The crystal cracked on impact. A second punch from his lower arm shattered it, pieces scattering to the floor. Was Aderen directing him now?

Kuyi's heart leaped, but she was torn. If they could destroy enough mirror crystals, Aderen could immobilize these vekorna with a thought, and they would be free. Was her life more important than the kolb's mental freedom?

The vekornan dropped the remains of the crystal and raised his wrist lasers, dropping a pit into the depths of her stomach.

"Stop!" she shouted, pleading.

"Stop the fighting," echoed Danosh, and both sides paused in their advance. Kuyi wondered if Aderen was pulling on them.

She turned to Danosh, twisting in his knife-like grip. "You don't know what to do with human hostages. Don't use Dairnehy's strategies to change who you are. I don't think you're willing to kill your kolb allies for this." Two eyestalks peeked out of Danosh's silver faceplate at her. She winced as the blade-like fingers of his lower hand cut into her arm. "You've never intentionally put my family in danger before. That's not who you are."

She frowned at him. "Remember what Kirina said the last time you neglected to protect our family. You can't surround yourself by mirror crystals forever."

"I do not fear Kirina," he responded, withdrawing all of his eyestalks. "However, these tactics may be too extreme."

Danosh withdrew his grip, and she pushed away from him, stumbling between the two kolbs to Aderen. Her heart was beating too fast, thumping in her ears. She'd done it, and without the powers that Aderen used so casually.

"Let's get out of here," Aderen whispered into her ear. "I don't have control of the kolbs. Can you move?"

Blood was running down her arm to drip from her elbow, but otherwise she was physically unharmed. She nodded, keeping an eye on Danosh's extended eyestalks. The two unresisting kolbs were now surrounded by his vekorna. The sea of mirror crystals advanced.

Aderen led her through the last tunnel to the shuttlebay, where Étar was waiting. Her heart skipped a beat as he looked into her eyes, inspecting her for... for what?

Satisfied, he ushered her forward as the tunnel behind them filled with mirror crystals, vekorna advancing like a plunger.

Treklay and Talmer were already at the shuttle, and raised their weapons as the winged burst into the shuttlebay, fanning out. Danosh was still using extreme tactics, but to chase them away, instead of holding her hostage.

Talmer fired at the advancing winged, shattering crystals, which were immediately replaced. The winged returned fire. Étar sheltered her as they ran up the ramp, but what good would it do if he was shot in the process? He left her in the care of Jye-Tan and Mai, and ran to the front of the shuttle.

Talmer crumpled to the ground at the base of the ramp. From the top, Aderen yelled at Treklay, "Into the shuttle. We have to leave. Now!" Treklay obeyed, not glancing at Talmer's body as the shuttle lifted off, ramp closing slowly.

Danosh's voice carried to them before it shut completely. "You know the route to these caves. But if you return, we will be gone, and they will be empty. Remember my offer."

"I understand that you are desperate, but you were a friend to my parents, and have betrayed us. I will not forgive you," Aderen said. The ramp was closed, and she wasn't sure Danosh heard.

Kuyi watched through a rear window as the shuttle flew off without chase. They had escaped with one casualty.

She looked up at a touch to her shoulder. Doj said, "You were good confronting Danosh. Let's clean you up."

20. Memories of Rykol 3

Head buried in his hands, Aderen searched his memories for anything he could have done differently. More than ever, he wished he'd gone to Rubiel with Tararnifal. He could have been confronting Dairnehy right now, advancing their mission, the reason they were on Rykol. But he now realized he had to get the Arais safely to Egalinsor, first.

He'd thought Danosh could offer him a birth chamber for experiments. Danosh undoubtedly knew how Bolob used birth chambers to remove the wingless genes, and could have helped them ingrain a prohibition on Terra. But his temper prevented that conversation from happening.

"What kind of new weapon does Danosh have, to defeat me so completely?" he whispered, wondering if he could protect anybody anymore.

Doj, cleaning Kuyi's arm, looked up at him.

"It's the mirror crystals –they were at Rubiel, too," said Jye-Tan, struggling against Mai to approach him. Aderen didn't realize he'd spoken aloud. "They inhibit vekornan telepathy, and it looks like they affect you, too."

"Have you heard of mirror crystals?" Aderen buzzed the

Arais. It was a long time ago, but maybe one of the original crews would know of them.

Immediately, Wandel, Pinoa and Penagel responded negative from farther south. Doj shook his head and returned his attention to Kuyi.

Aderen leaned over toward Jye-Tan. "So they're new," he said. "Tell me about the mirror crystals. Is there any way to defeat them?"

Jye-Tan withdrew from the intensity of Aderen's gaze. He looked to Mai and Kuyi, then stuttered, "I don't know." He ran a hand over his face, then through his hair. "I don't know," he repeated, voice steadier. "I'm not telepathic, but I used them to trick Dairnehy at Rubiel. He couldn't detect me."

At a look from Rogo, Jye-Tan added, "I only took the fragment to try it out, and it worked for me. Do you really think Ontral has one, too? We would know, wouldn't we?"

"I could read Danosh easily in the first caves," Aderen said. "But I missed his plan all along." He stood, pinching the bridge of his nose.

"It was harder in the obom cave," said Ketaris. Aderen stared at her. "You were having trouble there, and you were telepathically blinded by the time we reached the crystals."

It was true. He should have recognized the feeling of diminished power. Except that he'd been holding his mind closer in, tightening his circle of influence.

Monera said he was running. On Rykol, he was supposed to make one big change that would last lifetimes, and that was all. No more mental changes after that –to anybody.

Yet he'd done *only* that since arriving. First the kolbs in orbit, then Treklay and Talmer on Egalra, again with their winged attackers, and now the two kolbs against Danosh. He couldn't run from it, because it never ended.

When he'd *needed* to make a change, when human lives were at stake, he was haunted by Ret and the memory of Legionnaire Dalpah so long ago. He'd almost failed to control the kolbs.

"I should have stayed," whispered Sarenie. "Maybe they would have let me speak with Ret."

Another opportunity he'd missed, and just when Sarenie was starting to recover from the wound of her loss, now torn open again. If Jye-Tan could read minds using Dairnehy's fragment, would Ret be able to do the same?

Aderen considered what he might do with such a tool.

The fog of another vision washed over him, and he struggled to keep it at bay for a few more minutes, moving to sit as far from the others as he could in this cramped shuttle.

"I think the mirror crystals caused Bolob's lapse in telepathy when he was trapped on Esetek with your father," Doj buzzed, including Penagel in this conversation. "They were probably mixed in with the exploding crystals."

"It would explain why they remained incommunicado for so long," Penagel buzzed.

Would Bolob have told anybody about mirror crystals, if he realized what they were? He had been trapped in the Esetek caves for days, seemingly stripped of his tigal-en telepathy, unable to contact the outside world for help. Maybe his father wouldn't have been so sick after the encounter with the obom.

The feeling of disappointment washed away as he shut out his kennis and other senses, and let the vision carry him back to a time long gone.

*   *   *

Aderen was dropped once again into the grasslands of Tiroosae. Siims were studying the plant called vitonesse, which they'd learned had a healthy appetite for mirkonel. The siims that he currently shared minds with, showing him the fractured view of the portable lab, wondered how vitonesse got away with killing the insects without retribution, when a single capture by siims made them into mortal enemies.

He listened for the heavy voice, but there was nothing.

Mlurat stood in the center of the siims, projecting the vekornan mental buzz like a shield, which seemed to keep the mirkonel away.

Vitonesse swayed around the lab, another layer of protection. Mirkonel sometimes strayed too close, and the vitonesse would rapidly extend a sticky stalk, catching the red light and drawing it into a central digestive tract.

The siim was bitter that he couldn't do something similar to the mirkonel without being swarmed.

Aderen was amazed that the vekorna allowed siims back in Tiroosae after the devastating results of their last research mission.

Mlurat stared at the sky, nervous. The vekornan shuttles were absent, and Aderen realized that they were hiding from the kolbs, who had recently attacked nearby Metik. Was this research so valuable to continue it inside a war zone?

Then Aderen thought of his mother and Monera's mother, both of whom regularly ventured inside the Terran radiation zones for samples. The borderlands of the radiation zones were inhabited by dangerous and predatory mutant plants, yet the two women continued sampling there to understand how Terra-water spread through those areas.

Feeling secure in the presence of Mlurat and surrounded by vitonesse, the siim watched as a captured mirkonel sat fading in the glass jar on his work table, one of a handful extracted from a vitonesse after being caught, but before it was killed and digested.

He sat the jar next to a vitonesse plant, and watched as it reacted immediately, sticking first one stalk, then another to the glass. It could obviously sense the presence of the mirkonel. Would it get frustrated and give up? the siim wondered.

Mlurat broadcast a question that brought the siim's attention to the edge of the vitonesse field. **Whose siims are those?** he asked.

The work area was surrounded by siims, but they were of a lighter breed, something the researchers had never seen before.

The grey-skinned siims observed them curiously, eyestalks protruding and waving as they took in the research area.

What is your study? Mlurat called. **Where are your protecting vekornan?**

The grey siims didn't answer, and Mlurat advanced on them. Aderen could tell that the vekornan was puzzled by these new siims.

"You cannot read our minds," said one of the grey siims, a soft, gravelly voice that Aderen couldn't associate with the Rykolien species. "But we have been practicing against your kind."

Mlurat stopped as the grey siim raised its arms, similar to what Aderen did when he concentrated. Two small grey wings lifted from behind the siim, pushing aside the tall grasses and a couple of vitonesse.

The siim whose memory Aderen was sharing saw the grasslands on fire, his fellow siims burning, and Mlurat standing unaffected. The fire touched Aderen and he started to burn. All the siims on his team were moving about trying to put out the flames, but no matter what they did, the fire stayed on them.

"Strange, that we can affect kolbs, but not vekorna," said the grey siim.

The fire went out, and Aderen found that his siim body wasn't burned at all. What kind of illusion was this? He recalled Kezim talking about his experiences at the mind of Rolag, one of the long-dead rokels, and realized that this wasn't a siim that they faced, but the kolb counterpart —a rokel, created by the same asteroid impact as the siims.

Vekorna had never encountered rokels before.

The grey-skinned rokel raised a laser and shot Mlurat, who staggered back, raising his own weapon. The vekornan and the rokel exchanged laser fire while the siims watched in shock. Mlurat fell to the ground, his chest armor burned through to his brain.

The rokel staggered forward into the siims, and suddenly there was a mix of grey and black, siims running out of the field of vitonesse, rokels chasing them, but not firing their lasers.

Why? Aderen wondered. It looked like they were all armed.

Rokels were chasing the siims away from the vekornan shuttles, and from the sounds, it seemed like their vekornan escorts had been killed.

Frustrated by being unable to move the siim to strategic paths that he saw, Aderen was about to give up when he heard the sound of a swarm of mirkonel. He fought down panic, shared with the siim.

No matter that this was just a vision, Aderen had felt the stings himself, and it hurt.

The siim whose viewpoint he was sharing swerved and bolted through three rokels that were chasing him, reversing direction on four legs. They fired on him, but missed. He had to get to the safety of the shuttle before the mirkonel caught up with him.

Laser fire turned to silence then to trampling behind him, and he slowed, curious despite the danger. Other siims joined him, walking on two legs to get a higher view.

"Rokels are dying," said one siim, and others confirmed it. "The mirkonel are attacking them."

A swarm of mirkonel had ignored the rokels and was advancing on their small group, so they moved closer to the shuttle. A rokel came into view, and the swarm stopped its advance, pricking the rokel until it crumpled to the ground.

Aderen hoped his siim would move faster, not linger to watch, as the swarm continued its advance. At this speed, the vitonesse would not be able to catch the mirkonel with their sticky fronds.

Running up the ramp on four limbs, the siims watched the swarms of mirkonel. They waited until the last instant before closing the shuttle, locking the mirkonel outside.

"Why did mirkonel attack those rokels?" he asked.

"We know that the disturbance caused by the asteroid impact caused mutations in both vekornan and kolb birth chambers. Rokels and siims might be genetically closer than we thought."

"Close enough that the mirkonel cannot tell the difference?"

"We could not tell the difference, but we survived to report this information."

"This place is no longer safe for siim research, especially with the increased kolb presence near Metik, and rokels as their soldiers."

"Siims will never become soldiers of the vekorna," said the other.

"We will have no choice but to do what the vekorna tell us, just as rokels must follow the kolbs."

"This is not acceptable. There must be another way."

The loboms know, came the mysterious voice, the one that felt heavy, and wasn't associated with the vision itself. **Speak with loboms first.**

The vision faded, and Aderen returned his attention to the brightening sky, wondering who belonged to that sense of deep sadness. At Bol, he might have an opportunity to speak with loboms, but what would he ask?

21. Land of the Folems

Aderen descended first when Treklay landed the shuttle, eager to speak with Pinoa in person.

"I put everyone in danger by trusting Danosh," Aderen said. "So much about Rykol doesn't make sense anymore."

"Rykol never made sense," Pinoa responded, then turned to the Egalsan. She introduced the rest of the Arais, while Jye-Tan blurted out the names of his family again, with their generational order. Aderen stood aside, watching Étar and Kuyi standing close in conversation. That was good; they needed more tight friendships.

He went to comfort Wandel, to reassure her she couldn't have done anything to rescue Ret after his fighter exploded. At least he was alive. She nodded, but he could detect her guilt. Only time, and Ret's eventual return, would assuage that.

"Were the wingless and Danosh after the same thing?" Pinoa asked. "Danosh was never our enemy."

"He was never your friend, either, always following Bolob's instructions." Aderen looked down at the red grasses, practically glowing in the sunrise. They were among life again, different from what he had seen in his vision. "He's desperate, and maybe Kuyi was right that he was using Dairnehy's tactics. I didn't see it in his mind."

"You got through to his kolbs, though, so the mirror crystals can be circumvented?" Pinoa asked hopefully.

"I think I was far enough ahead of the crystals that their effect was lessened. I wouldn't trust him to gain me access to Dairnehy, nor any birth chambers. We'll have to do better with the wingless."

Rogo found them among the tall grasses. "Treklay has been granted access through the shield, and Étar hid all the weapons in that cave." He pointed to a rise nearby.

Rubiel was to the northwest, too far away. He should pile everyone into one shuttle bound for Bol and head the opposite way. They wouldn't agree, of course. His gut told him to leave them anyway, but now that he was so close he felt obligated to speak with Nalimai and Egalinsor.

They'd created birth chambers, modeled them on those the vekorna used. They had to have access, and maybe the knowledge to implant the prohibition he needed. Then he would confront Dairnehy.

He went to collect Ketaris, who was scanning samples with her palette and comparing notes with Illian. It was almost impossible to get them away from their work.

*   *   *

The transformation as they passed through Bol's shield took Aderen's breath away. It was like moving from Rykol to Terra, but an alien version of the world they'd called home for the last two hundred years. Rubiel was suddenly beyond his reach as the shield closed.

From space, the outline of the inland sea was visible through the shield, but it was blurred from the surface. Inside the shield, the blue sea stretched off to Rykol's far horizon in all directions, and anybody could be excused to think that they'd reached a Terran ocean.

Ketaris was out of her seat and scanning through the windows, a dozen panels open in her palette. Her sighs of frustration implied she wasn't getting everything she wanted. Aderen wondered how she would respond to his visions of killer insects in tall alien grasses.

He scanned Treklay's mind with the lightest of touches. To be sure the wingless vekornan didn't betray them the moment they arrived, he had to push deeper. Treklay seemed satisfied with Danosh's intelligence about Erim, to be delivered to the wingless leader.

Withdrawing, Aderen wondered how Tararnifal was faring. He hadn't heard anything from him and Sebenet since they passed through Rubiel's shield.

Seeing their awe, Jye-Tan, said, "Folems protected the inland sea before Alpro went unstable." He stood beside Aderen, who buzzed the commentary to the other shuttle.

"What life Alpro's heat didn't kill, war and Rykol-water did everywhere else," Mai added quietly.

"Illian is going nuts," buzzed Pinoa.

"Ketaris too," Aderen replied. Suddenly aware of a lack of updates, he added, "I've lost contact with the extars near Egalra. I suspect kennis signals might not get through these shields. It would explain Tararnifal's silence from Rubiel."

"Understood. We'll watch for openings and are deploying a new node now." They waited as Pinoa's shuttle slowed to a hover. The ramp opened slightly, and a package dropped to the ground. Communications beyond line of sight was restored as they continued, though they would have to wait for the shield to open again before it would synchronize with the outside world.

When he finally got to Rubiel, he would have to plan for communications interruptions. Hoping to keep them safe at Bol and negotiate by kennis, he now realized either Pinoa or Sarenie had to go with him. If he went alone, he would only have Tararnifal.

"I see a patch of folems," Jye-Tan said, pointing. The large yellow group seemed to move as one, shifting on an imaginary breeze. "They're all different colors, but from this altitude the patches always look yellow."

Mai was suddenly beside Jye-Tan, and they seemed in competition to point out parts of their home region, recent trauma momentarily forgotten.

"It's so blue," Ketaris remarked.

Mai explained, "The folems expend a huge amount of energy keeping this basin free of Rykol-water, so it doesn't contaminate the inland sea like the rest of the planet."

When the giant blue body of water broke up into myriad lakes and rivers, Jye-Tan pointed out some of the larger islands, and the main river that flowed eastward.

"What's that?" Ketaris asked, pointing to a black scar on the horizon. It reminded Aderen of the boundary lands to the former radiation zones on Terra.

"That's a burned pollen forest," Jye-Tan said, his voice suddenly somber.

Before Jye-Tan or Mai could add anything, Rogo said, "Dairnehy attacked the forests, which used to spread folem pollen around the world, recording all of its history." He looked sad. "For a long time, there were few new recordings. Folems have started producing it again, but these forests haven't recovered."

Finally, the blackened forest gave way to sand, then grasslands again, as far as the eye could see. Noting Aderen's interest, Jye-Tan said, "The inland sea has its own weather, and sends waves down the river. Do you see how sand on the beaches is rippled?" Aderen nodded at the youth's excitement.

"The river runs all the way to caves in the mountains," added Mai. "I've explored some of them myself. If you get caught in the rushing water, though, you'd end up in the ocean, where Rykol-water would kill you."

Mai painted a grim picture, and Aderen and the others were silent as they watched the river pass below. The Arais had used a derivative of Rykol-water to cure Terra's radiation zones, and were still monitoring the effects; the strain they used was supposed to be benign, but what if they'd done something wrong?

"I see the mountains," Doj exclaimed, bringing Aderen back to the present, and interrupting Jye-Tan and Mai's endless descriptions.

"The Temple of Spall is in those mountains," Mai said.

"Looks like we've taken the scenic route," Doj said, standing beside Treklay and Étar.

Surprisingly, it was Treklay who responded. **We would have normally turned east just north of Esetek, but I needed to avoid Erim, and get under cover of the shield as soon as possible.** Aderen was now curious about the intelligence he'd received from Danosh.

Étar moved his hands within the virtual controls, Kuyi at his side. "It seemed safest to cross early, based on where Pinoa's shuttle was hiding. The view is better this way, too."

The river widened, eventually shifting northward, where it would run through the caves Mai had described.

"We just passed over our home," said Jye-Tan. Aderen strained to see what he was pointing at, but by the time he oriented on the small lakes, they were past.

"Is that a vekornan city?" Doj asked. "I remember this as empty land."

"The wingless have taken over the plains between the mountains," Mai said quietly. She pointed left to right. "Reles, Miranee, Siftral."

"Ontral named a city after himself?" Aderen asked.

Rogo nodded. "It's normally the other way around."

The huge plain at the base of the mountains extended for thousands of square kilometers. Small towers and buildings clustered together to form three small replicas of Rubiel, but packed tighter than any other city on Rykol.

The shuttles hovered over the landing area for a brief moment before descending to the ground. Vekorna were gathered around the shuttles, weapons pointed.

"There's Ontral, leader of the wingless vekorna," said Rogo, frowning. "This is unusual; he must have been alerted to your presence. His mind is very sensitive, so don't try any of your tricks on him." Aderen would have to be subtle.

Follow me, Treklay said, descending the ramp into the heat outside.

22. Made, Not Born

Aderen stepped down to the hard-packed sand that served as a landing area. He'd expected it to be cooler under the shield, but the heat of the equatorial desert persisted. If anything, proximity to the inland sea added humidity.

As the others descended the shuttle ramp, he instructed his kennis to adjust his body to the atmospheric conditions.

Scanning Ontral's surface thoughts, he confirmed the wingless leader was here because of him. More specifically, he was guarding the landing because Aderen was like Kirina. Word had reached him quickly. Treklay stood in front of the wingless leader, transferring thoughts in a way few humans could imagine.

"I had hoped Nalimai and Egalinsor would be here to greet us," Aderen buzzed Pinoa, who frowned.

Ontral extended two eyestalks toward the humans. **Wait.** He held his two upper hands high, and a rectangular device crossed with horizontal rods floated over their heads. The Egalsan stood together, arms out, while Aderen and the Arais watched the device emit a falling mist.

Jye-Tan took Aderen's arm and held it out, saying, "The anti-pollen is harmless to us. Don't worry."

Aderen realized he was holding his breath, and released it. The mist smelled musky, and just to be sure, he set his kennis to neutralize any poisonous substances that might enter his lungs. He instructed the others to do the same.

Ketaris and Illian couldn't stand still, he noted in amusement, waving their hands through the mist as it fell, analyzing it until it left a brown smudge in the sand at their feet.

"That's deactivated spy pollen," said Mai, stepping

around it as the device floated to the shuttle.

Finally, Ontral came up to him. **You are called Aderen, born on Rykol half a generation ago.**

"Yes," Aderen responded. "I have returned to negotiate peace between the vekorna and the humans of Terra."

The vekorna can no longer travel to Terra. Your interference is not necessary.

"Vekorna must never travel to Terra again," Aderen insisted. "I would still like to ensure that the vekorna understand what –"

Follow my vekorna, where you will wait.

"I need transportation away from Bol," Aderen continued. He couldn't directly ask for access to the birth chambers.

You will remain here until we release you.

Rogo frowned. "I'm taking them to Egalinsor. There is no need to keep them here."

I have questions that must be answered.

Rogo's frown raised Aderen's suspicions. He scanned the thoughts of the vekorna around him. They were following orders, and didn't question Ontral's motives. They would be easy to control when necessary. Ontral himself hid most of his mind, necessary as leader of a telepathic species. Aderen could force it, but decided not to, just yet. He took note of interesting mental levers for when the time came.

What caught his mind's eye, though, was– "Nalimai asked for us to be separated," he said with surprise. "You should have started with that."

Nalimai asked to see you in her workroom. This also suits my needs. The Egalsan will leave.

"What do you want to do?" Pinoa buzzed.

"Nothing," Aderen buzzed back. "He's telling the truth."

"You fought hard to avoid getting locked up on Esetek."

"I trust Nalimai and Egalinsor." As long as they didn't hinder his efforts to get to Rubiel.

Rogo was ready to argue, but Aderen shook his head. "We'll go, and see you soon."

Immediately, Jye-Tan asked, "Can I go with the Arais? I'd really like to stay."

Keep him under control, said Ontral, and Rogo clamped two hands on Jye-Tan's upper arms. It was harder to separate Étar and Kuyi, but Aderen buzzed him to comply. Étar kissed her forehead and withdrew with the vekorna.

"Danosh said you have a piece of the stellar fragment," Jye-Tan called over his shoulder as Ontral started moving away. "Is it true?"

Aderen now understood why Jye-Tan wanted to stay. It seemed that Tararnifal was right. The stellar fragment was on a lot of minds.

The vekornan didn't answer, but the question propelled Rogo into action. "I'll contact Nalimai as soon as we get to our hover-scooters, to be sure she knows you are here. I have to get Jye-Tan out of the city."

Aderen nodded. "I think we'll be okay."

"I hope so."

It wasn't far to the room Ontral had designated for them, though it came as a surprise when Aderen was separated from the other Arais. It took rare coordination to surprise him, so he appreciated the effort required by their wingless escorts. Allowing it to happen, he weakened the will of key vekorna in case he had to force an escape.

"I'm fine," he quickly buzzed the others, before the

shield went up around his room, cutting off the local kennis link.

*   *   *

When he was young, Aderen couldn't penetrate shields with his mind; it had taken practice, and lessons from Bolob and the other Terran vekorna. The shield around this room didn't provide much of an obstacle after he'd probed it a few times.

More annoying was the loss of his kennis connection. Ontral hadn't been to see him, and he wondered if the others had been interrogated. He reached out to nearby vekorna, trying to get information from their thoughts, but on the surface they didn't seem to know anything about the Arais.

The room was rectangular and had a bench, which meant it was made for humans. He sat and waited. Empty, it couldn't be Nalimai's lab. Presumably that's where the others had ended up.

A split-second mental warning brought Aderen to his feet before the door slid to the side. A dark-haired human with a round face and sharp eyes walked in.

"Nalimai!" cried Aderen, emotions at the sudden reunion overcoming him. She enveloped him in her arms. He sobbed into her shoulder, allowing the unexpected release. As quickly as it had started, it was over. He disengaged from her and wiped his eyes. "I'm so glad to see you."

She smiled at him, brushing strands of black hair from her face. "I never expected to see you on Rykol again."

"We should have taken you back to Terra, no matter your stubbornness."

Nalimai shook her head. "No, we needed to stay,

176

although it might have been better in the end if we'd left."

He couldn't help his eyes as they drifted down her left arm to her leg, both of which she'd lost in a shuttle crash with his parents. The flesh of her hand showed no sign of the metal limb that had replaced it, and her hug had felt real.

"Real skin and flesh over a metal skeleton," she said, flexing her fingers, with a passing tic in the muscles of her left cheek. "You should have avoided Danosh."

Aderen nodded, trying to stay calm under her gaze, which reminded him too much of his mother's. "He rescued us, but I understand that now. Danosh didn't want to hurt us."

"He never does, but we end up hurt anyway." She adjusted something on the strap wrapped around her wrist. "The new shield modulation will confuse vekornan telepathy for a moment, if they're listening. We don't have long." Looking him straight in the eye, she said, "You are in grave danger here."

"Lusava told me the same thing. I'm so happy to see you, but we're here for one reason –to keep the vekorna away from Terra forever. But what about the others? Did Ontral talk to them yet?"

Nalimai nodded. "Yes, they'll be safe here; the vekorna won't enter our compound. I need to tell you about Kirina. Rogo explained our birth chambers?" He nodded. This was where he wanted to steer the conversation anyway. "Good. Unfortunately, he doesn't know the real reason why we use them."

"They aren't for genetic diversity?"

She tilted her head, shrugging. "Yes, but we had that technology on Earth, without needing the big setup we have here. The birth chambers are made to keep vekorna out of our unborn babies' minds."

He frowned, looking down at the floor. An old memory surfaced, vague and unclear, and older than anything he'd remembered before.

She studied his face and shook her head. "You don't know, do you? Jairon and Kym never figured it out."

"Figured what out?"

Nalimai adjusted something on her wrist again. "That the vekorna made you what you are –the telepathy, the ability to alter minds, to immobilize people. That's because Kopiv did something to you when you were in Kym's uterus."

She paused to let the information sink in, but he'd already rejected it. "Impossible. We've done research on Terra that indicates it's the Rykol-water in our blood."

"Not impossible." She shook her head again. "It's the truth. Rykol-water gives us extraordinarily long lives, which changes our brain chemistry, but we *all* have that. This is a different kind of change. Your Rykol-water theory can't support the facts. Is there anybody else on Terra who can do what you can?"

Aderen was about to say yes, but it wasn't true. Monera could detect emotions, but she was a third child, and her brothers showed no mental enhancements whatsoever.

"I thought so," she said, but he was distracted. It wasn't possible, but what if it was? What did that say about Monera?

"Come with me," Nalimai said, and pressed her wrist. A seamless door opened on the other side of the room. Nalimai walked quickly through it. Her left leg paused mid-motion, as if she'd changed her mind, but then continued into a laboratory. She picked up a long black tube of anti-pollen and peeled it open, withdrawing a seed pod, and squeezed it in her palm. A puff of powder escaped. She handed one to him, and indicated that he should do the same.

"That should be enough to keep the folems from recording us, even here," she said, nodding. "The shield is useless to us; the vekorna will have pierced it by now."

Moving to one of the machines, which looked remarkably primitive compared to anything he'd used on Terra, Nalimai deposited the rest of the seeds into a funnel. She nodded to the crate, so he picked up another and did the same. She pointed to her temple. Knowing that she didn't have a kennis, she could only mean one thing.

Pushing away his unease at entering another human mind, Aderen quickly scanned Nalimai's surface thoughts.

Dairnehy found Kopiv's memories from when he manipulated Tari's child, and you, while you were in the womb.

"What?" exclaimed Aderen, earning a stern glare from Nalimai. **Manipulated how?** he projected into her mind.

She nodded, and motioned to the machine. He deposited seeds into the funnel, as she'd done. Wheels turned below it, and he could see a thick liquid moving sluggishly through transparent tubes.

It's been a while since I've done this, Nalimai admitted. **I don't let telepaths pick up my thoughts anymore. With Kirina's training, it's hard to let go and allow you in.**

Aderen wondered how she kept him out, but saved that question for later. He fed more seeds into the funnel.

Kopiv's predecessor inadvertently made changes to

Egalinsor's mind before he was born. Kopiv did far more to you.

Eyes glazed, Aderen searched his earliest memories. They weren't clear, after so long. Was it possible that the vekornan leader at the time had created his mental abilities? He had organized the mass kidnapping of humans from Terra over the course of a thousand years. He might do anything.

Have you seen these memories? How do you know for sure? Aderen asked.

Nalimai moved to another device, and extracted yellow slime into a narrow tube. "Lobom algae," she said. It didn't look appetizing. The slime passed into the tube with the anti-pollen liquid, painting a narrow line down the remainder of the process.

Lusava, Aneya, Gavet and Nekken were normal pregnancies. Kirina was not. She controlled my emotions, and spoke to me –not in words, but in feelings and images. I remember Tari and Kym sharing similar experiences, but dismissed them at the time.

Aderen also remembered his mother speaking of her strange pregnancy, but he assumed all mothers thought they could feel their babies' moods.

He reached over and handed Nalimai a jar she'd indicated from his side of the processer, from which she extracted a thumb-sized white ball. It went into another part of the machine.

I didn't think more of it, Nalimai continued, her precise manner of speaking so easy to pick from her mind, compared with the randomness he usually encountered. **Even as Kirina did the same things you did as a child – which I remember very clearly.** Aderen frowned.

Everybody seemed to think he got away with too many things as a child for it to be natural, but he'd seen plenty of spoiled children. They always seemed to get their way.

My sixth pregnancy was extremely painful, for both me and my unborn child. She held her belly. **I thought that was the end, that we were going to die. Seven months in, he told me clearly that Dairnehy was responsible. It wasn't just images that time, but real communication.** Her face turned ashen, and Aderen rushed over to give her another hug. **In the end, he died before coming into the world. He almost took me with him.**

"Four of six," Aderen whispered, recalling Jye-Tan's list of Egalsan survivors. **That was your last pregnancy.**

She nodded, pulling away to concentrate on the spinning centrifuge. The translucent brown mixture being extracted looked remarkably like tea.

"That's not Joem's secret recipe for lemonade, is it?" he asked, trying to lighten the mood.

She smiled, at least.

No. The word was so clear in her mind that it came to him without effort. **This ensures the Egalsan don't get pregnant. Men and women take this supplement every two weeks. Dairnehy, and any other vekornan, will never be able to manipulate fetal humans again.**

The oldest of us don't really need it, as I think my daughters have reached menopause, and it turns the oldest men sterile after a time. "Years," she said out loud, making the word seem strange. What would Pinoa, sterilized through the Information War, say if she found out? **Nobody knows the real reason for this concoction, except me, Egalinsor and Kirina. The folems hid all memories for us of what Kopiv and Dairnehy did, to**

avoid passing the knowledge on. They assure us no related memory globes could have been released when the Temple was attacked. Hopefully that's true, otherwise we're still vulnerable.

Aderen shuddered. If her claim was true, any vekornan could manipulate a human fetus's mind as it was developing. That only Kopiv and Dairnehy had done it showed that the ability was a secret. They had to keep it that way.

But why keep it from her family? What would they do with the information? He thought of how he suddenly lost Ret's trust. Would the others ever trust his manipulations again, especially here, where the vekorna dominated?

She extracted the liquid into small vials, sucking her cheek. Aderen passed her vial after vial, until she had emptied the supply from the machine. She'd filled almost a hundred of them.

"That should keep us going for a while." She handed him a vial, and sipped one herself, though from what she said, she shouldn't need it. **It also makes it more difficult for the folems to extract our memories.**

Knowing the effect Nalimai's serum could have, he was reluctant to drink it. He was an only child; his parents had never managed another successful birth. If that trait hadn't been passed down to him, the vial would ensure it in time. Being a father seemed unlikely, now, unless his manipulation of Monera's ovaries had been successful, something he would never know.

He hadn't planned on sexual relations here, in case he passed on his "gift", but like Monera, they had inevitably discussed establishing a colony if they stayed on Rykol. It seemed that events had preceded them. If Nalimai was right, he had to remain celibate anyway.

How do birth chambers work? Aderen asked, his mind still reeling from the revelation that his abilities had been influenced by a vekornan. The way Nalimai told it, how could she be wrong? He had to replay his life, all of the manipulations, wondering if he gave the vekorna an advantage on Terra. He didn't think so.

Kirina hadn't been trusted, and was forced to leave Bol. Would that happen to him if the others found out? If he could find Kirina, maybe he didn't need Pinoa and Sarenie with him at Rubiel. She might know Dairnehy's mind better than anyone, if there was any residual connection.

"Female ova are fertilized with thawed sperm in the birth chamber," Nalimai said, and he had to focus on the question he'd asked. "We mix in relevant genes to ensure diversity using the folem method. It's not that different from ex-vitro births on Earth," she said it out loud, implying it was a safe topic to discuss with potential vekornan eavesdroppers. He picked up on her silent commentary, though: **Except that birth chambers were shielded from the vekorna.** She sealed the vials with his help. "When the wingless took over the Temple, they refused to let us back in, so we built our own birth chambers. Unfortunately, they didn't work as well as the folems ones. We stopped after maturing Jye-Tan and Mai. Something went wrong with the machines. You might have noticed the character and physical traits."

Aderen wondered about the use of the word "matured", which was how vekorna described the development of the seed-pods around their necks after they died, through the process of becoming a full-grown vekornan.

"You're talking about Jye-Tan's lack of attention, and

Mai's sarcasm and short stature?"

Nalimai closed the case of vials and picked it up. "All my children were sarcastic at that age," she said. "But yes, otherwise."

"And for diversity, you used our DNA without permission."

Nalimai sighed, hanging her head. "You weren't here, and we needed to survive. I am truly sorry. We discussed it at length, but we never expected to see you again." Her face was grim, but he wasn't convinced that she was sorry.

One last thing, he said into her mind. **Can you get us access to vekornan birth chambers?**

Her mouth gaped open. **No. I've never seen one myself. Why?**

We believe it's the only way to guarantee future vekorna don't go to Terra.

Their birth chambers will be well guarded. You won't get close to them.

She touched her wrist again, and his kennis connection returned as the shield dropped. Information instantly flowed both ways, distracting him, which was probably her intent.

He welcomed the flood of data from the others, but he couldn't tell them what Nalimai had told him, not until he came to terms with it.

"Ontral went to the others, but never saw me," he said, confused.

"He doesn't want to talk to you –ever. Not after Kirina," Nalimai responded, walking to the wall. Her leg paused for a fraction of a second again, something most people wouldn't notice. Aderen realized that her artificial limbs weren't as seamlessly integrated as she implied.

"Where is Kirina?" he asked.

"You are dangerous to us, just like Danosh, but in a different way," she responded, ignoring his question. "You will always choose yourself over others."

"That's not true," he protested.

"Think back on your life, your decisions," she responded without hesitation. "I don't know what to do with you, yet."

"Get me to Rubiel to negotiate with Dairnehy, and find a way for Doj to test vekornan birth chambers, but keep the others safe. I'd like to meet Kirina." His strategy would be different without Pinoa and Sarenie by his side, but he could manage, especially if he could find Kirina. The others couldn't know he was made by the vekorna; his judgement would be suspect. If Kirina was like him, they could watch each other for any bias toward the aliens.

The door to his former cell slid open to reveal two vekorna. Aderen gently touched their minds, but they were not a threat. Or did he think so only because of the way his brain was wired?

"For now, let's get you out of the city. Can you ride a hover-scooter?"

Aderen shrugged. "I guess we'll find out."

23. Creator/Destroyer

The octagonal vend'ok came to a halt, hovering over the ground, and although the windows were still opaque, Tararnifal could feel the two vekornan minds outside.

Disembark, said Punad, the first word the prin-el had spoken since Tararnifal left Rubiel's tower, and his first interaction since Dairnehy had welcomed him back to Rubiel.

Ahead, Dairnehy was perched on a slender piece of rock

jutting from the Rykolien desert sands, not far from the edge of the continent.

Show your wings, Dairnehy said, and Tararnifal did as was expected of him.

Sebenet was already perched on the ruins of old Rubiel, destroyed twelve generations ago, wings relaxed behind him.

Tararnifal walked to the ruins, and used his wings to assist in hopping onto one of the stone outcroppings. He let them sag, but didn't fold them, mirroring Dairnehy and Sebenet.

Punad remained on the sand, watching with five eyestalks extended.

The landscape around Rubiel's ancient ruins had changed. He could see pieces of large metallic structures in the distance, new ruins. They looked more human than vekornan. He was content to know that humans had lived here, for a while.

You and Sebenet came back changed, said Dairnehy. **What happened on Terra to cause this?**

I expect that Sebenet is less changed than me, having spent less time among humans, said Tararnifal. **But Rykol has changed, too.**

Dairnehy jumped from the ledge onto the sand, sinking down to his first joints.

How did you overwhelm Sebenet's vekorna? He was ignoring Tararnifal's claim.

I did not.

Tararnifal let loose the memory of the encounter with Sebenet's fleet, shuttles streaming from the invading extars, the tense atmosphere in his own control sphere. Sebenet had already divulged his experience, so Tararnifal showed

Aderen's arrival, how he had immobilized the tigal-en, and the compromise that resulted.

This matches Sebenet's report, said Dairnehy.

Tararnifal reached for Sebenet, who was so eager to regain Dairnehy's approval. Dairnehy was unreadable, as Tararnifal hoped his mind was to the vekornan leader.

I was unable to fulfill my objectives, Sebenet said. **I could only compromise, and bring those who volunteered so they could convince you to leave their planet alone. In exchange, they offered their expertise to bring stability to Rykol. I was blocked from gathering the thousands of humans you requested.** He extended three eyestalks and pointed them at the vekornan leader, who didn't react.

Your objective changed because we know that humans are independent, intelligent beings, said Tararnifal with urgency, sensing Dairnehy's paranoia. **Aderen used his power to avoid a protracted battle, and showed you that humans cannot be used as slaves.**

You were not surprised when I told you that I could create enhanced humans, Dairnehy said, turning his attention to Tararnifal. **Did you know that Kopiv created Aderen and Salma?**

Tararnifal had never met Salma, born dead. Could the vekorna be the source of Aderen's power? **I was unaware that Tari's child or Aderen had been manipulated by Kopiv before their births,** he said.

As had Egalinsor, said Dairnehy.

This announcement evoked shock inside Tararnifal. **Is that why Kopiv went to Terra for the six crews? Because he could manipulate them? For what purpose?**

Not Kopiv. I used a macrobot to tap into the folem

pollen. **My intention was to track wingless movements, but I found much more. Kopiv's predecessor created the ability in Egalinsor. Kopiv himself calculated the changes necessary to create human telepaths. He miscalculated with Salma, but succeeded beyond expectations with Aderen. You were aware of the potential.**

On Terra, I connected emotionally with Kezim and Yenine's child in her womb, Tararnifal admitted. He hadn't manipulated Monera, but the connection was undeniable.

My creation is more powerful, said Dairnehy.

You speak of Kirina, guessed Tararnifal.

I created her.

And she slipped from your control.

We are aware of her movements. When the time comes, we will recapture her.

They cannot be used in this way, Sebenet said, **much as we would not want to be used.**

You are wrong. We are Spall's warriors, and must follow his will when he comes again. Humans are inferior as a species, and we can make them into so much more! Dairnehy's mental projection was more intense than Tararnifal expected, and the vekornan leader jumped back up to the highest outcropping of rock amid the ruins, balancing on one leg, wings outstretched.

To Tararnifal, he said, **You have been deceived by the sample you lived with on Terra, and perhaps Aderen altered your mind such that you believe it. But the fact that we can do this shows our superiority!**

You have no idea what humanity is like, responded Tararnifal. He sent a shared memory of Kopykat, Es, the city of the Legion, and more. While humans could share limited thoughts by way of their kennis implants, vekornan telepathy allowed a more rapid, truthful sharing beyond dialog.

Dairnehy didn't believe what he saw.

There are more humans in that one memory than vekorna that have ever lived on all of Rykol, Tararnifal said. Dairnehy nearly fell from his perch, denying the truth of it.

I walked in a sea of humans, the way I did with fish in their rivers, fought fleets of fighters from their Moon. There is more variety in the city of Es than in all vekornan cities combined.

They are a swarm! exclaimed Dairnehy. He was still analyzing the shared information. **So many to choose from.**

They will not be overcome by simple manipulation, said Tararnifal, worried about the route this conversation was taking. He hadn't come here to show Dairnehy the opportunity Terra could give him for manipulating millions of fetuses for his own benefit. Dairnehy could not be permitted to go to Terra.

Dairnehy turned on Sebenet. **Tararnifal was with them for many human lifetimes. You were there for a day before you converted to their cause. Show me your wings!**

Sebenet stepped off his perch, and spread his wings.

You were supposed to bring me back a means to victory, but instead you brought back traitors. Do you see the missed opportunity?

He advanced on Sebenet and pushed him backward. Sebenet flapped his wings to rise over a pile of rocks.

Dairnehy braced himself on two lower legs and grabbed Sebenet with the other four, using his own wings to counter the large shift in his center of gravity.

Tararnifal began moving toward them, but Punad hopped onto a broken wall, reminding him that they were not alone. His lasers were lowered, but ready, as he watched. Wrist lasers could kill a vekornan without damaging the area around them, immediately stopping the flow of blood to his brain. The other weapon, held in two hands, could tear apart the rocks along the cliff, and shred vekornan armor as easily. From his perch, Punad had them all covered, though a touch to his mind showed distaste in what Dairnehy had just done.

Stopping mid-stride, Tararnifal called to Dairnehy. **Stop! Let us show you what we learned.**

I have no time for traitors or damaged vekorna. My old prin-el was damaged. Danosh lost two arms protecting humans, and he was never the same after they grew back. He betrayed us to the kolbs, and left Rubiel to wage war against me. That will not happen again.

He thrust Sebenet out over the cliff and threw him beyond the edge. Sebenet instinctively pushed back, his wings unfurling, but he was too far from land, and started falling.

Fly, if you can, like vekorna awakened of old. Let your true wings be freed by pure water, if you can find it.

With a wary eye on Punad, Tararnifal moved to the edge of the cliff, keeping his distance from Dairnehy.

What have you done?

I did what was needed. We have always killed

traitors.

Am I a traitor? Tararnifal braced himself against physical assault, but could do nothing against Punad's weapons.

That has yet to be decided.

Sebenet's wings were fully extended, and the flight was glorious as he spiraled down, down toward the deadly ocean. He drew close to the cliff wall, searching for purchase, then rebounded away. He managed to grab a rock outcropping near the bottom of the cliff, where the ocean was wearing away the ground, but it was too fragile to bear his weight.

A quick flap of his wings brought him to another grip, his claws finding six purchases on the wall. Maintaining proximity with strategic pulls on his wings, he scrambled to find rocks that wouldn't break free when he grabbed them.

Slowly, Sebenet crawled up the cliff, forced twice to regain the height he lost sliding as grips fell away. Tararnifal watched him, unable to help. Dairnehy was silent in contemplation.

Finally, Sebenet reached one arm over the cliff at Dairnehy's feet, and the vekornan leader stepped back. A second arm crested the cliff, bringing his faceplate into view. He pulled his massive body over the edge, gaining the help of his middle arms, and finally his legs.

He stood before Dairnehy, exhausted, wings sagging behind him.

I am yours to command, said Sebenet, and Tararnifal saw that he had capitulated. Without humans at Rubiel, he would focus on advancing Dairnehy's destructive plan for Rykol's stability.

Dairnehy turned away from them, and Punad hopped

down to the ground toward the vend'ok. Tararnifal thought he sensed relief.

He watched the red sea at the base of the cliff as Sebenet left, remembering his walks along Terra's ocean floor, looking up at the massive creatures that lived there. Bolob had thought they could reverse the effect of Rykol-water with more genetic engineering.

Sebenet had never walked Terra's oceans, and Rykol's ocean had nearly devoured hm. What else was Dairnehy willing to risk?

24. Cleaning Up

"They'll be on their way soon," said Egalinsor. "Kuyi, show them where to wash. You smell like anti-pollen." He frowned.

Nodding, Kuyi didn't move, breaking one more puppet's string. Most of the Egalsan had already dispersed, going to clean up and knowing that Egalinsor wanted to speak with the older Arais privately.

"Aderen will be alright. Nalimai has him."

It was a dismissal, but she was more amazed at how he'd misinterpreted her reaction. In her eyes, Egalinsor had always been larger than life. It was an illusion he often cast, but she'd also seen him as a normal man.

Having spent time with Aderen, though, she realized the two had a lot in common, and Egalinsor was the more fragile of the two. Egalinsor was the first human ever born on Rykol, while Aderen was the second to survive. Egalinsor was older than many vekorna, and just as set in his ways.

Egalinsor raised his eyebrows, and she noticed Étar staring at her. She turned, and said, "Come with me to the lakes."

By some unspoken command, Doj, Penagel, Pinoa and Wandel remained behind. All four had known Egalinsor from their previous time on Rykol.

They walked through the display room, with trophies from travels in a distant time. Sarenie stopped to look, and everyone gathered around her.

"There was peace, long ago, when my aunts and uncles could travel Rykol," Kuyi said. "They brought many things back. You'll probably find items recovered from the kolb islands, or Forbek and Rolm most interesting."

Akinuf's face perked up at the mention of the cluster of kolb islands, remnant of two minor continents that were blown up by the wingless as her grandmother flew against them.

"Isn't Forbek forbidden?" Étar asked.

Kuyi smiled. "It's forbidden to the vekorna and kolbs, but not to Lusava and Nekken at the time."

She'd thought they would be most interested in Rolm, from when the Egalsan could travel in extars, before the base was destroyed. Maybe not, if Ret was captured near there.

Tapping Étar and Sarenie on the shoulders, she said, "The display room will still be here after your baths." Reluctantly, they turned away and left the main house, onto the path in back.

Étar was beside her, but stopped suddenly when she shed her travel clothing, leaving them on the side of the path to be recovered later.

She turned when she realized the other Arais had also stopped. Rogo was walking up the path toward them, beckoning them on. His hair was wet, dripping down the rest of his body. "We don't have long. Kuyi, get them moving. It's all I can do to keep Jye-Tan and Mai in the water."

"Come on. We'll bathe in the hot pond, clean off the anti-pollen and desert sands."

Looks passed between the Arais, and she instinctively knew they were talking silently amongst themselves. Finally, Étar removed his shirt and shoes, but kept his pants on. The others did the same.

"We didn't realize you all went naturel," he said, looking from Rogo back to Kuyi. Something about the way Étar looked at her made her blush.

To cover her sudden discomfort, Kuyi frowned and responded, "It'll be hard to bathe with your pants on." She gestured for them to advance, and noticed that most retained their clothing until they reached the beach. There, they stopped to gasp in wonder.

Kuyi smiled again and said, "This is our home. I understand the original human crews thought of this as a home away from home, because it resembles Terra." She raised her eyebrows in question.

Étar came up to her, fully naturel now, and said, "It's beautiful. I hope that feels like Terran water."

"It's not Rykol-water, if that's what you're thinking," she responded.

Kuyi led him to the artificial steaming pond, where Lusava, Ontral, Jye-Tan and Mai waved at them. Rogo dove back in immediately. "All of Rykol is hot, of course, but Nalimai diverted a hot spring for this pond. It contains cleaning salts and minerals to keep our skin healthy."

"A wonder of engineering," said Akinuf, walking up to it, hands on her hips, observing the pond. "Where is the hot spring?"

Kuyi pointed at the lobom hills in the near distance, where the path eventually ended. "It passes not far beyond those hills. At its source, the spring will burn your skin off."

Jye-Tan splashed out of the pond and gestured at the Arais to join them, disappointed eyes searching. Kuyi shook her head. "He's not here yet, though Nalimai should have him back soon."

He nodded, and led the Arais into the hot water, joined by a muted Mai. Kuyi relished the heat that soothed her tired muscles as she stepped over the rocky edge into the pond. The long Rykolien day and night had passed without sleep, and more excitement than she'd ever wanted to experience.

Diving under the water, she let her hair shed the caked sand and anti-pollen residue. She sat on a submerged flat rock and ran her fingers through each clump, freeing it, watching the water get cloudy, then run off to the filters.

The noise of the others faded as she began her rite of solitude, closing her senses to everything.

"Do you mind if I join you?" It took a moment for the voice to register, and she sighed as the ambient talk and splashing came back to her.

Then she sat up as she noticed Étar standing chest-deep beside her. His beard was dripping, as if he'd just breached the surface.

Smiling, she said, "Certainly."

"Rogo and Lusava said we should get out of the hot tub soon, since we aren't used to it. But you look like you are positively enjoying it. I didn't realize you wanted to be alone. Sorry for interrupting your meditation."

As he turned to go, Kuyi touched his arm, holding him back. She shifted over on the flat rock and said, "Please join me. Do you not have hot springs on Terra?"

He gave a gentle laugh as he sat next to her, hips not quite touching under the water. "There are many hot springs on Terra, and many places where engineers have diverted them to make baths like this. I never expected to see this much normal water on Rykol, though."

"It's the largest concentration on the planet. Lusava's right, though, we can't spend too long in the hot water. My skin is already starting to crease. I usually move to higher rocks and dry off in the suns little by little, but it seems your friends have decided to play in the cooler water."

She reluctantly descended from the rock and swam to the shallows. Walking up the wide carved stairs, she took a chance and grabbed Étar's hand, guiding him from the pond, moving quickly across the scorching hot sand to the closest lake.

"How much cooler is the water?" he asked, looking from the hot pond to the lake.

She gave him a look of bewilderment. "Is anything cool on Rykol?"

"I guess not."

Moving away from the others, and assuming that Jye-Tan wouldn't bother her until Aderen returned, Kuyi walked into the water until it was above her shoulders, Étar at her side. He'd sought her out, so she didn't think she was mistaken about his interest.

"Is the water cool enough for you?"

He tilted his head. "It's warmer than most lakes I'm used to."

The water was still as they stood together silently, two

heads hovering above nothingness in the sunlight. Finally, Kuyi said, "I usually do more than just stand in the water."

Étar laughed. She wondered what he was thinking; if she had a kennis, would she be able to tell? It didn't matter, she realized, wondering if she could possibly be misinterpreting his look. She thought the intentions on his face matched her own.

"Don't worry about me," Étar said. "On Terra, I'm quite adept. You do your thing, and I'll follow along."

She pushed off the sand and flipped into the water, arcing around not too far from him. Popping her head above the surface again, she worried for a moment when she couldn't see him. Then he, too, surfaced, farther than she'd expected.

Feet kicking, she maintained her head above the water as she felt him pull closer. She looked longingly into his eyes, and thought she saw his own desire reflected there. But then his eyes grew cloudy, and he said, "Aderen has arrived. We should get back to the house."

The brief spell was broken, and she sighed in disappointment.

He took her hand and led her out of the water. The others seemed to have received the same message through their kennis, as they were also retreating from the lake. The Rykolien suns dried them almost immediately, but Kuyi directed everybody to a covered area where they could towel off the residual water.

She picked up her travel clothes from the path where she'd left them, and offered Étar a clean robe. It hung from his shoulders, sheer in places, opaque in others. While adopting the naturel style where it made sense, Nalimai had insisted on hygiene, safety, and what she described as decency. Human skin was much more sensitive to Rykol's suns and sand, pollen and other aerosols, compared with vekornan armor.

Étar pulled the cord closed around his waist and waited for her to don her own.

Nalimai passed them on the way back, leading the four older Arais toward the bathing pond. "Aderen is in the main house. He wants to speak with you."

Back straightening, Kuyi couldn't hide the smile that came to her face. She squeezed Étar's hand, though she didn't know why. It was her moment to be something bigger. She should relish it on her own. But Étar's touch and his smile somehow made the feeling more pertinent. She didn't let go.

25. An Old Friend

Nalimai's hover-scooter wasn't much more than an engine with control handles that snaked out the front. She leaned forward to embrace them, Aderen holding on from behind.

The engine hummed quietly as Aderen skimmed the ground, feeling an insanity of motion, especially when Nalimai maneuvered over shallow rocky dunes as they left the trio of vekornan cities behind. Sand whipped up behind them, leaving a trail anybody could follow.

Aderen would have liked to observe the landscape, but was distracted by holding on and assuring the Arais he was alright.

"I'm glad you're free," Pinoa buzzed him. "We feared the worst when you weren't let go with us."

"Nalimai brought me into her workshop to keep me away from Ontral, I think. I haven't figured out the relationship between the Egalsan and the wingless vekorna yet."

"From what I can tell, the wingless and folems have unequal control of Bol, and the Egalsan are allowed to move between their homes and workshops in the vekornan cities."

"What did Ontral want?"

"The stellar fragment," Pinoa buzzed. They were both silent for a moment, Aderen's senses now dominated by the wind rushing by his ears.

"It seems the fragment is on everybody's mind. See what you can find out from Egalinsor. The other Egalsan were either withholding what they knew or are oblivious, which I don't believe."

"I'm already on it," Pinoa buzzed. "Did you get any information about vekornan birth chambers?"

"No," he responded. "But I believe the discontinued human ones are not far from you. We should start there."

The stellar fragment had changed everything on Rykol, but what did the vekorna think they could do with it? From what he'd heard, it was a spying device, nothing more.

Dairnehy had more than one piece, but the largest was stolen by Jye-Tan. When the boy had asked Ontral about the fragment, the vekornan's surface thoughts confirmed that he also had one. The kolbs had excavated another piece from Rolm for Ret's experiments. Were there others?

More important was the fact that war still raged, despite each side having piece of the stellar fragment. It was obviously not a huge advantage.

A mind touched his, and Aderen looked up. He tapped Nalimai on the shoulder and shouted, "A shuttle."

She nodded and shouted back, the wind almost stealing

her words. "Ontral is watching you. We need to keep moving."

All the more reason to leave as soon as possible, he thought. Their mission had to take priority over everything else. Negotiating with two leaders was less than ideal, but they had no choice. He'd leave either Pinoa or Sarenie here to make the same deal with Ontral, while the others studied ways to introduce changes into the birth chambers.

Some of Nalimai's black, silky hair escaped its netting and flew back, tickling his face. He leaned away from it and watched the landscape blur by.

The desert plains had transformed into small ponds, which grew into lakes. At a narrow segment, Nalimai took an arced bridge just wide enough for the hover-scooter, revealing a human farming complex, without the big robotic machinery.

Backed by large lakes, the farm was composed of the rustic houses he barely remembered, supplemented by silos similar to those at Egalra, as well as barns and covered cylindrical buildings that extended out over the lakes. A rock wall, human-height and broken up by gates, bordered this side of the compound. Metal shone in the distance, where the land rose up into large rocky hills. More than anywhere else, this could have been Terra.

As Nalimai slowed, Aderen said, "You've been busy."

She turned to him, a smile on her face as she removed her goggles. "I built things for a living on Earth. Why would I stop here? Your father wouldn't have been surprised."

"You were a structural engineer, like Wandel."

"I'm way more than that, now, though I've been forcibly retired since the war restricted us to Bol." She advanced slowly to one of the barns, where she parked the hover-scooter, and they walked to the main house.

Aderen looked up to the sky again, but saw nothing, felt nothing. Nalimai caught his glance. "They know where to find you. Soon we'll go out on the lake, to keep you moving."

He'd been watching Nalimai, and knew he could operate a hover-scooter. Once Aderen was sure the Arais were safe, he would find a way through the shield, alone.

*   *   *

"Do you remember me?" Egalinsor's dark, larger-than-life features were imposing, even to Aderen. He recalled the man being huge, but assumed it was because he'd been a small child at the time. The perspective hadn't changed.

Egalinsor put a hand on his shoulder, and he could feel the touch in his mind. He jerked back, at which Egalinsor laughed. "You remember me, and can feel it, can't you?"

Aderen nodded. According to his parents, Egalinsor could influence people through touch, even through clothing or vekornan armor. He recognized the hypocrisy of not wanting to be influenced, and thought again of Ret and Legionnaire Dalpah. Yet there was something comforting in letting Egalinsor control the meeting.

"Do you remember what I said when you left Rykol?" Egalinsor asked. He hugged Nalimai across the shoulders, then sat in a chair, which groaned under his muscled weight. The man had been alive for a thousand years, and although his grip was strong and he showed no weakness, the cane leaning against his chair implied some physical degradation. Aderen couldn't believe his eyes as the big man seemed to shrink into the chair, massaging stiff joints. The imposing figure had turned into an old man.

"You told me to take care of my parents," Aderen responded, still standing. "You knew I would be like this?" Egalinsor had maintained independence from the vekorna and kolbs. Wasn't that a sign that he wasn't biased?

Egalinsor nodded. "I suspected, and warned your parents. I suppose that's why they did such a good job raising you, and warned you about using your influence selfishly."

Aderen fought the rush of blood to his cheeks with a kennis command. "I used my abilities to keep them safe."

"Has that task been completed?" Egalinsor asked. "Have they died, and no longer need your protection?"

He knew Pinoa had already provided him with that answer. Pinoa was gone for the moment, avoiding Nalimai. They hadn't said goodbye when she left Rykol, had never reconciled after the kolb war.

"I judged this to be the larger threat," Aderen responded.

"Good, you show no regret. You've made your decision, and don't look back." Aderen didn't let his doubts show, suddenly wanting to impress this man. Was he so susceptible to the influence of his touch? "As you can see, the vekorna are in no state to threaten Terra," Egalinsor continued.

"Yet there is another fleet of extars poised to arrive on Terra's doorstep as we speak."

The old man put a hand to his chin. "Yes, we had words with Dairnehy and Danosh about that, but it was far too late even for this body's influence to recall them." He stared at his hands, rubbing his thumbs against the first two fingers.

"We need a way to stop all vekorna from going to Terra," said Aderen, certain that was what he wanted. Would he be forever checking his decisions against what

202

the vekorna wanted? "Now and in the future."

Shaking his head, Egalinsor said, "As I told Pinoa, it can't be done. She wouldn't say more until you got here." He put his hands out, palms up. "Now you are here."

Aderen buzzed the original Arias to join them. Nalimai hugged Doj and Penagel, and nodded to Pinoa and Wandel, then sat beside her husband. She didn't shrink into the chair the way he had, and they appeared about the same size.

He took a chance that Egalinsor knew of Bolob's Plan. "Our best idea is to borrow from Bolob, manipulate their birth chambers to ensure newly matured vekorna avoid Terra, either through fear or respect."

The old man seemed to contemplate the proposition, and he hoped Egalinsor would approve. Did he understand what Aderen was saying?

"Maybe," Egalinsor said, revealing nothing.

"My last time on Rykol, I proved that they communicate with each other, and influence birth chambers in other cities," said Doj. "Even vekornan and kolb birth chambers had some connection."

"Now I understand why you brought a geneticist and programmer on a diplomatic mission," said Nalimai.

"Doj and I have had a lot of different careers since we married two hundred years ago," Penagel said. "We do a lot more than programming and cooking."

Nalimai rose to her feet and hugged them both again. "I'm so sorry. I've had to learn so much since you left, but you still haven't changed in my mind. Congratulations!"

Penagel nodded with a grim smile and kissed his husband, both squeezing Nalimai's hands.

"Do you think the stellar fragment could help?" Aderen asked. "If we found the one Jye-Tan hid from Dairnehy, if we found Ontral's, and brought them together, would we be able to do more?"

"I don't think Ontral has a piece of the fragment," said Egalinsor, frowning.

"He does. I saw it in his mind. Danosh knows about it, which tells me that Dairnehy does, too. Everybody seems to want it, which means it's more than just a telepathy crystal like the tigal-en use for long-distance communication. What's so special about it?"

His eyes bored into Egalinsor, along with a quick touch to his surface thoughts, which was rebuffed. He wondered how much mental force would be required to dive deeper. It would probably kill, so he refrained. There might come a time when that would be necessary, but he wasn't there yet.

"It's exactly like the other telepathy crystals," said Nalimai, frowning, hands on her hips.

Aderen was about to disagree when Egalinsor said, "Jye-Tan thinks it can do more."

"Jye-Tan thinks many things," Nalimai said sharply. "It doesn't mean they are true." Her look dared both of them to defy her. She was afraid of the stellar fragment. She wouldn't help him, not without a nudge to her closed mind.

Egalinsor rocked in the chair, and closed his eyes. "Yet he managed to sneak the fragment away from Dairnehy. He, Gavet and Aneya wouldn't have been able to carry it together, let alone sneak into the tower, so how did he get it?"

"It sounds like we need to have another conversation with Jye-Tan," said Pinoa.

"We need to keep Aderen moving, but I think he can safely spend the night here," said Nalimai, as Aderen frowned. The only place he intended to move was out of this shield and north to Rubiel.

"Where would we go?" asked Pinoa.

"Ontral is watching, but we should be able to get Aderen to Kirina's refuge." Aderen was suspicious, but the offer to learn where Kirina might be was too good to pass up. He could afford a small delay.

"We'll bring Jye-Tan with us to talk about Rubiel," Pinoa said.

"You will be staying here with me to explore our records," Egalinsor said to Pinoa.

Aderen didn't disagree. "I want Kuyi here for that, too," he said. He wanted to foster her friendship with Sarenie, gain some trust.

"Talk to Kuyi, then wash and get some rest," said Nalimai. "You've been awake far too long, and I don't need a kennis to see that your body is long overdue for sleep."

Unfortunately, Aderen couldn't argue with her on that.

26. Relations

"We're sisters!" Sarenie said, with more enthusiasm than she'd expressed up to now. Maybe the sudden change in hair color from blonde to red had affected her mood. She stood to give Kuyi a hug. The sudden attention was embarrassing, but welcome.

After the disappointment of watching Aderen and Jye-Tan disappear from the docks, Kuyi was surprised to discover how fun looking through their genetic records was, though she contributed little to the discussion. It was amazing how many surprises were hidden in that giant hologram, including the fact that she shared almost twenty percent of her genetic material with Doj.

Kuyi returned Sarenie's hug as Doj enveloped them both. "I now have two grand-daughters here with me." Several Egalsan shared his genes, but nobody else with such a high fraction.

Wandel glared at the hologram, then turned and stomped out. She'd been unhappy earlier at how the Egalsan had used their DNA indiscriminately. Egalinsor had apologized, but assured her that they needed the genetic diversity or else avoid reproducing at all, something Wandel seemed to think would have been for the best. Genetic defects could be corrected using folem machines, but with limited diversity it would eventually lead to a dead end.

"She claims to be upset at how casually you are taking this," Akinuf said, pointing to her temple. "But I think my grandmother is more insulted that her name isn't anywhere in your records. I think secretly she was hoping for another grandchild here, too."

Kuyi stared at the list of genes that had contributed to the third and fourth generation Egalsan. Akinuf was right; Wandel wasn't listed anywhere.

"I don't see anybody who took part in the assault on the rokels or the kolb continents," said Doj, inspecting the record. "Lituk, Breg, Wandel, Redinam, Teemar, Frejelle, Kekell –even Tari, who didn't fly." Kuyi knew Tari's name from her superb gardens, her stillborn baby, and the fact that she'd fallen under the influence of the militaristic Lituk.

"I make no apologies for that," said Egalinsor. "We have their genetic material, but did not want their traits passed on to our family. No offence to Wandel or to you, Akinuf."

Akinuf shrugged, noncommittal. "I can't say I'm not disappointed, given that everyone else on this mission shares something in that hologram, even Aderen. But there are only so many of you. If you ever decide to expand by another generation, I'd donate a part of myself. Wandel is a good person."

"That won't happen unless the folems rebuild our birth chambers," said Mai under her breath, but loud enough for everyone to hear.

Kuyi patted her shoulder, then sat down next to Étar, and took another look at the genetic record hovering above the table. She always thought of her family as large, but even including stillborns, there would have been no more than thirty eight Egalsan. Egalinsor, Nalimai and the six first-generation children were all natural unaltered births, so there wasn't a lot of room to add random genes.

"Including Nalimai," she said, "thirty-one people from the four crews lived on Rykol at some time." She gazed into Egalinsor's eyes, feeling brave. "Of your parent's generation, only Joem is represented, and only once." Firini was Lusava's child, their only attempt at introducing foreign strains in a natural birth.

Egalinsor nodded, but didn't say more, and she didn't press him. She understood Wandel's criticism better now that Akinuf had pointed it out. To her knowledge, the *Siberath* crew had arrived after the war, barely interacted with anybody, yet three of their crewmembers had unwittingly donated genetic material to her family. Wandel had been here much longer than them.

Kuyi tried to lighten the mood. "If only Jye-Tan and Orem were here now! What will they say when they find out they have some of Aderen in their genetic code?"

"Jye-Tan will be insufferable," muttered Mai. "I have some of Yenine in me, which means I'm related to Ketaris, in a way." She looked around. "No hugs for me."

The exobiologist Mai was referring to had excused herself before this meeting, not wanting to waste valuable time that could be spent analyzing Bol's flora.

She and Étar could be doing other things, too, if she'd excused herself. Their closeness from the day before, in the bathing pool, lingered at the surface of her memory.

Standing, Xeffeya rounded the hologram to embrace Mai from behind. Mai squirmed at the contact. "We share a tiny amount of Krefer's genes, which means we're related, too." Xeffeya gave Mai a kiss on the cheek, then let go, to Mai's obvious relief.

"It's not the hugging gene," Mai muttered. Kuyi thought she was the only one who heard, until she saw Étar smiling. She squeezed his hand again.

Was this what the older generation did when they weren't working? Kuyi was having fun discovering her heritage, giving more thought to the original crews than she had her entire life.

Except for the few times someone asked for her help with research in the vekornan cities, a break from watching Jye-Tan and Mai meant tending the gardens, gathering lobom algae, scrubbing filters, or any of the other tasks required to keep her family alive here. Most of those were shared with Orem and the twins.

This was different from any of that. It must be what Kirina found so interesting about Rykol's history when she was stuck here.

"I'm sure the others would love to know, too," she said, eyes bright. Winking at Mai, she added, "They might even like hugs!" Mai rolled her eyes and stuck out her tongue, eliciting laughs.

"Yes, I'm sure they would," said Egalinsor, nodding. "You've done well, and Aderen sees something special in you. I realize now that I haven't given you enough of a chance at our genetics research."

Aderen had pulled her aside privately before his turn in the baths. He wanted her to look for Ontral's piece of the fragment. It would mean sneaking into the Temple again, something Egalinsor and Nalimai would frown on.

Egalinsor looked at Lusava, who had been unusually quiet. She'd been involved in the original birth chambers, but had not been genetically manipulated. Kuyi was amazed at how she knew the entire genetic map with barely a glance at the hologram.

"I agree," Lusava said. "You've been very helpful since the Arais arrived. We think you should be among the first to receive a kennis."

Kuyi didn't think her eyes or her smile could get any bigger. Egalinsor and Lusava had both recognized her talents, beyond childcare. Now they wanted to make her among the first to take the next step into becoming an Arai. She felt more of her puppet strings falling away.

*   *   *

The hydrofoil raced across the water, wind whipping harder than on the hover-scooter, droplets splashing against them as the wind beneath the boat raised a spray.

Aderen stood at the bow with Penagel as their speed dropped so they could pass under a magnificent bridge, made from a single arc. He was reminded of his mother's renowned gardens on Terra, which melded nature with man-made structures, and which he hadn't visited nearly often enough. Politics had stolen so much of his life. He could happily disappear here.

"You built all these without vekornan help?" he asked, as Nalimai came up beside him.

"It was my livelihood before leaving Earth," she said, shrugging. "I trained my family when they were old enough, and the folems didn't seem to mind. In fact, I've seen them floating across my bridges often enough."

He looked down at the spray of water. "You made this, too?"

"I had a lot of time to go through knowledge bases the original crews left behind." She smiled wistfully. "The boat doesn't need a hydrofoil to rise above the water, but this was more fun to build." She knelt and looked over the edge, waving him down. "It has shuttle repulsors, if needed. The grandkids roll their eyes because I like to feel the randomness of currents and eddies. They prefer the stability of retracting the wing and avoiding the water altogether."

Jye-Tan was sulking just outside the control area. He knew why he was here. Illian kept encouraging him to look at the readings on her palette, but he turned away.

Beyond the span, they sped up again, the submerged wing lifting them higher out of the water. There was time to relax and enjoy the view.

Wandel and Akinuf would be studying the human-made birth chambers used to mature Jye-Tan and Mai, in preparation for gaining access to the vekornan version. With Egalinsor's help, Sarenie would negotiate Ontral's agreement.

Yet he couldn't help but think that Nalimai was stalling. "Are you sure you're not just showing off your magnificent works of engineering?" he asked with a smile. "I'm sure it would have been faster to take a shuttle."

She looked exasperated, and flexed the fingers of her left hand. "You, too?"

He shrugged, looking up.

Following his gaze, she asked, "There's another one tracking us?" He nodded, feeling irritably connected to the vekorna now. Fortunately, he was a distraction, which could help negotiations with Ontral.

"They know we're going to Kirina's refuge," she said.

Maybe it was time to talk with Jye-Tan, before the vekorna got involved.

"What will I learn about Kirina?" he asked. "Will you tell me how to find her?"

Nalimai turned away.

"The vekorna aren't the only ones watching us," said Illian, pointing to the shore of the river, palette floating in front of her. Orem went to the side, too, staring in awe.

Jye-Tan suddenly stood up on the deck and joined Illian. "Wow. I haven't seen that many folems together in a long time."

"Never this close," agreed Nalimai.

On Terra, a river that linked two lakes like this might be bordered by a dense copse of trees, with reeds poking their heads from the shallows. The folems lining the shore would put those to shame. They leaned out over the water, bobbing in the breeze, a multitude of colors melding into one. On the other shore, the folems were interspersed with small black pillars, unfurled loboms standing at attention.

Aderen reached out with his mind, sampling thoughts as they passed.

Danger… Trouble… Help… Choice… Memory… Exile… Death… Control… They came easily to him, but were incoherent. Were they thinking about him, or was he picking up on random thoughts?

He focused on one folem up ahead, two layers of petals, white and purple with alternating shapes and a black center over a green stalk.

Alirv. He picked the name from the male folem. Why had he chosen that one? He knew the name. Alirv was now the folem leader. **We will wait at the Memory Caves. Do not abuse your power here.**

Aderen raised his eyebrows. "What are Memory Caves?" he asked, putting his interest in Kirina's refuge aside.

"It's where they study memory globes," Jye-Tan offered. "Kirina spent a lot of time there, too, before the folems poisoned her."

Nalimai gave him a sharp look, and sighed. One more secret, Aderen thought.

"We never let Kirina leave Bol, for obvious reasons," she whispered. "She often studied in the Memory Caves, but moved closer to where the original memories are stored, in the forests. She pressed the folems for more history, more information, until they realized she was controlling them. They took matters into their own... vines." She looked out at the dwindling crowd. "We managed to get Kirina out, and now she roams the northern deserts."

"Sometimes we see her at Egalra," Jye-Tan said in a small voice.

"I'll have to be careful," Aderen said, wondering how far Kirina had pushed the folems.

The hydrofoil entered another lake, and the shores receded, leaving the folems and loboms behind.

212

"Technically, Alirv governs Bol alongside Ontral, but in truth, the folems are more interested in regrowing the forests and finding the missing memory globes, so leave the vekorna to their own," said Nalimai.

That explained why Ontral greeted them without a folem presence on their arrival. Turning to Jye-Tan, Aderen said, "It's time to talk about the stellar fragment."

Nalimai led them from the deck into the glass lounge. By now, Aderen was able to pick out the occasional hitch of her artificial leg. A kennis would help with that.

From inside, they continued to watch the water without noise or spray. Orem took over piloting from the blonde woman who had been at the controls, Nalimai and Egalinsor's second child.

Most of the Egalsan had black hair, and Aderen wondered what the genetics records would say about Aneya, whose hair took on a reddish tint when she turned in the sunlight. She smiled with half her mouth, the other half disfigured. The hair on the left side of her head had been burned away, the skin permanently red and bubbled down to her mouth.

Aneya touched the side of her head self-consciously, and Aderen realized he was staring again, like when he'd boarded the hydrofoil at the docks.

"Sorry," he said.

"This is still new to you," Aneya responded, enunciating every word carefully as she sat beside him, showing him only her unmarred side.

He was glad for the distraction when Jye-Tan handed him a soft spongy food, which he popped into his mouth. The sweetness of the lobom algae cake snaked down into his throat.

"We've been experimenting for a long time," the young man said. "The original lobom algae farms don't make things that taste this good."

Aderen barely remembered them from his childhood, and nodded. "You know why we're here, and it has nothing to do with lobom algae cakes."

Jye-Tan sighed and sat down. Aneya put an arm protectively around him. "Where do we start?"

27. Enhancements

The common room of the main house was empty, Egalinsor's usual chair unoccupied. Kuyi raised a questioning eyebrow to Rogo, who answered, "He insisted on being first to have kennis surgery, and is recovering."

That was typical of Egalinsor. He wouldn't ask his family to go through the procedure unless he'd tested it first. Kuyi was surprised he was letting her do it so soon.

Rogo led Kuyi to an adjoining room, which had been completely transformed. Strange and foreign equipment was neatly aligned near beds and shelves. Had Pinoa and Wandel brought all of this with them in their shuttle? It was a wonder Ontral hadn't confiscated it.

Lusava was already sitting on a bed, legs crossed, black bands around her neck, forehead and upper arms. She looked impatient, but Kuyi knew that she was actually nervous.

Kuyi sat down beside her as Ketaris rummaged through the equipment. Xeffeya connected Kuyi with the same black bands, and drew a rectangle in the air. Numbers, graphs and more leapt into the space above her palette. Xeffeya carried the figures with her as she moved about the room.

Finally, both women settled on Kuyi and Lusava. A second set of graphs sprang into the air above Xeffeya's palette, and she assigned one to each patient.

Ketaris held a thin tube in each hand. "Are you ready?"

Lusava shrugged, and Kuyi said, "I guess so."

Ketaris pressed one tube to Lusava's temple, just below the black band on her forehead. She studied the readout on her palette as Lusava closed her eyes, wincing with a bit of pain or discomfort. Kuyi grabbed her hand.

Since the kennis interfaced with their minds, did that mean Ketaris was affixing the implant directly into the brain? Kuyi didn't want to break her concentration to ask.

Lusava's eyes opened wide in shock, then she went limp as Ketaris withdrew the device from her temple. Xeffeya studied the numbers coming from her palette and smiled.

"She'll be asleep for the rest of the day while new neural connections are made with the implant," she said.

Lusava seemed either asleep or dead, completely limp and seemed very uncomfortable.

"She's perfectly fine," Xeffeya assured her.

"Can I lie down?" Kuyi asked.

They cleared off another bed for her, then Ketaris put the cylinder to her temple. There was no sensation for the first few seconds, and she couldn't tell when her skin was pierced.

Then she grunted as the pressure built in the side of her head. She moaned as it peaked, then disappeared with a flash of light. Breathing rapidly, Kuyi closed her eyes against the discomfort. Remembering how Lusava had fallen limp, she suddenly wanted to see the world around her. Forcing her eyes open, she looked at Xeffeya, saw the nod of satisfaction on the doctor's face, then felt the world receding.

Everything was concentrated on the white dot in her mind, as she created new strings, with herself as puppet-master.

*   *   *

Aneya wiggled the three fingers that remained on her left hand, bringing Jye-Tan close, exposing the scarred half of her face. "I was lucky. We escaped Rubiel together, thanks to Gavet's sacrifice."

Looking back at Nalimai, Aderen wondered how the folems could restore her entire arm and leg, but not her daughter's face and fingers.

"Why were you at Rubiel?" Aderen asked.

"The usual reasons," said Jye-Tan defensively. At a touch from Aneya, he added, "Mostly for harvesting."

"How did you get your hands on Dairnehy's crystal?" Aderen would have to pry the information out of him.

"Dairnehy used it to read my mind," he said. He looked imploringly at Nalimai. "It wasn't my fault. I'd just broken through my mental blocks, and hadn't had time to learn all the other blocking techniques."

Aderen raised his eyebrows. He sent a small tendril of a thought to Jye-Tan's mind, found it impenetrable. Hating himself for doing this, he skimmed the surface thoughts of the Arais with him. He saw Penagel's desire to get back to his husband, and Illian's distraction with the variety of life they were passing every minute. He was reassured that he could still see into people's thoughts.

Nalimai said, "To prevent vekornan telepathy with our family, Kirina put barriers in their minds when they were very young." Aderen's shock was likely reflected on his face. He didn't know that was possible. "They only last until puberty," Nalimai continued. "Jye-Tan's held a bit longer, but they always fail eventually. As adults, we rely on other techniques to resist. I imagine you've found it effective?"

Thinking of the serum he'd helped concoct, Aderen said, "I do." With knowledge of Kirina's blocks, could he find a way around the Egalsan defenses? He didn't want to risk damaging their minds. He immediately chided himself for the thought. He was here to change one mind –Dairnehy.

Coming back to Jye-Tan, Aderen concluded, "You were vulnerable at Rubiel, and Dairnehy took advantage of it?"

Jye-Tan nodded.

Taking another bite of the algae cake, Nalimai said, "The vekorna use special crystals to augment their telepathic abilities. With enough mental resonance, they can speak across the solar system, without the need for technology."

Tararnifal had found a weak crystal near Terra, but Aderen had never tried to enhance his skills by using it. He'd already been proficient without physical aids.

"Your kennis can do that, can't it?" Jye-Tan asked, temporarily relieved.

"With the nodes we dropped in orbit, we can communicate around the world," Penagel replied. "Without another node deeper in space, we can't get much farther."

"Dairnehy was experimenting, and we happened to be there at the wrong time," Aneya said.

"I felt his touch in my mind, and responded. The fragment is special." Jye-Tan leaned forward, clasping his hands.

"Stick to the facts," Nalimai admonished him, adjusting her legs with a slight wince.

Aderen put out his hands in a placating gesture. "No, I'd rather hear of his impressions. How did the fragment feel?"

Jye-Tan's eyes brightened. "Amazing." He took in a deep breath and let it out slowly. Aderen's kennis showed the euphoria through an increased heart rate, the flush in his face, and more. It was concerning.

"When I touched the fragment, I could see into vekornan minds. It was like being Kirina." He looked tentatively over at Aneya, who nodded. "I could see into Aneya and Gavet's minds, too. It was as if their blocks weren't even there."

Aderen could see how such a feeling could lead to obsession. He'd felt it himself, without the crystal fragment. Absent the guidance of Bolob and his parents, he could have gone through life adjusting minds on a whim.

Monera grounded him, trusted him completely, and he showed her the deepest parts of his mind. She would have seen if he was biased toward vekornan desires, wouldn't she? He'd let her see his fears and anxieties, the despair at those who reviled his ability, and kept it secret through his influence. Ret wasn't the first, but he hoped he would be the last.

Monera's advice in bed on that last Terran day stayed with him. Trust in his companions without violating their mental privacy. He'd failed at that. Adjust the vekorna only in need. Where did the need end?

"It's not one you want," whispered Aderen.

"But we need more people like you and Kirina, to keep our family safe!" Jye-Tan implored.

"I don't think Kirina would agree." Aderen looked up at Nalimai. "That's why she kept this refuge. Humans were not meant to have that kind of power."

"It felt so right," continue Jye-Tan. "The more I touched

it, the more power I had. I put my bare stomach against it, and I could see more, influence more."

"Stop," said Nalimai, and Jye-Tan quieted.

"How large was the fragment, if you could hug it like that?" Aderen asked.

"Half my height, and as wide around. Cylindrical." Aneya nodded at his description.

"How did you steal it, then? It must have been many times your weight."

"I influenced a vekornan, like Kirina could do –or Egalinsor."

As much as he wanted to condemn Jye-Tan's use of the stellar fragment, Aderen's hopes rose. The fragment could be the key to solving his dilemma. If it was that powerful for somebody who had no natural telepathic abilities, what could Aderen do with it? He now regretted never testing his telepathy with the Terran crystal.

Instead of admonishing the young man, Aderen asked, "Where did you hide the fragment?"

Jye-Tan shook his head. "I can't tell you."

Frowning, Aderen asked, "Why not?" He considered pushing harder against Jye-Tan's mental blocks.

"You are going to see Dairnehy, and I can't be sure your minds are protected against what he can see. Dairnehy can't get the fragment again."

"My mind is protected against the vekorna, I assure you," he said, surprised at the passion Jye-Tan evoked.

"What about them?"

Aderen was about to order Penagel and Illian out of the cockpit, when Jye-Tan added, "You let Tararnifal into your mind. Can you be sure he won't see this?"

The information Tararnifal and other vekorna could take

from his mind was carefully controlled, but their limits had never been tested. Was it possible the vekorna took more than he wanted from his thoughts, but he just didn't know it?

The hydrofoil slowed, sinking into the water, banking to the right.

"We've arrived," Aneya said. Illian had moved back to the window and was watching the shore closely.

Putting a hand on Jye-Tan's shoulder made him flinch. Was he this afraid of his great-grandfather's influencing touch?

"You can keep your secret for now, but soon I'll ask for your help, and you will give it freely."

Jye-Tan's face was pale as Aderen stood and joined Illian at the window, the yellow shore approaching.

Nalimai came to them, as Aneya embraced Jye-Tan.

"You didn't have to scare him," Nalimai said.

"I did. I've had this power all my life, and it's dangerous. You know this. He has to let go of his obsession."

"Have you?"

"One at a time," Aderen answered. Dairnehy would expect him to go for the hidden fragment at Rubiel, but Ontral had no reason to be suspicious. Before he left Bol, Aderen had to test the fragment. He'd subdued Sebenet's tigal-en in Terran orbit, but his grasp had been fleeting. Tararnifal was right that he couldn't control an entire city of vekorna. Not by himself, and not without help. He had to know what he could do with the stellar fragment.

"One at a time," he repeated.

*   *   *

Sunshine woke Kuyi from her sleep, but the world was

220

different. She was in her own room, but everything was enhanced.

Ketaris and Xeffeya immediately came to her, an endless stream of numbers moving across both their palettes.

"Did it work? Can I talk like a vekornan now?"

Ketaris laughed. "You'll need practice first. Let's pick a focus word to get you started."

"Baby," Kuyi said instinctively, not knowing why.

"That was quick." Ketaris adjusted something inside a palette frame and said, "Let's give it a try."

Kuyi spent hours with Ketaris, Xeffeya monitoring, drawing and redrawing the palette. It was exhilarating, and self-teaching. After the first hour, Xeffeya left, and Ketaris focused on showing her how to do the most basic things.

She synchronized with local time at Bol, connected to her private terminal, and accessed the local kennis node.

"It's within the shield, and can only synchronize with the nodes in orbit when the shield opens," Ketaris explained. "But it contains a complete set of information on Terra and Moon. We've been updating it as we gain more knowledge about Rykol. Eventually, all the kennis nodes will have the same information."

"Can I access it all?"

"Eventually. Keep your progress slow and steady. As you gain more experience, your knowledge base will gradually open up." Standing, Ketaris added, "Come outside and learn the basic exercises. One-on-one experiences will help tremendously."

Kuyi stood and walked steadily to the sheltered patio area, where Egalinsor sat with Sarenie, whose hair was now blue and black, writing on air. Kuyi wondered when she found time to change her hair color. Firini stood with Doj, palettes paired playing some kind of game.

She acknowledged them, noting their kennis identifications, but her attention was drawn to Étar, who was passing a small virtual ball from his palette to Lusava's, which she tossed back.

As Kuyi concentrated, her kennis identified both of them, and gave additional information on Étar. It was a strange sensation; was Terran society so open that people could show their identities before even meeting?

"Good morning," Étar said, but his mouth didn't move. He was speaking directly from his kennis to hers, the process they called buzzing.

"Hi," she buzzed back, forcing the word from her mouth and concentrating the way Ketaris had told her. His smile told her that she'd succeeded. "This is fantastic; I feel stronger, and I see things in a new way. Did you know your heartbeat is faster than when I first saw you?"

Étar tossed the virtual ball to Lusava and turned his attention to Kuyi, putting hands on both her shoulders. "Don't overstress yourself on the first day. Your brain needs to get used to the extra loading. We'll teach you how to do it properly, but it takes time."

She covered his left hand with her own, noting the spike in her own heart rate as their skin touched. "I won't. But there's so much new stuff here!"

Lusava said, "Careful how you are doubling your speech. I can't hear what you're saying directly to Étar, but you don't need to repeat it with your mouth."

Slightly annoyed with her older aunt, Kuyi saw Étar nod, and tried to be more patient with the lecture. Taking care of Jye-Tan and Mai had been a thankless job, but it kept her away from her older family's endless corrections.

"I had to take a refresher course on the simple exercises I did when I was a child so I could properly educate your family," Étar said out loud. To her frown, he added, "It's necessary to develop your basic kennis skills."

"Jye-Tan and Mai are going to love this," she buzzed to Étar and Lusava. She kept her mouth firmly closed, but felt her tongue move regardless.

She and her aunt laughed together.

"I'll let you continue your game," Kuyi said, and started to walk away, eyes lingering on Étar.

Étar followed, waving to Lusava.

"What about her?" Kuyi buzzed.

"She knew I would be taking on your kennis education. Akinuf will be back soon for her, now that Rogo has gone for the procedure. Do you want to eat breakfast? You'll need food to keep your kennis at full strength."

"I want to refresh in the water first, then we can go to the garden, where we'll pick our own breakfast," she buzzed. "We can supplement the fruits with algae cakes."

"I've tasted some of those delicacies," he said. On one frame of his palette, he pulled up images of fruits, vegetables, and the more elaborate lobom algae concoctions. "These are my favorites so far." He pushed some to the side, into another frame. "These I don't like so much."

Laughing felt good. She grabbed his hand. With the other, she drew a rectangle in the air. "Baby," she said. To his curious look, she buzzed, watching her palette appear, "Short for 'babysitting', because that's what I did until you arrived." It wasn't the complete truth.

She found the appropriate breakfast references in the kennis node and made them appear on one frame of her palette. "These are my favorites in the morning. I'll take you to the algae farms another time."

"You deserve more than just taking care of the youngest," Étar buzzed back. The conversation was much more intimate than speaking out loud. It gave her courage.

"I want to be useful to you and Aderen." It felt strange voicing that aspiration to another, even though nobody else could hear her buzzing. He put an arm around her shoulder, not judging her, not offering any opinion, the way her aunts and uncles would.

A sudden thought came to her. "I can contact Aderen through the kennis node, can't I?"

"Yes, you can. He's just arriving at their destination."

The path ended at the long beach, and they stopped to remove their clothing before it collected too much sand. Naturel, she saw his body flush as he watched her, and knew he wanted the same thing she did. He leaned down tentatively and kissed her on the lips. It was too short, but he pulled away.

"Not yet," he buzzed. "You still need to recover."

Disappointed, she changed the subject, urging Étar to keep his footwear so the hot sand didn't burn his feet.

"Let me show you how to protect your feet with a kennis input, then we can practice some kennis tricks in the water."

Kuyi smiled and accepted the offer.

Part IV: Overconfidence

28. The Refuge

The refuge was a mess. Aderen stepped carefully around glass marbles littering the floor, some smashed. Larger ones, the size of his head, lay in corners and against the walls. It was unlikely he was going to find anything useful about Kirina's travels here.

Without worries about rain, the refuge was airy, allowing the warm breeze to easily pass through high windows. Kirina must not have cared about folem spy pollen, though in the end it seemed she should have.

Aderen paused in the middle of the floor as he felt new kennis identities appear on the node. Xeffeya had activated the first implants. It would take time before the Egalsan could use them.

Penagel nodded, acknowledging that he'd felt it, too. He walked to the far wall and peeked into another room, avoiding globes and shards of glass. Illian remained at the open door, blue water at her back, while Jye-Tan cleared off a cushioned couch and sat down. He reached for one of the small glass globes, rubbing it between his hands.

"What went on here?" Aderen asked, taking in the sparse furnishings. He had time to tolerate Nalimai's obvious delaying tactics. Sarenie wouldn't see Ontral about birth chambers until after the Egalsan were attuned to their kennis. While that was happening, he'd asked Kuyi to do something for him. She and Mai had already admitted to sneaking into the Temple of Spall, which was the most likely place for Ontral to hide his piece of the stellar fragment. Was he acting selfishly, as Nalimai had accused?

"I helped Kirina make this place when she couldn't stand the noise of our thoughts," Nalimai said. She smiled in memory. "I wanted to make it as grand as the farming compound, but she shouted at me until I gave in to a simpler design."

"Kirina never shouted," said Jye-Tan defiantly.

"Not with you," Nalimai responded softly. "You didn't have to live with her."

"You didn't get along?"

"We got along the way a parent and child do, sometimes easily, sometimes not. She had a temper, and she rebelled when she couldn't go where others could. I guess she's better off in the desert with Nekken. It's a hard life, though."

Aneya put her head on Nalimai's shoulder, wrapping an arm around her in a calm embrace.

"You confined her to Bol," Aderen said absently, picking up a clear globe the size of his palm. How would he have felt if his parents shut him away after the debacle with Legionnaire Dalpah, instead of his self-imposed exile? "I'm surprised you let the others in sight of any vekorna."

"I couldn't have stopped them."

"I left Bol to train at Ban, like Lituk and Tari," said Aneya.

Nalimai frowned. "You and Gavet were drawn to vekornan weapons, rebelling in your own way."

"That part of my life is over," Aneya responded, deflecting a potential argument. "Gavet and I created a mechanical device that allowed us to hoist a heavy blaster without much muscle or bone stress, but it stayed at Ban."

She sounded proud of her achievement.

"Anyway, Rykol was dangerous to Kirina, especially when she was young," Nalimai continued. Her eyes grew intense, and Aderen took a chance, found her thoughts open. **I couldn't let her near Dairnehy after what he did.**

"Do you think she can take care of herself now? Danosh thought he knew where she was."

"They flew a few missions together after she escaped Bol. I don't think he'd betray her to Dairnehy."

"Do you know where she is?"

"Not exactly." Nalimai was being circumspect again, but it didn't bother him as much since his conversation with Jye-Tan. If he could test the stellar fragment, maybe he wouldn't need Kirina's help at Rubiel.

Putting the small glass sphere down, Aderen picked up another, colored by a touch of blue and green, like a marble. The sphere expanded and a face appeared inside.

Younger than Aderen, but older than Jye-Tan or Kuyi, the woman had long, black hair, small dark eyes, and a complexion very much like Nalimai herself.

"I'm out right now, collecting memory globes." Her voice was high pitched, but deepened toward the end of the short sentence. The young woman smiled, and looked happy. "You can wait, but I might be gone a while."

The image faded.

"These are folem memory globes," Aderen said.

"She recorded an away message?" Penagel asked, reappearing from the other room with Orem.

Nalimai carefully took the globe from Aderen, examining it. "She was much younger then, and very much into her research." She turned a full circle, arms wide, indicating the scattered globes. "She loved studying Rykolien history. The way Aneya loved weapons, she loved knowing what had happened on this planet long ago."

Aderen's face perked up. Kirina had been isolated from her family and her world, but she'd found refuge in the isolation and Rykol's history. She must have learned so many secrets about the vekorna and folems.

During his years of self-isolation after Legionnaire Dalpah's suicide, he'd also turned inward, but not to history. If he'd grown up on Rykol, would it have been different?

Penagel shifted his weight at the door. "There's a ground vehicle in here, a couple of rooms over."

"Is it functional?" Aderen buzzed, and Penagel nodded. "Do you think we could use it to get away from here?"

"I don't think it has access codes to get through the shield," Penagel buzzed back. "Those things are slow, and Ontral would find us quickly. What about them?" He nodded toward the Egalsan.

"Nalimai is trying to keep me away from the others. I don't think she'd object to me leaving."

"You've decided not to bring Sarenie and Pinoa, then?"

Aderen had to be careful about his response. As spouses, Penagel and Doj didn't keep secrets between them. "For now we wait, but it's an option if we can't get our hands on a shuttle."

Penagel acknowledged, and turned to the outside conversation. Their silent communication had taken moments, and Aneya had just started responding.

"Kirina used to drive to the pollen forests, not that she minded hiking for days on end. But it was hard to carry so many memory globes, so she used the small vend'ok as a cargo hauler."

The strange word meant nothing to Aderen, and his kennis didn't help. The local node didn't contain that reference.

"We used to call them security vehicles," offered

Penagel. "I vaguely recall the name, but I recognize the octagonal shape." He pointed to the other room with his thumb. "I've never seen one that small."

"I often insisted on going along," said Aneya. "She showed me how to tap into the roots of the folem forests, collecting memories on the spheres. It wasn't my interest, but she loved studying and analyzing them."

"That was before the vekorna attacked and burned the spy pollen forests?" asked Aderen.

Nalimai nodded. "We last used the vend'ok to smuggle her away from here and out of the shield."

"Find out how they accessed the shield," Aderen buzzed Penagel, who started up a conversation with Orem. He wondered why the folems felt the need to poison Kirina. What kinds of secrets had she uncovered?

"Now she spends her time chasing down the memory globes that escaped Bol," Jye-Tan said, still playing with the small sphere.

Aderen cocked his head. "What do you mean?"

Nalimai sighed and sat down beside Jye-Tan, her face strained. Aderen wondered how much pain her limbs were giving her.

"When the winged attacked, they didn't just burn the forests. They attacked the folem Memory Caves –you were asking about them earlier?" Aderen nodded. "As the side of the mountain sheared away, memory globes floated off in the wind." She tapped the globe in her hand, and it expanded. When she withdrew, it hung in the air like a balloon. Jye-Tan flapped his hands, and it drifted slowly, until Aneya stepped forward to catch it.

That's what Nalimai meant when she said she didn't know what information had been released in the attack.

231

Could knowledge of Dairnehy's fetal manipulations have drifted away into the desert?

"Can I access some memory globes?" Aderen asked.

"I expected you would." Nalimai stood with an almost imperceptible grunt, and started picking up the globes, placing them in baskets.

"She kept memory globe journals," said Aneya. "Some of these will be empty, others will have Rykolien history. Nobody has been here since she left."

Kirina would have seen thousands of memory globes in her lifetime. How many dissertations could she have written or recorded? What might she know about birth chambers that could help keep the vekorna away from Terra forever?

Had she tested the stellar fragment herself?

Unfortunately, Kirina was out of reach.

"Do you think she had visions?" he asked suddenly.

Nalimai paused in her tidying. "I don't think anybody has had visions since the rokels were destroyed. Jye-Tan, help me sweep up the broken glass."

Closing his eyes and sighing, Jye-Tan stood and found a broom, such a basic tool among beings who could record their thoughts on holographic spheres. Orem disappeared out the front door, heading back toward the hydrofoil. "Be back in a minute," he said.

"When they captured Kezim and I, rokels put frighteningly real visions into our heads," said Penagel. "I thought I was going to die often, when I was standing safely in our cell, or outside on the cliffs."

Nalimai licked her lips. "When *Alnevar* arrived, Tari saw visions of Pinoa's Information War. There no rokels."

Aderen buzzed Pinoa, who confirmed that she'd questioned Tari at length about what she'd seen. "The vision was accurate," she buzzed from the main compound.

"It would seem that something on this planet creates telepathic links," Aderen said. "I've had more than one."

"What are you seeing?"

"I think I'm witnessing the saga of the extinct siims and goses," he said. He didn't mention the mysterious voice. "More curious, they seem to be ordered chronologically.

"I saw the asteroid impact Rykol, disturbing birth chambers all over the planet, causing the initial mutation. Then I saw siims interact with mirkonel in Tiroosae, experiments that turned the insects into deadly enemies. I think mirkonel have genetic memory. They remembered and attacked unprovoked, even going after the genetically similar rokels."

Penagel nodded. "Kezim and I were saved from rokels in Tiroosae because of that genetic memory. They attacked Rolag before he could kill us."

"Mirkonel also tried to save my parents, until kolbs arrived," said Aderen, as Orem returned from the hydrofoil with drinks. Jye-Tan and Nalimai stopped cleaning, and Aderen took a sip. It was sweet and fruity, and probably supplemented with lobom algae. "This morning I saw the first siim-goses interaction."

"Your visions sound like memory globes, but without the globes," said Jye-Tan. "Sometimes I've wandered through a highly expanded globe without seeing it, experiencing the memory inside."

"If you were walking through random memory globes, they wouldn't be in order," said Illian, also sitting with a drink. "Did you record the mirkonel with your kennis?"

Aderen nodded, and sent her a kennis pulse with the data. She'd be lost to this expedition for days with new research, he thought affectionately. Illian and Ketaris were in their element on Rykol. Aderen was here for a very different reason, but his priorities kept changing. He needed to get to Rubiel so he could confront Dairnehy about the raider fleets to Terra. The stellar fragment might help, and so might Kirina, but they weren't essential. His visions were an annoyance, albeit an interesting one.

"I could show you the most recent memory if you had kennis implants. It would be much easier than describing it."

"Put it in a memory globe," said Jye-Tan, shrugging.

"Do you know how to do that?" Aderen didn't see any equipment. In fact, Kirina's refuge was devoid of most things he would expect in a technologically active home, things he'd already taken for granted in the farming compound.

"Sure, Kirina showed me at Egalra."

"Why am I not surprised?" Aneya said, standing and knocking his upper arm with her fist. He flinched, but smiled as she laughed. Tapping Penagel on the elbow, she said, "Come with me; I'll show you the vend'ok." Orem disappeared with them.

29. Memories of Rykol 4

Jye-Tan struggled to remember how to activate a memory globe recording, and Aderen suspected that it would have been faster for him to describe the vision in detail.

To Nalimai, he projected a thought, hoping she was open enough to receive it. **You don't know how to do this?**

I do, came the immediate response. **But Jye-Tan won't appreciate my interference.**

Everything was done from the memory globe itself. Finally, Jye-Tan activated the controls, a section of the sphere expanding with faint light. It darkened when he put his palm to it.

As he waited, Aderen responded to a tentative contact from Kuyi. "I wish I could join you," she buzzed. Her voice seemed awkward.

"You can help better from there," he buzzed back. "For now, get familiar with your kennis. Étar can help you."

"He's been a big help." Her kennis voice was colored with emotions. She was romantically interested in Étar, and just referring to him made her thoughts blush.

He disconnected when Jye-Tan withdrew his hand from the globe, handing it over.

Holding it in his palm, Aderen touched a finger to the reflective surface, and was enveloped by sensory deprivation –silence, sightlessness, even touch disappeared. He was suddenly alone in a garden. "Take me with you," Jye-Tan's voice said, and like the siim visions, it seemed to come from Aderen himself. The garden looked real, and when the viewpoint turned, he saw a red tower nearby, as real as the vekornan cities where they'd landed.

"Rubiel?" he asked as the globe collapsed.

Jye-Tan nodded eagerly, and Aderen shrugged, unable to make promises. Jye-Tan could prove a liability on any mission to Rubiel, but he did have knowledge of the city, and had stolen a highly-valuable artefact out from under Dairnehy's security.

He'd allowed Nalimai to bring him here thinking that he could find Kirina, so she could help force Dairnehy's cooperation. Jye-Tan's experience with the stellar fragment though, the way he longed for it years after he last touched it, made Aderen wonder. Could it be as simple as having a large piece of the fragment?

"When do you think you'll be able to get into the Temple?" Aderen buzzed to Kuyi.

"I don't think Xeffeya will let me out of here so soon after the procedure," she responded.

"I agree, but let me know when go."

Following Jye-Tan's procedure, Aderen put his hands on the memory globe. The interface was intuitive, made easier when he established a telepathic link. He was careful to block his mind, wondering if it would do any good against a machine that could record thoughts.

The deep voice that accompanied the visions had asked him to send somebody soon, but he kept that off the memory globe. Satisfied that he'd done it right, he called Penagel back into the room.

"Do you want to see it, too?" Aderen buzzed Kuyi. When she silently acknowledged him, he added his viewpoint to the kennis link.

They all touched the memory globe together. It expanded, and they were immersed in Rykol's past.

*   *   *

The siims were wandering the rocky plains of Metaspu in northern Depraf. The continent's desert extended to all horizons. The hot double suns didn't disturb the siims, even without protective gear such as what the vekorna wore. Their skin didn't dry out the way kolbs' did.

Kolbs and rokels no longer attacked the siims, so vekornan patrols were sparse, and no vekorna supervised them, a rare event. The siims were gaining more trust from

their vekornan masters, and were taking full advantage of
it.

Persinjali was a typical siim, nearly identical in features
to all the others, much as the vekorna were all physically
the same. Their mental signatures were much weaker than
those of the vekorna or kolbs, but it was enough for them to
communicate simple feelings.

Persinjali opened his mind to the different receptors of
his sensor head, catching the sparse life that still clung to
this vast desert.

Their research into the vitonesse of Tiroosae had led to
impressive results, though nothing that would protect siims
from mirkonel of that same region. Other research projects
were similarly exciting.

The vekorna would not give them leave to explore the
depths of Rykol's ocean for large creatures that might still
live there, below hundreds of meters of dangerous Rykol-
water.

Their next-best idea was to search for the rare flying
creatures that vekorna and kolbs used to see in Metaspu,
but whose numbers had plummeted, maybe to extinction.
There was a lot of ground to cover.

Persinjali loped on his four lower limbs, covering dozens
of kilometers in almost no time. His upper arms held
scanning equipment that could register outputs his sensor
head could not.

After six weeks on this rocky, sand-covered desert, they
hadn't found a single goses. Considering how large the
creatures were supposed to be, Persinjali was surprised that
they hadn't found any remains, either.

Rykol-water wasn't responsible for the decimation of
this desert and the goses, though it had certainly

contributed. After the vekorna disappeared from Rykol's surface, hiding from an intense flare-up of their unstable star, the kolbs had turned on each other. This desert, the goses primary habitat, had been broken and blasted by kolb inter-clan wars.

At the top of a low crest of rock, Persinjali stopped and extended several of his eyestalks, looking at the beige-brown desert all around. Hundreds of siims were out here, and Persinjali could connect to dozens at a time. He could only see seven from this vantage.

Turning to the east, the siim felt a compulsion, an invitation. Rokels could compel beings with weak mental defenses, which worried Persinjali, but this felt different. He followed the invitation down the rise and walked through a windswept dune.

Yellow grasses with deep roots were almost completely hidden, but managed to stay alive. For what purpose, Persinjali could not tell.

Sinking to his upper shoulders in the next dune, Persinjali stopped. Two large white disks irised open from the other side. The disks turned red almost immediately, making him think of the mirkonel, but this time he heard a voice in his mind.

Advance, came the invitation, and Persinjali decided to obey. He pushed through the dune and out the other side, shaking the sand from his limbs and light armor.

The next dune shook and trembled, bouncing as a giant flat shape emerged, red-white disks turning into eyes atop it, with an open yellow beak below them. Persinjali extended two eyestalks to match the visual receptors of this beast. The sand continued to shake as a wide body rose from the dune. Creamy white, the first segment of the goses matched the color of the Metaspu. Two contacts touched the ground, where its immense body tapered to a point.

"We have been searching for goses," Persinjali said.

Another segment of the goses emerged from the dune, arcing above the sand until another pair of contacts touched the ground. How large was this beast?

We watched you, observing your minds. We approve of what we see.

A third segment rose from the sand until it too was supported by another pair of contact points. A thin tail swept the sand behind the creature.

"What do you see?"

Curiosity, and non-violence, came the response.

"We are motivated by research," Persinjali replied.

You wish to create birth chambers of your own. The vekorna have not provided you with the means to propagate your species.

"It is our secret project, though we suspect the vekorna are aware of our efforts. What of you? We have searched weeks to find a goses."

We hide from all Rykolien species, because of what the soraen did to us long ago.

The invitation to walk toward the goses intrigued Persinjali, so he strode to its side, continuing to converse. The three large segments were as thin as a wing, rising in narrow arcs from the six points that supported it on the ground. The color was not uniform, but marred with dark and light patches that camouflaged it against the sand.

"The soraen split into vekorna and kolbs before the wars that caused this devastation," Persinjali said.

They have not changed.

He climbed on top of the goses, and secured himself

ahead of the first segment, behind the neck. **I am Nirk,** said the goses, and there was a female sense about it. He made a note that, like folems and loboms, goses were intelligent species with two sexes. It seemed that the sexless vekorna and kolbs and their mutations were the exception.

The goses lifted her first segment into the air, followed by the second and third, and suddenly they were as high as a vekornan shuttle. Persinjali sensed dozens of siims nearby, also rising into the air. The sky was cloudless, but they rose above a layer of haze that he hadn't been aware of.

They swooped and dove, and Persinjali noted he could discern thoughts not his own. His companions were too far away for the primitive telepathic connections siims were normally capable of. Other thoughts underlay those of the siims, more raw, untamed, wild. It could only be the goses.

Nirk banked hard, and the wind jerked at Persinjali, forcing him to react quickly to hold on. He used all six limbs to secure himself, and enjoyed the ride. Being a goses meant more thrill than a siim could experience, but due to the shared link among all siims and goses on the desert plain, he could get a sense of what the goses found exciting.

They had drifted east, toward the forested lands near the ocean.

Two soraen factions fought here, Nirk said, **while the others of the split race hid from the suns. They were destroying food and energy sources, so our people tried to intervene. The soraen didn't care that we flew between them, shooting us down like they destroyed their own.**

When the soraen left, we moved the bodies close to the shore, where they decomposed, and the great forest

grew over them.

That's a lot of goses, said another voice, siim.

We brought soraen bodies to the forest, too, but they didn't decompose like the goses. Their remains and armor are still piled at the southern point.

Many more goses fell to the soraen after that, and we brought them here, too. Our numbers are now very few. We have no more births, because all of our males have been killed.

You want us to create birth chambers for goses, as we work on our own, Persinjali said, speaking mentally for the first time, and knowing that the goses understood him. He now understood Nirk's earlier question. **It is a long project.**

We still have time, Nirk responded.

We cannot stay under the weight of the vekorna if we take on this project, said another siim. **We must be free to do our research.**

Persinjali agreed, sailing through the air on the goses.

*   *   *

The memory globe faded and shrank back to its original size. Jye-Tan held it, nodding.

"The vision is just like a memory globe," Kuyi buzzed.

"They never finished, and destroyed themselves together," said Penagel. Aderen's parents had told him of the memory globe showing Bolob helping siims escape the vekorna, only to watch them commit mass suicide –all siims and goses were destroyed that day.

"The vision ended with a siim report to the vekorna," he continued. "They lied, and said they never found any trace of the goses."

"Their escorts didn't see them flying around?" Jye-Tan

asked, surprised.

"Apparently not. Some were drawn off by kolb attacks farther south. The others didn't report anything."

"Or maybe, like Bolob, they were in league with the siims, helping keep their secrets, which led to their escape," said Penagel.

30. A Secluded Spot

The bright light of Rykol's suns woke Kuyi again, and she grumpily wondered why nobody had shuttered the windows. A smile grew on her face as she remembered leaving them open to stare at the stars, until Rolm rose in the west, washing them away.

She dressed in short brown pants and a semi-transparent top that Étar seemed to like. Then she connected to the kennis node. Aderen was already waiting from many lakes to the west.

"Mai and I will go to the Temple tomorrow," she said. I thought you wanted to get into the birth chambers?" Aderen's mission wasn't clear to her. He wanted to see Dairnehy but not Ontral. He wanted to enter Ontral's birth chambers. Now he wanted the stellar fragment. Which was more important?

"We will, but that's Sarenie's job. I want you to find the fragment for me. Be careful. I think I've convinced Nalimai to return tomorrow night. Jye-Tan is my ally –he wants a kennis badly."

Kuyi snorted in laughter. "I understand." Turning serious again, she buzzed, "Are you sure Ontral has a piece of the fragment? I've never heard of one here."

"He has a piece," Aderen buzzed back.

"It wasn't just in his mind because of what Danosh

claimed? You spoke openly in front of Treklay."

"On purpose," buzzed Aderen. "I wanted Ontral to think about the fragment, to reveal it to me. He did, thanks to Jye-Tan –it's there."

They signed off, and Kuyi went out onto the stone patio, where she could enjoy a view of the lakes and trees. She almost never spent time here, because the twins preferred to be out on the water. *My strings are my own*, she thought.

The patio was full. Xeffeya was flitting from person to person, guiding them through kennis exercises. As she passed the empty fire pit and abandoned instruments, Étar saw her.

"I hear you aren't going out until tomorrow," he buzzed. News traveled fast among kennis-users, she thought. "Do you want to go to the beach where we can practice alone?"

Kuyi blushed, and tried to control it with her kennis. She wanted very much to spend time alone with Étar. But Aderen needed her first.

"Yes, soon," she said. "I need to talk with Sarenie. Alone." She didn't know why she said that last part. She would have welcomed his company. To ease the sting of her comment, she embraced him, pressing the length of her body against his. She looked up and snuggled her chin into his short beard, enjoying the prickly feeling, and bringing her lips to his. "Later," she buzzed. "I have to finish something first." She didn't want to let go.

Thoughts of Aderen drove her to break contact, and she had to use her kennis to dampen the feelings. Turning away, she walked down the rocky path to the nearest lake. She did nothing to ease the abnormal beating of her heart.

*   *   *

It felt strange to search for someone mentally. She

followed Sarenie's beacon to a sheltered viewing spot, where she sat on a cushioned rock.

"Hi Sarenie," Kuyi buzzed, connecting directly to her kennis. She waved as the other woman took notice.

"Hi Kuyikal," buzzed Sarenie, her open palette remaining stationary as she turned. "Aderen said you might seek me out. I think I've finally found a secluded spot for my work." She gestured to the small field of sitting rocks, water visible through a break in the grasses on the other side.

Kuyi bristled a little at the use of her formal name and Aderen's presumption, but pushed the feeling away, turning instead to Sarenie's palette.

"I have different interests from Ketaris, who is out taking samples of everything," Sarenie said. "Or Wandel, who's out tinkering with Gemni."

"Gemni maintained our human birth chambers," Kuyi explained. "I didn't think Wandel would be interested."

"Give her time. Like Pinoa, she isolated herself last time she was on Rykol, and I don't think she's come to terms with the memories. Wandel has a mission, too, and we don't have access to vekornan birth chambers, yet."

Kuyi flushed. She watched Sarenie's fingers dance in the air as they manipulated one frame of her palette. Three others held pictures, Rykol most prominent, but also the image of a man Kuyi had never seen. She thought she knew who he was.

"This spot is too close to the compound," said Kuyi, "I'll show you a better one."

Sarenie stood, and her palette came with her. Streaks of blonde in her long auburn hair shone white in the sunshine. Kuyi brushed her fingers through the dark mass on her own head. Feeling bold, she said, "Yesterday your hair was blue."

Sarenie smiled softly. "My kennis is set to change hair color every day. Sometimes it follows my mood, otherwise it's randomized."

"Isn't that hard on your hair structure?" Kuyi asked.

"My kennis takes care of that, too. I've been doing this all my life." She ran a hand through the wavy strands, and it flew out behind her, returning gently to rest against her back.

Stepping from the grass path onto the sand of the beach, Kuyi removed her shoes, and Sarenie did the same, digging their toes into the sand. "I'll show you something more beautiful."

Sarenie hadn't shut down her palette, but her hands stopped moving. The image of Ret stood out. He had short dark hair, a different color than Étar. Where Étar's eyes were green, Ret's were very dark –brown, she thought. He was handsome, but without a beard.

"There's been no word since Danosh's cave?" Kuyi asked.

Sarenie wiped a tear from her eye and shook her head.

"Are you in love with him?"

Sarenie looked askance, but said, "Yes, we are in love, but it's been a rocky road." Her eyes glazed over. "The hextet broke us for a while, long ago."

A quick check of her kennis gave Kuyi the proper reference, a family of six adults, and wondered if it was worth testing out.

"There aren't enough humans here to create stable hextet groupings," Sarenie said, as if reading her mind.

"Nalimai says that love evolved so that people would

procreate. Now that we have human birth chambers, love is no longer needed for procreation. Is it just for our own enjoyment, then? Is that how it is on Terra?"

Sarenie put an arm around Kuyi's shoulder, bringing her close. "I'm surprised at her harsh assessment, but I think you mean sex, not love. With our longevity, love is more important than anything." She took a deep breath. "Many of our grandparents are still married after two hundred years."

Kuyi's kennis automatically translated the unit of time, which Nalimai sometimes used. It was a long time.

They turned onto a path that led away from the beach, pausing to put their shoes back on. It led to a place she didn't mind sharing with Sarenie.

"The physical part of a relationship grows less intense as we age," Sarenie continued. "It's more of a mutual burning than the instant flame you and Étar have."

Kuyi drew back in shock. "Did he tell you?"

"No, but I can see it in the way your eyes light up when you see him. His do the same."

Her kennis was doing a good job at keeping Kuyi's face from overly blushing. She realized that she wanted Étar as much as she wanted to be useful to Aderen. Could she have both? She looked at the image of Ret. If Sarenie's love was here, Sarenie would still pursue her mission.

The path opened up to water on their left, and Sarenie stopped to look. Kuyi thought of Étar's first kiss in the baths, and the way he pressed up against her this morning. She was addicted to him and the way he made her feel.

They continued walking in silence, Ret's image strangely joining them, the others fading away. The lake receded as tall grasses closed in on both sides.

"Cherish what you have," said Sarenie. "For me, love is

companionship, somebody to share my life with, to share our experiences. Although the hextet could do that, I wasn't ready for it. That's why this hurts so much. Ret and I were just coming back together when he was torn away. I can't share his experiences, just like I can't share my joy of this place."

"I hope he's okay," Kuyi said.

"Me, too."

They came to four flat sitting stones overlooking a round pond with flowers and grasses. It was like they were alone in all of Bol.

"It's beautiful," said Sarenie. "Thanks for bringing me."

She sat down, waving away the image of Ret, breathing in deep, exhaling slowly. "I could get used to this, but it won't last." She opened another frame in her palette. "I'll be negotiating with Ontral when Aderen gets back, and I need to know what I'm up against, to convince him Terra is out of reach and to gain access to his birth chambers. I've already spoken with Egalinsor and Lusava, but Aderen values your impressions, too."

Kuyi frowned, which made Sarenie laugh. "I'm sure the twins led you into unexpected places, and you don't even realize they were preparing you for reconnaissance. Let's see what we can do in the vekornan cities."

*   *   *

The beach was eerily quiet as Kuyi and Étar worked on her kennis exercises. She had created stacks of virtual blocks, some of them rotating slowly. It didn't take any effort to keep them there.

She drew the palette rectangle with and without her keyword, but hadn't reached the proficiency she wanted. Étar didn't have to draw an actual rectangle; it seemed to

Kuyi that he just waved his hand around and the palette appeared.

"Doj has taken a sudden interest in me," Kuyi buzzed, practicing her silent communication. It made the beach seem even quieter. "I hadn't noticed until Sarenie told me how important the Arai lineages are."

Poking at her palette, Étar added a block to her stack. He insisted that she practice revoking and giving him permission, so the next time he went to add something, his hands passed through her palette without changing it.

His face lit up. "That was great!" he buzzed. He sent her virtual flowers, which danced around like folems in a strong wind.

"It wasn't until the Arais realized that they would live long like Egalinsor that they began to care, and kept track of who would have that advantage. There's a lot of jealousy toward us on Terra." He looked at her seriously. "I'm not sure how they would classify you and the others. Are you Doj's daughter, or is there another term because there are more than two donors to your DNA?"

"Sarenie said we were like sisters. I never realized it would be so complicated," she said, giving him access to her palette again. They were quiet as she continued her exercises.

"Now it's your turn," she said, tired of manipulating her palette. Unfortunately, there was no way to test if Étar was doing his exercises correctly, as she couldn't try to read his mind. Kirina and Egalinsor had taught the family how to shield their minds from vekorna when they were very young.

Étar furrowed his forehead in concentration, and Kuyi tried not to laugh. She watched him through her palette, his eyes drawn to her every so often. He was taking the exercises very seriously, which she hadn't expected. She wondered if he was singing an annoying song, or doing complex mathematical problems, or something else.

As his eyes came back to focus on her, she curled up one side of her mouth. "You're not doing the exercises right."

"How do you know?" He leaned forward expectantly.

She leaned toward him, too. "Because I can tell what you're thinking."

Falling on top of him, Kuyi let Étar catch her, and they kissed. This was it, she thought, removing the kennis blocks she'd placed, and desire ran through her. He requested permission to alter her hormones, and she accepted, shaking. This was what he'd promised, enhancements to the physical relationship they hadn't had yet.

Somehow, they shed their meager clothing, shivering in the heat. She drew him tight, feeling his warm body under her, lips searching for release. He didn't need to alter her hormones for this to be glorious. This was not sexual experimentation. This was an urgent lust she had never felt before.

It was over too soon, but they lay facing each other, giggling. She didn't even know what was funny. Étar's chest and stomach were heaving as he took deep breaths of Rykol's warm air. She relished the slow retreat of what she was feeling, without help from her kennis.

"I have sand everywhere," she said, standing.

Étar followed her into the water. They dove together, touching and caressing, until they were making love again, partially submerged.

Now that their lust had been satisfied, his kennis touched

249

hers, and she felt the way he enhanced her nerves. His hands on her body made her glow inside. Every touch was like lightning, fading as he withdrew.

They fell into a rhythm, and he fed her desire until it peaked. He held her there, guiding her breathing as he kissed her gently.

As she descended from her extraordinary high, she explored her way into his kennis. Unfortunately, her control wasn't as fine as his, and his eyes widened as she unintentionally pushed him over the edge.

He laughed, eyes sparkling, and she kissed him again. After a quick moment, they were once more exploring each other's kennis. She allowed herself to get lost in his arms, his touch, his buzzed thoughts, and the unseen connection between their implants, forgetting Aderen and her mission for a time.

31.Crystal Search

Meditation had never been so difficult. On Terra, humans leaked their thoughts continuously, and Tararnifal preferred to be on his extar in space. He hadn't expected the same on Rykol. Vekorna were not supposed to emit the fear he sensed.

Abandoning his meditation, he reached out through the city, searching for any who felt more frustration with Dairnehy than fear. He easily found Paknef, a beacon of non-fear among them, exploring. Punad was another, but he wasn't ready to trust a prin-el who carried out their leader's horrific orders on other vekorna.

Sebenet was still in the tower, his emotions conflicted. He showed no fear after his near-death experience at Dairnehy's hands. By allowing him to climb back over the top of the cliff, Dairnehy had evoked loyalty in Sebenet, overshadowing the compromise that Aderen tried to instill.

Kular had a different mission. There were places in the city Tararnifal couldn't penetrate, even as tigal-en. Kular had found one, and his report was disturbing.

Keeping secrets from Dairnehy was nearly impossible, but Tararnifal had compartmentalized his mind, and urged the others to do the same. He imagined this was how Bolob had hidden what he was doing to the wingless from Kopiv.

Dairnehy's voice entered his mind, tigal-en to tigal-en. **Come to me in the lowest chambers.**

Tararnifal acknowledged and wondered if he'd been careful enough. The way Dairnehy had shoved Sebenet over the cliff still haunted him.

The elevator took him into the depths of Rubiel, almost as deep as the tower was high. Darkness enveloped him, and he wondered why he'd ever left space.

"You spent most of your life in space, even before Bolob took you away," Dairnehy said when he entered the room, standing amid red crystal dust. Perhaps his mind wasn't as compartmentalized as he thought. "Like Sebenet, you have returned to the city to help me."

His telepathic link to the outside world attenuated as the door closed, leaving him confused. What kind of power did Dairnehy have here? He was as unreadable as the Egalsan.

"Where are we?" Tararnifal asked aloud. There was no other way to speak. "It's as if I've been transported off Rykol."

"We are surrounded by mirror-crystals, which isolate us from the rest of the city and prevent spying on our conversations."

Mirror crystals also caused the voids he'd sensed around

251

Rubiel. Such crystals hadn't existed prior to his departure for Terra. "Did they come from the stellar fragment?"

Dairnehy spread his wings wide, thrashing them in anger, disturbing the dust and small crystals. "They are not of the fragment." He pointed three eyestalks at his lower feet. Was that stellar fragment dust? "Wingless kolbs grew them under Esetek before Kopiv's war."

Useful crystals for a paranoid leader, Tararnifal thought. How many of these rooms did Dairnehy have? If he kept his thoughts behind mirror crystals, he would appear unpredictable.

Calculating the effect it would have on Dairnehy, Tararnifal removed his faceplate, expressing vulnerability to the winged leader, placing it in one of the unnatural corners of the room. He shifted his weight and extended his wings.

Dairnehy's snapped the air of the small room with his wings. "I held the entire fragment in my hands when it was discovered. Now I only have tiny pieces." He glanced down again. The largest piece was the size of his hand. "When I stand among them, sometimes I feel connected to the other pieces."

"Jye-Tan took it from you," said Tararnifal. "Is this all that remains?"

"He left without the fragment," said Dairnehy. "It is hidden in the city. You lived a long time among humans, and know more about them than any vekornan."

"I have watched them," Tararnifal admitted, now knowing what was expected. He moved again, along one of the flat walls opposite Dairnehy. The vekornan leader matched his movement, stepping out of the dust, like two Terran crabs facing off. He was strong enough to defeat

Dairnehy in this sealed room, unless Dairnehy had another trick ready, something that could inhibit him physically like the mirror crystals inhibited telepathy.

Unfortunately, Tararnifal didn't yet know if the vekorna of Rubiel would accept him or kill him for taking Dairnehy's place. Perhaps in time, or with Danosh's support.

"Find the stellar fragment for me."

He stopped circling. Mai had also implied that the fragment was still in Rubiel. If he could find it, he could remove it from the city later. He couldn't allow Dairnehy to obtain the full stellar fragment.

"I will search for the stolen piece, though what I can provide that thousands of vekorna under your control could not is unclear."

*   *   *

Jye-Tan would have chosen a hiding place with emotional significance to him or other humans. Tararnifal sent Kular back to the ruins of the old city, not willing to revisit the site of Sebenet's near-death himself. It was a good hiding spot, though, as the original crews had often spent time there. To his surprise, Punad went with him. He sent Paknef to the gardens, which were now overgrown in the absence of human gardeners. Both had their instructions, and both had their guards.

Tararnifal watched the octagonal vend'oks leave in opposite directions, then folded his wings and turned to Rubiel. A familiar presence was waiting for him.

Dairnehy's teams have already searched the human rooms, said Sebenet. **What do you expect to see that we have not?**

Tararnifal wasn't going to argue with Sebenet, but had

to respond. **We shall see what a new perspective gives.**

I was a new perspective, and found nothing.

Tararnifal pushed past him to the small door, with direct access to one of four corridors that spanned the length of the city's arm. **I wonder if you are new enough, or if you are fully trusted.**

The experience brought my mind back into focus. I remember my place on Rykol. Do you? We need to use our leader's vision and influence to bring about stability, even if he his measures are extreme in the short term.

For a time, you were open to compromise, Tararnifal said.

If I see an opportunity to compromise, I will take it. Sebenet moved toward the automated transport, and Tararnifal didn't stop him as he walked to the narrower service corridor. He kept his mind closed.

The human rooms are this way, said Sebenet.

Entering the corridor, Tararnifal noted small lights in the distance, lights that were not installed by vekorna. **Would you think of taking the less efficient route? Humans take pleasure in long walks.**

A waste of time.

If they have someplace to be, Tararnifal admitted. **Like ours, their minds work best with movement. Unlike ours, their brains relish time spent away from communal thinking.** Was it ironic that he thought of the solitude of the solar system in his extar at the same time?

Will you tolerate my humanisms, or report me to Dairnehy?

Sebenet didn't answer. He followed Tararnifal down the corridor, illuminated by human lights.

He cast his mind outward, determined to do a thorough job, despite the potential consequences. Dairnehy would have no honest cause to throw him from a cliff. Searching for the power of a telepathic crystal with each step, Tararnifal moved slowly toward the old human section. On his mental command, doors slid aside or upward to reveal unremarkable rooms.

Dairnehy's teams have thoroughly searched these rooms, Sebenet claimed.

We are being shadowed. Tararnifal had felt the surge in communication as Sebenet requested information on the rooms. **Another team is following us from the second floor.**

Dairnehy is aware that you plan to deceive him. He will know the moment you find something.

He felt four vekornan minds above them. There would be little fooling Dairnehy if he found the fragment. He sent warnings to Paknef and Kular to be wary, as he took a crossing to the other side of the city's arm.

Patterns on the walls showed Tararnifal that he was entering the old human section. He had only been here once, to meet the human crews before leaving for Terra. He hadn't understood the significance of the artistry at the time.

Their art is different from ours, Sebenet said. His comment showed an interest in something other than pleasing Dairnehy.

Inspection of the drawings revealed a lot about the humans who had lived at Rubiel.

All humans from the four surviving crews are represented here, including those who never reached Rykol, he responded.

The scenes appear to be unrealistic.

Tararnifal now recognized many of the terrestrial scenes, especially those that Rykol lacked.

You have seen inside my mind, he said. **Do you not recognize their blue oceans, snowcapped mountains framed by green trees, birds in the sky and fish in the rivers?**

Why do you have a fondness for their fish? Sebenet asked.

Tararnifal clamped down on his thoughts, the elation he felt as Terran fish drifted up against his armored skeleton no longer leaking out. **They were unique,** was all he would say.

A wide variety of Terran animals, large and small, crossed the walls and ceiling. The four human crews had brought their world with them. Had Bolob's vekorna done the same at Terra?

What are these creatures? Sebenet asked. **Humans do not have wings.**

They are mechanical devices that allow humans to glide, just as we do, when they jump from a height. His thoughts went unconsciously to Sebenet's spiral dive from the cliff, wings supporting him as he sought purchase in the rock.

Sebenet stood staring at the parachutes and flexible wings humans clung to in their odd recreational time for several seconds, before turning to a large animal.

We will enter here, said Tararnifal, moving on. Sebenet followed him into the medical ward. All of the equipment was shut down, but he knew that it would have been active when Jye-Tan visited not long ago. Humans were notorious for getting hurt.

Crouch on that side of the chamber. Sebenet understood, and didn't question him, marching to the side of the room, flanked by machines designed to heal the human body.

As far as Tararnifal knew, Danosh was the only vekornan to have been properly healed from a crippling mutilation. Most vekorna would have been killed after those injuries, but Bolob had already learned compassion from humans by then.

Tararnifal settled himself on the opposite side of the medical ward, near chairs Yenine had used to examine her patients. He balanced his weight on four limbs, letting the upper ones hang limp. Things could get dangerous from here if he found the missing fragment.

Opening his mind, Tararnifal connected with Sebenet, touching the vekornan's thoughts, shielding the compartments of his mind. Although Sebenet was now wholly loyal to Dairnehy, some of Aderen's influence remained. Sebenet would still be open to Tararnifal's suggestions, if applied forcefully enough.

There is no amplification between us, he said, hiding his relief.

Dairnehy knew this already, Sebenet agreed.

They moved down the corridor, passing two-dimensional images of dogs and horses, rockets and asteroids.

This is the first human chamber, Sebenet announced, but Tararnifal bypassed it. The room had been used briefly by the *Siberath* crew, before the broken hextet moved to Bol.

Jye-Tan would not have any connection to that crew, Tararnifal said. He bypassed more rooms to enter the

Avenger quarters, Nalimai's original living space.

A small entrance led to the large common room, still furnished with seats and couches pulled together from the five spaceships. A table held well-worn tools. Originally each member of the crew was to have their own side chamber, private space and a bed, but couplings and deaths had changed that.

They walked to each alcove, all of which were in storage mode. The crew had left items behind, but nothing that could hide a crystal the size Dairnehy was searching for. Sebenet remained silent as he searched.

Assume a meditative position at this end of the common room, Tararnifal instructed. He did the same at the other end, ready to send his suggestive commands into Sebenet's mind through Aderen's remaining pathways.

Once again, he connected with Sebenet. Once again, nothing augmented their minds the way the fragment would. They could search the other rooms, but he was now certain the fragment wasn't here, and he relaxed.

A familiar feeling briefly caught Tararnifal's attention. Above Sebenet, he could sense some of the vekorna that had been shadowing them. But directly above his head, there was nothing. Was this another of Dairnehy's special void rooms?

What is above us? Tararnifal asked.

Storage, said Sebenet. **A team will investigate.**

The area is unimportant to our search, said Tararnifal, regretting his question. He should have sent Kular later. How would Dairnehy react to them violating his special rooms?

I would not have recognized such a small telepathic dampening, Sebenet said.

There are voids like this all over the city, Tararnifal explained. **They are not of Jye-Tan's making.**

Sebenet reached up to a seam in the white ceiling, and the panel came loose. **The void is between us and the team in the storage room,** he said, revealing a hidden compartment. He stood up to his full height and extended arms above his sensor head, pulling down a familiar oval body. **The compartment is human-made, and is far older than the Egalsan.**

He threw the macrobot torso to the side, and reached into the compartment again. Tararnifal's eyestalks were drawn to the table and tools in the common room. This had been Doj's workshop. At the time, Kopiv refused to allow macrobots within the city, but Doj had found a way.

Sebenet pulled down other components, defunct sensors, glass rods, and finally a flat crystal the size of his faceplate, handing it to Tararnifal. Two smaller crystals followed, revealing what he feared most.

Immediately, he pushed on Sebenet, a command to keep this secret and replace the fragment piece, but he was impotent. The suggestive influence never made it across their short separation, inhibited by the mirror crystals he was holding.

He threw them to shatter against the walls, but the delay had already cost him. Dairnehy must have been nearby, launching into the room within seconds. When he saw the oblong crystal, red as Rykol's ocean, his wings snapped out in anger.

They shattered the fragment! he exclaimed. **There must be more.**

Tararnifal backed away, suggestions to Sebenet now useless. The strange voids had distracted him, and now

259

Dairnehy had the fragment.

Reaching into the compartment, Dairnehy withdrew the small crystal, almost the size of his sensor head. **Useless! I can barely see further into your mind than before.**

Realizing he might not have failed after all, Tararnifal reached for the crystal, but Dairnehy turned away from him.

He thinks it makes him more like Kirina, Mai had said, speaking of Jye-Tan. Could the boy have used the fragment to discover other secrets, like mirror crystals?

I will add this to the other pieces we recovered, making it stronger, but we will continue searching. The power of Dairnehy's thoughts was more powerful. He was breaking through Tararnifal's compartments.

Tararnifal has discovered other voids like this around the city, said Sebenet. **The boy might have hidden more pieces there.**

Dairnehy extended three eyestalks toward Tararnifal, passing through the walls of his mind. **You've been spying on me.**

I was curious, Tararnifal responded, opening parts of his mind he'd held in reserve, distracting Dairnehy from those that were more important.

Dairnehy's eyes moved to Sebenet. **Search the city.**

To Tararnifal, he said, **Maybe Jye-Tan found them, like you did. I have not checked on my caches for some time. You have done well.**

Opening his mind to them both, Dairnehy added, **The only large fragment left on Rykol is in Bol. We will draw Ontral out, force the wingless to use it outside the folem shield.** He extended several eyestalks at Tararnifal. **You will lead the attack on Metik.**

Tararnifal was confused, and tucked his wings in close.

Metik is half a world away, and across the ocean from Bol.

It is the closest wingless city to the Temple of Spall, where they keep the fragment. You will draw them out, and we will capture it.

Hope filled the remaining compartments of Tararnifal's mind. He would be leaving Rubiel, but could he escape? He didn't regret that Sebenet was lost to him, thoroughly under Dairnehy's control. The vekornan had been an annoyance since before they left Terra.

He'd given Dairnehy potential hiding spots for the remainder of the fragment, locations Tararnifal knew Jye-Tan would not have used, as they were too distant.

Dairnehy was getting him out of the way.

32. Confidence

As she and Mai approached the gate, Kuyi buzzed Firini in his workshop. She recognized Treklay's mental buzz as he let her by. He had been their liaison for a long time before Aderen took control of his mind at Egalra and Esetek, and didn't question them as they passed.

When they met Firini, he said, "Lusava is in Siftral, adapting her genetics routines to the kennis interface. Rogo and I have been doing the same here, with help from Wandel and Akinuf."

Firini, last of the natural-born Egalsan, led them to the old shuttle pad that was unofficially designated for Egalsan use. It was cluttered with disassembled machinery, including vend'ok and shuttle parts.

At some time in the past, Firini had convinced Ontral to donate a shuttle cockpit, after the rest of it was destroyed in battle. More parts had been scavenged from wrecks dating back to the winged attack.

Rogo was in the cockpit mockup. He waved them over, which caught Kuyi off guard, and she wondered if his congenial attitude was because he believed he still held some of her strings, as she was ostensibly watching over Mai. Little did he know that this was just their first stop of the day.

"Did you manage to get this thing flying?" Mai asked, her voice carrying among the sounds from the vekornan city.

Rogo frowned, looking about. He was probably trying to decide how to respond to the comment, but Kuyi laughed at its absurdity. "Where are Wandel and Akinuf?" She hadn't seen Wandel since the older woman had stomped out of the genetics conversation.

"She and Akinuf are over in that vend'ok skeleton," Firini said. Then he pointed to his temple in what she interpreted as the universal sign for their kennis. "Even from there, Akinuf is always quick to answer questions, though."

"They're quiet, but they catch on fast," said Rogo. "At this rate, they'll have that skeleton operating by nightfall."

Kuyi nodded, understanding the idea of Wandel keeping her hands busy. Sometimes it helped sort through feelings of anger or inadequacy. It was curious that she wasn't still in the human birth chambers, though.

Rogo shook his head and returned to the front console, twitching his fingers. Firini put his arms around Kuyi and Mai, and whispered, barely audible, "Look, no helmet." His eyes were bright.

"Is he doing something?" Mai asked. "I don't see what's

happening."

"Open your mind," Firini buzzed.

Rogo glanced at them, and Kuyi's kennis opened up with a virtual layout of the cockpit panels, invisible to her eyes. Rogo was manipulating a diagnostic, which showed that the cockpit had been brought to life.

"If we had a real shuttle, then we could give it a short hop," Rogo said, forcing an attempt at humor. "Watch. I have some control."

The cockpit lit up with a soft white glow. It faltered for a moment, then stabilized. "Ketaris says not to strain our new abilities," he buzzed. "I think I'm almost at that limit."

Kuyi watched the virtual controls as Rogo pulled on one of them, and the indicators changed. If she was to be of use to Aderen, she had to be capable of flying a shuttle. She'd used the helmet a couple of times, but it didn't interest her, and she'd let any skills she'd once had atrophy. With the kennis, she would need to learn from scratch.

"What other telepathic controls can we tap into with the kennis?" Mai asked, touching the smooth surface. Her hand slid right through the virtual controls Rogo was manipulating, with no effect.

"I've connected to a few vekornan computers," said Firini. "The kennis leaves a smaller footprint in their system than our old interface. This could revolutionize everything."

Kuyi nodded. "Show me how to fly a shuttle," she said, surprising everyone. When Rogo hesitated, glancing at Mai, she added, "I'm not a babysitter. Mai and Jye-Tan are nineteen Terran years old, which might not mean a lot to you, but if you look it up on your kennis, it means they can take care of themselves. They have to start their own lives."

Rogo, Firini and Mai stared at her. After a few seconds, Firini smiled, and Mai buzzed her a silent congratulatory laugh.

Rogo shut down the cockpit, and she started to back away, disappointed. But he grabbed her hand and placed her in the center of the shuttle console. To her mind, he was willingly handing her the puppet string he'd formerly controlled.

"It's easier if you use physical cues, like holding out your hand. Look for the link showing telepathic contact, similar to what you might remember from the helmet." His voice was calm and instructive, patiently guiding her. In awe at the change she'd effectuated by standing firm, Kuyi's palette failed briefly before she regained control. Rogo caught her mistake and calmly emphasized the need for caution.

She found the telepathic link, which her kennis mimicked as a computer connection, and the world opened up to her.

"Wow," she said, and Rogo smiled, taking notice of her skills. "How far can we go with this technology?" she buzzed, imagining the cockpit taking off and flying around Bol, then out of the shield to circle Rykol, without Treklay's help or supervision.

33. Puppets

Excitement at learning to fly under Rogo's tutelage turned to wariness as she and Mai explored the Temple of Spall that afternoon. The search for Ontral's piece of the stellar fragment was long and boring, not to mention unfruitful.

"We need to split up to cover more ground," Kuyi

buzzed, hiding in a small hollow of rock, listening to mental leakage from vekornan minds on the other side. The back ways were too small for vekorna or folems, who probably didn't know these fissures existed.

In the darkness, Mai's eyes widened, reflecting the scant light from a small palette between them. She shook her head, frightened, not sarcastic. "No, we have to stay together."

"We've been here for hours, and found nothing. We'll be more efficient alone."

"Don't leave me."

Kuyi pointed to her temple, mimicking the gesture the Arais used. "I'll always be nearby." She stood and left the hollow, confident she could find the fragment for Aderen.

A tug at her shirt turned Kuyi around, and there was Mai. Exasperated, her face softened as the younger woman held up a pouch. "Folem pollen," Mai said. "For locked doors."

"Thanks," Kuyi said, annoyed she hadn't thought of that. Vekornan doors operated telepathically, but the Temple had been built for folems. Then, trying to add something wise, she buzzed, "Ontral won't keep the fragment in an unlocked room without guards. Find an area with more vekornan traffic, but stay out of sight, keep your mind small, and your body temperature the same as the air."

Mai rolled her eyes. "I've been doing most of that all my life," she buzzed bravely. Kuyi put a hand on her shoulder, more to reassure herself than Mai.

"Keep it up, and don't get caught. We'll share the kennis map, and mark off places we've checked."

She turned and left, tracing her path on the kennis map as it extended in two directions. She shivered as the implant matched her skin temperature to the cooler air under the mountains.

Regular corridors were mostly unoccupied and lit by the same diffuse light that permeated the Bol dome at night, but the back ways sometimes faded to pitch black. Kuyi enhanced her retinal sensitivity, and applied an infrared filter to see temperature differentials. It was as close to vekornan eyesight as she would get.

She'd expected more vekorna this far into the Temple. Had they given up on the folem machines and retreated completely into the three cities? Of course, on her previous trips, she'd always gone out of her way to avoid them.

While she used to let leaked vekornan speech relax her after watching Jye-Tan and Mai all day, now Kuyi listened intently. Vekornan telepathy was centered on the buzz she felt in her mind, not necessarily in words, or even feelings.

She understood enough that the area she was watching was dedicated to genetics and weapons research. The stellar fragment was nowhere in their leaked thoughts.

"I'm going deeper," Kuyi buzzed, leaving her latest hollow. Mai acknowledged her silently.

Sliding down a steep and rocky groove, Kuyi felt Mai's presence disappear. Her kennis connection had been interrupted. Kuyi scrambled to ascend the path, sliding more than she gained. Eventually, sweating with effort and panic, she crouched at the top of the grooved path. Her kennis reconnected. Predictably, Mai's repeated query to her kennis was getting more and more desperate.

"I'm fine, but I have to leave you for a while, after all," Kuyi buzzed, projecting more calm than she felt. "We've been separated before, when we didn't have a kennis."

Reluctantly, and without sarcasm, Mai relented. "We

should meet up again in two hours, when the first sun sets," she buzzed, and Kuyi agreed.

Ready for the disconnection this time, Kuyi descended the triangular groove again, watching her step, hands on one wall. She'd never gone so deep into the Temple, and wondered if the vekorna tested the fragment this far underground. If it had any power to enhance their telepathy, would the rock attenuate the effect, keeping it secret?

As she descended into silence, cut off from her brief time in the shared kennis world, she was determined to prove her usefulness to Aderen. She thought of Egalinsor's words, the way he'd praised her, and pushed on despite her fears.

The steep groove led her to a fissure, which only went one way. Infrared light shone ahead, and she popped into a wide hallway, instantly scrambling to get back into the narrow crack in the stone wall.

This deep in the Temple, the stone was a little darker. She was about to peer into the hallway again, when she felt a sudden vekornan buzz. Two vekorna were exchanging information, and stopped alongside her fissure. She didn't dare move, adjusting her kennis to ensure she was invisible to all vekornan senses. What were these vekorna doing, standing in the middle of a hallway for so long?

A minute passed, then two, and she wondered if she should risk movement. Vekornan hearing was very sensitive, and she didn't think she could be silent enough so close to them. If only she could pull their strings like Aderen, move them out of the way, so she could either retreat or move forward.

Although her muscles were cramping, her kennis indicated the vekorna had only been there six minutes as she waited, before moving on down the corridor.

Controlling her heart rate, she waited a long time before peering out again, searching with her eyes what her mind told her already. The vekorna were gone. Nearby, she noted the blue metal door, so different from other doors she'd passed in the upper levels, and likely where the vekorna had come from. Could this one be hiding a special project?

Finally deciding she had to do something or go back, she entered the hall, and sprinkled some folem pollen on the door, but nothing happened. Other doors had a panel which would sense the pollen, but not this one. She pulled and pushed on it, to no avail. Her mood brightened. This was a vekornan door. She couldn't get too excited, though, as Ontral could have many secret and secure projects.

The door would require a telepathic link. Using the new skills she'd acquired in Firini's workshop, she searched for an opening with her kennis, giving up after a couple of minutes. She noted its position on her kennis map, which no longer updated with Mai's excursions, and followed the wall away from her fissure, opposite to the two vekorna.

She noted other fissures along the walls of the corridor, places she could escape into if vekorna approached. The mountain was still causing cracks in the excavated hallways.

The next door was locked, but a sprinkling of pollen opened it. Empty, except for a glowing blue cylinder near the center.

Disappointed again, she made her way to other doors, turning to smaller hallways cut out of the mountain rock, wondering if the vekorna had abandoned the Temple altogether. She'd been expecting to avoid a lot more vekorna.

The Temple had been around since the first vekorna, so she shouldn't have been surprised that so many rooms were empty. Her thoughts kept being drawn to the vekornan door, unique among all that she'd seen on this level. Maybe it was time to return.

Unlocking another door, Kuyi sighed at its emptiness. She forced herself to enter, in case it wasn't altogether empty, and as she approached the far wall, she felt the telltale buzz of vekorna nearby. She dropped to the ground and crawled to a small alcove made by adjoining walls.

The vekornan thoughts were indistinct, as if they were trying to avoid telepathic leakage. Kuyi reached out with her kennis, the way she had in Firini's workshop, searching for a connection she could exploit. Why were these vekorna being so secretive in their own space, so far from prying eyes and other senses? Could it be the fragment?

Although her kennis wasn't true telepathy, it could mimic some aspects. It hadn't worked on the vekornan door, but other receivers weren't always so secure.

There —she found something, and tapped into the system. A viewing pane. Maybe she would be able to see what they were doing. Carefully manipulating the controls like Rogo had shown her, it wasn't so difficult.

The wall opposite suddenly turned transparent, and she withdrew her kennis connection, huddling deeper into her hiding place. Would the vekorna notice, or should she change it back? She touched the connection again. If she interpreted it correctly, the viewing panel was unidirectional.

Sliding against the walls until she reached the side of the window, she peered through, heart beating faster. Could this be it? The stellar fragment was supposed to be red, but the six crystals in the next room were clearly glowing white.

Something skittered along the floor between the crystals, and she hid from the one-way viewer. Peeking out again, she saw sparks reach from the nearest crystal to touch the creature. It picked its amorphous body off the ground, forming three rail-like legs, moving away from the crystal.

Another crystal sparked, hitting it so that it changed direction. Soon all six crystals were sparking, and the creature was skating back and forth.

Another creature entered the ring of crystals, six spheres extended on individual tentacles. They looked like eyes, and were ranging all around the room. Sparks made it dance one way, shifting direction in tune with them.

Kuyi frowned, thinking of her imagined puppet strings.

They respond well, but we need more samples, came a voice. Vekornan, but she couldn't see where he might be. Behind another one-way viewer, like her?

Something fell from the ceiling in the other room, hitting the ground with a loud splat that she could hear through the wall. It stood on its three rail-like feet and moved toward the first two, until sparks from the crystals forced it to change direction.

These were living creatures, and the vekorna were forcing them to do their will. She had to admit that it was similar to what Aderen and Kirina could do, and she thought of Treklay, immobilized at Egalra, at the mercy of the winged.

More creatures slapped to the ground as she watched. Some weren't even close to the crystals as they sparked, changing direction anyway, extending tentacles like perverse vekornan eyes without a faceplate. They were all moving in concert as the crystals sparked.

This was wrong. The vekorna were torturing them. When war broke out between the winged and wingless, the folems had released cloned creatures from their genetic zoo. They couldn't control the giant oboms, like those Danosh had displayed. Others still roamed the deserts, killing indiscriminately. These creatures had to be from the same cloning machines, and the vekorna were controlling them.

She watched them dance to the tune of the sparks, more joining in as they splatted to the ground from wherever they were perched.

On an unseen command, fifty or sixty of the creatures lifted two of their rail-feet from the ground, balancing on a single rail without effort. Kuyi found herself standing on one foot in sympathy, tears flowing from her eyes. This was horrible.

The innocent creatures dropped to their three rail-feet and froze, much like Aderen had done to the vekorna at Egalra, or Danosh's forces outside Esetek. Then one spit something at another, which dissolved into a smoking jelly on the ground.

Crouching with one hand on the floor, Kuyi screamed, a hollowness in her throat keeping the sound from escaping. She drew on her kennis to keep it that way, allowing a physical release without revealing herself through noise. Even the sound of her whimpering was suppressed, her suddenly running nose sniffling silently.

The air tingled around her as the swarm of creatures in the other room spat at each other, the crystals silently sparking around them. They dodged one another, spitting at their former dance partners-turned enemies. The brawl in the other room wasn't natural.

She turned around, looking for something to hit. She dropped into a lobomai pose, searching for an enemy. Her hands went out to the sides, elbows bent, ready, and she spat at the ground.

Knees bent, she took long strides, keeping her body close to the floor. She spat at the wall, but nothing happened. She spat at an outcropping of rock to no effect. Frustrated, she hit the rock with her hand. The pain caused her to spit again, but she stopped midway, spittle dripping down her chin as she realized she was mimicking the creatures from the other room.

The vekorna were pulling her strings like those of the creatures. Panic welled up inside her, and she drew on her kennis to keep calm.

Something splattered to the ground near her, loud in the darkness with only her minimal palette for light. She spat instinctively in that direction, then swore. This was wrong.

Another splat to her right caused her to turn suddenly and spit, hands ready. Blood dripped from her palm where she'd hit the rock, but she didn't dare lower her guard. She dampened the pain with her kennis.

Another splat startled her, but she refrained from spitting. Her mouth was dry anyway; there was nothing left to spit. The transparent wall was to her left, but she'd lost track of the door. Increasing the illumination from the palette that followed her movements, comforting her, she searched the walls.

While the door was lost to her, the army of small amorphous creatures on the floor was not. She screamed again, a small squeak overcoming the limits her kennis had placed on her vocal cords.

They shifted toward her, and she couldn't move, immobilized by fear the way the creatures in the other room had been immobilized by the crystals.

They were moving in concert, marching with their three rail-tipped feet, some with tentacle eyes extended, others not. She watched them in horror, eyes darting from one to the next, chest heaving, heart beating erratically, kennis unable to synchronize it. The implant was too new, she understood as it sent her warnings. She hadn't tested it enough, the way Étar hadn't practiced his anti-telepathy exercises.

She was surrounded by a sea of amorphous creatures, more dropping from the ceiling all the time in loud splats. They deftly avoided her feet and legs, but she could feel their mass as they scratched along the floor toward the viewing pane.

The creatures had climbed the wall from both sides, hugging and sucking on the transparent surface. She couldn't even check if it was one-way anymore. Her kennis wasn't responding.

Then the wall shattered, smoking from the same projectile acid that the creatures spat. The wall tumbled down and crushed hundreds of the creatures, but more surged through in both directions. The ones from the other side were spitting, while the ones on her side were dancing.

How could the vekorna not know she was here?

She ran to the wall opposite the activity, fumbling with the pouch at her side, throwing folem pollen everywhere, feeling for the door. As her heart raced and a full-scale battle erupted in the two rooms, sparks from the six crystals conducting it all, her palette disappeared. Pain erupted on her shoulder, legs and back.

Frantic, she tried to activate her palette again, drawing the rectangle in the air, mouthing "baby", over and over. She couldn't connect to the viewport controls she'd accessed earlier, and the kennis map wouldn't come to her.

She was alone. Abandoning her kennis the way it had abandoned her, she threw more pollen at the wall. Miraculously, a segment of the wall opened, and she fell into the corridor. Standing uncertainly, she ran down the hallway until she found a fissure, but it was too small to squeeze into, and the darkness on the other side was unnerving.

She hugged the wall, single-mindedly looking for a place to escape. A door interrupted her thoughts, and she passed her pollen-covered fingers over the panel. It opened into a dark room. There was no buzz, no glow, no noise.

She collapsed to the ground and closed her eyes, feeling the dirt beneath her. Sighing heavily, she knew she needed rest, if only for a moment, and fell into a heavy sleep.

34. Memories of Rykol 5

The kennis surgeries had gone well. Nalimai, Aneya, Jye-Tan and Orem were sleeping off the effects, creating new connections with the implant. Aderen spent the time reviewing strategy with Étar and Pinoa.

Étar was concerned that Kuyi and Mai hadn't checked in from their explorations in the Temple of Spall, but a discrete check with Sarenie revealed that she'd admitted to spending nights away before. It was more troubling that they'd turned their kennis off. Hopefully Nalimai and Egalinsor wouldn't notice until after the girls returned. Was that selfish, as Nalimai had accused?

Aderen hadn't expected a second vekornan leader on

Rykol. Ontral seemed content to harbor the wingless in Bol, and Sarenie shouldn't have trouble negotiating access to his birth chambers, especially with Egalinsor present. The intelligence Treklay had brought back from Esetek included an offer of alliance, and Sarenie wanted to exploit the possibility that Danosh was sincere, without offering Ontral's piece of the stellar fragment.

Despite the possibility that the two vekorna might depose Dairnehy, Aderen's mission would be more difficult if they failed. The current winged leader was unpredictable and more dangerous than he expected. He couldn't wait for them ignite a new civil war.

Kirina's vend'ok was run down, but could still travel. Unfortunately, Penagel couldn't figure out how to get it through the shield, so it wasn't a viable option to get to Rubiel. Sarenie would negotiate a shuttle, and he thought Ontral would grant it just to be rid of him.

It was clear that he couldn't go to Rubiel alone. He needed support, and unless they found a way to boost kennis signals through the shields, that support had to be with him.

Unless… If Jye-Tan wasn't exaggerating, and the stellar fragment could further enhance Aderen's skills, he could go alone. Ontral's piece had to be tested, though, so he was willing to give Kuyi and Mai time to locate it in the Temple. It would be worth the wait if he could subdue Dairnehy and at the same time reach into the birth chambers to ensure that future vekorna never went back to Terra.

Kirina's memory globes had offered insight into Rykol's past, but she had nothing about the fragment. While Sarenie and Pinoa were negotiating with Ontral tomorrow, he would take advantage of the folems' suggestion that he visit the Memory Caves. They would certainly have memories that could help him better understand how to use the fragment.

As if summoned by the thought of memory globes, his vision started to fade. He lay back and let it take over his senses.

*   *   *

Speak with the folems. The voice annoyed him, now that he'd already decided to go to the Memory Caves. The voice was too consistent to have lived through all this history, and had certainly been added later. But when, and why?

The voice was easily dismissed as Aderen floated, flying high above the desert, with a forest off to his right, and the red ocean beyond. He felt the fear the goses had at flying over the ocean.

There are not enough of us to take the chance, even to get to the land you call Rapk. The giant island, almost a minor continent of its own, was less than a hundred kilometers off the shore of Depraf, beyond the horizon, though from high atop the goses he could see land. Goses eyesight was better than that of siims. Nirk assured him the land was beautiful for a goses.

They flew north, over the giant crater that was all that remained of the asteroid that had created siims and rokels. They crossed two rivers, which flowed out to the sea, where its water would be buried beneath vekornan-made Rykol-water.

"This is the first time you speak of fear," yelled Persinjali, not connecting to the group mind of the siims and goses. "You have never shown any other fear."

276

There is another fear, for a species of less than ten thousand strong, said Nirk. **You have not made progress in goses birth chamber technology, so we fear our decline from vekornan lasers.**

Persinjali understood the frustration. Fortunately, the vekorna had more and more trust in the siims, allowing them to conduct their research in the deserts with minimal escort. Today they could fly higher and farther abroad than usual because their escort had been called south to fend off a kolb attack.

"We have completed the siim birth chambers, but are not permitted to move them out of vekornan cities. The vekorna continue to inspect them, unsure if they want our species to continue into a second generation. But they feel that they need us to counter the rokel threat."

The kolbs have bred a second generation of rokels?

"Yes, they unleashed a larger rokel army." Persinjali enjoyed the feeling of flying. His own wings wouldn't do more than slow his fall over a short distance. He envied the goses. "We won't fight rokels," he continued. "We are researchers."

Nirk made her quick rumble of a laugh, something the siims didn't fully understand. **An entire species of researchers, born from a race of fighters. You should have a goses birth chamber ready soon after you gain your freedom from the vekorna.**

"That is yet to happen," said Persinjali. Mentally, he added, **I fear it will never happen.**

A ripple went through Nirk's wings, and Persinjali felt it on her neck where he perched. **There is our second fear,** Nirk said.

It was rare to see vekornan boats, made of a material that

would ablate in the Rykol-water, allowing a short stay on the ocean's surface in the unusual event this was necessary.

Soraen, but not vekorna, said Nirk.

Kolbs?

They have beached their boats, and are hidden in the forest.

The goses let out a mental sigh of frustration that kolbs, most certainly accompanied by rokels, would desecrate the sacred forest with their presence. The kolbs had contributed to the goses bodies that gave life to this forest. Their own dead still sat in a lifeless heap at the southern end.

As Nirk flew over the forest, Persinjali could pick out the rokel presences. A fierce anger penetrated him, something he didn't understand.

Then a beam sliced into the air, and Nirk banked away. More beams followed as they gained some distance. Another siim-goses pair, alerted by the group mind, came to help.

More beams sliced into the sky, targeting the goses. The goses circled the forest, nervously passing over the beach to one side, the desert on the other, trying to count the kolbs and rokels.

Those are small boats, a siim voice came across the common consciousness. **No more than four can fit in each.**

There are fewer than sixty intruders.

Assuming they all came by boat.

Would we have noticed a shuttle landing nearby?

A laser cut across one of the goses, and the mental scream echoed in Aderen's mind. He almost fell out of his chair as he watched the goses-siim pair fall to the ground, dead.

We must withdraw, said Nirk. She turned away from the beach as another laser blast ripped through the space she'd just vacated. The laser tracked them, and Nirk screamed through the communal bond as her left side was ripped to shreds. She started to tumble, arching her segmented body to slow the drift.

We are headed to the ocean, and I cannot stop us. You must jump.

The compulsion of the goses forced Persinjali to leap from her neck, even though he wanted to find a way to help her. Persinjali extended his own wings, but they didn't slow him nearly as much as he'd hoped. Flapping them and tweaking their camber, his wings stretched their muscles to the limit, guiding him toward the beach, away from the ocean, where he heard the splash and sizzle of the goses body hitting the merciless Rykol-water.

One foot touched the edge of the beach, but Persinjali rolled up the sand, folding his wings and arms into his shell of a body. He stood in a fluid motion, and reached for his connection to Nirk, but failed to find it. He was no longer connected to the collective voices.

Lasers were still slicing into the sky, but the goses had moved out of range. Without time to mourn, a concept unheard of among the vekorna, Persinjali knew he had to move. He could sense rokels hiding among the trees, but knew there must be kolbs, too. He took stock of where he was, on the beach near the southern part of the forest, as they had come up from the fold of the continent near Sumo.

The dead patch of land was nearby, so he moved to the edge of the forest and the rocky outcropping. Only it wasn't rock, it was armor. Thousands of kolb bodies were piled here. Persinjali didn't have to search long to find what he was looking for.

He lifted an ancient kolb weapon, checking the laser's charge as he entered the forest. The anger and hatred he'd felt from above had multiplied, helping him kill three rokels and one kolb before they enemy knew what was upon them.

Some withdrew from the forest, where they were picked off by the returning goses before they could shoot. Then the kolbs and rokels turned on him, realizing what he was. Persinjali didn't care. He fought them, leaping high into the trees when they were on the ground, floating to the forest floor while they searched the treetops for him.

He connected with a goses mind, and the others quickly ascertained what he was doing. His anger joined theirs, and the hunted became the hunters. More siims followed him into the forest, picking up old kolb weapons as they did so.

Persinjali recognized the irony that siims had turned into fighters.

Knowing that he was no longer alone, Persinjali became bolder. He turned from behind a giant, goses-colored tree to shoot a kolb in the back. But another of the yellow-skinned kolbs had been hidden by that one's bulk, and Persinjali hadn't sensed him. The kolb shot Persinjali as he dove to the ground and rolled again. The blast hit him in the arm holding the weapon, and he lost feeling in that arm.

His consciousness faded as Aderen saw the kolb torn apart by another weapon. This had never happened before. It was his kennis, pulling at his attention. It seemed less important right now. He had to know what happened to Persinjali. Was the siim dead? He knew the kolb had used wrist lasers, which could kill a vekornan with a single blast, designed to stop blood flow to the brain deep in the armored chest cavity. Were siims susceptible to the same weapon?

The consciousness Aderen associated with Persinjali reappeared, and he wondered if the kennis intrusion could really wait. Two of the siim's arms were gone, both on the right side, but he was otherwise alive.

The goses were nowhere to be seen, but it would be hard to keep their existence a secret now. The vekorna were loading siims onto shuttles, inspecting kolb and rokel bodies. From the other siims, Persinjali learned that the kolbs and rokels had been completely destroyed, though they had lost a large number of siims. The siims didn't talk about goses losses, but Aderen knew there had been many.

Aderen was saddened for this beautiful, giant species. From Bolob's story, he knew they had survived a little longer, only to die in their own way.

As the vision cleared, Mai's buzzing intruded on his awareness. "Aderen, what are you doing?" She was distraught, sobbing. "I've lost Kuyi. You have to come to the Temple and help me find her. I can't tell anybody else!"

35. Emergency Mission

A quick check with Étar confirmed that he still hadn't heard from Kuyi. If Aderen told him that Kuyi was in trouble, he'd race off to the Temple and get himself killed.

He didn't realize the vision had taken so much time. Everybody was up, practicing their new kennis. This would make sneaking away more difficult. He put a small bag over his shoulder and added a couple of things, trying not to be suspicious about it.

Xeffeya and Ketaris were with Nalimai, and he steadfastly avoided them. They were using her palette to study the schematics of Nalimai's artificial limbs, and the muscles covering her left ribcage down to the hip.

"I think I see the attachment that's causing you pain when you stand," Ketaris said. "When the connections are complete, you'll be able to adjust them using your kennis, adding strength and endurance."

Frowning, Nalimai asked out loud, "You mean I can increase their power?"

"Yes, until your bodily reserves are gone and can no longer provide that energy."

Studying her skeleton, Nalimai nodded absently.

Aderen found Aneya, practicing kennis games with Penagel. "I'll take over, thanks," he said, and Penagel nodded, moving to watch Orem and Doj shuffling a palette ball around.

"I need to get to the Temple," he buzzed. "I think I can count on you to be discrete." She nodded, and they moved off the patio to a more secluded space.

"We have to tell Nalimai and Egalinsor," she buzzed when he told her Kuyi was missing.

"No, Nalimai is already hindering my mission, keeping me isolated because of what she thinks I'll do, afraid I'll be Kirina all over again."

"It looks like you're already a worse influence," buzzed Aneya, folding her arms across her chest.

"Guide me to the Temple, and you can tell them when I'm gone. I need you to take care of Mai while I find Kuyi."

"Fine," she said, hooking her blonde hair over her one ear. She led Aderen to the barn where they stored the hover scooters, and they got on.

"Aderen!" Jye-Tan buzzed, running up to them, a dozen frames bouncing above his palette. "It's just as good as you said. I've been talking to everyone, and discovered so much about Terra." He was talking out loud at the same time.

"Slow down –you sound like a lobom," Aneya said, admonishing him verbally. "Buzz or speak, not both."

Jye-Tan nodded somberly.

"I'm taking Aderen to the Temple to join Mai and Kuyi. Grab Étar and get to Firini's workshop. We may need your help with the vekornan computers."

Aderen frowned at her. "What are you doing?"

"He won't leave us without a good reason," Aneya buzzed. "I'm giving him one."

Jye-Tan's eyes lit up. "I'll bet I can hack deeper into their computers with a kennis. I almost did it at Rubiel with the fragment."

"Keep quiet though," Aneya buzzed, nodding. "Don't tell anybody else. You know how protective Nalimai and Lusava are."

Jye-Tan nodded again.

Aneya kicked the hover scooter into motion, and buzzed, "Étar and Kuyi have become intimate, so he deserves to know that she's missing. I don't like what you are doing, and I need backup plans."

*   *   *

"They look like Rubiel," Aderen buzzed as they stopped, checking for vekornan surveillance.

Three tall towers rose above the plain, still shining in the faint glow of the dome's wanlight, as the suns began their slow rise.

"I don't think any other Rykolien cities have been built so close to each other," Aneya said. The three cities were connected in a triangle, each sharing two of their characteristic five arms. "There's the Temple of Spall. Mai is inside the Memory Caves, where their secret tunnel runs."

Aderen was chilled by the tentacled figure glowing above the entrance to the Temple of Spall, cut into the steep rock of the mountains that separated Bol from the edge of the continent. Over those peaks, the mountain range sloped down more gently, through a second set of rippled hills to the dangerous ocean.

"It glows a little," said Aderen.

"It'll fade as the sun hits it," Aneya responded. "The vekorna don't care about their god." She pointed to a broken peak, destruction from the attack centuries ago. "I don't see any vekorna, do you?" He reigned in his senses, shaking his head.

She took off again, kicking up dust in their wake. She didn't stop again until the Temple of Spall rose high above them on its sheer slopes. Aderen could sense vekornan guards at the ground level main entrance, and told Aneya.

"We're not going in that way." She pointed to the broken peaks to their right, the folem Memory Caves. The folems had gone out of their way to line the side of the lake when he was on the hydrofoil. Why did they want him here? Or were they evaluating him, judging him the way they'd judged Kirina? It looked like he'd arrived.

They hid the hover scooter beside the one Kuyi and Mai had used the day before. Aneya led him easily to the uneven, debris-filled path that led up. "The Temple used to be filled with folems and loboms," she buzzed. "Folems aren't permitted inside anymore, which is how Kuyi, Mai and Jye-Tan can wander around so freely, as long as they avoid the vekorna. Now folems only live in the Memory Caves and communities along the river."

Face wet and grimy, Mai met them at the boulder-strewn entrance to the memory caves, pressed up between a giant rock and the wall, as hidden as she'd been in the trees of Egalra when he'd arrived.

She ran to Aneya, enveloping her in a panicked hug.

Aderen put a hand on her shoulder and said, "Have you been using your kennis to calm yourself, to think straight?" He hated to be uncompassionate, but he had to find Kuyi.

Mai nodded, and buzzed, "Come this way." Eye rolls were absent from the distraught young woman.

"Folems to the right," Aderen buzzed.

"They know I'm here, covered in their spy pollen," Mai responded, more composed, holding Aneya's good hand. "I think they know why, too. Are you sure you can find her? Kirina could find us even when we were hiding. You'll have to block your mind from vekornan telepathy."

"I've been doing that since I was young," he answered patiently as they came to a dead end. Mai braced her body and pushed one of the boulders out of the way with a grunt. "Your secret passage?" She nodded.

"Show me where you last saw Kuyi," Aderen said, and when Mai went to enter the tunnel, he stopped her and pointed to his temple. "Show me on your kennis."

"I want to help you rescue Kuyi," she said. "I need to know where she is."

"I'll keep in contact using this repeater node," he answered, revealing the small device from his bag. "When I get too far under the rocks of the mountain and lose access to the Bol node, I'll plant it somewhere so I can stay in contact. We'll never be apart."

"That's what Kuyi said," Mai grumbled, but activated her palette and showed him the shared map that she and

Kuyi had been creating. "We went this way until we split up, and I lost contact with her here." Both Mai and Kuyi's paths were indicated on the map. Kuyi's ended abruptly.

"I checked the rooms near there," Mai continued, pointing to Kuyi's last known location. From her path on the map, she'd gone much farther than that, putting herself in danger, especially if she was panicked.

"Thank you Mai," buzzed Aderen. "You have to go back now. Aneya will take you to the workshop, where you can monitor my progress." To Mai's reddening face and obstinate expression, he answered, "You've done your part. Now, I need to you monitor from far away, in case things get tricky." He pointed back the way they'd come.

"I was stopped by loboms," Mai buzzed. "They want you in the memory caves, not the Temple."

Aderen stopped short. "Why?"

"Something about your visions," Mai buzzed.

"How do they know about my visions?"

"The spy pollen," buzzed Aneya. "They know everything short of getting into your mind."

The folems wanted him to come to the Memory Caves, and the loboms were interested in his visions. What did they know about the siims and goses, and how was it relevant?

"Thank you for telling me. Now I have to leave. Go to Firini's workshop, and monitor from there with Jye-Tan."

She frowned and put her hands on her hips, shaking her head. Eyes threatening to overflow with tears, she yelled, "Why are you always sending me away? I know my way around better than her." She pointed at Aneya. "Why don't you want me with you? I can be useful!"

"I have to rescue Kuyi alone," Aderen buzzed, resenting

the time it took to explain. "But you can help me with the loboms. If I don't get to the Memory Caves, you will have to meet the loboms for me. What is it about the siims that they find important?"

Mai's eyes widened, and the unshed tears disappeared. The expressions contorting her face showed that Mai was struggling between her desire to continue, and obeying Aderen.

"I'll still need your help, but I can't protect all of us."

Finally, Mai nodded, one curt dip of her chin. She glared wordlessly at Aneya, then abruptly pushed something into his hand and motioned him into the tunnel. The rock moved back into place, leaving him in darkness.

*   *   *

Aderen shimmied through to the other side, clothes and hair full of dust. Mai actively followed his progress through the kennis, offering unnecessary tips.

Her map led him deeper into the Temple of Spall, through a corridor that she warned was occasionally used by the vekorna. Aderen kept his senses wide open.

"Are you getting close?" Jye-Tan's voice came into his head. Aderen stopped, annoyed at the interruption.

"Jye-Tan has hacked into the city network," Étar buzzed. "I wish you'd told me Kuyi was missing." Étar put some condemnation behind his words. "It looks like the vekorna are still unaware of her, so she hasn't been captured as far as we can tell."

"Sorry, but I need to do this by myself. Are you alone at the workshop?"

"Wandel and Pinoa were already here with Firini. Aneya and Mai will be joining us soon. Why?"

"Too many people already know that Kuyi is missing.

287

Soon we'll have all the Egalsan here. Nalimai is going to keep them locked away from me forever."

He thought about Aneya's statement that he was already far worse than Kirina's influence on the young ones. Maybe she was right. It was time for him to get out of Bol anyway, and make his way to Rubiel. "Get ready to run," he added. "After this, we won't be welcome here anymore."

36. Under the Temple

Aderen moved in the dark like a shadow, turning through narrow passages with rough floors that had probably never been traversed until the youngest Egalsan found them. They were too narrow for most folems with their large blooms, though maybe loboms would have crunched their way through single file.

The kennis map was easy to follow to the point where Kuyi had gone too deep and lost her connection to the local node.

He shuffled down the small slope where the map had stopped updating, and felt his kennis connection grow spotty. He activated the small repeater in his bag, and it grew stronger as he hid the device in a crevice.

"Did you find her yet?" Mai's concern was buzzed along with her question.

"Not yet," he responded patiently. "I'll let you know when I do."

"I hope the vekorna haven't found her. I don't know what Ontral will do."

Frowning, Aderen hoped he wouldn't need to deal with that. According to Aneya, Ontral and the vekorna didn't know the Egalsan sometimes infiltrated the Temple. What kind of punishment would he mete out if he found Kuyi here?

Aderen reached out and found vekorna in the tunnels beyond. He touched their minds, and saw no recognition of humans in this part of the Temple. Their mental buzzing increased as they reviewed experiments with their nonhuman senses. Aderen ignored them.

He tracked other vekorna as they moved down nearby hallways, and added those to the kennis map. Some vekorna were stationary, and he suspected they were in rooms doing research or other experiments. Although he'd lived among vekorna all his life on Terra, he still didn't understand the theoretical research that happened when they interconnected their brains.

As usual, he couldn't detect Kuyi's mind, though he searched anyway. Had she moved from this section of the Temple, gone deeper still?

He waited patiently from the fissure that broke through into a wide hallway. There. It had taken longer than expected, but her kennis had finally connected to his repeater. He tracked its emergency signal from his location, filling in the expected layout of this level.

"Xeffeya," Aderen buzzed, the repeater signal clear. "I need your help. Can you coax Kuyi's kennis back to activity? I think she's hurt."

"I have her emergency access, but are you sure?" After a second, she added, "Her kennis is in emergency standby, almost out of power. I think she overloaded it. See to her physical condition first, and I'll try to find out what happened."

Ensuring there were no vekorna along his route, Aderen left the fissure and strode through the center of the corridor, turning off at one passage, then another, until he got to the door closest to Kuyi's faint emergency signal. All the while, he waited for Xeffeya to coax information from her kennis.

Passing his hand over the contact didn't do anything. "Any ideas?" he buzzed.

"Use the folem pollen," Mai responded immediately, her mood anxious.

He put his hand in the pouch she'd hastily given him and traced a finger over the contact pad again. The door opened.

He rushed inside and found Kuyi's prone form. She was still breathing, curled into a tiny ball.

"She's physically fine," he buzzed Xeffeya, sending her the readings his kennis took of Kuyi.

"She has multiple skin burns," Xeffeya said. "I'm reactivating her kennis," A second later, Kuyi gasped, her eyes opening wide. Aderen reached over and put a hand on her forehead. She sat up and hugged him, a fierce movement that momentarily took his breath away.

"She's okay," Aderen buzzed the others, getting relief from all of them.

"Where's Mai?" Kuyi croaked, putting a hand to her throat.

"I sent her to Firini's workshop," Aderen whispered. "She was scared silly for you."

"Me too," she whispered, breathless.

Aderen handed over a bottle of electrolytes, which she gulped down. "This will stimulate your kennis, which will help you heal. Besides the burns, is there anything else?"

Kuyi shook her head. "No, I'm fine." She stared off into the distance, her gaze indicating otherwise. He let her decide her own pace.

"I can stand. We should get out of here. I think the vekorna saw me the last place I was... exploring."

She made to stand, and Aderen caught her as she stumbled. She couldn't leave like this.

"Tell me what happened," he said, and she flinched as he put a hand to her shoulder. It came away bloody.

She tested it with her own hand, and said, "I guess I was caught by one of those spitballs." She inspected the rest of her body, and found another scrape on her leg. Aderen found burns on her back, but they didn't look too bad.

"My kennis is already dulling the pain and healing them," she added.

"What happened?"

Tears formed in her eyes. "It was horrible. They were dancing, then fighting, and the wall broke and I was caught in the middle. Are you sure the vekorna didn't see me?"

"Not the ones I came across," he answered. "What were the creatures doing?"

She sent him an image that she'd captured with her kennis. "The vekorna were pulling their strings, making them do things they didn't want to do. I couldn't stand it."

She pleaded with him to do something.

Scanning the area near them, Aderen shook his head. "I don't sense anything. I think the vekorna have finished their experiment."

Kuyi sighed, and stood again, this time without stumbling. She looked strong enough to move.

"Let's go."

"I want to show you something else," she said, and led him out of the room.

*   *   *

Kuyi warily guided Aderen down the narrow corridor as she exchanged information desperately with Étar.

"I'm so glad you're okay," he buzzed, repeating himself. "It's bad enough that you had to go through that, but I couldn't forgive Aderen if he hadn't found you."

"I'll be fine," she buzzed back, cutting him off. "Trust me to do the right thing. Right now, I need to concentrate on where I'm going." She felt happy, though, knowing he cared.

They followed the branch into a much wider corridor, something the vekorna could have driven a small vend'ok through. She was growing stronger every moment, though the memory of those creatures turning on each other still haunted her. She ignored it for now, repressing the memory with her kennis.

She remembered turning a corner –and there was the door.

"Most doors in the Temple have a switch to sprinkle folem pollen," she buzzed, calling on her kennis to give her more energy. "This one is vekornan-made, and I think it's secured by a telepathic lock to keep other races out. Can you access it?"

"You should go back to the surface," Aderen said. His face was lined with worry. She could tell that he was going inside, his interest as piqued as hers. If there was anything she'd learned in the last day, it was that nobody should be alone down here.

She sent him a kennis report of her physical status, to prove that she could stay with him, at least until the door opened. She omitted brain indicators, knowing that he would see her mental scars, which would take far longer to heal.

"Jye-Tan," Aderen buzzed. "Can you see what's behind this door?"

"I can't see into the Temple, only the cities," Jye-Tan buzzed. "But that door is part of the city. It's a tunnel connecting the Temple to Siftral. I can open it for you."

His response surprised her, and she deflated again. "I thought it was a room, somewhere the vekorna would hide the fragment."

"I don't think the fragment is in the Temple," Mai buzzed with excitement. "I didn't see any trace of it."

"Me neither," Kuyi admitted. "The Temple is almost abandoned. The fragment has to be in the cities. Jye-Tan, do you see any place where it might be?"

"How would I–" he began, then was silent. She hoped he was sifting through vekornan data. She moved to the fissure that had led her here. Aderen reluctantly followed. Kuyi reconsidered her desire to accompany him to Rubiel. She'd had enough adventure for a little while, and just wanted to lay on the beach making love to Étar.

"Jye-Tan can see heat signatures, but we haven't broken into activity logs yet," Étar buzzed, and her heart raced to hear his voice. "There's a lot more activity in the city than where you are. We've identified a few interesting locations, and will try to narrow it down to those close to the tunnel."

"Two vekorna left the tunnel six minutes before you got there, entering the Temple," Jye-Tan buzzed. "No others are nearby. I can't see into the Temple itself, though."

"I have that covered," buzzed Aderen. Kuyi watched him intently in the half-light, not seeing any outward sign that he was concentrating mentally. She wiped yellow sweat from her forehead. Residue pollen or the creatures? She could move easily, if not completely without pain.

"We're clear for now," Aderen finally said. It looked like he'd accepted her decision to remain. At the moment, she was much happier to go into the city, where the vekorna were less likely to keep those creatures. She shivered again.

Aderen dashed into the corridor. Kuyi had trouble summoning that kind of trust in his mental abilities or Jye-Tan, and ended up behind him.

The door to the tunnel opened as they approached, sliding into the wall. Confirming that it was empty, Kuyi ran ahead of Aderen, touching the smooth white walls that contrasted the raw rock of the Temple corridors. Aderen easily kept pace with her. The tunnel looked shorter than the distance between the Temple and Siftral, but that was obviously an illusion –it felt like it took forever to traverse. They were completely exposed; there was nowhere to hide in here.

The other end was also open, and they stepped carefully through. Jye-Tan closed the door to the empty tunnel before she could make the suggestion. Ignoring the sting on her shoulder as she leaned against the wall, she pulled up her map of Siftral. If she'd oriented it correctly, she knew how to get to Nalimai's lab, and they might be able to pretend they'd been visiting it all along.

"Get out of that corridor!" Jye-Tan buzzed, sending them a location on the shared map. "Vekorna are coming."

"Understood." Kuyi reviewed the map in her head, noting the placement of the approaching vekorna, and took Aderen through a couple of turns that led to another open door, which slid shut immediately behind them. The steady lights of vekornan equipment lit the room in dim colors.

"Alright," Aderen said, speaking out loud for the first

time since he'd awakened her. "We're inside the city. We're committed now."

She nodded.

"This was supposed to be a rescue mission, not another search." He was disappointed in her, and she understood why. Depleting her energy such that her kennis failed, getting lost, and still coming up empty-handed? No wonder he looked at her that way.

"If Nalimai finds out I spent the night in the Temple – and she will– we'll never get another chance to search in here," she said, holding back her exhaustion. She wondered if he could tell.

"Aderen," came Étar's familiar buzz. "I've looked at Jye-Tan's analysis, and we have a potential location. Unfortunately, there are a lot of vekorna."

"Are you sure it isn't just a briefing, or more genetics research?" Aderen asked.

"Ontral doesn't keep records the way humans do," Pinoa buzzed, joining the conversation. "There is no way to know if you're in the right area."

"Can you draw them away?" Kuyi buzzed. There was no way she was turning around now.

"I don't see how. They can confirm any computer instructions telepathically within moments. They'll know any lie we feed them, and our advantage will be gone."

Aderen sighed. "Then it'll be up to me. I can do it." It sounded more like he was trying to convince himself, which worried Kuyi. She suddenly didn't feel as safe with him as she had moments ago. Thinking of the deadly creatures in the Temple, she knew she didn't want to go back.

"If it is the fragment, any vekorna touching it might be

harder to control," buzzed Jye-Tan. "Be careful with those ones."

37. The Ambush

Flying a fighter was much different from commanding an extar, and Tararnifal wasn't overly fond of the experience. He'd spent most of his pre-Terran life in space, either chasing zonguan grids or exploring other planets.

Now he flew lead in the fifteen ship formation to attack the wingless vekorna. He was helping Dairnehy destroy Bolob's Plan, which had been going strong for two generations.

Tararnifal was relieved to be away from Rubiel, and wondered briefly if he could escape, maybe find Danosh. Sebenet was still there, though, and although he had turned to Dairnehy's side much too quickly, there was still some empathy toward the humans in him. Tararnifal couldn't dismiss Sebenet's curiosity of the murals in Rubiel, as well as his uncertainty at searching the void areas. He had touched the fragment, while Tararnifal had not. Had he seen into Tararnifal's mind? Did he understand what Tararnifal had been trying to teach him on the voyage back from Terra?

Extending three eyestalks toward the empty sky, he opened his thoughts to where he knew the Black Moon orbited. Were kolbs waiting for the vekorna to wipe themselves out, so they could take control of the planet, or would they hold to Bolob's Plan?

Dairnehy had sent him out as a test. The test was not about winning or destroying Metik. He would pass only by returning to Rubiel, with or without the wingless piece of the fragment. He would prefer to keep his pilots alive, too.

Cutting across the northern part of Megnat, Tararnifal took advantage of his proximity to the Vamurel remains to contact Samlar, still hidden with their extars.

Report, he said, sending his thoughts kilometers to the south. It took a moment for Samlar to respond, but it wasn't from the ruins of Vamurel.

We were unsure you would come back, Samlar replied. A tigal-en like Tararnifal, Samlar could also speak across distances without help from a crystal. **Dairnehy's soldiers attacked, forcing us from Vamurel. We now hide in orbit.**

Anger flared from Tararnifal, and he fought to contain it before it was projected to Samlar. Maybe he put too much faith in Sebenet's sympathy.

What of the kolbs?

We are undisturbed for the moment. Have you escaped Dairnehy, to lead us away from this winged war?

No, the war continues.

Tararnifal opened his mind to the rapid-fire burst of telepathy that would send Samlar his experiences of the last few days, from the mirror crystals to Sebenet's fall, the fear at Rubiel and the role of the stellar fragment. In turn, he learned of Danosh's attempted human kidnapping at Esetek.

Stay clear of the kolbs, and be ready —we will move against Rubiel soon. Send Aderen a kennis message with what I told you.

Always being watched, Tararnifal had not been able to access the hidden node in Rubiel. The city wasn't safe, yet he had to return, if not for Sebenet, then for Bolob's Plan.

The support fleet from Fulk is approaching, said

Kular from above his left side.

Tararnifal severed his connection with Samlar and turned his attention to the sensors. Nine metelek fighters and six rolp-class shuttles had risen from the city as they passed over, doubling the size of the fleet from Rubiel. Their commander acknowledged his authority.

Guiding the small fleet southward along Megnat's eastern coastline, Tararnifal discussed strategy with Kular and Paknef. He knew they wouldn't be sufficient to capture Metik, but could it be enough to draw out the wingless piece of the fragment, if it even existed? Some of their pilots were eager to destroy the wingless, but all would follow his orders. Which were watching him for Dairnehy?

Tararnifal fed his pilots instructions as they approached Erim. Very close to Bol, but controlled by the winged, the city had somehow escaped attack by the wingless as war erupted around it.

There is no support from Erim, said Paknef.

Tararnifal thought of Samlar's report, and how close Esetek was to Erim. Could Danosh be hiding here, influencing its leaders? The city was quiet as they passed near, not responding to his queries. The minds he touched were reluctant to join, risking Dairnehy's wrath.

Monitor Bol for a response, Tararnifal said, turning his fleet eastward. As with Erim, there was no sign of activity, and the shield remained closed. There was still time, once they realized the threat he posed.

The stretch of ocean from Megnat to Depraf was smaller here than it would have been to the north, as the two continents tapered closest just south of Bol. It also made their ultimate destination all too clear. Metik, on the other side of the world from Rubiel, would be ready. Tararnifal didn't expect anything less than a full-fledged battle.

The fleet poured on more power, to meet Metik's defenses at full speed in an attempt to balance the lack of surprise.

The enemy is waiting, Kular said as Metik's defenders appeared on their sensors. Tararnifal reached for the opposing pilots; his fleet would be outnumbered two-to-one.

Continue to watch for activity from Bol, he said. To the rest of his fleet, he ordered, **Engage all shuttles and fighters.** His pilots paired off as they threaded their way through the enemy fleet under his direction, firing all the way. As expected, they inflicted only minor damage at that speed, but all of his pilots survived.

Tararnifal turned his fighter, enjoying the quick response compared to an extar, and brought it above the fight. The two sides were reorganizing, changing direction for another pass.

A moment later, Kular and Paknef joined him. He noted six wingless tigal-en matching their position, hovering on the other side of the battle. He reached out to them, but they refused to acknowledge his call for a peaceful resolution. He couldn't blame them, with the forces he'd brought.

Support ships have launched from Erim, Kular said, bringing Tararnifal's attention to the long-range tactical display. He wondered if Dairnehy's side had won a power struggle in that city.

Watch them, and assign positions when they arrive, Tararnifal responded. **A second wave could win this battle.**

The defenders pursued Tararnifal's forces, but never went so far that they let the winged through to the other side. They were willing to let damaged targets go, to hold the defensive line. The strategy would work until Erim's shuttles arrived.

In time, three pairs of his fighters had been cut down, and the enemy had lost more of theirs. Attrition would only get them so far. If the wingless tigal-en would not talk, he would have to end this another way.

Follow me, said Tararnifal, diving into the melee, feigning to join the battle. Instead, he looped back up and above it, then dove across to the other side, feeling for weaknesses in the other minds. Kular followed, and his forces briefly lost cohesion before Paknef took control.

Half the wingless tigal-en pursued, and Tararnifal dodged them using techniques learned from human opponents at Terra. He might be able to save the wingless pilots if he distracted their tigal-en.

Through his telepathic connection, Tararnifal guided Kular. Working together, they destroyed a wingless pursuer, but their single-minded concentration left them open to others. Tararnifal's fighter bucked as he was hit.

He opened his telepathic senses to momentary overwhelm their pursuers, rising above them, Kular on his wing.

Divide their attention, he said, defending against a telepathic attack from above. **Go.**

Kular mentally sent confusion ahead of his fighter as he flew past their pursuers to the east, away from Erim's approaching fleet.

Tararnifal drew the attention of the three remaining wingless tigal-en, hoping it would be enough. He engaged them with all his senses, giving them no choice but to pursue at three-to-one odds, to try and remove him from the battle. War was not all about technology, and he was one of the most powerful tigal-en on Rykol.

Two fighters dove on him, the third wavering until he resumed his mental attack. Certain he had all three tigal-en, he turned suddenly and raced for Metik. He couldn't make it to the city, but that wasn't his goal. He looped around, dragging them lower, keeping their focus away from the battle.

Without the full coordination of their tigal-en, the wingless defense started to fall apart, much as his own had when he left his position. Some of his ships were now getting through, and the battle turned into chaos.

A laser blast clipped one of his wings, and he returned his attention to the fighters around him. He spun and lifted his nose, his attacker following so close that laser-fire lit up the forward view.

Tararnifal loosed his other senses in another telepathic barrage against the ones following him. His enemy deflected much of the attack, but the laser barrage slowed.

He tried to evade, but was being boxed in.

Here comes the second wave, said Kular, tossing his fighter around, turning prey into predator, damaging an enemy ship.

The pursuit paused as Erim's metelek fighters plowed into the battle, firing intensely between combatants without hitting any, forcing evasive action. They came out the other side already spinning around, ready to re-enter the fray.

What are they doing? Paknef asked. His fighter was enveloped in fire a moment later, and Tararnifal was shocked as his mind disappeared from their telepathic link. He'd just lost half of his trusted vekorna. Kular immediately took control of their forces, and he considered having the vekornan fly to safety.

Tararnifal turned from his fallen commander to study the tactics of Erim's meteleks. They interfered with targeting from winged and wingless alike, forcing both sides to back off.

The nose of Tararnifal's fighter was hit by a laser barrage from ahead, his attention split too many ways to concentrate on this deadly dance. He fired his own lasers and saw the enemy fighter disintegrate. An instant later, he flew through the debris, and knew his fighter was dead.

The damaged wings held him aloft, if sinking, a tribute to its human designers that no other vekornan would acknowledge. He nudged the crippled fighter into a wide spiral, though it barely responded to his mental commands.

An enemy shuttle descended toward him on an intercept course. The telepathic brush against his mind confirmed they knew who he was, and probably would not fire. Was he to go from trapped winged to prisoner of the wingless?

As it drew within range, one of Erim's shuttles flew between them, but stopped shy of firing on either. It danced with his attacker, allowing him to gain some distance.

Three shuttles are hanging back, Kular said, also waylaid by a fighter from Erim. It kept between the two opposing sides.

Tigal-en from Erim. He reached out to them, and identified himself.

Withdraw your forces, and land in the deserts north of Metik.

Danosh, Tararnifal said, skimming the vekornan mind.

Danosh's shuttles and fighters were forcing the winged and wingless fleets to regroup, strategically turning the wingless lower and southward, beating the winged fighters higher and toward the northern desert. Tararnifal didn't interfere, allowing his forces to withdraw.

I will keep the wingless at bay, said Danosh. Tararnifal wondered at that, but Danosh had been prin-el to Bolob, who had led kolbs and vekorna, secret winged and oblivious wingless. He must have learned from that powerful leader.

Their strategy is to hinder the battle, Tararnifal told Kular. **We can do nothing until I deal with Danosh.**

The bottom of his fighter cracked as he corrected his attitude for a heading north of the city. The two sides flipped up to meet, wingtip-to-wingtip, spilling its pilot from the bottom.

Immediately, Tararnifal pointed his faceplate in the direction he wanted to go, and opened his own wide wings. They stiffened in the breeze of his descent, almost too much to handle. The memory of Sebenet falling toward the deadly ocean forced Tararnifal to twitch his wings and level off. The hard desert was no less deadly if he couldn't bleed off his vertical speed.

Tararnifal had time to survey the remaining ships. The withdrawal was slow, but progressing. Erim's fighters formed a wall between the two sides. He skimmed under the wingless fleet, watching their movements. They didn't shoot at him; either he was too small a target, or Danosh was keeping his promise.

Tararnifal continued his descent in a staircase fashion, dropping, then bleeding off speed. The ground was still a patchwork of desert browns and greys, too far below.

A mind touched his, and a shuttle flew under him.

Hold the top of my shuttle, and I will guide you down without harm, said Danosh.

Tararnifal dove quickly for a fraction of a second, grabbing six contact points on the shuttle roof, and folded his wings to avoid being yanked off.

He reached his mind into the shuttle, and was surprised that Danosh was alone.

What happened to you? Danosh asked.

I am under orders from Dairnehy, Tararnifal responded, watching the ground approach from this unique vantage point. Kular reached out to him, but would hold their forces in the air until he figured out what was going on. **Why are you here?**

Gaining the trust of the wingless, the way I gained trust of the winged. Would you join me?

I need to gain Dairnehy's trust, Tararnifal said, wondering how this chance of escape had presented itself, when he'd rejected it earlier in the day.

Join me. I can only confront Dairnehy with more vekorna under my leadership. You have provided them.

You are exploiting the fear Dairnehy creates, Tararnifal realized. **Where do you take the pilots? It cannot be Erim, or Dairnehy would have attacked already.**

Our location remains secret, Danosh responded. **Erim's proximity to Bol directly shields us from Dairnehy. The wingless would not tolerate an attack so close to their shield. The strength of your fleet was surprising, given how close it came to our city.**

Tararnifal considered telling Danosh about Dairnehy's planned ambush, to capture the stellar fragment he thought the wingless would deploy. Had that been thwarted by Danosh? It didn't seem like the wingless planned anything special to defeat his fighters.

The shuttle came in to land, and Tararnifal released his hold, once again extending his wings, pulling him back into the air. He glided gently to the ground, something probably not seen on Rykol in many generations.

Dairnehy is testing my resolve, Tararnifal said, revealing part of his motivation. The shuttle ramp descended, and he entered.

As he did mine, Danosh said, opening his senses. Tararnifal tentatively connected with them. Communication would be faster this way. **We both failed.**

My plan was to gain his trust and depose him from within, Tararnifal said. **That seems impossible now that I've failed the task he set for me.**

Realization emanated from Danosh as they shared thoughts. He closed the shuttle's ramp and began to take off, saying, **I don't think you failed. Dairnehy had other plans for you.**

Tararnifal stiffened. He had believed Dairnehy's story about the wingless piece of the stellar fragment, but the fleet's deployment had been too poorly executed for that.

He isn't after Ontral's fragment.

He's after me, said Danosh, checking their ascent into a hover just off the ground. Tararnifal accessed the shuttle's sensors, noting more shuttles hovering directly above them and to the sides, boxing them in.

Tararnifal reached for Kular, instructing him to send this new information to Samlar. To Danosh, he said, **He anticipated your tactics, your desire to recruit from both sides.**

The trap has been sprung, said Danosh. **There is no escape, only death.**

Or the struggle to remain alive, as humans say.

305

Dairnehy will make me wish for death. I have made my last mistake.

Surrender to fight again. We may need your help before this ends, said Tararnifal, knowing it was not the vekornan way, and that Danosh would have trouble accepting it.

The shuttle above them descended, mimicking Tararnifal's earlier connection with a loud noise, forcing them down. The ceiling buckled.

As Danosh prepared to die fighting, Tararnifal lifted his weapons, embarrassment filling his entire being.

You can only surrender, he said, taking telepathic control of Danosh's shuttle, settling it on the ground and opening the ramp. Their ceiling continued to buckle, so they crouched on their upper arms and rushed out into the desert.

Sebenet stood in the sand as a massive terebar shuttle completely crushed their defenseless ship. For a moment, Tararnifal thought it was Dairnehy, but the vekornan leader wouldn't leave the safety of Rubiel.

This was better, though, as Sebenet could easily be overcome with no effect on the winged leadership.

I have captured the traitor, said Sebenet, firing a short, diffuse, laser blast, not killing Danosh, but weakening him as the blood slowed to his brain.

The wall of shuttles from Erim fell apart, and Tararnifal struggled with Sebenet for control over the winged tigal-en. But it was foolish of Tararnifal to think that Sebenet would be sent here alone, and Dairnehy's other tigal-en overwhelmed him, forcing Danosh's vekorna to surrender. Those who resisted were quickly destroyed. Wingless shuttles fled to regroup closer to Metik.

You were planning to join Danosh, but when you saw Dairnehy's strength, you were loyal to him, said Sebenet. **As I have also proven my loyalty.**

Tararnifal seethed, but didn't deny it. He lowered his weapon and strategically allowed Sebenet to pick parts of the conversation with Danosh from his memory.

The fragment was never Dairnehy's target, he said.

The fragment is always his target. But this ambush was for the traitor. He warned you that this was a test.

More shuttles landed, the standard rolp design, and emptied their troops with weapons raised. Now was not the time to resist and die.

Take me back to Rubiel, and leave Metik alone, Tararnifal said.

Sebenet agreed; was he risking Dairnehy's wrath by doing so? Maybe Metik didn't matter to the winged leader, but it was possible Sebenet also wanted to avoid needless death, and still thought Bolob's Plan was worth defending.

We have passed Dairnehy's loyalty tests, Tararnifal said. **Where do we go from here?**

Sebenet didn't answer, but removed Tararnifal's weapon. It seemed that none of Aderen's influence remained. He could not defeat Dairnehy and Sebenet alone. He had to keep Danosh alive.

38. Quick Withdrawal

The first vekorna were easiest to fool. They never noticed Aderen's mental touch. He felt a new connection with the vekorna since Nalimai's revelation that his telepathy was created by them. Could that be why this was so easy? It wasn't clear if the awareness went both ways. He'd have to be careful.

Now that they'd snuck inside the city and were committed, he was excited about testing the stellar fragment. If it worked as well as Jye-Tan described, he could go to Rubiel alone, stop Dairnehy and maybe even reprogram the birth chambers so that all future vekorna would inherently steer clear of Terra. It was more important than ever, now that he knew why Dairnehy wanted humans.

He was concerned about Kuyi, but she was determined, and far stronger than her family gave her credit for, even after what she'd just suffered.

Tugging on mental threads from sensor head to the vekornan brain buried deep in their chests, Aderen forced the guards to reinterpret what they sensed, forgetting they'd detected humans. Confident, he walked right by them. Kuyi, resolute but wary, padded silently close behind. One of the guards shifted, and Kuyi ducked below his middle arm in an instinctual evasion. Aderen frowned, rechecking his alterations.

Beyond the two guards, just before a slight bend in the corridor, Aderen sensed six stationary vekorna, sharing minds for research like only vekorna could. Securing his hold on the two guards behind them, he carefully touched the fibers of the vekornan minds ahead. He was like a whisper, allowing them to continue their research while ignoring the two small shapes that would soon draw near.

Rounding the bend, they came up short, and Kuyi gasped. "You didn't say anything about a machine," she buzzed, shivering.

The corridor ballooned wide. The six vekorna were standing around a large device with pulsing balls of white static on two ends.

"Why are they in the corridor?" he buzzed back.

Despite the width of the passage, the machine was large enough to block most of the way forward. To the open side, they would need to slip between three of the large alien bodies, and he wasn't sure they would make it.

"How will we get by?" Kuyi buzzed.

Aderen took a deep breath, and dove once more into their minds. What were they doing? There… It was some kind of transmitter, or maybe a receiver.

The fragment. Aderen froze as he sensed incredible power nearby. Jye-Tan was right. The fragment was nearby, and it multiplied vekornan telepathy. He had no doubt now that it had enhanced Jye-Tan's mind. He was eager to find out what it could do for him. Was this why the folems had tried to kill Kirina?

The twitch of a mental nerve sent one vekornan to inspect another part of the machine, never knowing it wasn't his own idea. Aderen nodded, the only outward sign of his invisible activity.

"No," Kuyi buzzed, but he had to ignore her, concentrating on the second vekornan. Uncharacteristically, the first one changed his mind and walked back, blocking the corridor again.

Aderen took a calming breath, and instructed his kennis to keep him in that state. He reached out again, touched the two vekorna. Both stopped moving at his intrusion, but reverted to normal before he got any further. Kuyi was shaking her head, obviously wondering why he was failing.

He was afraid to try a third time. Frustrated at how long this was taking, he tried the same trick he'd used on the two guards, blinding them to humans.

"Go," he buzzed. After a quick look to see if he was serious, Kuyi moved forward. She couldn't fit between two vekorna, but managed to slip through a small gap underneath the machine. She came out the other side, grasping her hair as it shot straight out. She ran to the next bend, beckoning him.

Holding all the vekorna blind to them was getting trickier. It had something to do with the machine, which was connected to the fragment.

One vekornan moved, creating a small opening. Aderen quickly flattened his back against the wall, holding his breath, sucking in his belly, and came within a hair's breadth of the blue exoskeleton. Just as he shuffled past, the vekornan shifted back, closing the gap. He ran quietly to join Kuyi.

"That was too close. You turned them into puppets, didn't you?" she buzzed, angry.

"It didn't work," he buzzed, shaking his head. "I think the fragment is disrupting my efforts through the machine. It should enhance me when I connect to it, so we won't have trouble getting out of here."

Despite what he'd been able to do at Terra, here he felt like his mind was being stretched thin. Reducing his mental output to the vekorna behind them, Aderen reached inside the next room, finding twelve more vekorna. Étar wasn't kidding when he said it was crowded.

"Is the fragment in there?" Kuyi asked.

He nodded, taking a deep breath. He couldn't hide from the new connection he felt with the vekorna. They shouldn't have this kind of effect on him. Hiding himself, but making sure he could still reach them, he instructed the vekorna inside to let go of the fragment and move aside.

It didn't work. They were more resistant than those working on the machine in the corridor. He couldn't even blind their senses. Worse, the vekorna touching the fragment were now aware of them.

"Close your mind tight!" he told Kuyi. He needed to touch the fragment, too, and gain the upper hand.

To Jye-Tan, he buzzed, "Open the door on my mark."

"They've triggered an alarm," buzzed Étar.

The vekorna in the corridor extended several eyestalks and turned their armored sensor heads, looking for the intruders, unable to detect them. Aderen held their perceptions tight. It was something he didn't want to make permanent.

"Our connection is being traced, but we'll stay as long as we can," Étar added.

"Get away before they find you, but clear our escape route now," Kuyi buzzed, nervously crossing and uncrossing her fingers. He realized that the fragment was slipping through his fingers. Jye-Tan wouldn't be opening this door.

Whether or not he gained physical access, he had to do this first. He reached for the fragment with his mind, shying away from the vekorna touching it. Physically smaller than he expected, it was immensely powerful. The fragment was elation, easy to use. No wonder the intact fragment had allowed Dairnehy to see into all minds on the planet. This was just a taste. He blocked the vekorna from his mind and Kuyi's, ready to release their touch on the fragment.

Something came at his mind from the shadows, and his back arched as he was overcome by chaos. He tried to scream, but was physically stuck.

"What's wrong?" Kuyi asked, afraid to touch him. Aderen couldn't answer. He saw into her mind, too, for the first time since arriving on Rykol. He wove between her questions and the chaos, trying to find an anchor. She was a mixture of wonder and terror, anxiety and horror. He thought of Ret's horror on Sebenet's extar, hoping it would break him away, make him stronger, as Monera had suggested to him so long ago.

There. He found a similar place in her mind, her experiences in the night, the horror at how the vekorna turned those creatures into puppets like her, completely removing their free will. She'd been affected, too. That's why she called out at the machine. She didn't want him to force the vekorna to do anything. If they were to get out of here, she needed to accept that some things were necessary.

Monera had been right. Kuyi's fears anchored him, like Ret's anger, and he reached out to silence the alarm, but it was too late. The fragment didn't give him access to all the vekorna in the city, but even if it had, he wasn't ready to try something that large again, especially if the connection might be two-way. He relaxed his body.

He made the six vekorna at the machine turn and march to the side of the corridor, faceplates against the wall. He had the vekorna inside the room do the same, except for one that he forced to open the door.

Running into the room, Aderen tried to lift the fragment, but it was too heavy. Swearing, he called to Kuyi, but she wasn't behind him. There was nothing in the room to help him carry it.

"Stop this!" Kuyi cried. "Look what it's doing to you already."

"It works. It's the only way I can defeat Dairnehy."

"What about negotiation?"

"This is faster." If only he'd known about the fragment before departing Terra –he could have come to Rykol alone, and forced the vekorna to forget about humanity!

Kuyi was gone again, and he turned his attention back to the vekorna. One of them could carry the fragment out of here, and back to the Temple. From there, he was certain that they could find a trolley.

His connection to the fragment faltered, and his eyes opened wide in alarm and surprise. The vekorna around the room started to turn, and without the fragment, he couldn't control them. What had happened?

Kuyi.

He found her at the machine, pushing her body through the static spheres, her nerves tingling. He reached to stop her, but she rebuffed him, pushed him out of her mind. He was impotent, and the vekorna were approaching, raising their arms, readying their wrist lasers. He started backing away.

The door closed behind him. Jye-Tan? He didn't know, couldn't focus on his kennis connection. Kuyi was straddling the machine, disrupting the static with her body amid vekorna who were completely oblivious to her presence. At least that much of his control held.

"What did you do?" he asked, running up to her, ready to shake some sense into her. "Get off the machine." Her hair was sticking straight out from her head. She looked at the vekorna, and both ways along the corridor. Jumping off the machine, her hair fell back over her shoulders, unnatural curls dominating.

"Did you see what you were doing?" she asked out loud, shaking her head. "Turning them into puppets? We have to leave. Forget about the fragment. You don't need it." She grabbed his hand, pulled him down the corridor, unresisting. Was she right? The fragment left a hole in his mind that needed filling.

"A lot of vekorna are converging on your position," buzzed Jye-Tan. "The whole city has been alerted."

"We're on our way out," Étar buzzed. "Sorry, but you're on your own now. I know you can take care of yourself, but take care of *her*." He emphasized the last part.

Aderen stumbled as he was pulled forward, no longer sure. Kuyi saw a danger in him that he couldn't ignore. She was sensitive to his total control, just like Ret, just like after Legionnaire Dalpah. Was she right? Could he trust his judgement that mass manipulation was the best way to do this? Was his mental ability compromised by the way it was created as a fetus?

Kuyi guided him around corners, always taking the easy paths. All doors were closed, cross-corridors sealed away. They could only go one way, thanks to Jye-Tan.

Unfortunately, they were being followed.

"Run," he shouted, and Kuyi took off. She crossed a large unfamiliar corridor, and down two more. When she was almost out of sight, he pushed on the minds of two vekorna behind them, a brute force attack, and they went down.

They came to the crossway at the tunnel door, which was wide open. A single vekornan stood in their way.

"Treklay," breathed Kuyi, almost in relief. "You have to let us by."

Treklay didn't move aside.

I saw your secrets through the fragment, said the vekornan, and Aderen froze. He was acutely aware of more vekorna approaching from behind. If Treklay saw into his mind, and now knew what Nalimai had told him about his origins, the Egalsan would no longer be safe from Ontral.

Your kennis was unknown to us. It serves an interesting purpose.

Aderen breathed a sigh of relief. He could give up that secret.

Did *she* see your secrets? Treklay asked, extending three eyestalks toward Kuyi, still pleading with him.

It was confirmation that Treklay knew about more than just the kennis. Had Kuyi seen into his mind the way he'd looked into hers? The fragment had shredded his defenses before he mastered it.

Reaching into Treklay's mind, he searched for details, intent on erasing what the vekornan knew. He could still do that, and Kuyi would have to forgive him later. Laser fire hit the walls around them, the vekorna afraid to kill Treklay, but still aiming for the two humans.

"Let us pass," said Kuyi, hands on her hips, trying to find a way around or under him.

You will be brought to Ontral, said Treklay, and he reached out to grab them.

No! shouted Aderen, freezing Treklay, Kuyi and the vekorna approaching from the rear. It was the very first thing he'd learned to do with his mind in fear, and it still worked, when nothing else did.

"Sorry," he buzzed, releasing Kuyi. Horror-struck, she ducked between Treklay's leg and lower arm, and he did the same.

He reached for the knowledge Treklay had stolen from his mind, wondering how many others had seen it in that brief moment of uncontrolled telepathy. Maybe it was only Treklay, due to their special bond, created when he'd first held the vekornan's mind captive on the way to Esetek.

Kuyi gasped out loud as Treklay fell to the ground, dead.

Aderen stared at Treklay, dumbfounded. He'd overcompensated, but how? This had never happened before.

"You can't kill with it," Kuyi said, shaking. She thought he was still connected to the fragment, that it was too powerful for him. There was no time to figure it out, so he pulled her down the tunnel.

The open door to the Temple was ahead, as were three loboms, large black balls protruding with spikes. They let Aderen and Kuyi pass, then rolled into a line to block the exit.

*   *   *

Bursting out into the light of day, Aderen looked over his shoulder. Kuyi nearly knocked into him as she emerged, walking backward, but there was no pursuit. She hopped from one precarious perch to the next, and Aderen followed. She hadn't said a word since the tunnel.

"Why is there no pursuit?" he asked.

"They're focused at the entrance," Kuyi said as she boarded her hover-scooter. Aderen climbed on behind her, and she pointed back from where they'd come. Aderen stared at the scene unfolding at the Temple's main entrance, far from their exit point. Shuttles were hovering in the area, octagonal vend'oks moving back and forth. From here, they couldn't make out individual vekorna.

When they didn't find anything, Ontral's forces would fan out and search the surrounding area.

"We have to go before they turn their attention this way," Aderen buzzed, and Kuyi nodded. She took off at the hover-scooter's top speed, surpassing the thrill that Nalimai had given him on his arrival. He had to hold on to her waist for fear of being tossed off.

The hover-scooter produced a high-pitched whistle that made him cringe, but Kuyi assured him it attenuated quickly over the sand and soft rocks that dominated the space around the Temple.

Kuyi didn't initiate a kennis conversation, and Aderen didn't push her. He'd seen this reaction before, most recently with Ret. He used the time to review his interaction with Treklay, but no matter his analysis, he didn't understand what had happened.

They were almost at the Egalsan compound, and there had been no pursuit. Was it possible they'd gotten away?

"I need a hiding place," Aderen buzzed. He sent a message to Sarenie.

"Ontral knows about Kirina's refuge," Kuyi buzzed back, anticipating his next move. If he was that predictable, he would never make it out of Bol.

"Get me out the same way you did Kirina," he buzzed.

"That was long before I was birthed. You'll have to talk with Nalimai, but we'll never get there in time."

Kuyi stopped within sight of the farming compound, pointing at the main gate through the rock wall. Three vend'oks floated above the ground in their path.

"Stay away from the main house," Sarenie buzzed. "Ontral is here, and he is looking for you."

39. The Chosen Path

How had Ontral beaten them back? Kuyi hadn't seen any vend'oks pass their position, nor heard the telltale sound of a shuttle over the plains. Her only conclusion was that he'd been on his way before the emergency started.

For what? Surprise negotiations? Access to the birth chambers?

"Is Ontral just looking for me?" Aderen buzzed. "Not Kuyi?" Kuyi held her breath waiting for the answer, heart beating loud in her ears.

"Just you for now," Sarenie confirmed. "But he knows Kuyi is with you. His vekorna surround the main house, inside the wall, and he's not letting anybody out. He won't talk with me yet, but Egalinsor and I are working on it."

As far as Kuyi knew, the vekorna had never locked her family in, and had rarely crossed the rock wall. Were Nalimai's fears justified? Had she just been part of a catalyst from which they wouldn't recover? She forced herself to remain with Aderen, hoping distance from the fragment would bring him back to normal, stop him killing vekorna.

She'd already forgiven him for turning her into his marionette, like those poor lethal creatures in their labs. She'd thought herself a puppet of Lusava and Rogo when they assigned her menial tasks, but Aderen had done it literally. She didn't want to repeat the experience, even if it had saved their lives, but he had to learn.

They couldn't ride any further. She had to keep Aderen away from Ontral. She had to teach him control.

Swinging her legs to the ground, she motioned for Aderen to do the same. The garage was too close to the vend'oks; the vekorna would spot them if they approached that gate. She looked around, thinking. Jye-Tan used to hide near a shallow pond on this side of the compound, near where the wall ended. The small copse of trees would provide sufficient shelter, assuming Aderen would continue.

"Is anybody outside the houses?" Aderen asked as he put his feet on the ground. Kuyi turned to the buildings of the compound, searching, before realizing the question was not directed at her. She was still getting used to the way they could be alone, but also part of a larger conversation inside her head.

The question had been for Sarenie, but there was no answer for a long moment, and Kuyi worried about what was happening inside. Finally, Sarenie buzzed, "Ketaris is out near one of the lakes, taking samples. Doj and Penagel are at Kirina's refuge, working. Some of the Egalsan are in the lobomai caves with Illian and Akinuf."

"Thanks." He motioned Kuyi forward, but she pointed to the sheltered pond, and started walking the hover-scooter that way. When it was hidden, she forced her feet to move from tree to tree, the sparse vegetation not quite sufficient to hide them from vekornan infrared vision.

She led them farther from the houses, knowing that Aderen would be abandoning Arais and Egalsan alike, trying to keep them safe as he left, the way Kirina sacrificed her comfort so long ago. They finally reached thicker vegetation, which in her experience would keep their heat signatures hidden.

From cover, they could see the hydrofoil waiting at the dock. It looked prepped and ready to go. Kuyi turned to Aderen, who nodded. "Ketaris is a capable pilot," he said, "She can take me the rest of the way. You don't have to come." He put a hand on her shoulder, trying to be reassuring. "Ontral isn't looking for you. Étar escaped the laboratory –you can meet up with him and stay safe."

Étar was currently out of her reach. He'd briefly sent her a message that he was okay, but had since gone silent. She worried for him, but couldn't ignore the greater danger.

"If Ontral can't find you, he'll turn to me," she

319

responded. "I need to get us both to safety." If only to make sure he was okay, she added privately. He nodded, as if he'd read her thought, as if he understood her concern. "I was your anchor," she said, eyes blazing. When he looked surprised, she added, pointing at her head, "I felt you here." She didn't dare say it aloud, so she buzzed, "After Treklay, do you think you are in control? You need help."

"Doj and Penagel will help when I get to the refuge." She glared at him, and he nodded in acquiescence, but wasn't happy about it. "Come on."

A figure stepped out of the shadows and into their path. Kuyi immediately adopted a lobomai defensive posture, surprising herself. Aderen stood completely motionless.

"Nalimai," he said, relaxing, but looking around for others who might have snuck up on them. Kuyi's eyes widened with sudden worry about what her grandmother might have done.

"You are quick to put us in danger," Nalimai said. "You took Kuyi into the vekornan cities, but hesitate to use her outside the Temple? Why not?" Kuyi wondered how much she knew about what had happened.

"Sarenie didn't tell me you were outside," Aderen said.

"I wasn't, but we have ways of evading the vekorna." Nalimai shook her head at Kuyi. "I suppose this is my fault, for trying to keep you innocent for so long. You started to resent us, felt like you were left out. Then he came along." She nodded her chin in Aderen's direction. "Your chance to experience the thrill of danger. But you don't understand." She looked into Aderen's eyes. "When we first met, I said you would think only of yourself, and you've proven it with every decision. You only know part of what the vekorna are capable of doing."

Eyes scanning beyond their small shelter, Kuyi said, "You should come with us."

Nalimai barked a soft laugh. "I'm not leaving Bol, and neither are you." To Aderen, she said, "You bargained on finding the stellar fragment, when I told you not to, when I told you how dangerous it was. You lost, coming back here to hide, while antagonizing the vekorna, putting my family in danger.

"Your mission was ill-conceived from the beginning," Nalimai continued, angrier than Kuyi had ever seen her. "We are a constant reminder to the vekorna that humans exist, and there is a planet full of us two hundred light-years away. When the current war is over, they'll go back into space, and they'll surely return to Terra. It can never end."

"Only if all traces of humanity are removed from Rykol," Kuyi said with some anxiety. "You have to take us away. Is that it?"

Aderen's eyes were cast down. "I don't know yet. Doj and Penagel will try and use vekornan birth chambers to enforce a prohibition, but we don't know if it'll work. That's why Wandel and Akinuf are studying yours."

She could tell he was still thinking about the fragment, how it could help him enforce the change.

"If you go to Rubiel, Doj and Penagel will be killed," said Nalimai. "Keep them here until Sarenie and Egalinsor convince Ontral to open his birth chambers."

Kuyi raised her eyebrows. Nalimai was not that optimistic. Kuyi's courage rose as she realized her grandmother didn't have all the power she pretended to.

Aderen's gaze went suddenly toward the houses. "I have to go. Ketaris will take me to Kirina's refuge. You stay and hide here."

It was tempting. The folem lands were large, and she could hide for a long time, build another refuge farther from the vekorna. But even Kirina had chafed at her restrictions. She thought of Mai, who had agreed to leave only when Aderen had given her a mission.

"What would I do here?" she asked.

"Stay safe."

She shook her head, tears forming –real angry tears, not the kind Mai seemed to be able to produce at will. Aderen didn't realize he needed support. "Don't you understand yet?" she asked.

"Did he tell you what's happening outside this compound?" Nalimai asked, clearly exasperated. Kuyi looked up at her through tears. "Ontral has taken control of our laboratories and workshops."

"I know Étar escaped," she said.

"Did you know that Tararnifal captured Danosh, who is now a prisoner at Rubiel?"

Kuyi's eyes widened, tears suddenly dry. "Is that why Ontral is here?"

"Ontral is furious at what he thinks is our betrayal. Aderen's betrayal."

"My betrayal, too." Did they know about Treklay's death?

Ontral knew she'd been inside the city with Aderen, trying to steal the fragment. If Tararnifal had captured Danosh and brought him to Dairnehy, what did that mean for their chances at Rubiel?

"Your grandfather will reinstate our freedoms," Nalimai said, her voice resigned, not showing the bitterness her words expressed. Egalinsor needed to touch Ontral for proper influence, but he'd been practicing all his life. He could be subtle, and she had no doubt he would succeed.

"Will you tell Ontral where Aderen is going?" Kuyi asked. "He wants Aderen to leave Bol anyway."

"I don't know. Stay with me," Nalimai said.

"You helped smuggle Kirina out of the shield once," Kuyi said. "Would you do the same for Aderen?"

"Yes," Nalimai quickly responded. "I owe it to his father. We were best friends, and almost fell in love, until Egalinsor and Kym came along." She shook her head, as if to wipe the memories clear.

"Good luck," Aderen said, looking over his shoulder at the docks. "I'm sorry I brought this on your family."

Kuyi grabbed his hand in solidarity. She saw the sadness in her grandmother's eyes, and said, "I don't blame you for settling down, but our freedoms have been eroding for a long time. We need to do something. I need to pull my own strings."

Nalimai grabbed her away from Aderen, enveloping her in a tight hug. "You will always be welcome here. Stay safe." To Aderen, she said, "Keep her safe. Ask Doj how to get clear when you reach Kirina's old refuge."

"We aren't going to Kirina's refuge; it's too predictable."

"You must. Doj will know what I mean."

Kuyi released herself from her grandmother's grasp. Together, Kuyi and Aderen ran along the path, hidden from vekornan eyes by the thickening underbrush. They would be exposed briefly while approaching the docks, and who knew what would happen when the hydrofoil launched?

"I'm not sure you've chosen the right path," said Aderen. "I've already reached into the compound to make

323

Ontral more pliable to suggestions. That's all I can do right now."

He was still pulling strings, even after what happened to Treklay, but Kuyi kept silent, thinking about what was to come. Her eyes want to Nalimai, who was not heading back to the main house. She was going to a different lake, and the lobomai caves beyond.

40. Overcompensation

Like Kuyi, Ketaris wouldn't let him leave alone. As soon as Aderen stepped on board the hydrofoil, she had it untethered and racing through the water, ignoring his suggestion that she hide in the caves with Nalimai.

Aderen kept his mind focused on pursuit, hoping that Sarenie was keeping Ontral's attention away from the docks. He'd recoiled when touching the vekornan mind, wondering if Ontral already knew how to manipulate fetal humans thanks to Treklay. Kuyi was right about one thing – he needed to get all humans off this planet. He would deal with that after his main mission was completed, and that had to be done at Rubiel. Tararnifal's apparent betrayal complicated matters. He needed time to think.

"I'm discussing new tactics with Ontral," Sarenie buzzed when he enquired on the status inside the Egalsan houses. "Ontral has changed subtly; I assume that was your doing?" He acknowledged her. "Ontral's people are still looking for you, but they're mostly searching inside the Temple."

"Kuyi's passage probably isn't on their maps," Aderen agreed, watching the young woman stare into the water ahead, her hair blowing in the wind.

"Ontral has forbidden human travel outside the

compound and the lakes," Sarenie told him. "The city and Temple are out of bounds. I think we've lost our chance at his birth chambers. I don't suppose you could help?"

Aderen reached out, but across this distance, minds were fuzzy, indistinct. He needed a tigal-en's range, something he'd had in Terran orbit for a brief time, before he realized he was the product of a vekornan experiment.

"We're too far away," he buzzed, cursing himself silently for ruining their chances. "I can't do any more at the compound."

"We'll find another way," buzzed Sarenie. "Nalimai suggested a neutral location for our talks."

"Keep me up to date," he buzzed, and she was gone.

The hydrofoil rose higher out of the water, and crossed into a deeper lake. Ketaris was silent, and Aderen didn't initiate conversation. He watched the shores, wondering if he should have tried harder to leave Kuyi behind. She was still traumatized by her experience in the Temple, and deeply disturbed by his accident with Treklay.

She probably didn't know that Mai had slipped away as Étar and the others escaped the workshop, talking about loboms. Wandel and Firini were out searching for her. He regretted giving her a mission, but it seemed like the right approach at the time.

"You've been discovered," Sarenie buzzed him. "How far are you from your destination?"

Aderen checked his kennis map. "Too far." He nodded to Ketaris, and she increased speed, bringing the hydrofoil out of the water completely, activating its thrusters. Nalimai had designed an impressive craft.

Catching her balance, Kuyi stumbled back to the cockpit. She didn't say anything, but looked worried, braiding and unbraiding her hair.

"We'll have company soon," he said.

"We were too predictable."

"It's too late to change plans now," Ketaris shouted over the noise.

He detected vekornan minds above them before his enhanced vision saw the two shuttles. He knew the stakes now, and couldn't stay here, either by his own free will or under Ontral's control. Nalimai was right. He'd gambled with all of their freedom, and failed. He wasn't strong enough, or lacked preparation to deal with the fragment. He needed time, but it wouldn't happen inside the Bol shield.

Other minds drew his attention, more judgement in flowery form. Folems lined the shore, much as they had the last time he'd made this journey. He shied away from their musical thoughts.

"Two shuttles approaching low," Ketaris buzzed.

They were close enough for him to comfortably reach the six minds aboard each. Ontral hadn't made the trip, but probably wouldn't be far behind.

Diving into the vekornan thoughts, he found two pilots, but others were ready to take control if necessary. He would have to immobilize them before he could act.

"Two more shuttles behind them," Ketaris buzzed, keeping her observations short. Kuyi searched the skies.

The effort would increase geometrically if he didn't act now. Reaching into the sky, Aderen took control of one pilot, ignoring the other vekorna, as well as Kuyi's grim look. The shuttle turned aside, but came back on track almost immediately. Aderen reached out again, took a firmer hold.

Laser fire reached out for them, vaporizing the water as

the second shuttle fired across their bow. Ketaris was forced to maneuver, but to her credit, didn't slow down.

"They're too close. Are you going to do something?" she asked, and Kuyi shook her head.

He ignored her, finding the vekornan gunners. More lasers shot out, closer. The vekorna were under orders to bring him back, but would not hesitate to sink their boat.

Still reeling from his failure with Treklay, Aderen tried to ignore Kuyi's misplaced comparison of her own experiences at being controlled with what he could do. He tried not to think of how he had obtained that ability, and gently forced the gunners to stop shooting.

Without leaving the gunners' minds, he reached out once again to the pilots. The shuttles slowed, and the hydrofoil pulled out ahead.

More vekornan minds encroached on his awareness, overtaking the shuttles that he had just incapacitated. He searched in vain for a way to change their minds, and was coming to the realization that he might have to kill them.

He avoided looking at Kuyi, his gaze going to the judgmental gazes of the yellow flowers lining the shores instead. He wished Ketaris would steer farther from them as he prepared himself. They were a poor substitute for the raw anger Ret projected toward him, but they were far more numerous.

More lasers shot out at them, one hitting the side of the hydrofoil, causing it to dip. Ketaris moved in the other direction.

Searching for the new gunners was more complicated than it should have been, and he cursed his newfound timidity. One last mission, he'd told Monera. But he'd needed to change so many minds on Rykol, alter so many perceptions.

He tried a different tactic, blinding the vekorna to the hydrofoil the way he'd blinded the ones in the city to him and Kuyi.

The first shuttle turned away, as if suddenly expanding its search pattern, but the second one didn't veer off course.

The shuttles fired again as he lost control of the gunners. The shots pinged the hydrofoil, though Ketaris managed to keep out of the densest parts of the deadly rain from above.

Frustrated, Aderen looked around for more solutions. The folems just stared at him. "Why don't you help me!" he shouted. Then he looked into their minds, seeing indifference. Their interest in him had waned.

So had his interest in them. Why did he have to go to the Memory Caves, instead of them coming to him? For now, they could be of other use. The vekorna had been stopped in the Temple by a line of loboms. It was the only explanation for their escape. What would they do with a line of folems?

As he entered their minds, the multi-colored flowers leaped off the shore and drifted on unseen currents to create a curtain above them. Ketaris and Kuyi gazed at the yellow cloud that started to block the sky.

"No, not again!" Kuyi exclaimed, aghast, and moved toward him. Ketaris intercepted her, and the hydrofoil began to drift.

The folems twirled as they continued leaping into the air, filling the sky with their unique petal colors and arrangements, but blending into the undulating yellow mass above them.

The lasers stopped after tearing through a couple of folems on the edge. The whine of shuttles dissipated, and

Ketaris let go of Kuyi, pouring more power into the engines.

"I think they've given up the chase," she said, looking back. "Do you think that was a good idea?"

Aderen shook his head, shoulders sagging, looking at Kuyi on her knees, tears running down her cheeks. "No, it was a terrible idea. I can't come back here, ever. I might have ruined your chances with Orem, too."

Ketaris bit her lower lip, but nodded wordlessly. He sat down and ignored Kuyi's tear-filled glare. It was too similar to what he'd seen on Ret's face, to her judgement after accidentally killing Treklay.

At this speed, it didn't take long to reach Kirina's refuge. The sky was clear here, no folems clouding the view, no shuttles giving chase. Had Ontral truly given up so easily? Or did he have to answer to the folems for shooting them in their haste to get at Aderen?

Doj and Penagel had the old vend'ok ready.

"I thought Akinuf would be here helping you," said Aderen, looking it over.

"She was here a while ago, but left for the mobile labs near the lobomai caves. She's probably still there."

Aderen shook his head. "I hope she's safe."

"Me too," Doj said. He pointed to the vend'ok. "It's slow, but will get us to the shield."

"You aren't coming with me," Aderen said, shaking his head adamantly.

"You need us to reprogram the birth chambers," Doj insisted.

"We don't know how to do that yet, do we?" Aderen asked, knowing the answer. Nalimai was right –Rubiel was too dangerous to bring so many people. "I may have ruined our chances at getting into Ontral's birth chambers, but there are others. Concentrate your efforts with Wandel and Akinuf so we'll be ready when the time comes."

"My birth chamber is next to the lobomai caves, in one of the camouflaged silver pods," Kuyi volunteered. "I hope you can get something out of it." She looked out over the lakes, then back at Aderen. "We need to go."

Disappointed, Doj acquiesced. "We'll take you as far as the shield, where we've been doing experiments with the kennis, trying to counter the shield's blockage. I'll show you something special."

They drove due north into the daytime suns, following an overgrown trail directly to the shield. The two men nodded without comment when they heard what he'd done. They knew his power from Terra, and his mistakes, and thankfully never passed judgement.

A small camp had been set up near the shield. Ketaris frowned as she saw the cleared area, with uprooted plants and tall reeds flung aside.

Doj frowned a pained apology, then said, "Nalimai gave us these coordinates for our work." He pulled four small devices from the tall grasses, covered by mounds of earth.

"Shield interrupters?" Kuyi asked. "Is that how they got Kirina out of here after the folems poisoned her?" She shivered and rubbed her shoulder.

Aderen stood with one of the active devices in his hand, and placed it on the shield. It hung in midair. Doj placed the second one, also without any noticeable effect. The third opened a triangular hole to the dry grasses outside the shield. A fourth one enlarged the hole to form a doorway large enough to drive the vend'ok through, hovering over the low ground, brushing grasses as it passed.

"Get to safety," Aderen told the Arais. "If you can program the kennis nodes around the shield frequency, I'll be looking for a connection inside Rubiel's shield. Contact me."

"Knowing that these interrupters can pierce the shield gives me confidence that the kennis can, too," Doj said. "The shield is more complicated than a single frequency. There are myriad secondary modulations, which is what makes it so effective against attack."

"Except when the vekorna got through to attack the Temple," said Ketaris, still staring at the camp. "Good luck."

She went back inside the shield. Aderen smiled as he saw her fall to her knees and start to replant grasses.

Doj took Kuyi's hand. "I have many children and grandchildren on Terra, but I'm glad to have found you here on Rykol, unexpected. Sarenie is happy to have found a sister, too."

She enveloped him in her arms. Aderen could see tears in her eyes as she was overwhelmed by his grandfatherly love. She was leaving her home, maybe forever. Searching the sky inside and outside the shield, Aderen was eager to leave, and considered abandoning her with Doj, Penagel and Ketaris. But he waited, calming his impatience.

"Tell Étar I love him," Kuyi finally said, probably feeling the same urgency, and pulling away.

Doj saluted them, and said, "Don't activate them too close to each other. I've detected energy surges in small slits."

"It's as if you read my mind," said Aderen, and Kuyi looked at them both in horror.

Aderen reached inside and pulled one of the interrupters

off the shield. Doj disappeared when he removed the second one, leaving a thin line barely a hand's-breadth thick. He reached carefully through and yanked the third interrupter to their side, and the hole disappeared. There was no way to get the fourth, but they wouldn't need it.

Nalimai had given them a chance to escape, true to her word. Would the vekorna or folems know?

"Don't they need the interrupters?" Kuyi asked. "What if the wingless come for them?"

"They're probably safer without admitting they can get through the shield," Aderen said. "Ontral should be more open to suggestion, and between your grandfather and Sarenie, he won't be chasing humans. I know you don't like the way I force them to do things, but sometimes it's the only way." He tried to sound more confident than he felt.

They boarded the vend'ok again, and drove north. Inspecting his increasingly detailed map, which grew with every new place his kennis explored, they found the location where they'd met with Pinoa's shuttle after escaping Esetek. There was a cave in those rocky hills with Étar's weapons. From there, they could plan their next moves.

Part V: The Fragmented Crystal

41. Rendezvous

"You've lost concentration," Aderen said.

Squirming to get more comfortable, Kuyi took a deep breath. Aderen squeezed her fingers tighter.

"Sorry," she said. "He's so close."

"Curb your anticipation, which will make it more enjoyable when you come together." Kuyi tried, yet didn't believe him. Anticipation made the meeting even sweeter. Her heart was pumping faster, she had goosebumps, even though it had only been a few days since she'd last seen Étar.

They'd both gone through danger to get here, and that made all the difference. For a few brief hours, she didn't know if he'd been captured, or even survived.

Aderen had been surprised and upset when he found Étar and Pinoa's kennis signals outside the shield. Kuyi had had to point out that they were safer from Ontral out here, compared with the Egalsan workshop. Up to then, they'd had no news from within the shield since Doj closed it. She'd been upset with Aderen for a few hours after learning Mai was still in danger, but knew from experience how resourceful the young woman could be. She'd know how to avoid the vekorna.

Concentrating, Kuyi allowed Aderen inside her mind again. It was full of thoughts of Étar. Would Aderen judge her for what they'd done together on the beach? She felt like he would see little else.

He seemed to be concentrating on her displeasure, though, at the way he'd treated Treklay, and the folems after that. She was certain it was the effect of the fragment, something he had to understand. She allowed him to see her breakdown in the Temple, and how she felt used by her family, always being told what to do, as if she was their puppet –but not as literally as the way she'd fell into the rhythm of the cloned creatures. She couldn't allow him to make puppets of the vekorna, and certainly not the folems. Kirina had always been able to manipulate vekorna, but not like what Aderen had done in the Temple of Spall.

It was hard not to block him, the way Kirina had taught her. She was so used to blocking the vekorna that it took a lot of concentration to let him through. She wondered what she would find in his mind if she could do the same to him.

As it was, there was no physical sensation of his efforts. He didn't poke at her nerve centers, and as far as she could tell, didn't stir up old memories.

Every so often, she would feel turmoil that wasn't her own, interspersed with peace. When he'd approached her for help, to regain focus after what he'd done to Treklay and the folems, she didn't hesitate, but after hearing from Étar, it was more difficult. She wanted to jump up and look for the hover-scooters at the cave entrance.

"Count backward from one hundred," Aderen instructed, and she did so. It wasn't the first strange request he'd made while inside her mind, and she didn't question him. She knew meditation took many forms. Most of her family preferred lobomai meditation, as taught by Nalimai, who learned it from Kezim before he returned to Terra. Aderen must have created his own for mental balance.

"Who's Monera?" Kuyi asked, when a melancholy loving thought came to her, unbidden. She'd only reached halfway through the countdown.

Aderen released her hands so suddenly that she rocked back, squinting against the faint light. He was already on his feet, pacing, a little flushed.

"Sorry," he said as she stood, unwinding her legs in a fluid motion, pushing dark hair from her face, shaking her head so it would flow over both shoulders. "Monera was special to me, the way Étar is to you. She used to help me like this, keeping me centered, especially after I made mistakes."

"I think you're still suffering the effects of the fragment," she said. "You say Treklay was an accident, not a mistake, though I don't know what you were looking for in his mind that caused you to kill him. Turning the vekorna at that machine into puppets, forcing them to the wall, was no accident, and it wasn't necessary. The folems were also not an accident. You shouldn't have done that, though it saved our lives. I'm still willing to continue, if it will help you be more careful exercising your power."

"I appreciate your support. I'm feeling more balanced, as if the void created by my sudden withdrawal from the fragment is closing. You may be right about it, but that doesn't excuse what I did. I can never return to Bol."

Finally, he was taking her seriously. Kuyi thought of what she knew about Kirina's exile. She hadn't taken control of a group of folems, but they'd poisoned her anyway. Kuyi realized she'd always taken that story at face value, that she didn't know why Kirina had been banished, except that she had the power to do what Aderen could.

"Your boyfriend is here," Aderen said, causing her cheeks to flush.

The three hover scooters drove into the cave without slowing, followed by clouds of dust, and stopped beside the octagonal vend'ok. Kuyi and Aderen waved in greeting.

"Thanks for coming, but you shouldn't be here," Aderen

said. "Especially them." He pointed to Aneya and Jye-Tan, who jumped off their shared hover-scooter.

Disembarking, Étar hugged each of them, a more formal gesture than what Kuyi had been expecting. "I'm glad you're safe, but we couldn't leave them behind. Ontral has taken over all the Egalsan labs and workshops, and he knows that the lower levels of the city were hacked from there. We barely got out in time."

"And Mai and Wandel?" he asked, cringing.

"They also got away, to the Memory Caves with her loboms, I think. I would lock Mai up myself to curb her recklessness."

"Don't even say that," Kuyi said, hugging him tight.

When she wouldn't let go, he gave her a passionate kiss that left her trembling. He pulled away and winked at her. "I missed you, too," he buzzed. She kept hold of his hand.

"I've never seen the vekorna like that," said Aneya, ignoring the display of affection and brushing a strand of hair from the unblemished side of her face. Her kennis had started healing her burned skin; Kuyi could already see tiny hairs poking from that side of her head. Unfortunately, Xeffeya said there was nothing it could do about her missing ear and fingers so long after the fact.

"Wandel's decoy worked?"

"We believe so, though we haven't had contact with those inside the shield since we escaped. Nobody followed us out."

"I thought we were going out in the scrap of a vend'ok that Wandel got working," Jye-Tan said, coming up beside her. "But the hover scooter ride along the shield wall was much more exciting!" He grinned.

Kuyi wondered how many more escape or decoy

vehicles Wandel and Akinuf could fix with their skills. Rogo was right –they worked fast!

"I don't think Wandel's work on the vend'ok was a secret from Ontral," said Étar. "The controls are telepathic, and there's a good chance visiting vekorna could detect them when activated."

"They never visited the labs," Jye-Tan insisted, with the certainty of youth. Kuyi ignored the fact that she was only a little older.

"You don't think the vekorna visited in the night, or any other time the Egalsan weren't there?"

Jye-Tan pursed his lips, but remained silent.

"It seemed to work," said Aneya. "The vekorna didn't follow our hover-scooters, and Mai escaped on foot until Wandel found her."

Jye-Tan was beaming, proud of the fact that he'd managed to hack into the shield system, opening a hole for them. He'd maintained his kennis connection with the city controls all the way to the edge of the shield.

"Hopefully Ontral will think you're hiding in the hills beyond the city, where the vend'ok likely ended up; I hope they don't take it out on Nalimai and Egalinsor."

"Ontral made it known that he killed all the vekorna who were working on the fragment, and were potentially influenced by you," said Pinoa. She put a hand on Aderen's arm. "I'm sorry."

Kuyi looked sharply at Aderen. "See the result? No more puppets!" she buzzed. More gently, she added, "Use my strength," and felt him gently caress some of her worry away. How that helped him, she didn't know, but she saw him nod in appreciation.

"He hasn't threatened any humans yet," Étar said.

"Egalinsor and Sarenie are making progress, thanks to your influence. They know how to take care of themselves. The folems reminded Ontral that vekorna are not permitted within the compound wall, and suggested a more neutral place for further discussion. I think Ontral will agree, but it's going to be harder to get into his birth chambers now."

He glanced away from Aderen, looking uncertain. "After what happened at the Temple, are you sure you're up to this?"

Aderen nodded. "Kuyi has been helping me. I'll be ready by the time we reach Rubiel."

Anxiety once again gripped Kuyi, the way it had when they'd first left the shield. She didn't mind admitting that Dairnehy scared her, much more than Danosh had.

Aneya put a hand on Aderen's arm, eyes stern. "They aren't looking outside the shield yet, or they would have seen us. Every minute we wait allows for greater chance of discovery, especially when we take a vend'ok into the open. We have to leave."

She looked at the old vend'ok, a grim smile on half her mouth. "I remember when we smuggled Kirina out in that thing. We wanted her to take it, but she refused." She patted her hover scooter. "We smuggled two of these out a day later, which gave her and Nekken more freedom."

"Can the vekorna trace this one?" Aderen asked.

"No, it's almost as bad off as the one we sent from the workshop, stripped of everything the vekorna could use to track it."

That was a worry off his mind, something Kuyi hadn't been able to answer. Unfortunately, it added a new one. "Will it survive the trip across the continent?"

Aneya shrugged.

340

"I've been gathering grasses from outside the cave," said Kuyi, pointing to the vend'ok, and wondering what Ketaris would think of her uprooting them, but put the thought aside. "Their roots might not taste great, but will sustain us."

"Good thinking," Aneya said. To Aderen, she added, "Those are Nalimai's genetically engineered grasses. They're thriving here, but haven't spread into the desert."

Jye-Tan made a face, and took two algae packages from his hover scooter. "I grabbed these on the way out, but they won't last long."

"Unfortunately, Doj and Penagel didn't have time to pack us extra food," Aderen said. "But that's not our biggest problem. We still need to find a way across the ocean. Is there any chance we can contact your family to steal us a shuttle? Or have them tip Ontral off to where we are, so I can take control of the pilot?" Kuyi gave him a warning look. It was obvious that he hadn't taken her concerns seriously yet.

"I think he would send an overwhelming force, after what you did," said Aneya. She looked around at their surroundings. "He'd likely destroy the cave, sealing us under tons of rock."

A look from Étar silenced everybody. He'd cocked his head, as if he didn't understand what he was hearing. Aderen walked over to him. "What is it?"

"Ret, I think," Étar whispered.

Kuyi searched the kennis node for Ret's signal, the way Étar had shown her. It was strong, but far away, at the Black Moon.

"Let us all in," Aderen instructed, and Étar nodded. He frowned.

Kuyi wondered about a man who could survive alone among kolbs for so long. According to Djaxtal back at Esetek, he'd chosen to cooperate with them. Sarenie didn't believe it, because she knew Ret wanted to keep an eye on what Aderen did. Kuyi understood his position a little better after what she'd recently experienced.

"No, Sarenie is still with the Egalsan, under the Bol shield," Étar buzzed as she was brought into the mental conversation. "Pinoa is here for our talks with Rubiel. There's so much to tell you."

"Have you made any progress?" Ret asked. He was directing his questions to Étar, barely acknowledging Aderen and Pinoa, and completely ignoring the Egalsan, whose unknown presence she thought should register on his kennis.

"No, the vekorna at Bol weren't willing to send us to Rubiel. We've escaped, but now have to walk a third of the way around the world." He gave a depreciating laugh. "How did you get on the kennis node? Have the kolbs finally let you go?"

"No, I'm outside their shield, being transported to Rolm. I think we're going to see my fighter, which they destroyed when we first arrived. I don't know what'll be left."

"You know your first duty, right?"

"Is it to survive, or escape?"

"You can't do one without the other. If you get away, come to Bol. I'm sending you a data dump of all we know so far. We'll find a way to get you back, otherwise."

"That's a promise you can't keep," Ret buzzed, but Kuyi knew Étar meant it. If he could, he'd get his friend back.

Ret linked them in to what his eyes saw, lagged as it went through the kennis buffer.

Kuyi braced herself against the vend'ok as her mind tried to grasp what she was seeing. Dozens of shuttles, broken and mixed in with the debris of the vekornan structures, showed devastation from the first battle for the stellar fragment at Rolm. The base was breached from explosive decompression, where the kolbs had attacked hardest, seizing the fragment. She wished now that they'd destroyed it.

"These images confirm what Étar and Wandel recorded from their fighters, but I don't see the excavated fragment." Aderen buzzed, to her alone. She nodded, trusting him.

The resolution suddenly increased, and she could see incredible detail, like being in a memory globe.

Ret shifted his gaze left to right, passing over the giant kolb pilot as he did. The dry, yellow skin was nauseating to Kuyi, who had only ever seen live kolbs recently, in Danosh's cave under Esetek.

"Do you see those areas that look like more recent construction?" Ret asked. The image froze.

"Yeah, maybe," Étar answered. Kuyi had difficulty seeing beyond the debris. "Ret? Are you still there?"

Étar let go of her hand and shot a worried look at Aderen.

"Ret's signal has disappeared," Jye-Tan said, eyes darting in every direction.

"We only have two nodes in orbit, which isn't enough for detailed tracking," Étar explained.

"It didn't seem like they were under attack," Pinoa said. The shared kennis space had disappeared. "I think he entered another shield."

"Let's hope so."

"Doj and Penagel are already working on improvements

to the kennis nodes so we can buzz across shields," said Aderen. "Unfortunately, we can't wait for them to be done."

"Did you see the warning Tararnifal stored on the kennis node?" Pinoa asked.

"Yes, and Samlar repeated it. He's now in orbit."

"Probably not the best decision, with the kolbs out to repossess his extars," Pinoa said.

"Tararnifal says if we go to Rubiel, we may never get out," said Aderen. "I don't know if he was forced to capture Danosh, or if he's a traitor. Either way, I need to get into Rubiel and confront Dairnehy."

"If we surrender outside the shield, you'll never get the chance," said Pinoa. "We need to get in some other way."

"That's why you took the shield interrupters, isn't it?" asked Kuyi.

Aderen nodded. He turned to Aneya. "Do you know how far Rubiel's defenses extend? When we first arrived, they destroyed an extar kilometers from their shield."

"At least that far in all directions," she responded. "I'm not sure if they would detect somebody on foot, though."

"Because no vekornan would ever cross the desert on foot," Aderen said, and she smiled. Jye-Tan nodded, and Kuyi wondered how he knew. She'd spent most of her adult life taking care of him, but didn't notice details like he did, wasn't drawn to explore beyond what was right in front of her. Maybe she shouldn't have resented his rebellious nature.

"What about our weapons?" Étar asked, picking up a small laser. Kuyi had never fired a weapon, relying on being boring to defend herself. But after Danosh and the cloned creatures in the Temple, maybe she needed something more.

Aderen looked toward the weapons cache thoughtfully. "They might be useful as we cross this continent, but we can't afford a firefight inside Rubiel's shield. Take as many as you need to defend us."

Étar offered her a small hand weapon, but although she reached out her arm, in the end she refused. Étar nodded and put it in his waist.

"I want to take a hover-scooter with you, spend some time together," she buzzed. She hadn't told him about her experiences in the Temple, though he knew all about their flight from the compound. He took her hand and nodded.

The vend'ok came alive as Aderen entered and connected by kennis. It was under-maintained, sitting at Kirina's refuge for so long.

Aneya checked the grass roots Kuyi had gathered, and congratulated her on good choices. Kuyi nodded, already immune to her family's conciliatory thanks. After what she'd done with Aderen in the Temple, she didn't need them to acknowledge that she could succeed.

Pinoa boarded a hover-scooter and left the cave. Kuyi smiled at Étar, tying her hair back, as they waited for Aderen to drive the vend'ok carefully through the small opening. They would be moving slower than usual, matching the aged vend'ok's pace.

They stayed close to the shield, hoping their energy signature would be disguised by proximity. Amid the grasses, they didn't kick up any dust, but it might become a problem as they entered the deeper desert.

Finally, she was alone with Étar again. She buzzed him little by little what had happened to her in the Temple. To her surprise, it was the hardest admission she'd ever made.

Étar was compassionate and incensed, and sent her emotions through the kennis she didn't know was possible. It was as if she was in his arms, though he was flying beside her.

"I don't mind you accompanying me to the edge of the continent," Aderen buzzed from inside the vend'ok. "But you'll stay on this side of the ocean. I'll find a way across with Pinoa and Kuyi. I don't want to risk more than I have to. I should have insisted on going to Rubiel with Tararnifal straight from Egalra."

Proud as she was to be included, Kuyi didn't want to be separated from Étar again, so soon after reuniting. Yet she didn't know how to protest without being left behind.

"At least you know what you are up against now," Jye-Tan buzzed. She shouldn't have left him in the vend'ok with Aderen. All of her work distracting him from the stellar fragment would be undone. His mission was to stop Dairnehy from going back to Terra, which would require some kind of mental control. She could reconcile her feelings about that if he limited himself to making Dairnehy more pliable to Pinoa's suggestions. She didn't want him taking control of the winged leader's body and thoughts.

Étar shook his head and buzzed, "I wasn't there when you took control of Sebenet's extars and stopped the fighting. It upset Ret, but I was impressed by what he described. Something happened since then, but I know Sarenie has been helping you to fix that." Kuyi almost volunteered that she'd taken over that role, but refrained. "If you could control all those tigal-en in Terran orbit, then you should be able to handle Dairnehy and his guards." Kuyi disagreed, and wanted to contradict him, but he continued. "But Danosh had tricks up his sleeve that you didn't expect, so you'll need backup. It might even be an opportunity to find some birth chambers. At this rate, though, it'll take months to get to Rubiel, if ever."

"I've left a kennis message for Samlar, in case he checks the node," Pinoa buzzed from up ahead. "I'm hoping he'll send us a shuttle."

"Good idea," Aderen said.

"Dairnehy knows what you can do, that you're like Kirina," Jye-Tan buzzed. "If he uses mirror crystals against you, then you'll need us."

"True," buzzed Étar. "I know that's how you hid the stellar fragment from Dairnehy, which means you know how to be subtle. I want to review how they work."

"They reflect telepathy," buzzed Jye-Tan earnestly. "The kolbs created them on Esetek with the exploding ones."

Aneya projected an image of her hands into their shared kennis, forcing Kuyi to note the prominence of her missing fingers. "I didn't know what they were," Aneya buzzed. To Jye-Tan she added, "The question is how *you* knew."

"I'm not telepathic like Kirina, if that's what you're asking," said Jye-Tan, his kennis presence uncomfortable. The silence dragged on a little too long, so he added, "But when I connected to the fragment, I *was* like Kirina, just for a moment."

"The stellar fragment is very powerful, and very dangerous," buzzed Aderen. Kuyi was glad to hear him say so, and nodded emphatically in agreement.

"I saw blank spots in Rubiel," continued Jye-Tan. "I searched the vekornan minds to understand what they were."

"And the vekorna haven't found the stellar fragment all these years because of mirror crystals?" Aderen asked.

"Hopefully."

"I think we would know," buzzed Étar, looking over at Kuyi, his face questioning in the wind of their passage. Kuyi shrugged. She hadn't been on that trip, one of the few times she'd been asked to help in the genetics labs instead.

"I'm not sorry I couldn't extract Ontral's fragment," said Aderen, as the vend'ok cleared the red grasses. "I'll do better with Dairnehy. The fragment is just a distraction from our original plan. I thought I could use it to dissuade the vekorna from going to Terra, but it's harder to control, and I don't want to rely on it. But I don't want to be blocked, either. How can I defend against mirror crystals?"

"They only work when oriented correctly," buzzed Jye-Tan. "That's why I had to use a lot of them. If you turn them away, or crack them like the kolbs at Esetek did, you should be able to get through." In true Jye-Tan fashion, he changed the subject, buzzing, "But if you're looking to connect with the birth chambers, I can hack into Rubiel like I did at Bol. The kennis just slides through their security."

"Our first priority," buzzed Étar, "will be to find an escape vehicle."

"If I can get into their network, we can do both," Jye-Tan challenged.

The vend'ok slowed, increasing its distance from Pinoa, and forcing Étar and Kuyi to slow behind them. Pinoa circled around, asking "What's wrong?"

"We have company in the sky."

Kuyi looked up, but didn't see anything. Étar pointed at a black dot that was getting larger. The vend'ok would be visible from the sky in this open area.

"Samlar?" Pinoa asked. "Or Ontral?"

"Neither. Kolbs."

The vend'ok stopped and Aderen, Aneya and Jye-Tan exited to the desert sands. Pinoa and Étar descended from their hover-scooters, while Kuyi turned hers toward the shuttle, wishing now she'd taken Étar's proffered weapon. His hand was reaching to the back of his waist.

"Djaxtal and Thirp'inc," Aderen said as the two kolbs descended the shuttle's ramp. "I was wondering what happened to you after Danosh was captured."

He was one ally among many, said Djaxtal. **For the moment, we have no base of operations, and continue our surveillance of Rykol,** said Djaxtal. **However, a message reached us that you needed help getting across the ocean.**

"From Samlar?" Pinoa asked.

From Arnatak, who heard it from the human on the Black Moon.

"Ret arranged this?" Étar said, laughing. "That shouldn't have been a surprise." It was good to hear Étar laugh, and Kuyi reached for his hand, but he was too far away.

We believe Dairnehy will harm Danosh, but we do not know what he hopes to gain.

"Information," said Aderen, shrugging. "Will you take us there?"

Nepral is not safe for us. Can you fly a shuttle?

"Yes," Aderen nodded. He didn't bother to explain his kennis to the kolbs, who probably didn't even know Egalsan needed helmets to connect. "But what will you do?"

We will take your vend'ok until another opportunity arises.

Étar took Aderen by the shoulder. "We're coming with you. That's not negotiable."

42. Memories of Rykol 6

Despite the composition of their party, Aderen was confident they would succeed. Bol had made him complacent, and raised new doubts. Now over the ocean, they were back to the original plan.

"Big flame up ahead," said Étar, his voice even as he flew the shuttle, as if he was pointing out scenery.

Aderen stood to see, but Jye-Tan met his eyes, and bounded to the front of the cockpit, putting his hands on the front window. The others followed more sedately.

With three hover-scooters in the cargo hold, the shuttle smelled like machinery, and they already occupied the forward section near the window.

It was more than a flame; it was a massive erupting volcano, with tongues leaping hundreds of meters into the sky, ash falling from the giant cloud into the deadly ocean.

"What is it?" Jairon asked.

"It's Tilireval," said Aneya, jaw clenched. "Long ago, the winged and wingless fought for control of the tower." She turned away. "I've seen it before."

"That happened before I was birthed!" Jye-Tan exclaimed. "It can't still be on fire now."

"It started long before that. They must have broken through the mantle for it to be fueled for so long," said Aneya, shrugging. "The island was sacred, used by kolbs and vekorna alike to burn their dead leaders and inaugurate new ones. Respect for all things has disappeared in this war. Not for the Temple of Spall, and not for Tilireval."

They watched in silence as Étar gave the burning island a wide berth. Most of it simmered in roiling flames or lava, but a powerful energy source from deep within fed the higher torches. It was more evidence that Dairnehy couldn't be reasoned with directly.

Then it was behind them, and Étar said, "We're halfway to Nepral. The extars didn't stand a chance against Rubiel's outer defenses. I'm veering south, but we'll have to be quick."

While Étar offered to teach Jye-Tan how to fly, Pinoa and Aneya moved to the cargo hold to ready the hover-scooters.

*   *   *

Aderen welcomed the latest vision as he contemplated the significance of the vekorna destroying their sacred places.

The shuttle dissolved around him as he let the vision overtake his consciousness, leaving the giant torch behind.

By kennis, he had revisited the asteroid impact that had created the siims, to their discovery of the mirkonel genetic memory, the attack of the rokels, the discovery and bonding of the goses, and another attack by rokels, the first time siims had taken up weapons.

Viewing Kirina's memory globes had shown him how to identify timescales. He knew that the vision he was falling into now took place more than seven hundred Rykolien years after the asteroid impact, near the end of the first siim generation, and about one hundred years since the rout of the rokels and kolbs in the goses forest.

We are dying, said the now-familiar voice. He suspected it was somebody who wanted to find the siims, who hoped he would drop everything and go out in search of their remains. They would have to be disappointed.

Persinjali was nowhere to be seen, but not everything could be from that siim's point of view. Aderen knew that most vekorna and kolbs injured the way he had been would be put to death, their seed-pods harvested for the next generation. He wondered if the vekorna followed that practice with siims, too.

Three vekorna escorted five siims down a long corridor that opened into one of the multi-level rooms that the vekornan leaders used for energized thinking and discussion.

This generation of vekorna didn't have wings, so they used single-person lifts or climbed segmented ladders to get to the next levels.

One vekornan, Aderen wondered if he was the vekornan leader, called down to the siims. **Your research has reached a plateau in the Metaspu. It is time to move on. The goses are dwindling faster than before, and soon there will be none left to study.**

"We have shown our worth to Rykol," one of the siims shouted up, his mellow words echoing off the different levels. "It is time for our independence."

The vekornan climbed down to the lower level. **You have shown your vulnerability, and weaknesses that the vekorna do not possess. You require our protection and guidance. During your early research, you provided us with a weapon against the rokels in the form of mirkonel, but they are of limited use outside Tiroosae. You lied to us about the existence of the goses, and half of your research group was wiped out in a kolb/rokel ambush. Your species has shown recklessness and poor judgement. You are not ready for independence.**

"We wish to expand the research station in the Metaspu and move our birth chambers there. We are nearing the end of our lives, and you have not seen fit to mature a new generation." The siim who identified as Flaorniti wanted to flutter his wings in frustration, but it was not permitted in here.

The new generation of siims will be matured in Metik, under the watch of vekornan experts. Your birth chamber will be filled with the seed-pods of your dead well before the last siim dies.

Flaorniti was confused. "Then how will we teach them?"

You will not teach them. Vekorna will show them how to fight kolbs and rokels, and they will not be researchers like the first generation.

Now Flaorniti was insulted. "How can you do this? We are siims, not vekorna. We have our own distinctiveness."

So do rokels, and they were bred for war by the kolbs. Your initial time at Ban was not put to useful efforts. We will start again.

Flaorniti and the others were dismissed and brought to the research station in northern Depraf. The goses were waiting for them.

Have you brought parts for the goses birth chamber, one of them asked.

A siim with two missing arms walked up to them. Aderen's heart rose to see Persinjali again, though he didn't look well. His other arms were emancipated, and his sensor head shriveled.

He put a hand on the goses beak. "No, Thof, it is too dangerous at this time. But we will be ready. The hidden city is progressing, and you've assured us that the tunnels will be ready in time."

Impatience glowed through the shared spectrum.

"We must be subtle, or the vekorna and kolbs will continue to hunt us long after we are gone."

"I met with a vekornan while at Metik," said Flaorniti.

"He will help us. But I am concerned about what the vekorna told us in the last meeting. They could create siims at any time with the new birth chambers."

"The siim birth chambers at Ban will not function; they have been misled on the construction," said Persinjali. "Only the six at Metik will successfully mature siims."

"How will we ensure the vekorna have no siim genetic material with which to mature new siims? Even the false tanks at Ban contain our seed-pods."

There is only one way, said the goses. **You must destroy them all.**

"But how? The moment we sabotage one tank, the vekorna will know, and will understand our plan. They will never let us out of their sight."

You must do it the same way in which you were brought into this world.

"An asteroid?" Flaorniti asked.

An asteroid is not necessary, just a seismic event that will rock all of the birth chambers on Rykol, destabilizing them.

"How would we do that?"

Leave the seismic disturbance to the goses. You must ensure that all of your dead are accounted for, and all siim seed-pods not currently in a birth chamber have been collected and brought to the underground city. We will be waiting.

Aderen knew the end of this story, how Bolob helped the siims escape Metik by smuggling a functional birth chamber out of the city under the cover of an ambush by kolbs and rokels. He wondered if the next vision would show how they committed mass suicide, destroying their races forever.

43. Slipping Through

This is not the vekornan way, Tararnifal said, feeling more helpless than the last time he'd said it.

Dairnehy, five-sided sensor head completely exposed, the black spots flaring on his four back faces like nothing Tararnifal had seen before, turned three eyestalks toward him.

Vekorna have evolved, much as your humans. They introduced the idea of bodily reconstruction, and we learned the concept of torture from them, too.

Danosh stood still as a statue on three legs, one arm hanging limp. The two that had been regrown by the folems long ago, having been severed by the same shuttle crash that cost Nalimai two limbs, had been severed again, this time intentionally.

Vekorna were not meant to be tortured, continued Tararnifal, aghast at the sight of the vekornan who had once been prin-el to Bolob, and friend to the humans.

Vekorna were meant to die in battle, and to give their lives instead of living crippled, returned Dairnehy. He activated the electrical impulses that seared like lightning over Danosh's exposed body. His armor might have protected him from the worst of the effects, but he had been stripped of it on arrival.

Tararnifal could sense Dairnehy probing his adversary's mind, but the focus was so intense that he could not tap into the thoughts being transferred. What secrets was Danosh giving up? He barely dared to think himself, for fear that Dairnehy would cut into his thoughts.

Dairnehy had to be removed, probably killed, but Tararnifal had to make sure his prin-el and other supporters were also subdued. Without his own supporters ready,

Tararnifal himself would be killed. His only true ally in Rubiel was Kular, who had made small inroads with others who secretly opposed their leader. Unfortunately, none among them were leaders, and certainly none could take over Dairnehy's role if Tararnifal was killed for his insurrection.

Although he'd seen moments where Punad might have secretly questioned their leader's methods, the prin-el had never shown disloyalty to Dairnehy, and couldn't be counted on to support a coup.

Maybe Aderen could repeat the impossible feat he'd accomplished with Sebenet's fleet in Terran orbit. But it was too dangerous for Aderen here. Tararnifal studied this torture device. A human would not live long in such a machine.

The vekornan leader went to another machine, and Tararnifal moved to stop him. **That will kill Danosh.**

He is dead to us, except for the information that he carries, responded Dairnehy. **As with our wrist lasers, this will slow the blood flow to his brain. However, it will not kill all of the blood cells. At its lowest setting, small numbers of cells will die, making it more difficult for oxygen to reach his brain. It will not kill him until I desire his death.**

Physically, Danosh didn't change when the device was activated; psychologically, he was suffering. The intense pain, which few vekorna had ever experienced, was seeping out of the telepathic emitters on his sensor head. Tararnifal wondered again what information he was giving up.

Despite instructions to the contrary, Dairnehy's prin-el entered the isolation chamber. Punad glanced at Danosh with three eyestalks as he turned to their leader. Tararnifal didn't hear the exchange, but Dairnehy switched off the torture machines and turned to leave.

The humans have finally arrived, he said, and Tararnifal was disappointed at yet another defeat. Aderen had not received his message about the dangers of coming to this city. **Punad will greet them, and we will watch their approach from the control room.**

*   *   *

They have come to take the remains of the stellar fragment, which was left behind in their haste to escape the last time, said Dairnehy, watching the scene outside the shield.

The shuttle, which had come from Megnat, over the remains of Tilireval in the deadly ocean, and crossed over Nepral's shores, was following a similar trajectory as Tararnifal had many days ago, intent on infiltrating Rubiel.

They are moving exceptionally slow, said Sebenet.

They know of Rubiel's defenses, and do not want to get caught as we did, Tararnifal responded. Normal telepathic interfaces to the defense command computers refused to accept his mental imprint.

They come willingly, said Dairnehy. **Once I have Aderen, I will send troops to get the other like him from the deserts of Megnat. I will use them to regain the kolb and wingless pieces of the stellar fragment, and harness their power to eradicate all who oppose me.**

Keeping his thoughts compartmentalized so Dairnehy couldn't reach them without a tremendous struggle, Tararnifal said, **Aderen is here to negotiate a treaty with you, an agreement that will keep all vekorna away from Terra forever. He is not here for the fragment, and will be wary of a trap.**

The shuttle suddenly jerked to a stop high above the desert. It pitched down precariously, cracks appearing along its hull.

And yet he is caught, said Dairnehy, extending one eyestalk toward Tararnifal.

It appears that Aderen isn't as wary as you believe, Sebenet added.

Tararnifal watched as the shuttle was forced to the ground, and Punad led five vekorna to the ramp.

"The shuttle is empty," said Punad as his troops entered.

Dairnehy turned to Tararnifal. **What game are they playing?**

Tararnifal was just as confused, and extended four eyestalks to look at Punad's screens. He then realized that he and Dairnehy were alone.

Where is Sebenet? he asked.

*   *   *

The interrupters formed a triangular door over the ramp-shaped hump of sand at the base of Rubiel's shield.

"Do you think they took the bait?" Étar asked.

"We would know if they spotted us," Aderen answered. Kuyi was still sifting sand from her hair after rolling through a dune when she'd jumped from the shuttle.

"They'll know where we entered," Étar said, pointing at the three hover-scooters. "Are you sure you don't want to bring them inside the shield? We could go anywhere, fast."

Étar was right, but two of them were damaged from the fall, despite the makeshift padding they'd used. The trek had taken longer than expected, and they were all tired.

"How far to the ruins of old Rubiel?" he asked. Aneya and Jye-Tan looked to the north, shading their eyes against the bright desert sands.

"A couple of hours on foot," she said. "Then a full day along the road to Rubiel." Distances within the shield were larger than he'd realized.

Only Jye-Tan and Aneya knew where they'd hidden Dairnehy's piece of the stellar fragment, and it was not guaranteed to be inside the city. The single undamaged scooter might be useful if he had to take off quickly.

"Okay, we'll take them."

Étar and Kuyi smiled as they crossed through the hole again and brought the scooters inside.

Jye-Tan looked at the hole. "Do we just leave the interrupters there, too?" he asked.

"Unless somebody stays outside, we'll only end up with two of them in here," Aderen said. "And that's not going to get us out. Either we leave the hole, or we destroy the interrupters."

"We're here to negotiate with Dairnehy," Pinoa reminded them. "If we are successful, he will let us out. If not, I doubt we will have a chance to get back to this hole. I think we should destroy them."

"I agree," said Étar. "We can't let Dairnehy get his hands on these. It would give him direct access anywhere in Bol."

Jye-Tan looked disappointed, but watched without complaint as Étar slid the two lower devices up to meet the third, and they all started humming.

"That's the energy buildup Doj mentioned," said Kuyi.

Aderen watched in fascination, but frowned as nothing happened, even as the sound rose in pitch. "Maybe it's not as dangerous as he thought." He felt his mind descending, and warded off what was surely another vision. Now wasn't the time, though he regretted what might be cut off as the shield closed.

"I think it just needs a little help," said Étar, pulling the small laser from his waist. As Aderen nodded, committing them to this course, Étar fired. The three interrupters exploded in sparks, and the view outside the shield disappeared.

"I see red from Rubiel's tower over there," Jye-Tan said, pointing. He pulled his feet from the sand irritably.

Étar and Kuyi were already on one hover-scooter, and Aderen joined Pinoa on a second. Aneya and Jye-Tan had trouble getting the third one to stay upright, but after a few tries, and a bit of leaning, they managed to get started. It would be a long ride like that.

Predictably, Aneya's hover-scooter failed first, dropping them to the ground suddenly, not far from the ruins. Fortunately, Aneya had anticipated the drop, and pitched them up and to one side. She skidded the scooter to a landing, keeping it upright as she scraped a trench in the sand.

"I guess we walk from here," Jye-Tan said, extricating himself from the trench. "At least I can stand without sinking." Aderen wondered how long the hard track would last.

"We all walk from here," Étar said. "We can't afford to be separated."

"Watch out!" Kuyi yelled. Laser blasts scattered them, Aneya and Jye-Tan falling into the small trench for cover.

Aderen reached for vekornan minds in the shuttles that had appeared out of nowhere as Étar and Pinoa split up, their hover-scooters weaving to get away. He felt nothing – no thoughts, no disciplined minds. Was he so predictable to the vekorna because Dairnehy knew the secret to his mental abilities?

Pinoa almost threw him off as she dodged their pursuit, but Aderen knew she had to circle around to protect Aneya and Jye-Tan. Their scooter bucked as it was hit.

"Jump!" Pinoa buzzed, already up from her seat. Aderen jumped with her, rolling as he hit the hard surface. Their scooter fell to the ground, scattering pieces across the sand.

Running back as best they could, they watched helplessly as Étar flew through a hail of laser fire, disintegrating their scooter's front end. He and Kuyi flipped over, narrowly escaping their engine as it flew over them.

They had regrouped near Aneya's scooter when the shuttles landed and ramps descended.

"This was always a risk," Aderen reminded them. As he stepped behind Pinoa, he noted Kuyi's satisfaction amid her fear. Thanks to her, he was falling back into his role as influencer, not manipulator. She didn't realize it was because he was limiting vekornan access to his thoughts.

One mind grew clear among the mirror crystal dampening, and Aderen seized on it, softening his resolve, making him more susceptible to Pinoa's suggestions. The mind was familiar.

This time I have *you* at a disadvantage, said Sebenet.

Aderen pushed deeper into his surface thoughts, seeing everything he'd changed back in Terran orbit gone, flushed out by loyalty to Dairnehy. Then Sebenet's mind faded from his vision.

Étar fired his laser, cracking two mirror crystals as more vekorna disembarked from the shuttle. Sebenet raised his wrist laser and returned fire. Hit in the arm, Étar dropped the laser as his hand grew numb. The other vekorna fired on them indiscriminately. Aderen toppled Pinoa to the sand, trying to get them under cover. He felt the diffuse beam wash over him, and instructed his kennis to keep the blood flowing.

The effects of vekornan wrist lasers had not appeared immediately on the few humans who had been hit before the kolb war. Designed to stop blood flow from vekornan skin, where it was absorbed, to the brain, where it was used, on humans it temporarily depleted blood oxygen, causing tingling and eventually fainting and sickness.

With the diffuse hits they were taking, Aderen felt faint and confused. He reached fully for Sebenet's mind, but the mirror crystals inhibited his reach as they closed around the small group.

Aderen flinched as he felt a sharp vekornan pincer hand grab him by the shoulder.

44. Surrender

Tararnifal watched the shuttle descend to a smooth landing between the city's arms, amid more than a hundred vekornan soldiers, many of them holding mirror crystals. How was he supposed to combat this kind of devotion?

Punad stepped forward as the shuttle's ramp opened.

"Parachutes and artificial wings," Sebenet said as he exited the shuttle triumphantly, his metallic voice, necessary amid so many mirror crystals, loud in the otherwise silent space. "That is why they slowed their approach."

It must have been. Why hadn't he seen their strategy, and distracted Dairnehy and Sebenet? Tararnifal vowed never to explain human customs again. He extended three eyestalks toward Aderen and Pinoa as the humans stumbled out, clearly still dazed after being shot. Tararnifal's reassurances that he was still working to help them were attenuated before his thoughts extended far. It was unfortunate that vekorna couldn't connect directly to kennis nodes; his interface was still hidden on the extar they'd brought to Rubiel, dormant.

Étar was next out, falling to his knees and vomiting onto the tarmac, more affected by wrist laser hits than the others. Kuyi rushed to help him up.

Tararnifal was surprised that Aderen would bring Jye-Tan to Rubiel, giving Dairnehy another chance to find the missing fragment. He'd never met the last human, but Dairnehy recognized Aneya as an Egalsan who had helped Jye-Tan escape after hiding the fragmented crystal.

Sarenie was not here, so negotiations would fall to Pinoa, if Dairnehy gave her the chance. Aderen would not get to influence Dairnehy to her advantage, the way he had with Arnatak in the kolb's orbital fleet. It was likely that Aderen knew about mirror crystals, and had been hoping to circumvent them by sneaking through the shield. Thanks to Sebenet's brief education in the human corridor, that plan had been thwarted. Dairnehy would be doubly protected by mirror crystals from now on.

"This isn't the welcome I was hoping for," said Aderen, standing defiantly, as if Dairnehy had agreed to a meeting of equals.

"But it is probably the one you were expecting," Dairnehy responded immediately, his metallic voice reverberating across the landing pad. "You are here with the thieves. I have turned your allies to my side; they will not help you steal the rest of my stellar fragments." To the guards around them, he added, "Take him to the tower."

Punad extended two eyestalks toward Aderen, and

another two toward the elevated platform where Tararnifal and Dairnehy stood. Was he wondering about the torture machine? With the mirror crystals, maybe he was reading too much into the gesture.

"We don't care about the stellar fragment," Aderen shouted from below. "Pinoa is here to negotiate the enforcement of Terra's borders, forever."

"I told you that was his goal," Tararnifal said.

"There will be no negotiation," said Dairnehy. "I will find the remains of the fragment, and use it to see all of your thoughts." He made a hand gesture, and six guards detached from the circle around the shuttles, cutting Aderen off from the others with their mirror crystals. Punad went to grab Aderen, but he shook him off and, with an intent look at Pinoa, probably buzzing her, he walked ahead.

"Will we house the others in their usual place?" Tararnifal asked. He needed to get Pinoa alone. Bringing Jye-Tan and Aneya here made him doubt their intentions. While Aderen was imprisoned, would they go searching for the missing piece of the stellar fragment?

"Take them to their rooms, while I deal with the telepath."

His first task would be to convince Pinoa that he was not a traitor, even if she knew he had a role in Danosh's capture. If they worked together, Tararnifal might be able to depose Dairnehy while he was distracted by the humans. Kular was now running out of time in his search for vekorna willing to help them.

"Sebenet will accompany you," said Dairnehy. To argue would have raised Dairnehy's suspicions, but he couldn't confide in Pinoa with Sebenet around. He would have to wait, or try to convert Sebenet, something he had been unsuccessful at so far.

*   *   *

They took the high-speed passage down the arm of the city where the first four human crews had once lived. Tararnifal tried to scan their surface thoughts, but the Egalsan were as opaque as at Egalra, and the two Arais had jumbled, incoherent thoughts. He didn't chance a telepathic conversation, for fear that Sebenet would pick up on it.

The four humans didn't speak either.

Instead, Tararnifal questioned Sebenet privately. **Why did you betray them?**

Their scooters were failing, and I saved them the difficult walk in the sand. They are here to negotiate with Dairnehy. Sneaking into the shield was counter to their purpose.

So is holding them hostage. You do not have their purpose in mind.

I have Rykol's purpose in mind, snapped Sebenet. **Dairnehy is our leader, and needs the stellar fragment to bring stability. The humans know where the rest of it is, and want to establish Terran boundaries. Negotiations are already under way.**

They would have been easier if you had not interfered.

I would not let Aderen do to Dairnehy what he did to me. They entered the human corridor, and Sebenet pointed two eyestalks at the murals, singling one out in particular.

Parachutes and artificial wings, Sebenet said,

"Yes, you were very clever," Pinoa responded, keeping her eyes straight ahead.

Initiating contact, Tararnifal asked, **How did you break through the shield?**

"Special folem tools," Pinoa said, taunting him. It was unlikely the folems would sanction an infiltration like this. She didn't trust him, rightly so.

I saw you destroy something attached to the shield, said Sebenet. **The folems did not give you sufficient tools to complete your task.**

"How can you be sure?" Pinoa asked with raised eyebrows, entering *Avenger*'s old quarters. Her face flushed. "What happened here?" Tararnifal was almost glad for the distraction. "Are we supposed to live in this disaster?"

Jye-Tan's gaze went directly to the ceiling, and he frowned.

"We found the crystals you placed in the hidden compartment," said Sebenet. "There is nothing left for you here." He didn't mention the void areas, nor their suspicion about a second part of the fragment.

He took advantage of Sebenet's distraction to send a private thought to Pinoa. **I am working to remove Dairnehy from power.** She didn't react, but was watching Jye-Tan.

Jye-Tan's reaction told him that they were right –the fragment they found in the ceiling must be a decoy. Aneya was holding him close, worried, but his face did not show the kind of disappointment it should have if they'd found everything.

Tararnifal was thankful that Sebenet didn't have the experience to read a human's facial expressions, yet they had been operating on this assumption all along. Sebenet had not found anything in the void areas around Rubiel, but he hadn't stopped searching.

How long did he have before Dairnehy was finished

with Aderen? He thought of the torture device currently holding Danosh. How long would Jye-Tan last there before revealing the location of the missing fragment?

Defiant, Jye-Tan wiggled out of Aneya's grip to step forward. "So Dairnehy returned the fragment to the crystal room in the basement." He was playing a charade, but it was interesting that the boy knew about Dairnehy's secret room. He had regained strength quickly after being shot with vekornan wrist lasers. It confirmed that the Egalsan had received kennis implants, which could heal them much more rapidly than natural.

We found macrobots and other human equipment, most of it explicitly prohibited, in the ceiling compartment, said Sebenet, still watching Jye-Tan with three eyestalks.

Pinoa nodded sharply, but said nothing. Perhaps she hadn't known about the compartment, like the vekorna. Pinoa hadn't been popular during her time on Rykol, coordinating the human side of the kolb war. Many from the older crews resented her assigning them tasks, and did not follow her lead. It was possible the *Avenger* or *Kamsar* crews had hidden some of their activities from her.

"You may dwell in any of the human quarters. The others are in storage mode since the last time humans were here," said Tararnifal.

"When will I see Dairnehy for negotiations?" asked Pinoa, stepping forward.

I will try, but you know what he wants, Tararnifal chanced privately to her. At the same time, he opened his telepathic voice to all, hiding his private message. **There will be no negotiations. Jye-Tan and Aneya must remain in the human section. Shields have been erected at**

367

either end to prevent you from leaving. Vekorna will come to debrief you about the last time you were here. Jye-Tan's eyes widened in surprise, and he was about to say something, but Tararnifal cut him off. **Pinoa, Étar and Kuyi may be asked to participate in other discussions.** He would insist on being present, and would allow them to turn those discussions into negotiations.

"I want to go to the garden," said Jye-Tan. "We need food."

You may go hungry, said Tararnifal. What was the boy after? He wasn't aware of any void areas near the garden. Maybe the boy was thinking of his human stomach, but maybe there was more to it. **However, I will see if Dairnehy will permit it.**

He turned and walked away from the humans, Sebenet following. Interrogation would come quickly, and he needed to be part of it, to find out what the humans were doing.

He ensured the forcefields were active at either end of the corridor, and that guards were monitoring all human activities. Dairnehy would not be able to accuse him of being a traitor, yet kennis signals would still penetrate, as shields did not encircle the rooms on all sides.

45. Rebel Thoughts

"Aderen is safe, but confined, and surrounded by mirror crystals," Étar buzzed, displaying an image of Aderen's room.

Kuyi hoped Aderen was alright, as he wouldn't buzz her. Dairnehy might do anything to him, but if Aderen found a crack in the mirror crystals, would he take full control of the vekornan leader's body? Their situation had changed since his promise to be subtle.

She put a hand on Étar's shoulder, hugging him. She was a little light-headed from being shot by the vekornan wrist lasers, but that was dissipating thanks to her kennis. Étar had been affected almost immediately, but whispered, "I'm fine."

He was recovering quickly, but his mind was distracted, and she knew he'd been negligent about his mental exercises. Any secrets he harbored would be known to Dairnehy by the end of the day. Including...

"How is the kennis node still active if Sebenet and Tararnifal have turned on you?" she buzzed. "Do you think he can monitor it?"

"No," Pinoa buzzed immediately. "Tararnifal sent me a telepathic message telling me that he was still on our side. Maybe hiding knowledge of the kennis is part of his strategy. I need to get him alone for a proper assessment."

Jye-Tan walked through the debris, pushing it to the side to make a path. The hole in the ceiling had dropped tools and pieces, stale food and medicine, and shattered mirror crystals.

"Look at the mess they made," he said aloud.

"I'm surprised that Dairnehy didn't repossess these rooms after we left Rykol," said Pinoa.

Kuyi followed the path Jye-Tan and Aneya were making to the personal alcoves, small rooms off the main one. They had been ransacked, but were free of debris.

"We used these rooms when we visited Rubiel to harvest from its garden," she said.

"I think we used the old *Alnevar* quarters," Jye-Tan corrected. She turned away from him as he shifted a mattress back into place in one of the alcoves.

Étar and Pinoa started picking pieces from the floor, examining them. If they were buzzing, Kuyi wasn't part of the conversation. They would have to move fast, before the winged fished any strategies from the two Arai minds.

Putting a long white tube with wires at one end onto the worktable, Pinoa said, "I'm going to check the other rooms. I'll let you know when I need your help. So far, Dairnehy is keeping Aderen isolated, impatient." She smiled gravely as she disappeared from *Avenger*'s quarters.

"I'll join you," said Étar, squeezing Kuyi's hand and running after her, leaving the three Egalsan alone.

They started tidying up. Jye-Tan moved into another alcove, and buzzed Kuyi and Aneya. "They found the decoy, and I think Tararnifal recognizes that it wasn't the large piece of the fragment."

"There's more?" Kuyi asked.

"One more," Aneya answered. "Why did you ask about the garden? That's the last place we should go."

"Because it's always the first place we go," Jye-Tan said. "It would be more suspicious if we didn't."

Neither Aneya nor Jye-Tan would reveal where the fragment was hidden, but Kuyi now had a good idea. It was the most obvious location, because it was where humans spent the most time at Rubiel. Why hadn't Dairnehy found it, then?

Aderen's goal was to prevent Dairnehy and future vekorna from ever going back to Terra. Trapped between mirror crystals, he would have to use words and arguments, with little to trade, until Jye-Tan could hack into Rubiel's network, the way he'd done at Bol. But it would only work if Pinoa could join him as negotiator.

That wasn't Kuyi's goal.

Aderen had brought her to keep her safe from Ontral. He hadn't given her any tasks, the way he'd instructed Pinoa to negotiate, Étar to find a way out of Rubiel, and Jye-Tan to hack into the network. Kuyi and Aneya were bystanders.

The side effects of using Ontral's piece of the fragment had been severe, but Aderen didn't realize how badly he'd been affected. He still thought it was like any other long-distance telepathy crystal the vekorna used.

Aderen admitted that chasing after Ontral's fragment had been a mistake. He didn't need the fragment to make the mental changes, assuming he could get away from the mirror crystals. Aderen still hadn't connected Treklay's death with his use of the fragment, only the way he'd been disconnected from it, thanks to Kuyi's efforts with the electrostatic machine.

But Kuyi saw the temptation in his eyes, the same look that still haunted Jye-Tan at times, even as he talked about the decoy fragment. If Jye-Tan went to the garden, he wouldn't be able to hold back. He would seek it out, and then Dairnehy would have it. Aderen wouldn't be able to do anything.

Grabbing the white metal tube that Pinoa had been handling, Kuyi wondered how Aderen had been able to control all of Sebenet's fleet at Terra. How had he made mental changes to all those vekorna, spread across five extars, when he couldn't control a handful of wingless so close by? Something had happened to degrade his abilities. She couldn't believe it was her influence, or the trauma she'd experienced with the cloned creatures. He'd managed to control the folems, after all. No, it had to be more fundamental than that. Had Danosh's mirror crystals affected him? Or something the kolbs did? Or even before that, like cryo-sleep? He wasn't forthcoming about what he could do, just like Kirina, so she could only guess.

She knew, though, that even though he feigned wanting to complete his mission without the fragment, he was still hoping for a way to get it and use it.

Slapping the white tube into the palm of her other hand, she used her kennis to start calculations beyond what she'd ever done before. She didn't know the formulae, but her kennis did. It made assumptions based on generic data about stellar cores, fused carbon silica, diamonds, and more.

The rod in her hands had been part of Doj's macrobot. Lightweight and strong, it wouldn't be enough. Nothing on-hand had the strength to destroy a piece of a star. The kolbs had used shuttle lasers to break it into smaller pieces, but little of it had been destroyed. She sat down on a mattress in one of the alcoves, hand on her forehead, as she realized she would need a large explosion to vaporize the fragment. It would be impossible, even if they weren't being constantly watched.

"Are you okay?" Aneya asked, coming up to her.

"I'm overwhelmed," she said out loud. Silently, she buzzed her aunt, "You were here last time. What did you think of Jye-Tan's behavior? Why did you help him?"

"He and Gavet had already stolen the fragments when I got involved. They'd stuffed mirror crystals in the ceiling and –" She stopped suddenly.

"And in the garden. I figured that much out, and Tararnifal will soon, too, I think," Kuyi buzzed, making Aneya start. "You had no choice but to go along when Jye-Tan and Gavet went for the fragments."

Aneya stared at her, but used her kennis to show she was

mentally nodding. "Do you think Gavet touched the fragment?" Kuyi asked.

"We all did."

It was Kuyi's turn to stare at her second-born aunt. When she recovered, she asked, "Did you feel what Jye-Tan did?"

"Yes, but not as much as Jye-Tan. Gavet neither. We had to get it away from Dairnehy."

"How did you come in contact with the fragments in the first place? I can't believe Dairnehy let a human near them."

"He did. I don't know why, and he didn't tell us what it was, but he brought us to the crystals himself."

Still staring at her aunt, Kuyi asked, "How much of this did you tell Nalimai and Egalinsor?"

"All of it. They forbade us from saying anything, and even suggested that Egalinsor could help us forget the incident –permanently. I was too afraid of his ability, even now. Every time he touched me, I wondered if I would lose part of my mind, so I kept quiet."

"Even though Jye-Tan talks about the fragment all the time."

Aneya was keeping tears out of her good eye by force of will alone. Kuyi leaned over and hugged her.

"I'm sorry to have brought it up, but thank you."

Aneya withdrew. "It feels good talking to somebody about it. When did you get so good at listening and probing our feelings?"

It took a moment to respond. "The moment Aderen stepped out of that shuttle on Egalra," she buzzed.

"From babysitter to spy," Aneya said, pulling her fingers through Kuyi's fine black hair.

"Now I have to ask about your much younger life," Kuyi buzzed. "You, Gavet and Lusava did research with weapons at Ban way before I was birthed."

Aneya nodded, and Kuyi knew they had to start doing something. If the vekorna were watching, they would get suspicious of the long silence.

"Are any of your inventions at Rubiel?" She flashed her desire to her aunt.

"The mechanical hoist to heft a vekornan blaster? I don't think so. Why? What are you thinking of doing, young one."

"Don't call me that," Kuyi snapped, not able to put the appropriate emphasis to her kennis voice. "I need something that can destroy the stellar fragment. It's the only way to help Aderen and Jye-Tan. It's the only way to reduce this war to something that can be negotiated."

"The fragment gives each side hope that they can win," Aneya buzzed, understanding. "I know the pull it has on Jye-Tan. I see the same pull on Aderen. I'll help you."

Kuyi put a hand on Aneya's deformed one, and stood, relishing her decision to do something, rather than wait around for somebody to pull her strings.

Walking over to Jye-Tan in the common room, where he was organizing tools, Kuyi asked out loud, "Did you find anything useful?"

"Most macrobot pieces have been removed," Jye-Tan buzzed. "I was hoping to use them."

"For what?" Kuyi asked.

Jye-Tan shrugged as he gathered some tools onto a worktable, thumbing a laser welder on and off. "I'm not sure yet," he said.

Buzzing this time, and sharing with Aneya, she asked

Jye-Tan, "Any luck breaking into Rubiel's systems?"

"No, but I'm still working on it. It would be easier if I had access to their telepathic controls. The kennis interface is being rebuffed without a tactile link."

Walking toward them, Aneya brushed hair out of her eyes. "Everything useful has been removed," she buzzed. Out loud, she said, "I'm going to check the medical ward."

Kuyi's kennis whirled down a different path from lasers and explosives. She suspected even if she could gather the right materials, only Étar had experience building a bomb. But Yenine had accumulated many different chemicals in the medical ward for procedures, not just on the body, but on tissue and blood samples. Was there anything in those rooms that could dissolve the diamond-hard stellar fragment?

She asked for status reports from Étar and Pinoa.

"The hidden compartments in *Alnevar* and *Siberath*'s rooms have not been touched," Pinoa responded. "We have not inventoried them, but Doj said he hid macrobot pieces in each of the crew quarters."

"Is there a functioning macrobot anywhere?"

"I'm not sure," Pinoa said. "Étar is looking."

"According to Jye-Tan, he might need to touch an interface for a proper connection," Kuyi buzzed. "A macrobot might be the solution."

"We'll need a distraction to get into the compartments, though," buzzed Pinoa.

"We'll work on that," Kuyi responded. To Jye-Tan, she asked, "Did you hear?"

He nodded, still examining the parts on the worktable.

"We should have brought Doj," Kuyi buzzed. It was another mistake in a pile of poor decisions by Aderen. Her grandfather would have identified everything he'd hidden so long ago.

There were no vekorna in the hallways, probably not in the entire human section. Kuyi didn't have any illusions as to their freedom, though. She'd been here a few times when she was younger, always overnight, to harvest from the gardens. She'd never been allowed to tag along with Nalimai and Egalinsor and the others to spread genetically modified seeds or to take samples. When she wasn't too young, she'd been watching over Jye-Tan and Mai.

Looking over her shoulder back into the room, Kuyi saw Jye-Tan hunched over the worktable, engrossed in his task. Things hadn't changed that much, she sighed.

The drawings and paintings in the hallway had always fascinated Kuyi, even as a young girl. There were things here she couldn't conceive, like the large animals, water dropping from the sky, the concept of ice and lakes freezing over so a person could walk on it, and the depiction of sports played in front of thousands of people –not on a beach, but in a place built specifically for that. Nalimai told stories about each of the drawings, but only when asked. Terran society was so much richer than what they allowed on Rykol.

If only the birth chambers had remained intact, they could have made a true human colony on Rykol. Nalimai and Egalinsor had been afraid to do it, understandable given the indiscriminate way the vekornan wars destroyed everything. But humanity wasn't starting from zero. She looked at the drawings of huge technological machines, thought about what Nalimai had created near their homes, and wondered if they could have carved out a minor continent or two of their own. It wouldn't be as easy as that, she knew, moving down the hall.

"Kuyi, come see me," buzzed Aneya. "I may have something."

Kuyi turned immediately toward the medical ward. What she was planning was very dangerous, and she hated keeping this from Étar, but his mind was too open to the vekorna.

She couldn't wait for Jye-Tan and Étar to crack Rubiel's network security. She had to be prepared for Aderen to fail, because he was too worried about the fragment.

46. Debate

Wanting to pace and rage against the walls at his stupidity, Aderen reigned himself in. He'd learned at a very young age to channel his anger mentally, and avoid outward signs of how he felt.

Instead, he lashed out with his mind at the mirror crystals lining his prison. The honeycomb panels absorbed his mental energy, giving nothing in return.

Despite his anger, Aderen was impressed at Dairnehy's preparedness. Having Sebenet shoot them with wrist lasers reduced their ability to concentrate, as they dealt with uniquely human side-effects, which his kennis was still countering.

Meanwhile, the room was completely sealed, mechanically and telepathically. Despite Jye-Tan's advice, the room didn't contain anything that could shatter the crystals. His limited experience at Esetek hadn't led him to believe a room could be made from them.

For a moment just before their capture, the crystals had been misaligned. Sebenet had done that on purpose, to taunt him, but he'd managed to slip into the vekornan's mind.

Surprise at how much of his earlier changes had been reverted slowed him down, and by the time he'd touched a few sensitive thought centers, the mirror crystals had closed in. He didn't know if the light touch had achieved anything.

Aderen had no illusions as to their fate in Rubiel. At the same time, he wondered what kind of experience Dairnehy had with Kirina that made him so cautious. Did he know the full extent of her abilities because he'd nurtured them before she was born?

How he longed for Monera's mental touch now, cut off from the world!

In the silence, worries about those still inside Bol tugged at Aderen through his guilt. He'd made too many mistakes, too many changes, and left in too much of a hurry. What price were they paying for his actions?

Tararnifal's single message showed that it was hard to synchronize the kennis when one shield blinked open. The chances of getting through two shields in time for useful communication were miniscule. Doj was a miracle worker, but the kennis wasn't designed for those modifications.

Fortunately, Tararnifal had managed to smuggle a kennis node into the city, which meant none of them were truly alone. Yet after helping to capture Danosh, Aderen wondered if the vekornan could still be trusted.

"Jye-Tan is busy with something, but he won't say what," Pinoa buzzed. He welcomed the distraction. "You should speak with him."

"Not now; with the mirror crystals, I can't influence Dairnehy, and I don't know how well my mental blocks will hold. I'd rather not have too much information."

"At Bol, he hacked into the city using a tactile interface that responded to vekornan telepathy."

"Have him try the doors. They are telepathically activated, and may be connected to the city."

"I'll do that," Pinoa buzzed. "I'm also helping Ret look for a distraction for when we need to get to a shuttlebay in a hurry. At this rate, I'm not going to be doing much negotiating, but buzz me if Dairnehy talks about Terra."

"I'll see what I can do," buzzed Aderen, signing off. What other surprises did Dairnehy have for him?

He stood and stretched, paced the circular room with its domed ceiling, then sat back on his knees, cradling his body between the deep soles of his feet. His kennis ensured they wouldn't be stiff if he needed to move fast.

Closing his eyes, calming his mind, ignoring his kennis, Aderen probed for holes in the room where his telepathy could reach outside to other minds. Not all of the panels were mirror crystals, but the fields overlapped, reflecting his thoughts and probes back. They were strongest in the center, and faded at the edges, never weak enough to let his mind through. He wondered when the vekorna had become proficient at keeping prisoners.

Was this why the siims had rebelled and tried to escape vekornan control? Maybe they were always like this, and his parents hadn't known the vekorna well at all.

When the door slid open, Aderen wasn't ready. He enlarged his consciousness, seeking the hole that the door created, but wasn't fast enough. He detected three vekornan minds outside before the door shut, skimming their surface thoughts, revealing an underlying fear. Of what?

His mind walled up again, Aderen remained seated and looked up at the imposing figure of the approaching vekornan. Dairnehy's mind was blocked.

Dairnehy stopped three long vekornan paces from

Aderen, and lowered himself onto all six of his supporting limbs. He spread his wings wide, casting shadows over Aderen's face.

This was what Tararnifal meant, saying Dairnehy had changed. Vekorna didn't understand human psychology enough to try intimidation. When the kolbs had captured his parents, they used terror to torture, but not intimidation. Dairnehy had spent the last two centuries learning this somewhere.

"Do you know your origins?" the metallic voice pierced the silence of the room. Aderen had his kennis damp out part of the voice, so the edge didn't hurt his eardrums.

"Do you know yours?" Aderen asked, shifting onto his knees, suddenly glad for the mirror crystals. How could he get Dairnehy to tell him if there was a more fundamental connection than he'd realized?

"I contain the original genes of my species, ensured pure through the efforts of the winged vekorna in Metik. But you were manipulated within a living incubator."

Even though he knew that Dairnehy was trying to get him angry, that slight on his mother upset him. He wanted to lash out at the vekornan. There was no way, though, not yet. They were both handicapped here.

"Kopiv manipulated my brain as it was forming, making me into what I am now," he said instead, breathing evenly to calm his anger. He knew the vekornan could read his heart rate and blood flow through ancillary senses, and had his kennis do a better job of regulating it. He'd already given away too much. "I'm lucky to be alive."

"That is correct. Kopiv's first experiment failed."

"Salma died, you mean."

"Was she ever alive?"

The fact that Kopiv had been able to manipulate his brain meant he *had* been alive, and so had she. That he'd been able to communicate with his mother, and how Nalimai connected with Kirina and her next, unnamed child, proved that they had all been alive. Dairnehy was keeping his thoughts focused on one thing, the wrong thing.

It was time to change the subject.

"I'm here to negotiate an end to your intrusions into Terra's solar system. But you've locked me away from my chief negotiator."

He wanted to let Pinoa into the kennis link, but not if Dairnehy was going to talk about his origins. He didn't want to think about what would happen if others found out that his abilities were due to vekornan interference. They wouldn't trust his manipulations, any more than he did anymore. Worse, other vekorna might learn of it and try their own experiments. But his failure while trying to keep it from Treklay still haunted him.

"Pinoa was good at strategy, which helped us win the war against the wingless kolbs," said Dairnehy. "I am interested in the strategy she intends to use this time."

"Let her in here and we can start negotiations."

"There are no negotiations. You cannot stop me from sending extars to Terra."

"Except that you have no extars, do you? You let the kolbs have them all, in exchange for your stellar fragment, which you promptly lost to the wingless."

Dairnehy's wings shifted.

"How much of the fragment is still on Rykol?" Aderen asked, wishing for Pinoa's input. "How much do the wingless have compared to you? Ontral wants your piece of the fragment. He thinks we can negotiate it away from you."

"Impossible. You would do better to negotiate theirs away from Bol."

"Ontral would say that's impossible."

"The youngest Egalsan hid the largest piece of our fragment, but it has been found. Your negotiation tactics are poorly formulated."

Was Dairnehy convinced that the piece they found was the only one? Pinoa hadn't said if the vekorna were still searching.

"But you would like a way to gain the other pieces, wouldn't you?"

"Why promise something that you cannot obtain?" Dairnehy asked, his wings twitching again.

Aderen had never seen the Terran vekorna twitch their wings. Were Dairnehy's wings like a dog's tail, unconsciously showing his thoughts? He had to be careful attributing human emotions to vekorna.

"Ontral doesn't have mirror crystals," Aderen said, sweeping his arm around the room. "He has other defenses, but I found a way inside the Temple of Spall, and found his piece of the stellar fragment. I've touched it."

Dairnehy's wings twitched again, and he moved his front arms closer to where Aderen knelt, neck straining to look at the vekornan's silver faceplate.

"You have no fear of me," Dairnehy said. "Your pulse and heartbeat have stabilized to an uncompromised rhythm. Is it because you believe that you can defeat the mirror crystals? I assure you that you cannot." The vekornan leader raised his upper arms off the ground, stretching high enough that Aderen decided to stand. He moved from knees to feet, backing up so he could see the four eyestalks peeking out of the triangular faceplate.

"Tararnifal assures me that you only want my promise that we will not return to Terra. Are you willing to kill for that promise?"

Aderen frowned. "What do you mean?"

"Your equal, the one that I created, wanders the deserts of Megnat. She is eager to kill vekorna. She holds her telepathy against us. But even as we speak, I shape her. With the stellar fragment back in my possession, I will complete her transformation, and the two of you will enforce my will."

"You're delusional," said Aderen in awe, wondering if together, their connection to the vekorna would be enhanced. Could they fall under Dairnehy's power? "The fragment enhances your existing telepathy, which for a vekornan is to read minds, not control them. You could not control Kirina, and you cannot control me." He poured conviction into his words, ensuring his body didn't betray him.

"I disagree. I've been controlling Kirina since she left Bol. We know where to find her. She kills those I periodically send to check on her mental development, which trains her by emotional reaction."

"Are you too scared to go yourself?" Aderen asked, wondering why he was provoking Dairnehy.

"As tigal-en, I can see into vekornan minds from a distance beyond her range. She killed my soldiers. You, however, are reluctant to kill. Bolob often felt the same, allowing enemies to remain close, even to gain power."

He extended his wings to the full diameter of the room.

"He made mistakes," admitted Aderen. "But he saved me in the end, sacrificed his life so that Terra could survive.

Would you do the same for Rykol?"

"I would save Terra, but not by sacrificing my life."

"You would save it to enslave it," said Aderen. "But we are no use to you, especially at the distance and time it takes to get to Terra and back. Kirina and I are the only two of our kind." He swallowed, pushing thoughts of Monera from his mind. "You sent Sebenet for an army of human slaves to fight in your war, but the war hadn't even started when they left Rykol."

"The fleets were sent long before the fragment revealed our plans to the wingless," Dairnehy answered, raising his middle arms, the top of his faceplate touching the uppermost part of the domed room. Aderen wondered if he would scrape through one, watched for a misalignment of crystals that would open his mind again.

"I was supposed to have eight extars full of humans," said Dairnehy. "Instead I got eleven individuals, some of whom cannot breed. I should have gone to Terra myself, where there are probably thousands of pregnant women for me to take and manipulate!"

His kennis wasn't strong enough to counteract the blood loss to Aderen's face, even as he almost laughed at Dairnehy's estimate, not understanding the scale of humanity. He turned pale, and his breathing came more rapidly. He needed support from everyone at Rubiel, but couldn't let them in on the debate. The thought of Dairnehy targeting pregnant women, altering their fetuses, was too much of a secret to bear alone, but he couldn't tell the others. He believed he wasn't compromised, but they might not understand.

He pushed that thought away, buried it deep to refocus on his purpose here. Without mental manipulation, he only had words.

"The war would be lost before you could return, and where would that leave you?" he asked, straightening his shoulders and staring at the fixed expression on the faceplate. "No fragment. No control over the humans you have here. I should be negotiating with the kolbs instead. Only they have the capacity to go to Terra."

A flick of his wings pushed Dairnehy away, back to the wall of the circular room. The gust of wind almost knocked Aderen over backward.

"Kolbs don't have the will to go to Terra. They don't understand the power you possess. They would bring back an army of weak humans."

"Humans who helped you win the war against the wingless kolbs," pressed Aderen.

Dairnehy dropped down in front of him again, wings outstretched. He flapped them so they nearly touched Aderen, and they settled half outstretched.

Blinking to adjust his eyes after the double onslaught of Dairnehy's wing-wash, Aderen was forced to take another step back.

"Humans hastened the end of that war, but it only needed hastening because Bolob was stalling," Dairnehy said. "We would have won in the end. My war is more honest."

"The war you've been losing since you used the fragment to peer into every mind on Rykol?" asked Aderen.

"If I combine the three remaining pieces of the stellar fragment, I can end this war."

"And you want my help to do it. You can't force me to manipulate either the wingless or the kolbs. Are you offering me a moratorium on travel to Terra if I help you gain them? How could I trust you to keep your word, especially after you gain the fragment?"

"I am not offering you a deal," said Dairnehy. "I told you there would be no negotiation. I now have human hostages."

"They knew what they were getting into."

"But did the fetus inside the female agree to those terms?" Dairnehy asked.

For the second time, Aderen was shocked. He went through the list of people he'd brought with him. Pinoa was sterile from the Information War on Terra before she came to Rykol. Aneya was probably too old. Was Kuyi pregnant? They hadn't been here that long. If true, Nalimai's birth control serum wasn't working. How could Étar be so careless? It took all his effort not to buzz Kuyi or Pinoa, to keep the information to himself.

He needed to get out of this domed room. Dairnehy would go to any length to gain the stellar fragments. Would he then return to Terra? Aderen's words were no good against Dairnehy. He'd always worked in the background, which was why he'd brought Pinoa and Sarenie. But he couldn't let them negotiate with Dairnehy, in case he brought up the fetal manipulation.

Would he kill Dairnehy to keep that secret, to protect human babies? He thought he would. But not here. Here he had no power. He had to give Jye-Tan time to crack vekornan security so they could get into the birth chambers.

Aderen turned around and settled again on his knees, his back to Dairnehy. "You're right," he said. "Negotiations are over. Come back when you have more than threats."

47.Supplies

The medical ward was probably the most human place on the planet, Kuyi thought, walking through the sliding doors. Vekorna didn't have doctors, as they almost always died within hours of a serious injury. Those who didn't were killed, the almond-shaped seeds around their necks harvested for the next generation in birth chambers, more important than their lives. Danosh was a particular exception, living and allowing the folems to regrow the two arms he lost in the shuttle crash with Nalimai.

Kuyi reached up to her own neck. She didn't have seed-pods, though she was also matured from a birth chamber. Would she die here, like Gavet, trying to do something with the hidden fragment?

Humans had used this room often. Kuyi remembered coming here so Nalimai could check her insides after she started vomiting. It was still the place most suited on Rykol for medical inspection. Yenine, at one time the only doctor on the planet, had stocked the room with everything she could think of to ward off human ailments on a hostile alien planet. Xeffeya could probably use some of these supplies.

The chairs and beds were familiar, similar to what was used in the Egalsan homes. The machinery for looking inside a human body, testing tissue and cell samples, treating the problems of aging and decaying organs, had always looked fascinating, and she'd pestered Nailimai until she received some limited training. It suited her role as caregiver. Vekorna wouldn't know what to do with them.

Kuyi paused at the fetal ultrasound monitor, a device that hadn't been used since Tiralie died in Rykol's last natural childbirth. Everyone else came from birth chambers, a much safer way to bear children, and which allowed simpler introduction of alternate genes.

After Mai and Jye-Tan's unexpected genetic problems, though, Nalimai had stopped trying. The twins were the last. Kuyi thought she would be interested in trying again, creating life with Étar, implanting a fresh genetic mix. When she got back to the Egalsan compound at Bol, she would join Wandel at the birth chambers, and study what had gone wrong.

"Over here." Aneya's voice startled her out of her reverie, and she gripped the ultrasound machine tightly for a second before moving on.

Aneya was standing in front of large jars behind a glass door.

"Those are strong acids. What did Yenine use this for?" Kuyi asked, confirming the chemical structure through her kennis, as well as the limited potential medical uses. "Never mind," she said. How many of these machines and chemicals did humanity no longer need thanks to the kennis ability for diagnosis and treatment, she wondered. "What are you thinking?" she buzzed.

"Can we dissolve the fragment with these?"

She consulted her kennis again. "I don't think that would work, but even if it did, we'd need a lot more. The vekorna would catch us before that happened."

Smiling at her in the way an older aunt could, Aneya buzzed, "I love the way you're a natural with your kennis. I still struggle with it." She looked down at her hand and opened three fingers. "We don't know what the stellar fragment is made from, probably fused carbon ejected from deep within the star. I think acid might work, but we'd be very suspicious walking out of the city with all these jars. And you're right, it would take far more than this, and too much time."

She nodded down at the small cylinder in her hand. "This is a lot less conspicuous." She put it to Kuyi's palm where she felt a soft buzzing. "Ultrasonic waves, for breaking up hard cells and kidney stones, for the time before a kennis would prevent that kind of buildup." She knew about these.

"I thought about using a large hammer, but this would be easier," Kuyi buzzed. "I don't want to shatter it into pieces that the vekorna can gather again, to fuse into another telepathic crystal."

"Is it better than doing nothing?" Aneya asked. "Dairnehy will find the hidden fragment eventually, especially if Ontral is experimenting with the one in Bol, and Ret is testing the one the kolbs have." She passed the small cylinder to Kuyi, who pocketed it immediately. Aneya passed her a second. "I have two as well. Assuming we can crank them up strong enough, I think we'll need as many as we can."

Kuyi's mind raced. If they could somehow hide the smaller fragments, if they could crush it into dust that mixed into the soil, if they could get the crystal dust into the garden, bury it there, where it would be gripped by the powerful roots of the genetically engineered plants and vegetables, would it be gone forever? She shook her head. The vekorna would never let them bring shovel-loads of crystal dust into the garden.

"I've been thinking about normal crystals, too," buzzed Aneya. "We've altered the internal structure of crystals before, cracked their interiors."

Kuyi stared at her aunt, eyes narrowing as she fingered the small cylinder against her leg. "You think we can crack the insides instead of breaking it apart? How will that help us?"

"I think we can alter the fragment's structure, turning it into a regular crystal, making it useless to Dairnehy." Kuyi liked the idea, but worried that it was a theory based on scant evidence. "I've been running calculations on my kennis," Aneya continued, pointing to her temple. "I think seven or eight of these will be enough, which means we'll need help."

Kuyi felt her spirits drop. "Jye-Tan will never do it, and I'm not sure we can count on Pinoa and Étar for this. They'll tell Aderen, and I don't think he's given up on finding the fragment for his mission." She dropped her eyes to the ground. "I don't think he'll destroy it, or its usefulness."

Aneya grabbed some large elastic straps, the kind they would use to temporarily restrict blood flow to a large artery for downstream inspection. "We don't have extra arms like a vekornan. So if we can't get more arms, we'll have to attach them manually ourselves."

*   *   *

Tararnifal didn't return that night, though they were certainly being watched. Jye-Tan sat with his limited snacks, sharing with everyone. That, and the small roots she'd saved from the shuttle before she jumped, was all they would get until the vekorna allowed them into the garden. Fortunately, the medical ward still had running water, which Aneya provided.

Kuyi and Étar snuggled up together in one of *Kamsar*'s alcoves, taking advantage of the privacy the others accorded them.

After they'd made love, Kuyi gave them time before

breaking the bliss she felt, feeling his warmth.

"How are your mental exercises holding up?" she buzzed.

Étar knew what she meant. His mission was tenuous without the vekorna poking into his thoughts. "I think I'm holding the blocks in place," he buzzed. Fortunately, or maybe because of the lingering post-coital kennis euphoria, he wasn't insulted by her question. "I can't help the odd stray thought, but hope the rest of you are providing enough of a distraction so I can make my own."

Kuyi nodded, touching his nose, dragging her finger up to his forehead. "The vekorna will get bored with your mind if all they pick up are thoughts of me," she teased.

"That's the plan," Étar buzzed, kissing her. "I can't stop thinking of you, and hopefully that's all they'll get."

She regretted hiding her plans from him, but his inexperience dealing with Rykolien vekorna could put them all at risk.

"They know we want to get into their birth chambers, and to secure a shuttle to get away from Rubiel," he buzzed. "We've made that clear to Dairnehy's watchers already."

"We'll never get into Rubiel's birth chambers, even if Jye-Tan breaks through their security," she buzzed. "But do you think Dairnehy will let us go afterward?"

"It depends if Aderen can make him more susceptible to accepting the ultimatum. He needs to get Pinoa up there." His eyes rose to the ceiling, though he was certainly referring to Rubiel's tower.

Kuyi's kennis kept her heart beating steady, at the accelerated rate it always assumed in this state with Étar. "I've been gathering medical supplies and equipment to bring back to Bol," she said honestly. Every time she handled something in the medical ward, she wondered if it could be used to destroy or alter the structure of the fragment. She left that part out.

"That reminds me…" he buzzed.

She admired his physique as he slipped off the mattress and out of the alcove. He came back seconds later with water. She accepted, and replenished what she'd already lost to their private activities.

"We weren't counting on Jye-Tan, but it would have been nice," Étar buzzed, stroking her cheek, then her chin, and down her neck. As instructed, her kennis didn't stop the goosebumps from forming on her arms. She enjoyed the tingling sensation when he did that.

"It would make things easier," she responded, pressing up against him.

"I can't hide what I'm physically doing from the vekorna. As it is, I might be able to create a distraction with what I found in Doj's other hidden compartments."

"More of a distraction than this?" she asked, as she kissed him again, bringing him closer. He smiled as they reconnected their kennis, then their bodies, adjusting the chemical release into their brains that made the experience so much more than purely physical.

"There can't be more of a distraction than you," he buzzed.

48. Memories of Rykol 7

Bereft of anything useful to do, Aderen viewed his recording of the most recent vision, which had come to him just before Rubiel's shield closed. Due to the effects of the vekornan wrist lasers, and the importance of the moment, he'd managed to shift it to another part of his mind and record it through his kennis.

The vision started without a narrative lament about death, but maybe that had been cut off as the shield closed. The siims were saying goodbye to Bolob between the arms of Metik. Kolb shuttles were dropping bombs all over, and vekornan shuttles were giving chase. Goses had unexpectedly crowded the tarmac, and siims were climbing on their necks and backs. A single birth chamber was strapped to the goses named Thof.

The kolbs are already losing the battle, said Thof. **We must leave now. Signal the others to evacuate the city.**

This was it. Aderen's parents had seen this same memory before they left for Sumo crater. It was the end of the siims and goses, their mass suicide.

With siims on their backs, the goses lifted from the ground and flew north toward their research station, which they now called Siilat. The vekorna had fortified it after kolb and rokel attacks, giving it a shield.

The vekorna recognized that something significant was happening with the siims. While kolbs attacked Metik, most vekornan shuttles chased the siims and goses – whether as escorts or defenders, the siim named Flaorniti didn't care.

Riding Thof, Flaorniti watched too many goses fall to the ground, while most of their siim riders floated to safety on their wings, picked up by other pairs. They knew the risk if a single siim body was recovered by the vekorna. All traces of siims must be eradicated from Rykol.

The city is empty, Thof told him as they evaded kolb shuttles, which had now recognized the easy targets in the sky, and that there were siims on board. Fortunately, vekornan shuttles came to their aid.

Siilat was in view, so small compared with Metik. Flaorniti watched the goses dive into the small hole in the shield at the top of the city.

It was his turn. As Thof rose to find the hole, circling the perimeter, they were tailed by a kolb shuttle. Either they would make it or they wouldn't. The goses didn't have any weapons, and Flaorniti didn't carry anything that could affect a shuttle.

He felt the electric buzz of the shield as they passed through. The kolb shuttle tried to squeeze in behind them, but the operators closed it, destroying the shuttle. Thof swerved to avoid its debris.

Landing near the newly opened goses tunnel, Flaorniti watched as the city's shield was lit up by laser fire.

"How long can it hold?" he asked.

"Not much longer," said the two-armed Persinjali.

Aderen struggled to retain his objectivity while watching the scenario play out. The memory globe the folems had shown his parents was from Bolob's point of view. They'd watched the siims and goses commit mass suicide, destroying both species. What was happening inside the shield?

We must keep the shield closed, said Thof. **Eighty one goses remain outside. We cannot get to them, and there is a high risk of kolb or vekornan shuttles entering if we reopen the shield.**

"Then it is over," said Flaorniti. "Overload the generator." To Thof, he said, "You are certain the blast will destabilize all birth chambers?"

Down to the kolb continents in the south and Rubiel on the other side of the world, replied the goses. **You will**

be the only siims.

"Then we can mature the second generation, in the way that we decide," said Flaorniti.

The generator started pulsing, a loud humming noise that dwarfed all other sounds. The goses and siims outside the shield hugged it so close that the goses' wings were singed.

Flaorniti and Thof flew through the goses tunnel as its entrance collapsed.

The point of view shifted, and one building on the edge of Siilat exploded. A chain of explosions circled the perimeter of the city, and moved steadily inward toward the center.

Aderen saw that the goses must have rigged all of the buildings in Siilat to explode on their own. The pressure inside the shield was increasing such that shuttles and research equipment were being squeezed, imploding and adding to the general powder keg that was the roiling atmosphere trapped within.

The shield tower was the last to go, exploding in a cascade that ripped it top to bottom. The largest flash illuminated the interior of Siilat as the generator finally exploded. The shield collapsed, but the vekornan and kolb shuttles withdrew to avoid getting caught.

A giant crack formed with the last explosion, digging deep into the continental shelf, breaking the land far to the north, east and west. The trembling would be felt all over the world, destabilizing birth chambers of all species, just like the asteroid that had created the siims. The land would be broken for generations, and Aderen knew he would see no life if he visited the area today.

The siims and goses that were hugging the outside of the shield entered the conflagration, instantly boiling until there was nothing left.

The vision faded, and Aderen replayed the last few seconds again from his kennis, exhausted. The way vekornan stories described it, the siims and goses committed mass suicide, all getting caught inside the blast that shook the planet.

But the view from inside was much different. There were no siims, no goses in Siilat when it exploded. There were no vekornan supervisors, either. Had they all been killed before the tunnel was opened?

The siims and goses had retreated down a goses tunnel. The large burrowing animals had left tunnels under every continent. The siim conversation after the meeting in Metik implied that they were creating another city underground. Had the siims and goses survived, after all?

Our survival is not guaranteed, the voice in his head responded. Emotion came with it, great fatigue, and he felt like he was flopping his head down on the ground because he didn't have the energy to support it anymore.

He no longer thought the visions were coming from somebody who wanted to find the siims. It felt like a giant had been talking to him. It could have been a siim, but more likely he'd been touched by a goses mind.

If so, where were they?

49. The Garden

By morning, their limited food was gone. Fortunately, Aneya found some powdered protein and vitamins in the medical ward, which didn't sate anybody's appetite when mixed with water, but allowed them to forget about hunger for a few more hours. Pinoa wondered if medicine or supplements could last this long, even in the sealed storage

Yenine had put in place before leaving Rykol.

Close to mid-day, Sebenet came to get Jye-Tan, who was grumpy and short-tempered.

"What do you want?" he asked, fiddling with tools on the workbench.

Dairnehy will allow you into the garden to harvest food, Sebenet said. Jye-Tan's face perked up.

As wonderful as that sounded to her as well, Kuyi was suspicious. Had Tararnifal read more into Jye-Tan's request to go to the garden than he should have, and reported it?

Or worse, had Étar noted it, and let his suspicions slip? As much as she loved having him here with her, he was still a liability. She and Aneya had to keep their plan secret.

"The three of us will go," Kuyi said, pointing to Jye-Tan and Aneya. "We'll bring you back something tasty and filling."

"Thank you –I love you," said Étar, kissing her. Buzzing, he added, "It will also split their attention, and maybe distract them."

"I'll let you know if we need a distraction," she buzzed with a flirtatious smile. He returned it, but with more of a question. She kissed him again, cursing herself for revealing even that much.

Pinoa was less eager to stay behind, feeling more useless now than the previous day. "Stay in the city," Aderen buzzed, his frustration showing. "If Dairnehy returns, we might have a very small window to negotiate. Continue to help Étar. If we can get a physical interface with something other than a useless door control, maybe it'll give Jye-Tan a better chance to hack in when he gets back."

Kuyi put her arm around Jye-Tan's shoulders. "Give yourself a break, and maybe it'll work better when you've

397

eaten."

She touched her kennis intimately to Étar before Sebenet guided them out into the space between the city's habitation arms. She looked up at the red tower of Rykol's capital city. Aderen was up there somewhere, and the only reason Dairnehy was keeping him there was because he wanted the rest of the stellar fragment. As far as she knew, there were three large pieces left.

She would tackle the one at Rubiel first, then think about the other two.

Kuyi was surprised to see Kular, one of Tararnifal's vekorna, in the vend'ok. She didn't know if he recognized her, and remained silent, but shied away from Sebenet as he entered after her. The vend'ok brought them quickly to the empty desert beyond the arms of the city. Turning north, it didn't take long to get to the garden, which was more of a vegetable farm, now.

Originally created by Egalinsor's parents in preparation for the six human crews Kopiv was bringing back after his journey across the generations, it had been supplemented since then. Tari, still recovering from her problems after emerging from cryo-sleep, had found solace here for a time. It was a well-known secret that she'd stashed supplies near the water collection control station during her most paranoid moments. Jye-Tan glanced at the twisted grove of trees and bushes hiding it as soon as they disembarked.

The collector had been modified by Egalinsor and Nalimai, and Kuyi's aunts and uncles, intent on bringing better irrigation to the deserts inside Rubiel's shield. They'd dug wells to catch deep water and bring it to the collector. Wind traps gathered trace amounts of dew in the mornings, dripping them into the garden. The edges of the grasses, out closer to the shield, were held by physical barriers, so the desert could not so easily encroach on them.

In the time since Jye-Tan and Aneya's escape from Rubiel, the garden had overgrown. Kuyi stepped over thick vines, noting where they needed to be pruned to prevent choking others. Gigantic fruit hung from sagging branches, while big fat vegetables lay on the ground.

"Look at the size of this!" Jye-Tan exclaimed, rolling an orange vegetable around. He let it fall back with a disgusted look when he saw that its bottom was rotting. The smell wafted over her, and she put an arm to her nose.

Sebenet was lucky he didn't have an olfactory sense, the only thing missing from that vast array of sensors on his head. He was the baby sitter now. She almost felt sympathy for him. Was this a demotion from extar fleet commander, or did he prefer being a spy for Dairnehy?

"Imagine how Illian and Ketaris would react."

They would be tripping over themselves to get specimens. Many of these plants were unique to Rubiel, and since the city had been closed to humans they had no way of getting the harvest to Bol. Kuyi took some recordings for the exobiologists.

It wouldn't take long for the five people at Rubiel to harvest everything, and she thought of bringing seeds back, too. There were varieties she hadn't realized her taste buds were missing.

Jye-Tan was busy running from overgrown patch to overgrown patch, commenting on how they should look, how the fruit bushes and trees shouldn't be intermixing, and more that she tuned out, even as he sampled many of them, gorging himself. Kuyi picked a round fruit and took a delicious bite.

Aneya found the supply of tools and presented them with small shears. Without supervision, life found a way to expand. Was that how the Arais felt about her family?

"Eventually, the garden might reach the shield, if left untended," Aneya said, surveying the withered vines near the barrier, crunching on a vegetable. It had been Egalinsor's dream that Rykol could be made green by genetically engineered grasses and plants. That dream had been crushed by Dairnehy, who restricted everything they did.

Kuyi moved back to the center of the garden, pulled some errant stalks away, revealing a nice husk that would keep well for days. She shook it, noting with satisfaction the faint sound of sloshing within, and put it aside.

Jye-Tan was moving in the other direction, his gaze continually wandering to the nearly-hidden water collector control station. On the other side, the garden had managed to creep into the grasses meant for the deserts beyond Rubiel's shield. She absently noted its progress for Egalinsor.

Aneya hadn't said anything, but Kuyi was certain Jye-Tan's hiding spot and Tari's old supply cache were one and the same. Thick tangled trees and bushes had grown up in a large grove around the building, thicker on the garden side, close to the only source of water nearby. A wide band around it was kept clear by a static field so the machinery could function. If that failed, she doubted the vekorna would continue to clear it, and the garden would die. The grasses were meant to function on minimal water, and might survive.

Handling the sonic disrupter strapped to her waist, Kuyi buzzed Aneya. "Jye-Tan can't resist, can he?"

Aneya turned around, still pretending to inspect a withered vine, but undoubtedly watching Jye-Tan. "He's getting awfully close."

Kuyi was acutely aware of the two vekorna in the garden, watching them. Their weapons were holstered, wrist lasers inactive, but that would change if Jye-Tan made a sprint for the grove.

"Are we ready to do this?" Kuyi asked, watching their watchers. She was about to go to Jye-Tan, to warn him against doing anything rash, when Aneya picked her way to him, putting a hand on his shoulder, whispering in his ear.

"We have to make it look natural," Aneya buzzed. "I've told Jye-Tan to avoid that area."

"Which means he'll make his way there eventually," Kuyi concluded. Aneya acknowledged her comment, agreeing.

*   *   *

Something brushed at Tararnifal's mind, distracting him. He'd been standing out in the area between two of the city's arms, following Kular's ongoing reports from Rubiel's garden. So far, the humans were harvesting food for their stay, which seemed likely to be long. Sebenet hadn't shared any thoughts, and Kular didn't press him.

Although Dairnehy professed to trust him, Tararnifal had not been allowed to see Aderen. By contrast, he had seen Danosh again; the vekornan was in worse shape than before. How long could a vekornan last like this? Tararnifal doubted anyone knew.

Dairnehy's tactics went against everything Bolob had entrusted him to do. He couldn't be permitted to continue leading the winged vekorna. However, Kular had not been able to find enough vekorna to support them if they took action.

Tararnifal had already come to the conclusion that to restore Bolob's Plan, he would need to kill Dairnehy. So far, the opportunity had not presented itself, even when they were alone together. Dairnehy was always armed and unpredictable. Tararnifal, unarmed like most other vekorna in Rubiel, wondered if he could win a hand-to-hand fight against the vekornan leader.

Had Kezim had ever thought of teaching a vekornan his lobomai style of fighting? Tararnifal had observed it many times, but never thought to apply it.

The second soft touch against his mind was like a whisper at the edge of his awareness. He wondered if it could be Aderen, somehow peeking around the telepathic interference of the mirror crystals, but discounted the possibility from his own experiments in Danosh's crystal cell. He perceived that the touch came from far away, maybe Samlar in high orbit. He could be in trouble, especially if the kolbs had finally decided to retrieve the remaining extars. He had to try for a clearer connection.

Vekorna were sparse as Tararnifal entered Rubiel. Doors were closed where they had remained open in Kopiv and Bolob's time, another sign of Dairnehy's paranoia. Tararnifal was used to opening doors with a mental touch, though, as the doors on an extar, his natural home, remained closed for safety reasons. It was an unconscious impulse.

More vekorna mentally scanned Tararnifal's surface thoughts as he wound his way to the elevator shaft that would take him to the room at the top of the tower. The scans were a normal extension of their telepathic network, but seemed more sinister now, without knowing their true intentions, or if they were spying for Dairnehy.

The shaft opened into a wide corridor, and he turned toward the room that housed the crystals that tigal-en used for ultra-long distance telepathic communication. It was Tararnifal's only way to see if kolbs were about to attack, or if Samlar was still in orbit high above Rykol.

He nearly walked into the door, as it didn't open to his mental touch. The door, keyed to telepathy, should have opened for any tigal-en. Other vekorna wouldn't think of coming here. There was only one reason for Dairnehy to lock the room against him.

He doesn't trust me after all, Tararnifal said, feeling the presence of another vekornan in the corridor behind him.

He doesn't trust anybody in the crystal room, said Punad. **Even his prin-el cannot access it without him.**

Tararnifal turned to face Punad, keeping his eyes retracted in case of a confrontation. **I need a crystal to communicate beyond Rubiel.**

This room cannot be used, Punad responded. **Rubiel is effectively cut off from the rest of Rykol, except for strategic links with other cities. Who do you need to contact?**

The question was an obvious trap, but how could Tararnifal refuse to answer? **I need to find out what is happening with the extars I left behind. Without reassurance that I am still alive, they have no mission.**

Walk with me, Punad said, leading him back toward the elevator shaft. **You are an effective leader. Samlar undoubtedly has instructions in case you do not return. I will not ask about them, but I have been monitoring the three extars above Rubiel, circling in an orbit that**

keeps them two hundred kilometers above us at all times.

I believe they are in trouble.

They are, confirmed Punad, entering the elevator car. Tararnifal followed. **A small fleet of kolb extars has left the Black Moon and is on its way to their position. They are almost in range, but there is nothing you can do for them.**

They began their descent, and Tararnifal braced himself for a physical confrontation in the confines of the lift. Their car changed shafts and resumed its descent for a few seconds, before the door opened and Punad stepped off.

Aderen and Danosh are in danger, as are those you left in the garden. I do not care for humans, but if you want to save what is left of Rykol, you should escape from here while you have the chance. There is another crystal room in the lowest level of the tower. It is guarded, but you have been there before, and with access to that level you should have no trouble.

He stepped off into another small hallway, and the doors closed again. If Dairnehy wouldn't let him in the room with the normal crystals, why would he allow Tararnifal to enter the basement room with his precious stellar fragment?

Punad had become prin-el after Danosh rebelled and was exiled from the winged cities. Tararnifal recalled the glance at his tortured predecessor as Punad come to give news of Aderen's approach. It had never occurred to him to recruit Punad, but he now wondered if the prin-el was as close to the winged leader as was usual.

He suspected a trap, but to what end? The foreign mental touch brushed up against his thoughts a third time. He needed to find a communications crystal.

50. Contact

Silence descended as the door to Aderen's cell closed, leaving him alone. Dairnehy brought nothing new to their discussions, and it was wearying. He cited his willingness to accommodate humans by allowing them to gather food in the garden, but was playing games with Aderen, nothing more.

Aderen probed the mirror crystals again, checking for weak spots, but as usual there weren't any. He'd mapped all the crystals on his kennis, and they hadn't changed by an appreciable distance. There were no gaps.

Without Jye-Tan's hack into the Rubiel computers, which had always been a long shot, his only chance at getting out of this cage was letting Dairnehy think he was wearing Aderen down. It wasn't far from the truth.

He had no friends here, unless Tararnifal was playing at being a double agent. He didn't know if he'd touched enough of Sebenet's mind to be useful, and wasn't aware of any other friendly vekorna in this city.

Étar wasn't ready with a backup plan in the city's arm, yet, which gave them a little more time if Aderen couldn't find a solution on his own.

"Dairnehy is only interested in you and Kirina," buzzed Pinoa. "I don't think the kolbs would exchange their piece of the fragment for a bunch of humans."

"Me neither," Aderen buzzed. His ears rang from the silence outside his kennis connection. He'd risked allowing Pinoa into the latest conversation, and was thankful that Dairnehy hadn't mentioned his origins. "I don't think Dairnehy would honor his agreement to send you to the Black Moon for passage home, regardless." He stood, stretching muscles that he hadn't used enough while locked in this cell. He assumed a lobomai pose, then shifted his weight.

"I can't negotiate like this," Pinoa buzzed. "We came to Rykol thinking we could force a treaty with the vekorna. Any treaty he agrees to would be entirely suspect."

"There was always going to be the problem with later generations, which is why we need access to the birth chambers. I was right to keep Doj and Penagel away from here, but doubt they have access to Ontral's birth chambers yet. I was hoping Danosh could help find us some in another city, but that's impossible now. Somehow, we'll need to find another sympathetic vekornan."

Étar intruded on the conversation. Aderen hoped he'd made progress, but his urgency suggested another problem.

"Aderen," he buzzed. "Link with Kuyi in the garden."

*   *   *

Kuyi piled loads of fruits and vegetables, especially the more voluminous ones, precariously near the edge of the garden. The piles grew in size, much more than they could use among five people, but the vekorna didn't object.

At a sign from Aneya, Kuyi approached Kular and Sebenet. "We need help loading these onto the vend'ok," she said. She grabbed a few of the small fruits, leading the way. Sebenet indicated that Kular should help her. The way she'd piled it ensured they would not be able to pick anything up without everything falling over.

After two trips with arms full, she said, "Sebenet, I may have messed up some of the controls when I was packing the fruits."

We will clean your mess as we return to Rubiel, he responded.

"Are you sure? It might take a while to get things back

to normal." Kular extended two eyestalks toward her, arms full of fruit. How could she know if he was on her side?

I believe we should verify the controls, Kular said. Could he guess her intentions? **On Terra, allowing humans inside our vehicles unsupervised often led to disaster.**

They drew artwork inside my extar, Sebenet complained, apparently agreeing. He turned toward the vend'ok, and in that moment, Jye-Tan and Aneya disappeared. Sebenet sensed something was wrong, turning back to the garden immediately, searching.

The others have stopped harvesting, he said. **Why have they left the garden?**

"They're checking the water supply," Kuyi lied. To Aneya, she buzzed, "Sebenet is more suspicious than I expected. I can't delay him."

"We just got in here, and haven't started digging, yet," Aneya buzzed. Why were they digging?

Kuyi faced Sebenet and Kular, keeping her voice and pulse steady. "I'll go check on them. You should keep loading so it's ready to go when we get back."

That is not necessary, Sebenet said, but Kuyi was already making her way through the garden, avoiding rotten fruits and tangling vines, using her kennis to keep her pulse steady. When he inevitably followed, she hoped Sebenet would take the same care with his much larger body.

"Kuyi, where are you going?" She winced as Étar buzzed. Of course he was tracking her. She needed more time. "What's happening?" he asked.

She decided to be partially honest with him. "Jye-Tan went to check on the hidden fragment. Aneya went after him."

"So why are you going, too?" he asked. "You have to allay vekornan suspicions. Quickly!"

"I tried that. I don't think Sebenet is buying it, and I can't tell if Kular is on our side." She looked over her shoulder as she entered the tangled grove. The vekorna were still loading the vend'ok. How did Jye-Tan get in here so easily?

Kuyi swore as a branch whipped at her face, drawing blood. She pressed a finger to the cut, and directed her white blood cells to clot and heal it quickly. She rubbed the blood absently onto her pants.

"Show me what you see," Étar buzzed. She didn't want to, especially for what came next, but at the moment she could oblige. She connected Étar to her kennis, the way they did when making love, but linked only to her vision. He would see what she saw.

She bounced along, avoiding branches and twisted tree trunks and roots, in what must have been a nauseating image on Étar's palette. She reached a small clearing, where Aneya and Jye-Tan knelt amid the green and purple foliage. The walls of the water station were visible not far off.

Jye-Tan was reaching into one of the old wells, next to a very large rock.

"We have to hurry," she said out loud. "Kular and Sebenet won't be far behind me."

Jye-Tan pulled up a large bag.

"Is that the fragment?" Étar asked. "It's much smaller than I thought. Why did Aneya let him dig it out?"

Kuyi grasped the sonic disrupters in her pocket and sighed with relief as Jye-Tan spilled out the contents of the bag –supplies, not crystals.

"I think we could use a distraction about now," she buzzed Étar.

*   *   *

Aderen saw what Kuyi was projecting to Étar, and was disheartened.

"How could she let that happen, after all our caution?"

"I don't think she could control Jye-Tan," Étar buzzed. His judgement was biased, of course, but he was probably right. "I don't know how large the fragment hidden in the garden is," Étar continued, "but you know what will happen if Dairnehy gets it."

"Maybe this is for the best," said Aderen, sighing. "Look at Aneya and Kuyi's hands."

They were holding sonic disrupters. The women were taking matters into their own hands. They would try to destroy the stellar fragments. He couldn't blame them, after what they'd already been through, and what Kuyi had seen him do at Bol.

Only it wouldn't work. Palm-sized disrupters wouldn't have nearly enough power to destroy the fragments. These were pieces of a star. They couldn't use conventional means of destruction.

Étar's was right, though. If Dairnehy gained control of the fragment, and fused it with the pieces he already had, he would become more powerful. He would assault Ontral first, doubling his fragment, then use his hidden extars to go after the kolbs.

More important to Aderen, however, was the threat to Kuyi's embryonic child. If she failed to destroy the fragment, as she must, it was most important that she escape Rubiel. If nothing else, Aderen had to give her that chance.

"Étar, if you have a distraction ready, this might be the time to deploy it," Aderen buzzed.

"We're trapped in the human corridor in one of Rubiel's arms," Étar buzzed. "I don't know what good it'll do."

"Try anyway. Kuyi's life might depend on it." If that didn't get Étar moving, nothing would.

Aderen wished he'd been able to visit the garden before being locked in this prison. What he saw from Kuyi's viewpoint was beautiful. Although her life was on the line, he took time to record some of what he saw to his kennis. His parents, after all, had often been in that very space.

The bag that Jye-Tan dumped was full of supplies, probably left over from Tari's more paranoid days, before the kolb war. According to his parents, Tari had begun hoarding anything she could get her hands on, when she thought the vekorna were trying to kill her and her baby. Knowing what he knew now, she was right to be paranoid.

Jye-Tan wasn't interested in the bag, though. He reached down and brought out a large crystal, twice as large as his hand.

"Is that–" Étar started, but Kuyi stopped him, saying, "No, that's a mirror crystal."

Aderen looked around his cell. The crystals were on the outside of his walls. From his probing, they were probably about the same size, a little smaller than those Danosh had used in Esetek.

Jye-Tan lifted three more mirror crystals out of the pit. There was noise in the distance. Dairnehy's spies were coming.

*   *   *

Grunting with effort, Jye-Tan reached deeper into the pit and struggled to lift something out. Kuyi stopped on the

410

edge of the hole, saying, "No, leave it in there."

She took out two sonic disrupters, and activated them at maximum power. She motioned Aneya to do the same.

"What are you doing?" Jye-Tan asked. "I'm only here to check on it. Get away, or you'll damage it!"

"That's the intention," Kuyi said. "It's for your own good, and that of Aderen."

Jye-Tan stepped one foot into the pit, pushing her over. He was stronger than she realized. One of her disrupters fell to the ground, and she reached for it. By the time she stood up, Jye-Tan had the tip of a red crystal peeking out of the pit. His face was flushed with effort, probably straining his kennis to augment the energy from his muscles. The tip of the fragment became a cylinder, then narrowed irregularly.

Aneya knelt at his side, whispering urgently, "Sebenet is coming. I think he senses it! Put it back."

Kuyi looked to the non-existent path she'd traversed, and heard the noise of a much larger creature tearing at the branches. At least Sebenet hadn't fired his laser to clear the way. But Aneya was right. If Sebenet didn't know what they were up to before, he would have undoubtedly sensed the fragment when it was clear of mirror crystals. She picked up the sonic disruptor and leapt back to the pit.

Panicking, and looking up at the disturbance in the trees, Jye-Tan tried to dump the large fragment back down the hole, but it got caught, and now stuck out. It wouldn't matter, though, because without mirror crystals, the approaching vekornan wouldn't be using his eyes to sense it. Kuyi applied the disruptor, placing a second in a crevice so it wouldn't fall, taking two others from her elastic belt.

"Hurry up," she called to Aneya. Jye-Tan scrabbled to remove the ones Kuyi had already placed, but she batted his

411

hands aside.

Two vekorna came crashing in from bushes, the first one tearing them apart as he stomped into view. Kular, right behind, grabbed Sebenet by the upper shoulder. Sebenet lunged forward, breaking free, and slapped Kuyi to the side.

She didn't know how she ended up on her back, dizzy, tears blurring her view, wet hand over her belly. She couldn't focus, couldn't stand. Jye-Tan would be helpless against the vekornan –she had to help him, but couldn't figure out which image of him was the real one.

"Kuyi! Kuyi! Are you alright? Get out of there!" Étar yelled. She couldn't figure out how Étar had arrived so quickly. She put her bloody hand to the side of her head, smearing it on her face, confused.

Jye-Tan's eyes rolled up into his head, hands flat on the fragment. She felt something in her mind as Sebenet slammed into him.

*   *   *

Tararnifal descended all the way to the lowest basement level, where Dairnehy had taken him when they'd retrieved the stellar fragment from *Avenger's* quarters. The door opened and he walked carefully down the short corridor.

The two guards were probably alerted to his presence before the lift reached this level. They weren't tigal-en, but could contact minds in closer quarters.

Tararnifal had no laser, and would quickly lose any fight with armed guards. But as Punad predicted, while they tracked him with their lasers, he wasn't challenged entering the crystal room.

The large red crystal, remnant of the much larger stellar fragment, was supported by a narrow pillar at the level of his middle arms, and surrounded by countless smaller pieces and crystal dust. Tararnifal picked up two small shards, and circled the pillar so that he was facing the open door. He planted himself on the ground without removing his faceplate or armor. The mirror crystals were out of alignment, letting his mind through.

The combined fragment was extraordinarily easy to connect with, as if it had been made to synchronize with a vekornan mind. Not for the first time, he wondered if the crystals had helped shape his species after their god Spall created them.

He could see into many minds within Rubiel, but refrained from doing so, not wanting to accidentally connect with Dairnehy and alert him to his motive. He tried to find Danosh, but the connection to the vekornan's mind was weak and intermittent, fractured by the mirror crystals. About to move on, he felt a faint stirring.

Allow me to die, Danosh said. **The mirror crystals have shifted, but I cannot escape. Come up here and kill me.**

Surprised, Tararnifal answered, **The humans are in trouble and need to escape.** He trusted that Punad had informed him honestly. **Can you still pilot a shuttle?**

A shuttle will not permit escape.

His connection with Danosh trickled away. Tararnifal wondered if he should leave now, as Punad suggested. Had Punad shifted Danosh's crystals, giving him this chance? Aderen had never been close to Punad, so his mind was free of manipulation. This was what fear did, when presented with a little hope.

Immediately he was drawn to a more distant mind, the one that had brushed against his earlier. **Bri'dan,** he said, recognizing the touch of a kolb, their leader. **You have been probing me.**

Tararnifal, you have failed Bolob, came the response. **We gave you time, but it was wasted. We will now take your extars.**

No —come get the humans.

The connection quickly disappeared, so he searched for Samlar.

Kolbs are coming for us, his extar commander said. **What do you want us to do?**

I need a distraction, and the kolbs will do, Tararnifal said. **Break orbit, and bring them with you.**

"Who are you contacting?" The connection dissipated as a metallic voice intruded into the crystal room an instant before Tararnifal saw Dairnehy's glinting faceplate. The fragment had taken so much of his concentration that he hadn't noticed the vekornan leader's approach. He dropped the two shards he was holding. One clattered to the ground, while the other fell into a fold of his armor, which he sealed with a thought.

The kolbs are going to seize our remaining extars, he said, deflecting the question.

You should have brought them all to me, within the confines of Rubiel's shield.

You have already hidden some away. Do you need more?

That's irrelevant; these are crewed by winged vekorna. We need them more than we need extars. He froze, all his thoughts distracted.

The garden! The young human has revealed another piece of the stellar fragment, much larger! Come!

Then Tararnifal felt it. A human touch, similar to

414

Aderen, but not the same. It was young and raw, and could only be Jye-Tan. He'd claimed that the fragment made him like Kirina and Aderen. Tararnifal hadn't believed it, but here was proof.

Dairnehy was enraged and thrilled at the same time. **I told you this was why they came back. You said they wanted to negotiate, but I knew they would take the fragment for the wingless. This is how the boy stole it the first time! Come with me to the garden, and we will recapture it.**

51. Released

Struggling to her knees, Kuyi saw Jye-Tan go flying, his body doing a somersault before Aneya got to him.

Sebenet reached into the pit with two arms and pulled the fragment out with little effort. It was more than a meter long. This was how Jye-Tan had moved it to the garden in the first place, but then what? Had he erased vekornan memories?

With help from Aneya, Jye-Tan stood up, stunned, and stumbled back toward the pit. Kuyi wiped her face, looking at the blood on her hand. She watched Sebenet hold the fragment high above his head in triumph. The buzzing in her mind increased in intensity.

He was calling to Dairnehy. She had failed, and worse, she'd given the fragment to the one vekornan they couldn't allow to have it.

A blur to her left caused her vision to swell, but then Sebenet was on the ground, Kular standing above him. The fragment rolled away from them. Kuyi found two of her sonic disrupters not far away. They wouldn't be enough, but she had to try.

Jye-Tan arrived first, putting his hands flat on the fragment, closing his eyes again.

Her kennis pinged with updates from several sources. Kuyi saw a fighter launch from a kolb extar, Rubiel in the distance. It was being piloted by a human, who was broadcasting to everyone.

Sarenie was talking to Ret. Was he the pilot? She didn't understand his words, but the meaning was clear. He was in danger, and couldn't last against Rubiel's defenses.

Doj intruded into her mind. "We've solved the kennis problem, and can connect across shields, thanks to Jye-Tan," he buzzed. "How did he do it?"

Kuyi gathered her strength, watching the two vekorna struggle on the ground. Sebenet was armed with wrist lasers, but Kular, unarmed, was too close for him to aim.

"He's using the stellar fragment," she buzzed. "I think we're in trouble, though."

"Ontral will send ships against Rubiel," Doj buzzed back.

"I don't think that's a good idea." She rubbed her head, directing her kennis to restore equilibrium. "Where's Étar?"

"I'm here, and getting a lot of data from outside the shield," Étar buzzed. "Ret's out there. The kolbs attacked Samlar's fleet, but they broke orbit, and are now circling Rubiel, kolb extars on their tails."

"What about your distraction?"

"I'm not sure I need one, now. The shields around our hallway just went down. Can Jye-Tan free Aderen, too?"

"I don't think he's hearing anybody right now."

"You have to get him to safety. Dairnehy is on his way."

*   *   *

The human mind couldn't penetrate Aderen's thoughts,

though he felt the barrage against his mental shields.

"I'm using the fragment," Jye-Tan buzzed. "I've threaded the kennis through the shield. What should I do next?"

"You should have left the fragment hidden," Aderen responded. "But it's too late for that. I'm still stuck in this room, and can't do anything. Can you get the guards to release me?"

Jye-Tan's tone was uncertain and he sounded scared, even over the kennis link. "I don't think so. I can't even find you. Wait, I found someone. Punad can help."

"He's Dairnehy's prin-el. You can't trust him."

"I can see the truth in his mind."

"We'll head to the garden to help," buzzed Pinoa.

"No," Aneya responded. "Get us a shuttle. If Sebenet gets the fragment back, it will end up in Dairnehy's hands. Then nobody in this city will be safe. That's why we hid it in the first place. Are you able to help?"

"No, I can't–" Something changed. Aderen felt the whispers of vekorna around him. "Yes, I think I can. Some of the mirror crystals have turned away from me." He reached beyond the walls to his room and found a vekornan. It was Punad, and Aderen saw that Jye-Tan was right. Dairnehy's prin-el was looking for a way out of this situation.

Get me out and I'll help you, Aderen promised.

The door opened.

"Come with me," Aderen said, and Punad followed. No longer looking for stealth, he ran down the corridors to the conveyor. He sensed two more vekorna ahead. Not waiting for Punad to issue orders, and hoping he was up to the task after being locked up behind the mentally dampening mirror crystals, Aderen removed the fear and anger that held these vekorna to Dairnehy's will. That his abilities had been made by the vekorna didn't seem to hamper their connection.

The mental threads of the next two were easy, especially when he could look them in the faceplate. Better yet, they were still alive after his efforts. He ignored the part of his mind that repeated Kuyi's objections.

"By revealing the stellar fragment, we no longer have any power to negotiate," buzzed Aderen. "We need to get out of here."

"We think we can change the fragment's internal structure, rendering it useless," Aneya buzzed.

Aderen paused. Could they? Should they try to destroy it instead? The fragment might be the key to resolving all the problems on Rykol, including any future raiders to Terra.

"Do it if you can, but otherwise have Kular take it. Dairnehy can't have it. I've seen enough of him to know now that I was foolish. I should have listened to Tararnifal."

"We're going to the shuttlebay," buzzed Étar. "I'll find something we can use to get out of here. Setting off my distraction now."

"If Jye-Tan has hacked into Rubiel's systems, he needs to disable Rubiel's shield and defenses," buzzed Aderen. "A shuttle will not last long against those lasers. I'll be there as soon as I can."

"I can't do that," Jye-Tan buzzed. "The kolb extars will tear the city apart, and us with it!"

Turning to Punad, he said, **Go to the control room and make sure the city's defenses ignore our shuttle. We can't be caught again. Then meet Ret in the shuttlebay.**

Punad acknowledged him, and Aderen considered bolstering the order with a mental touch, but refrained. The prin-el seemed to be loyal to Tararnifal now, and without his mind being altered.

Punad remained in the conveyor when they reached the ground floor, and the chaos of vekorna responding to the crisis outside the shield. None questioned his four remaining guards, and he thankfully didn't need to alter any minds.

Outside, smoke was rising from about halfway along the city's arm. He didn't know what Étar had done, but it seemed effective for the moment. Vekorna were boarding vend'oks to reach it.

"We need to get that vend'ok to the garden," Aderen said, pointing at the line of waiting vehicles. His four guards guided him there, and they were just one more vend'ok among a dozen others. They split from the flow, in the direction of the garden.

Looking up, Aderen saw a shuttle pass overhead, heading the same way. He swore as he recognized the mind on board.

"Dairnehy will be with you soon," he buzzed. "You'll have to find a way to deal with the fragment one way or another until I arrive."

*   *   *

This was only the second time Tararnifal had seen the human garden outside Rubiel. The first time, the greenery and vast colors seemed out of place and unnatural.

Then he'd been sent to TenSik, homeworld of the zonguans, which was greener than any world should be. He'd almost been overwhelmed. Finally, he'd spent so much time on Terra that he'd forgotten what a real desert

419

was like. There, he could be immersed in all the green he wanted, at any time.

The Rubiel garden seemed so small now.

It was empty of people, human or vekornan, but Tararnifal saw three of the slower vend'oks converging on it.

Dairnehy was piloting their shuttle, and had given orders to the three vekorna who were on board already. They were to seize the fragment at all costs.

Jye-Tan was still in their minds, a strategic error that might cost him his life. Now that he could read their thoughts, what was he doing?

The shuttle came down in the middle of the garden, flattening dozens of genetically engineered plants and their ripe fruit. The five vekorna descended, Dairnehy and Tararnifal in the lead, all trampling more vegetation.

With his heavy blaster, Dairnehy shot at the giant mass of bushes on this side of the water station, disintegrating them until they provided scant cover for those hiding within.

Tararnifal saw Kular holding Sebenet down, Jye-Tan hunched over the fragment, palms flat on its surface as it lay on the ground. Kuyi looked up frantically, fumbling with something on her knees near the fragment, while Aneya stood in front of them as a symbolic human shield. The symbol would mean nothing to Dairnehy.

It grew harder to approach, and Tararnifal wondered if Jye-Tan had gained the ability to freeze vekorna the way Aderen could, through the properties of the stellar fragment.

Hand over the fragment, said Dairnehy, uncharacteristically willing to give the humans a chance to surrender. **You do not have control over my mind, and I will kill you for it.**

"You'll kill us anyway, so we must resist," said Aneya. "I know your mind, even though I can't read it. You will subjugate every being on Rykol, and kill those who don't have wings."

You are not entirely correct, Dairnehy responded. **I was willing to let humans go. The kolbs might be convinced to send you home on their extars.**

Tararnifal was frozen to the ground, unable to move his legs. He extended three eyestalks and saw that the vekorna with them were similarly immobile. Yet Dairnehy continued to advance, albeit slowly. Kuyi was mumbling, shaking her head.

This was the only chance Tararnifal was going to get. He projected his thoughts to the three humans. **He is now vulnerable. Release me, and I will kill him.**

Tears were in Jye-Tan's eyes as he looked at Tararnifal's faceplate, shaking his head. "I can't… all or nothing."

The boy was losing control, visibly weakening. Even now, Tararnifal found that he had minor control over his body.

More vekornan presences arrived in the garden, approaching slowly, but apparently not under Jye-Tan's control. Tararnifal counted ten trampling the garden toward the water station.

"I can't," whimpered Jye-Tan. "Too many."

Suddenly the vekorna were free. Tararnifal leapt forward and knocked into Dairnehy, who opened his wings for balance, allowing his heavy blaster to fall to the ground.

Tararnifal reached for the abandoned laser, but Dairnehy pushed it away. **You would be unable to fire it,** he said.

Sebenet broke Kular's hold and brought his wrist laser to bear, but Kular shoved at the armored limbs, locking their aim to the side. They grappled with their free arms, unable to gain advantage over the other.

The arriving vekorna spread out in a semi-circle, but otherwise didn't get involved in the struggle. Vekorna rarely practiced in-close combat, and were poorly equipped to do so. Maybe Jye-Tan was partly responsible for holding them away.

Dairnehy was moving toward Jye-Tan again. Kuyi was between them, small vibrating cylinders in her hands. Aneya ran to Dairnehy's discarded blaster, but couldn't lift it.

"You were right," she said, grunting. "I could use my old designs here." Instead, she tipped it over and was pivoting it on the ground toward the approaching vekornan leader.

A faceplate landed at Tararnifal's feet, and he saw Kular's bare sensor head get smashed by Sebenet's clawed fist. The two vekorna were still swiping at each other, and Kular was losing.

Nobody had fired a laser, either the blood-stopping wrist lasers or the flesh-shredding heavy blasters. Was this why Dairnehy had abandoned his weapon? Unable to stop the vekorna completely, had Jye-Tan inhibited their ability to fire them?

Unfortunately, that didn't stop Dairnehy from approaching. Kuyi leapt onto his torso, putting all her weight on one of his middle arms, bringing one of the cylinders down at the base of his sensor head. She might be hindering his movement, but was otherwise doing no damage.

Aneya managed to get the laser turned and started firing, but with the poor angle did more damage to the frayed bushes around them.

Tararnifal extended his wings in a powerful flap that brought him off the ground just enough to escape a burst of Aneya's laser fire. Dairnehy did the same.

Dropping to the ground, Dairnehy reached over and picked Aneya up by the head in one of his free arms. She grabbed at him, shrieking in pain. Kuyi tore at his faceplate, which cracked where she touched it, but Dairnehy ripped her from his arm with another free hand, tossing her to the ground. She landed hard, her devices scattering. She lifted her head slightly, then lowered it and closed her eyes.

A wrist laser lay next to her, and Tararnifal noted one missing from Dairnehy arm; had she ripped it from him as she was thrown away?

I will create a human slave from your unborn child, Dairnehy said, starting forward again. Tararnifal was distracted, taking a moment to search Kuyi's mind, following the small thread of awareness to her uterus, where a tiny, almost imperceptible spark of life was hanging on by a thread. If he kept throwing her around, there would be no baby.

Returning his attention to the vekornan leader, Tararnifal grabbed Dairnehy around the torso, dragging him backward. Dairnehy threw Aneya to the other side, where she hit the shredded remains of thick branches, and slouched down.

He heard Jye-Tan yell, "No!"

There was laser fire. Jye-Tan's concentration had been broken. Tararnifal heard Kular fall to the ground with a laser blast to his exposed sensor head, part of his body disintegrating.

Sebenet aimed his laser at Jye-Tan, who had abandoned the fragment and was running to the fallen Aneya. Tararnifal was forced to loosen his grip on Dairnehy to pick up the wrist laser near Kuyi. He activated the telepathic switch, regretting this necessity. He'd been unsuccessful with Sebenet, and could no longer delay. Just as he fired, though, Dairnehy dropped to four limbs, dragging Tararnifal with him. The beam his Sebenet's left foot, and the vekornan tumbled away, his heavy blaster thumping away from him. Sebenet roared telepathically, but the hit was diffuse, and would only restrict blood flow to his lower body. However, it would take time to recover.

Dairnehy swung around and freed himself of Tararnifal's uneven grip, tossing him to his knees and ripping the wrist laser from his hand. The vekornan leader lurched forward to touch the fragment.

Tararnifal felt Dairnehy enter his mind, whipping past his mental blocks, seizing anything and everything. Tararnifal locked his limbs and tried to resist.

The assault stopped as a voice penetrated his startled thoughts. Punad was calling to them. **Rubiel is under attack. Our defenses cannot deflect all the extars. We must send fighters to defend the city.**

Dairnehy's voice, calm despite the attack, responded, **It no longer matters. Get me outside the shield and with this fragment I will give us victory.**

He picked up the fragment and carried it out of the clearing into the charred trees and bushes. Tararnifal stood with tremendous effort and, one foot at a time, wings flapping uselessly, slowly followed.

He sensed a familiar mind stop Dairnehy in his tracks.

52. Duel of the Fragment

The vend'ok coasted up the hill that led to the garden, much too slow for Aderen's taste. He'd been in such a rush that he'd taken the first available transport, instead of thinking of alternatives. His four vekornan guards from Rubiel were ready, weapons active. It was as if they had no will of their own. He brushed aside the guilt. Yes, they were doing as he wished instead of what they wanted, but this was to save Kuyi.

Cresting the hill, he saw the shuttle that had passed them as he'd left the tower. It sat in the middle of the garden, plants and vegetables flattened by the massive bulk and trampled by Dairnehy and the vekorna who accompanied him. Three other vend'oks were parked nearby. He sensed twenty five vekorna just inside the small grove. Dairnehy's mind shone strongest. He already had the fragment, and was heading out.

He unconsciously picked his steps between the rows of undisturbed vegetables, the way he would have among the paths of his mother's garden back on Terra. The vekorna he'd brought with him didn't take such care, not noticing the squashed mess that stuck to their feet.

Kennis traffic had suddenly returned to normal, the chaos replaced by their local node within Rubiel's shield. He shut his connection down in case the chaos returned, especially the visuals from outside the shield. Ret wouldn't like what he was about to do, and he didn't want distractions.

Before reaching the path burned into the grove, Aderen found the nearest vekorna and forced their six limbs to the ground, immobilizing them until he said otherwise, weapons trapped underneath their massive bodies. He didn't trust himself to keep active control over so many vekorna, and they would only distract him from his true goal. He forced the four who had accompanied him into the same positon, even though their loyalty was now to Tararnifal. Let him deal with them.

I'm forcing them to do my will, too, but they are not puppets, he thought, feeling guilty as he sought out Kuyi. She, Aneya and Jye-Tan were injured, behind Dairnehy in a clearing. He sensed Sebenet's unprotected mind, too, not far back, but the vekornan was unconscious.

I see inside you, came a voice as he inspected the open wedge of burned bushes that had been cleared from the overgrown grove to the side of the water station. **You will now pledge yourself to me.**

Aderen didn't respond to Dairnehy, stepping into the still smoking foliage, careful of sharp branches that could tear into his skin. The wedge of cleared bushes narrowed to limit his vision, but two vekornan faceplates shone at the other end. He took in Dairnehy holding the fragment off the ground in four arms, while Tararnifal stood behind him.

Dairnehy had risen to his full height, his silver faceplate high above Aderen's head, slightly cracked at the top, no eyestalks protruding. Dairnehy probably thought he could see everything he needed to through the minds he was violating.

Kuyi was lying prone to the left, scratched and bloodied. Jye-Tan knelt beside Aneya, whose eyes were half-open and unfocused.

They were not strong enough to keep the fragment from Dairnehy, said Tararnifal. **You should have sacrificed them, and me.**

You know humans better than that, Aderen

responded, thankful that Tararnifal would not be fighting for Dairnehy, but frustrated that he hadn't done anything to stop this, either.

Once again, Dairnehy intruded on his thoughts, breaking through his guard with little effort. The violation sickened him, and Ret's disgust echoed in his mind. Was this how others felt when he wormed his way into their minds? He liked to think he was more subtle, but glanced over his shoulder at the prostrated vekorna he'd left behind. Did they feel this way when he changed them, broke their loyalty to their leader? He felt his muscles tighten up.

You second-guess yourself, said Dairnehy, and suddenly Aderen was frozen in place –he couldn't move. Had the fragment given Dairnehy the power to reach a hidden part of his mind, something Kopiv had put there as a safeguard? With an effort, he shifted his eyes to glance at Kuyi, her face contorted in pain, even unconscious. Were they all to be puppets, now?

Vekorna created you to be strong, but you fear to be unique, to be judged by others. You could destroy me, if not for those doubts, said Dairnehy.

Aderen hated the way Dairnehy used just the right phrases, taking information from his mind to augment those doubts. What did he want from him? So what if the vekorna had created him. It didn't mean he wasn't human. He could still ascribe to human values.

"My doubts are gone," he said. "Don't you see what I did out there?" He waved back at the kneeling vekorna at the entrance to the grove. *Puppet*s, he flinched. "You cannot understand all that I've done since coming to Rykol."

But of course, Dairnehy *could* know. He could see

427

everything now. Thoughts of Ret passed again through Aderen's mind, the horror on his face while he'd changed Sebenet, reliving Kuyi's terror in the Temple of Spall. Dairnehy opened old wounds that had never really healed, despite Monera, Sarenie and Kuyi. The suicide of Legionnaire Dalpah and those she worked with, holding Treklay and Talmer and the vekorna at the machine against their will, killing Treklay with a thought, moving the flock of folems at Bol. Had he been selfish, to prize his life over theirs, knowing that if he died or was taken prisoner that others would have a harder time stopping the people that threatened them? Dairnehy saw the guilt, knew his fears of being used because of the way his mind had been altered.

He heard Monera's words again, asking what he was running from. She was right. He'd walled himself up, avoiding people who knew what he could do so he wouldn't see their judgmental thoughts. He'd even pushed Monera away after the incident with Dalpah, so she'd married someone else. Facing Ret on Sebenet's extar made him want to avoid his ability altogether, go to a place where nobody knew him. Except he'd allowed Ret to come with them. Ret said he wanted to keep an eye on Aderen. Was that why he'd allowed Ret to come? Kuyi had echoed those thoughts, and here she was, too. Who was manipulating whom?

Nalimai's revelation that his abilities had been created by Kopiv came long after that.

Where was Monera right now? he wondered. Was she still alive after all this time? *What am I running from?*

Humans have intimate connections that make them strong, yet their reliance on those connections make them weak, said Dairnehy. **You are weakened because**

you long for lost connections. Your own people have turned against you. Your intimate refused to follow you here because of the monster we created in you. Look at how your team has turned against you, even the Egalsan.

Aderen's eyes flicked over to Kuyi, who wanted to destroy the fragment rather than let him be tempted by it again. Jye-Tan was on his knees, cradling Aneya's head. She was awake, and aware. Were they willing to be sacrificed?

Kuyi, get up and leave while he's distracted, Aderen said, hoping to nudge her from unconsciousness. **Save your unborn child.** He couldn't tell her why, not yet. It would have been better to buzz her, but couldn't take the chance of reopening his connection, lest he be overwhelmed.

Another voice intruded into his mind. **Vekorna cannot control thoughts, nor can they freeze your muscles,** said Tararnifal.

How could that be true? Aderen wondered. He was frozen, the same way he'd frozen the vekorna behind him, the way he froze everybody in the Legion as they tried to arrest the Arais when he was just five years old. Tararnifal didn't know how his mind had been altered, did he?

Illusions were unique to rokels, and are gone with them, Tararnifal said, as if from a distance. Dairnehy couldn't stop him from communicating with Aderen. Maybe he was right.

But... Dairnehy is sending me illusions, and he is controlling my muscles through some secret switch, he said, still unsure, hating himself for revealing that much.

There is no switch. The illusions are yours. He is driving your thoughts, making you think Kopiv put

something in your unborn mind to keep you loyal. I assure you he did not. Vekorna cannot control minds, not even yours. Release yourself!

How could he be inhibiting his own motor control? Monera's words came back to him. He was running, but from what? The judgement he felt when Ret and everyone else looked at what he could do? The failures with Legionnaire Dalpah, Treklay, and the folems? Could he have given them the choice, as Kuyi suggested? Monera said she thought Rykol might help him realize who he really was. Since arriving, the doubts had hindered his ability to manipulate people.

Any yet, he'd successfully manipulated kolbs and vekorna to the benefit of the mission, from the moment they were ambushed in orbit, to the prostrated vekorna in the burned out path just behind him. Doubts weren't hindering his ability. Was he was hampering himself? Was he his own puppeteer?

Jye-Tan gave him a pleading look, holding Aneya's scarred face. He drew on their waning strength, willing himself to move, get free by the knowledge that it was he himself who had been freezing his motor controls, literally self-paralyzed, torn between who he was and who he thought he wanted to be.

He had to accept his abilities, no matter how he had come by them, but he also had to accept responsibility. Like Ret had said, there were consequences. He had to avoid mass changes, like he'd done to Sebenet's tigal-en, or the folems, or Legionnaire Dalpah and her staff. He had to be more careful than he'd been with Treklay. He still didn't know if there was a greater connection with the vekorna because of how his abilities were created. If he was selective, though, maybe it would only go one way. With a surgical influence, he wouldn't be able to control them like puppets, but that might be a good thing.

If Dairnehy wasn't using a secret switch in his mind, then he should be able to move. First a finger, then his arms. He turned to look directly at Tararnifal. His leg lifted off the ground.

Aderen burst into a run that covered the distance to Dairnehy in four strides. He reached up and touched the fragment, feeling the power it gave him, beyond what he normally had. At Bol, he'd been overwhelmed. This time, he knew what to expect, and let it in carefully. He used the fragment to search his mind, found nothing that would make him favor the vekorna. Relieved, he expanded outward.

The world opened up to him as he saw every mind in Rubiel without effort. He touched Punad, still in the tower, scared but determined to follow Tararnifal's lead. Étar and Pinoa were also in Rubiel, not far from a shuttlebay. And just beyond the city he saw Ret's mind, engaged in battle. He shied away, keeping his senses within the city, in case his paralyzing doubts returned.

Snapping back to his immediate surroundings, he looked into Kuyi's mind for the second time, and nudged her from unconsciousness. She needed more help than he could give right now, so he opened his kennis briefly, saw how Jye-Tan had bridged the obstruction across shields, and did the same, contacting Xeffeya. The kennis chaos returned, and he almost lost his hold on the fragment. What had Doj done with the nodes? All their buzzing had echoes, but this was impossible to control.

Kuyi stirred, but didn't open her eyes. She recognized

his touch, though, and was grateful for his rescue. Then she realized what he'd done, and he saw her disappointment that he'd chosen this path. He quickly withdrew before his doubts returned.

53. Diversion

Aderen was here, and he was using the fragment again. She'd failed. She was as disappointed in herself as in him.

Lying on the ground in pain, forgotten by the vekorna, Kuyi tried to assess the damage to her body. It was too much for her kennis to remedy quickly. She couldn't see clearly, so she kept her eyes closed, concentrating on other senses.

There was motion all around, breaking branches, and heavy footsteps. Dairnehy's voice had lost interest, leaving her mind. She felt her belly. What did he mean by an unborn child? What did he know that she didn't? It wasn't supposed to be possible, but what if it was? Had her body been grown defective, too, like Jye-Tan and Mai, allowing her to conceive despite Nalimai's precautions? Admittedly, she hadn't drunk the serum for some time, but the effect should have been permanent by now.

"Kuyi," Étar buzzed. "Stay with me. I can help you get out if you follow my instructions. Aderen is there, but I don't know if he'll be strong enough, after being trapped in mirror crystals for so long."

Kuyi nodded her head, which made her dizzy, and repeated the motion within her kennis. He was strong enough, using the fragment. Her sonic disrupters hadn't damaged it at all.

"I see outside the shield," she said, still dazed, and wondering if she was dreaming. It looked like she was flying a fighter.

Doj had news from within Bol, but she couldn't focus on siims right now. She had to fly the fighter.

"Tararnifal said you needed help," buzzed Ret. "I can't take credit for the fleet beyond the shield, but I'll do what I can."

Ah, so it was Ret fighting, and Kuyi was seeing his point of view. That made more sense. She laid her head back on the ground, resting a moment.

"Stay out of the fight!" Sarenie yelled. It was a good idea. Kuyi had to get out of the line of fire.

"I'll fight for any humans Dairnehy has locked up inside that shield," Ret said. "I love you and will see you later."

He loved her, and was coming for her. That was good. But he wasn't Étar. That was Ret. What applied to him also applied to her. She had to get Jye-Tan and Aneya out of here.

Xeffeya intruded into her thoughts, showing her how to use the kennis in an emergency mode, instructing it to clear her mind, alleviate the signs of concussion so she could stand. Jye-Tan was still kneeling over Aneya, who looked very bad, crumpled up against a broken tree.

"Can you help her?" he asked, looking longingly at Aderen and Dairnehy, joined together by the fragment in the vekornan's arms.

Kuyi asked Étar, who in turn asked who had Aneya's kennis override. Kuyi didn't know, but helped Jye-Tan lay their aunt flat on the ground. "Activate healing on your kennis," Kuyi murmured, then buzzed Aneya for good measure. She listened for breathing, found it shallow. Aneya groaned when she pressed on her chest.

"She probably has broken ribs, the way she was

thrown," Étar said, as Xeffeya used her doctor's emergency override. "The kennis can only do so much. You'll have to get her back here." He paused. "I've made a mess of the medical ward, though, assuming we would never get a chance to come back."

Kuyi wondered what he meant, but didn't ask. Ret's vision overwhelmed her again, and she couldn't focus on how to reduce its impact. She saw extars attacking the shield around Rubiel. Ret was screaming at someone, presumably Samlar. "You can't win against five-to-one odds. Get closer to the city and force the kolbs to defend themselves, too."

One of the extars ahead was damaged and started listing to the side. The sky was suddenly swarming with shuttles and fighters. Kuyi had no trouble getting a lock.

She didn't fire, though, and wondered why. Her head swayed, and she was thankful that she was already on her knees.

"Finally," Ret muttered, and she remembered she wasn't flying a fighter, but inside the shield, safe.

"Are you still in the vekornan computers?" Kuyi asked. "Can you let Ret inside the shield?"

Jye-Tan shook his head. "Not without touching the fragment." He was split between stroking Aneya's face and watching the fragment, only a few steps away. "I don't know why it's so much more complicated than at Bol."

"Maybe because Dairnehy is much more paranoid. The kennis are reaching across shields again, though."

"I used the fragment," Jye-Tan said. "I think Aderen is doing the same. I don't think it'll hold if he lets go." He ran a finger across Aneya's cheek.

"Do you think Dairnehy is too strong for Aderen?"

"Vekorna can't do what humans can with the fragment. I could hold them still like Kirina and Aderen, but not for long. Dairnehy can read our minds, but he can't control our brain functions."

"He can't turn us into puppets or slaves," she murmured. She would warn Jye-Tan against using that power.

She watched a mixed group of extars, shuttles and fighters fly as a mass against Rubiel's shield, flocking over it like birds, illuminating the surface with their lasers.

Two extars were hit and fell, disintegrating into the ocean.

"Watch your back," buzzed Sarenie. Kuyi glanced over her shoulder. Her gaze took in the two dead vekorna –Kular and Sebenet. She wasn't safe, even on the other side of the shield from the fighting. Aderen wanted them to leave, and she agreed.

Ret checked his back, too, and she saw more fighters streaming toward him. Sarenie and Étar were talking, but she managed to shut them out.

"Ontral sent shuttles to Rubiel," buzzed Doj, probably talking to Ret. Why was everything so open right now? It didn't make sense.

"That won't make much difference in the fight," said Étar.

"He's more likely spying," Doj replied, and Kuyi agreed. It was more like Ontral to stay out of the fight and watch for whoever was victorious.

She looked at the single sonic disrupter in her hand. Dairnehy had been the victor in the garden.

"You were trying to destroy the fragment, weren't you?" asked Jye-Tan.

Kuyi nodded.

"Both of you? That's why you let me come in here?"

"Yes, I'm sorry we couldn't tell you."

Jye-Tan frowned. "It didn't work, though."

"We didn't have enough time to see if it would work. This thing cracked Dairnehy's faceplate, though."

"Ret just shot down a kolb shuttle," said Jye-Tan, changing the subject.

She stood, watching Aderen. They had to get out of here. Aneya opened her eyes as Kuyi and Jye-Tan lifted her, moaning as her feet scrambled to gain purchase. Kuyi was relieved she wasn't screaming, and thanked their kennis implants, and Xeffeya's help.

They walked around Tararnifal and Dairnehy, Aderen stretched to touch the fragment in his arms. She tore her gaze away from them as she guided her family to the edge of the clearing.

They stopped suddenly on seeing the crowd of vekorna guarding the garden. They would never escape like this.

"He's frozen them," Jye-Tan said, and she noticed the way they were prostrated at the edge of the grove, bowed down as if honoring them.

Aneya tumbled back to the ground as Kuyi let go of her aunt, shaking her head, hands to her mouth, mumbling incoherently. Aderen would have all their strings if he continued this way.

*   *   *

Aderen reached for Dairnehy's mind, seizing it. There was no need for surgical control; the vekorna had no influence over him. He froze Dairnehy's motor control just as Kuyi's emotions flowed over him, weakening his resolve enough for Dairnehy to enter his thoughts again. What if his self-analysis was biased, and he missed a way vekorna could dive into his mind?

I see your betrayal, your desire to seize everything from me. Tararnifal calls it paranoia, but it's not paranoia if it's true. You turned my prin-el against me and freed Danosh. He is as good as dead, his artificial limbs removed once again.

Aderen reached out for Danosh, but Dairnehy blocked him.

I have known of Tararnifal's true loyalties from the start, yet he did everything I asked of him. He is not yours, is of no use to you or the other humans. He wishes to rescue Danosh, whom he helped capture, but despite the chances I gave him, he did nothing. He is mine.

"Use our strength," Kuyi yelled, not out of forgiveness, but necessity. "Like in the cave."

Aderen reached for Kuyi, then Aneya and Jye-Tan, taking their horror the way Monera had suggested almost a lifetime ago, but also their support. He was distracted by an image of Kirina in the Egalsan minds, but refocused his efforts. Kuyi had done this before, restoring his confidence outside Bol, but the fragment also allowed him easy access to the others.

My connections are my strength, he said, more to himself, but the thought leaked out to Dairnehy. He pushed, the way he'd pushed against Sebenet in the largest mass manipulation of his life. This was harder. The fragment gave Dairnehy huge powers of resistance.

Still, Aderen saw deeper than the vekornan had probably ever allowed anyone to see.

"You don't care about humans at all," he said, the realization hitting him as he saw Dairnehy's thoughts. "We were a means to an end when you sent out the fleets, but since you found the fragment, you've changed. You don't care about human babies! That was just a ruse to keep me off-guard."

Not a ruse, responded Dairnehy. **I will use your abilities to make the winged supreme on Rykol. With the full fragment, I could control you all.**

"The fragment doesn't give you that kind of power. Even if it did, it would take too long, and you never had that kind of patience. Humans grow much more slowly than the seed pods of a vekornan, maturing in decades rather than months."

Then Dairnehy's plans were laid bare to Aderen, and he was disappointed. Control. That's all Dairnehy wanted. Control of Rykol, and of this solar system.

"Is that all you long for?" Aderen mocked. "To wipe out the folems and loboms, to destroy the kolbs, until only winged vekorna remain on Rykol? What then? What are your ambitions? To run the vekorna into the ground serving you as slaves? Bolob had a vision, as did Kopiv before him. Where is your vision?"

He pushed deeper into Dairnehy's mind, but found only hatred. There were no plans beyond control of Rykol. He didn't want to travel the stars to Terra, had no interest in controlling the unpredictable human masses. He would wait for Spall to arrive and claim him as leader.

"You are weak," Aderen said in realization, and he pushed that weakness into Dairnehy's very being. Dairnehy was envious of what Aderen could do that a vekornan could not.

All of Dairnehy's eyestalks extended at once through the three pairs of slits in his faceplate. He lowered the fragment, a movement that Aderen tempered so the vekornan didn't hit him over the head. Aderen bent over and struggled to keep his grip on the fragment.

I am strong. I discovered my own wings, when Bolob and the others had to be shown who they were by others. While they hid their wings out of weakness, I hid mine to better attack my wingless enemies. As tigal-en, I found other winged and awakened them to their genetic superiority. I reached beyond Metik to find Bolob, not the other way around.

Aderen saw that Dairnehy never believed in Bolob's Plan for the secret ascension of the winged. He only wanted power, and to eradicate the wingless. He thought that would trigger his god's return to Rykol.

Vekorna are stronger than humans by our very nature, physically, mentally, in innovation and creativity. We do things you cannot. We have traveled the stars to your homeworld.

"With nothing to show for it," Aderen responded. He took a step backward, hands still on the fragment, and wondered if Dairnehy realized that he was following. It took Aderen two steps for every one of the vekornan's, but they continued to move out of the grove through the wedge-shaped path he'd razed in his hurry to get to the fragment.

I will use the humans retrieved by my second fleet as soldiers, and continue to raid your planet to replenish them until my plans are concluded.

They stopped at the crowd of prostrated vekorna as Aderen considered the veracity of the claim. It went against Dairnehy's core being, but he could act on the threats, if only to spite Aderen. Dairnehy had no patience to wait for

439

humans to be born with Aderen's powers and mature to an age where he could use them effectively, so did he really have the patience to wait another four hundred years to get humans soldiers?

"I don't believe you would do it."

Do you believe that I would send a fleet of extars to bombard your planet and push humanity into extinction?

The image that Dairnehy sent into his mind was so powerful that Aderen withdrew his hands, only for a moment. He was still inside Dairnehy's mind, but lost all control. The vekornan stepped away from him, raising the fragment out of reach.

Even without the fragment, Aderen felt the minds of all the vekorna in Rubiel alerted against them, despite the defense of the city against kolb extars.

Aderen could release the vekorna in the garden to fight for him, but they couldn't hold out against the numbers that would come to Dairnehy's aid from the city. With the large piece of the fragment, he would see into all their minds, weeding out those Aderen had changed.

Help me, Aderen told Tararnifal. Was the vekornan waiting to see who came out of this match victorious? Why did he have no weapon? With the fragment, Dairnehy was too strong, his mind closed to Aderen.

The fragment is only a tool, and can be deflected by another tool, said Tararnifal. **My tools are not strong enough to take advantage of his paranoia.**

He was right. Aderen's tools were more powerful. He just had to find a way to get around the control the fragment gave Dairnehy.

You will not escape, and then I will conquer the

world, Dairnehy exclaimed. **After that I will send fleets to destroy yours.**

The words threatened to overwhelm Aderen, but he'd seen into Dairnehy's mind and knew that they were false.

"In all the time since the fragment was found, you failed to conquer Rykol," Aderen said. He saw the paranoia in Dairnehy's surface thoughts, almost overwhelmed by the confidence the fragment gave.

If he survived long enough to conquer Rykol, Dairnehy would forget about humans, and would certainly lose his motivation for revenge. Aderen tried to push deeper, make the changes necessary, but with the fragment, Dairnehy blocked him.

Something slammed into Dairnehy's back, forcing the winged leader to lower the fragment to the ground, holding it crookedly in three hands. Sebenet held him tight, revived from unconsciousness as both Aderen and Dairnehy were distracted by each other.

In one last desperate lunge, Aderen touched the fragment and poured all of his power into Dairnehy's mind, overwhelmed his blocks, and removed his motivation to go to Terra forever.

You dare to change me? Dairnehy twisted his lower left arm, and aimed his remaining wrist laser behind him, shooting Sebenet in the chest.

Shocked, but still holding the fragment, Aderen halted Dairnehy's motor control as the weapon was pointed at him next. Sebenet fell to the ground, dead.

Another mind surfaced behind them, and Aderen smiled.

"Yes, I changed you. Sebenet finally saw you for who you are, and we're not the only ones to overcome the fear you've instilled in Rubiel."

The grove shook as a giant extar descended to hover above them, dwarfing the garden, the shuttle and the vend'oks.

54. Through the Shield

The control that Dairnehy held over Tararnifal was similar to that with which he'd momentarily controlled Aderen. He used doubts and threats, but more than that, he let Tararnifal hope that he would loosen his control over the winged vekorna.

Tararnifal had helped capture Danosh, but kept a connection with their prisoner. He had not contributed to Danosh's freedom, though. And now Danosh had the automated extar he's brought to Rubiel, come to rescue the humans. It was more than Tararnifal had been able to do. The extar hovered above them, casting a huge shadow over the garden.

A shuttle launched from its forward bay, settling into the garden next to the one Dairnehy had flown here.

Tararnifal hadn't realized until this confrontation how much Dairnehy had delved into his mind, keeping his fears alive. He'd feared to act too soon, so he didn't act at all. He'd squandered his one chance in the brief fight that had killed Kular and maimed Sebenet. Yet even Sebenet, who sought to gain Dairnehy's trust, had finally seen the injustices their leader was exhibiting. His actions had given Aderen the edge by lowering the fragment to his level.

Now Tararnifal could take the fragment away from Dairnehy, to kill the vekornan leader, but again he did nothing, watching Sebenet's dead body fall to the ground with a thump.

Tararnifal had ignored the dropped blaster as he

followed them out of the grove –was that Dairnehy's influence? He couldn't control Tararnifal with the crystal, but was clouding his thoughts.

All nearby vekorna were kneeling on their weapons, making them useless. Dairnehy held the only weapon, and it was now pointed at Aderen. All Dairnehy needed was a moment of telepathic control to trigger it. A wrist laser would not kill Aderen, but might make him weak for a moment, which was all Dairnehy would need.

Help us escape, came the voice into his mind, vekornan, and in more pain than he'd ever felt from one of his kind. Danosh's intrusion broke the spell. Tararnifal launched himself into the air, wings spreading to pull him forward as his four lower limbs flexed to give him the speed he needed.

They both toppled to the ground with a loud thud. Tararnifal struggled to hold the wrist laser pointed away as Dairnehy fought to throw him off. Aderen was thrown clear as the fragment landed with another thud beside them.

Tararnifal was aware of Jye-Tan running to the fragment, Aneya calling for him to stop, Kuyi trying to hold him back.

"Get out of here," called Aderen. They would abandon him, and it would be an acceptable loss.

Come quickly to the extar, said Danosh in a general call. **Shuttles have launched from the city and will be here soon. The city's defenses are being rerouted in this direction. You already know that they can destroy an extar.**

An unfamiliar touch came into Tararnifal's mind. From the sudden start Dairnehy gave, Jye-Tan had entered his thoughts, too.

Dairnehy continued his push before Tararnifal recovered, forcing them onto their sides. Tararnifal grappled with the vekornan leader, in a rare display of hand-to-hand combat. Having watched humans fight with lobomai techniques, Tararnifal thought he might have an advantage.

With two eyestalks, Tararnifal saw Jye-Tan close his eyes, both hands on the fragment, while Kuyi held Aneya upright nearby. Dairnehy struggled to aim his wrist laser at the young human. Aneya pushed away from Kuyi with unusual strength, throwing her to one side, knocking Jye-Tan to the other, breaking his contact with the fragment.

Jye-Tan fell to the ground, but Aneya was hit by three shots from Dairnehy's wrist laser before she landed. In her current condition, even if the laser strikes weren't fatal, she would need serious treatment.

Dairnehy turned his attention again to Tararnifal, aiming a laser at his chest, the deep housing for his precious brain. One shot would be deadly.

Then Dairnehy relaxed, his arms falling to the ground.

"Come on," said Aderen, removing his hands from the fragment, and helping Jye-Tan to his feet. "We have to get out of here."

Tararnifal stood up and looked to the quiescent wrist laser, grabbing the fragment instead. It was heavy enough that he needed four arms while moving. He paused a moment as the thoughts around the garden were opened to him. No wonder Dairnehy was willing to risk everything for this, he thought. He could see into Danosh's mind easily, all the secrets the exiled vekornan wished to hide. He saw the audacity of Kuyi and Aneya, who had planned to destroy the fragment, probably the only sensible thing given their fears. He saw Samlar, forces joined with the kolbs, evading attacks from Rubiel defenses. Aderen's mind was open to him, all the doubts that Dairnehy had spoken about, but he didn't have time to push deeper.

Sebenet was dead from a final moment of devotion to Aderen, maybe some residual effect from his alteration in Terran orbit. Dairnehy wasn't dead. Aderen had used the distractions to freeze him physically, but it wouldn't last. He should have gone for the laser first, but the choice was made.

Hoisting the heavy fragment into the air, Tararnifal walked around the genuflected vekorna, toward the newly-arrived shuttle.

Pinoa ran down the ramp to help lift Aneya from the ground. Aneya had been hit in the chest, the side and the back, probably in sequence as she spun while falling. Her lungs would be affected, her blood flow slowed, in addition to her many other injuries. Tararnifal hoped her kennis was automatically making the proper adjustments.

Étar was impatiently watching from the controls as Kuyi ran on board, hugging him.

"The extar can't land here," Pinoa said, returning with Aneya. "We need to fly. Quickly!"

Lay Aneya down and strap her in for liftoff, Tararnifal said. **It's too late for Danosh to open the shuttlebay.** He extended several eyestalks to point behind the extar; Weapons fire was already scorching the ground around the garden.

Tararnifal didn't want to release the fragment, but somebody had to ensure the shuttle would reach the extar tantalizingly close above them. Étar and Pinoa had this one under control, but it wouldn't be enough to ward off the forces from Rubiel.

Take this, he said to Aderen, opening the fold in his armor and letting the small shard fall into the man's hand. Aderen looked at him with raised eyebrows, but remained silent.

Tararnifal hoisted the fragment to his chest, pausing again to marvel at the way the world was open to him, and motioned to the only other shuttle sitting in the garden. **I will cover you from there.**

He ran to Dairnehy's shuttle. Setting the fragment on the floor between his lower legs, Tararnifal powered it up and followed Étar into the air, scattering their attackers as he opened fire.

How will we leave the city? Tararnifal asked Danosh.

Punad helped me escape and sabotaged the capture field outside the city. He will be ready to open the shield. Can you contact him directly with the fragment?

Tararnifal put one of his lower hands to the fragment and made contact. The extar temporarily sheltered the two shuttles from Rubiel's defenders, but that wouldn't last. Speed was their best defense, now. Punad made sure the large batteries would not target them, but they needed time to get inside the extar.

Below, Tararnifal saw Dairnehy regaining his feet and making his way to the remaining vend'ok.

We should have killed him, he said, reaching Aderen's mind in the other shuttle.

I'm not a murderer, and it wasn't necessary. I got what I came here for.

Not everything, Tararnifal responded. **I should have done it.**

You still fear Dairnehy, as do all the winged vekorna

in Rubiel. I don't think you could do it. After a moment's pause, Aderen added, **Now you're free of his influence.** Tararnifal didn't feel different, but knew Aderen had made a change in the threads of his mind.

They rose higher into the sky, leaving the garden and Rubiel behind. The extar huddled over them as they moved south-west, where the shield wasn't so far away.

Tararnifal's sensors showed a small opening, and the three craft moved through it into the desert. Unfortunately, the shield didn't close, allowing their pursuers through, too.

His holographic screens activated suddenly as they joined the fray of kolbs, Samlar's forces, and Rubiel's defenders. The huge batteries lit up the sky around them.

Punad is dead, Tararnifal said. **Dairnehy has retaken control of Rubiel.**

*   *   *

An unfamiliar face popped up on the hologram of Étar's palette as they flew through the shield. Kuyi wouldn't let him get more than arm's length away from her, though she refrained from disrupting his movements on the invisible controls.

"Étar! I have your back. Follow me."

A big smile lit up Étar's face at Ret's words. Kuyi was momentarily jealous, but shuttered those thoughts. Étar had other friends, but what he shared with her could never be taken away.

Now that they were outside the shield, the kennis had stabilized. Ret's intimate connection had stopped suddenly when Aderen released the fragment, but he was now talking with Étar through his palette. She listened through her ears, not her mind, a refreshing change.

She could no longer reach Doj, Sarenie or Xeffeya in

Bol, and assumed Jye-Tan was right; the connection had only been opened through their use of the fragment.

"We're coming out hot!" Étar responded.

Activating a threat display in another frame of his palette, Étar identified their two shuttles and Danosh's extar, which were being pressed against Rubiel's shield. Ret's fighter was just below them, firing on another shuttle. Kuyi couldn't tell which ones belonged to Rubiel, Samlar or the kolbs.

"Go for higher altitude. If you stay here, you'll be hit by Rubiel's guns in a matter of seconds. What have you got that Dairnehy is so keen on keeping you? Is it his piece of the stellar fragment?"

"The fragment is with Tararnifal in the other shuttle," Étar buzzed, dropping in altitude as their attackers pressed them.

"We can't let Dairnehy have it," Étar continued. "Give us enough space to enter the extar's shuttlebay. I have a full complement of survivors here."

"Understood."

Étar couldn't fight offensively with the passengers they carried. Was this shuttle more important than Tararnifal's? Would he save her or the fragment? She thought Ret would choose to save his friends.

Kuyi knew this was her fault. She'd planned to destroy the fragment. She should have boarded Tararnifal's shuttle, taken all of Aneya's sonic disrupters and finished the job they'd barely had time to start.

Rising back into the protective shadow of Danosh's extar, Étar buzzed, "It was nice of the kolbs to send a distraction outside the shield. It allowed us time to escape."

"I was against the idea at first," Ret buzzed.

"What happens to the extars, now, and the fragment?"

"I don't know about the extars, but the farther we can get the fragment from Dairnehy, the better. I was experimenting with the piece the kolbs have, and it's scary."

"How so?" Étar buzzed.

"Too much temptation, and way too addictive. I'll tell you more when we get out of here."

Kuyi stared at him in awe. If he shared her conclusions, would he help her destroy the remaining pieces?

Étar concentrated on evading his attackers. Too many of Rubiel's shuttles were getting through, and Danosh wouldn't open the shuttlebay while under attack. He was as much a target as they were.

"That's the problem Ret had with the kolbs when he was hit as we arrived in orbit," Étar said, pointing at the fighters that were harassing them. "If Danosh opens the shuttlebay, their fighters can get inside just as easily as we can, and cause terrible damage. We need more altitude."

Samlar's extar was rising to join them. Ret fired on a shuttle that had locked onto theirs, and it broke off. Étar kept them moving. Tararnifal's shuttle was rising faster, firing on everything around him. It was an impressive sight.

"I just hope Punad's sabotage is hard to fix, so we're not immobilized by their capture screen." She'd heard about the extar that had been caught and held as Rubiel's lasers fired on it, unable to take evasive action. Dairnehy wouldn't destroy them, though, not while they had the fragment.

This was much worse than the brief firefight against with winged forces north of Esetek, which was Kuyi's first. She was frozen in place, as much as if Aderen had frozen her muscles. She looked back at him. He was strapped into one of the side benches, eyes closed, beside Jye-Tan and Aneya, who was hunched over unnaturally. She'd vomited onto the floor, and Kuyi suddenly noticed the smell.

Shuttles were veering away from them. As much as she was against Aderen using vekorna and kolbs this way, Kuyi was grateful for his influence. She wondered if Tararnifal could be directing the enemy pilots through the fragment. Had he seen into *her* mind?

"You're clear," said Aderen. "Get inside now."

The two shuttles and Ret's fighter were sandwiched between Danosh and Samlar's extars. There were no enemy fighters.

Opening the shuttlebay, came Danosh's voice.

She saw the white opening against the darkness under Danosh's extar, but it was too small, only a thin line, before it closed again.

"What's going on?" Étar shouted.

Another wave of shuttles was on them, racing in from behind, all weapons blazing. The shuttle rocked as they were hit. Aderen waved his arms, and the attackers broke off, but their shuttle had already drifted away from the shuttlebay.

"We'll go to the forward bay," Étar said. "Meet us there."

I cannot risk opening the shuttlebay doors with this many attackers, Danosh's voice came into Kuyi's mind. **Cover our front and I will open the shielded maw of the extar and catch the shuttles there.**

More fighters found their way between the two extars, all coming from behind. Étar was already moving between the two control spheres, where the front of the extar could open. Unlike the shuttlebays, this opening was protected by a particle shield, used to deflect stray pieces when the vekorna were collecting things like fragments of their star. There were other risks associated with this technique.

Ret hung back to dissuade their pursuers, and with Aderen's help, they were not hit again.

"There," Kuyi pointed. The maw was opening, something they didn't normally do in an atmosphere. The extar started buffeting, making Étar's job more difficult as they both danced around.

"That's how they captured *Avenger* and the other original fleets from Terran orbit," Ret buzzed. "Looks like there aren't enough vekorna on board to keep it stable."

"Could Danosh be flying it alone?" Étar asked.

"Tararnifal had this one automated when he went to Rubiel. Get inside, and I'll cover you."

"This time, we go together."

"You got it."

Étar, Tararnifal and Ret positioned themselves in front of the open maw, and reduced power so the extar could scoop them up. Suddenly four fighters swept in from the side, firing a maelstrom of lasers and projectiles. Ret's fighter jerked, and Aderen cried out. Kuyi clutched at Étar's arm as he swore.

She saw Tararnifal's shuttle hit and start to dive.

Étar grabbed her and dropped her to the floor in a perfectly executed lobomai technique, just as an enemy fighter glanced against the front of their shuttle. The explosion threw them backward, and she felt the air rushing by as it abandoned them through a gaping hole.

Étar held her tight, but his hold grew weaker as they struggled to stay conscious.

*   *   *

Unable to maintain control of his shuttle, Tararnifal used the fragment to hide his mind as it dove. Étar's shuttle had been hit as well, but he saw it and Ret's fighter get swept into the maw of Danosh's extar.

"Étar, are you there? Étar!" came Ret's voice. Tararnifal was still receiving communications, but could no longer transmit, could no longer fight.

"We will guide you out of here," said Samlar. "My fighters will find Tararnifal."

The fighters would be too late. Tararnifal decided that Kuyi and Aneya had the right idea. He'd seen what the fragment did to Dairnehy, and what Aderen could do with it. He knew Kuyi's fear at what she'd seen at Bol. The temptation was too great for misuse. He poured more power into the shuttle engines, diving straight for the ground outside Rubiel's shield.

Hiding his mind with the fragment hindered his tigal-en senses, the opposite of what he'd achieved in the garden. He relied on the shuttle's sensors to watch for pursuit. Rubiel's forces followed the extars higher.

Focused above, he wasn't expecting an attack from below. As Samlar's fighters were entangled with Rubiel's defenders, three shuttles rose from the ground to quickly destroy his engines and harness his shuttle, bringing it to an abrupt stop. They lowered him slowly to the desert sands.

The best way to destroy the fragment was to resist, and force his shuttle to be destroyed. Dairnehy would not get the fragment. But even as he had this thought, the ramp to his shuttle exploded inward, and he was surrounded.

Unveiling himself in the fragment, Tararnifal stretched out. He could still detect Samlar's fighters, and with the fragment he could see Samlar, now safely in orbit.

Dairnehy has recaptured me, but I will not go back to his cells, he called. More vekorna came to the front of the shuttle and touched the fragment, easily removing his hands. He was hidden again, by vekorna who knew how to use it. Dairnehy would never teach his people to use the fragment. These were not his troops.

You are winged, one of the vekorna said.

You are wingless! Tararnifal answered, shocked. What had they hoped to gain by coming to Rubiel? Feeling the power of the fragment that they were using to hide his awareness, Tararnifal realized he already knew the answer.

The fragment will be safe at Bol, the vekornan said. **You will come with us. Fusing this piece of the fragment with Ontral's, we will be the most powerful vekorna on Rykol.**

55. Memories of Rykol 8

Watching Kuyi in the medical bed, Aderen was content with what he'd achieved at Rubiel, but disappointed he hadn't had the chance to go farther. Thanks to Sebenet's sudden discontent, or some lingering loyalty to Tararnifal, he'd managed to execute the first half of their mission. Dairnehy would not go to Terra. But the larger problem remained. They'd wanted to get Doj and Penagel into a birth chamber, to program pre-matured vekorna into ignoring Terra altogether.

But wasn't that the same as what Dairnehy had done to Nalimai to create Kirina's mental abilities, and what he wanted to do with Kuyi's unborn child, now lost? Wasn't that what Kopiv did to his mother to create him? Did they have the right to impose their will on maturing vekorna like that, before they even entered the world?

That's what the wingless were fighting against –genetic programming to ensure only winged vekorna were matured. Why shouldn't all vekorna object to Aderen's mission?

Jye-Tan had tasted too much power. Now sitting at Kuyi's bedside, refusing to leave, he blamed himself. It wasn't his fault, though. The fault lay entirely with Aderen.

"She's waking up!" Jye-Tan said, and all eyes turned toward the young woman. Her kennis had repaired what it could, and the medical bed and tools had done the rest.

If it hadn't been for Ret, the only human to survive the battle unscathed, they would all be dead. Ret should have blamed him for Étar's death, but somehow he didn't. Aderen didn't press for reasons, but didn't avoid him, either. The looks that Ret gave him were different from before he'd been captured by the kolbs.

"Don't try to sit up," Jye-Tan said. Kuyi winced as she ignored him.

She caught sight of Aderen, Pinoa and Ret. "Étar?" she asked, eyebrows raised hopefully.

Aderen shook his head, sadly. "He took the brunt of the blast, shielding you."

"Aneya died, too," Jye-Tan said, tears in his eyes. "She died because of me, just like Gavet died the last time we escaped from Rubiel."

"There's a lot of blame to go around," said Aderen. "But what happened is not your fault." To Kuyi, he emphasized what he knew of her guilt, from the brief moments he'd seen inside her mind when touching the fragment. "You were right to try and destroy the fragment. I should have chosen that path, too, and the others could have supported you."

"I should have told you," she said. "But I didn't think you would agree."

"I probably wouldn't have. You did everything right."

Ret stepped in front of them. "Let her grieve, for Étar and her aunt." Aderen nodded and stepped back.

"I want to know what happened, though," Kuyi protested. She put a hand on her belly. "Am I really pregnant?"

Ret lowered his eyes and shook his head. "You were already weak from the fight in the garden. It didn't survive the blast." He was almost in tears himself, and Kuyi started bawling. Not only had she lost her lover, but the part of Étar that he'd left with her hadn't survived, either.

When their crying subsided, Ret said, "One of Rubiel's fighters was hit, and it collided with your shuttle." He sat at her side, brushing hair from her face. "I didn't get to it in time. I'm sorry."

Aderen hadn't caught it in time, either. Concentrating on the myriad fighters behind them, deflecting their minds away without doing permanent damage, he'd neglected the forward space, assuming the extars would cover them. Clearly, he had been too selective about his targets.

"Étar was my best friend, and he saw it coming," Ret continued. "He threw his body on top of yours, and held on as you were both thrown back. We couldn't keep him alive. You were very special to him, which makes you special to me, too."

"Aneya was caught in the explosion, too," Jye-Tan said, his eyes once again wet with unshed tears. "She never had a chance." He paused, emotions threatening to overwhelm him again. "Aderen and I were lucky; we're already healed. I had a piece of metal embedded in my arm, but Ret got it out with the help of a bed just like this one."

"Xeffeya insisted on these medical beds before we left Terra," said Ret. "She's been guiding me on how to heal you." He unconsciously tapped his temple, where the kennis implant was located.

"What about the fragment?" Kuyi asked, wincing as she coughed. "Did Tararnifal destroy it?"

Aderen dropped his eyes. "Tararnifal was recaptured. Dairnehy has the fragment again."

Kuyi flopped back down on the bed. "That's terrible."

"Maybe," said Aderen. "Or maybe not. The vekorna can't do what humans can with the fragment. It might be better off separated amongst the three major powers here."

"There will be time to think about that later," said Ret. "Now, she needs to rest." To Kuyi's continued protests, Ret said, "I'll stay to answer any questions you have, the way Étar would have done. I can talk about Étar, too, his life and the kind of person he was."

Kuyi nodded tentatively, eyes on Ret.

*   *   *

"Come with me," said Aderen as he led Pinoa and Jye-Tan out of the room. "Doj is adamant that I see an old memory the folems found."

"Why? What is it?" Pinoa asked.

"I think it's a memory about the siims and goses."

"Like your other visions?"

Nodding, Aderen said, "This may be why the folems wanted me in the Memory Caves when I arrived."

"Why are they so interested in your visions? Didn't the siims commit racial suicide generations ago?"

Aderen had shared all the memories he'd recorded on his kennis with the others, except the last one. "Maybe not.

You've seen the memory where Bolob watched the siims destroy their city, themselves and the goses."

Pinoa nodded. "The folems showed it to your parents before sending them to Sumo crater."

"I saw the same memory from *inside* the shield, but the goses flew through an escape tunnel, carrying siims with them. The tunnel was sealed before the explosion. I don't think they were all killed."

"Interesting, but why do we care?" Pinoa asked.

"I don't know yet, but the memory is my father's." Pinoa looked at him sideways. It couldn't be a vision, could it?

They stood in one of the human common rooms, walls painted with murals. Aderen wondered what the kolbs would do to the artwork when they finally claimed this extar. It was on loan to Samlar so Kuyi could recover, thanks to Ret's agreement with the kolbs. Sarenie was already impressed and eagerly awaiting his return to Bol.

Kennis signals still couldn't cross Rykolien shields, but Doj had managed to pass a weak beam through the single interrupter left at Kirina's refuge. The orbital node boosted the signal, though the quality remained poor.

Aderen raised a hologram on his palette.

Egalinsor and Nalimai stood beside Doj and Penagel. Nalimai refused to look in Aderen's eyes, and he didn't blame her. His apologies would never be enough.

"Thanks for doing this now," said Doj. "I know it's not a good time, but the folems won't let you back in Bol, so there may never be a better one."

"Why is this so important?" Aderen asked. "I never made it to the Memory Caves. What do the folems want me to see so badly?"

Egalinsor shook his head. In the hologram, he didn't seem any larger than the others. "The folems will never forgive what you did, but they are still interested in siims and goses."

"Why so much fuss over extinct races?" He thought again of the goses tunnel in his last vision.

"I asked them the same question a long time ago, when they sent us to Sumo crater to search for siim genetic material. We barely found anything, and it wasn't worth the price we paid for it."

He hugged Nalimai around the shoulder. That was the mission where she'd lost an arm and a leg, and where Danosh lost two arms.

"However, it seems that our mission to Sumo wasn't the failure we thought it was. Before he left Rykol, Jairon shared some of his experiences with the folems. Nobody was aware of the suppressed memory." Not a vision, then.

"He wasn't keeping it a secret," buzzed Penagel. "He honestly didn't know. We stayed with them for three days as they found us a new shuttle to escape with."

"What are you saying?" Aderen asked. "That the siims are still alive, and they erased your memories?"

Egalinsor nodded, grabbing Nalimai's hand. "The folems called us to the Memory Caves, where we saw Jairon's memory. It released the block on all three of us. We now remember the truth —the siims and goses survived!"

Jye-Tan's eyes opened wide, and Aderen looked to him, frowning.

"Why is this important?" Aderen asked. "What am I missing?" Was it that Ontral had allowed them freedom to travel to the Memory Caves?

"The siims are like you," Doj buzzed. "They added memory blocks and created new memories to replace them. But more importantly –"

"Dairnehy didn't see them with the stellar fragment!" Jye-Tan exclaimed.

"We could see vekornan, folem and loboms minds all over Rykol, and we found out about the hidden kolbs," buzzed Egalinsor, nodding. "Siims remained hidden."

"Show me," Aderen said, hoping this piece would complete the saga of the siims and goses, even if he didn't understand what it meant. Were the folems sending him visions so he could search for them? That wasn't his mission.

Doj sent his recording of the memory globe to the kennis node. Aside from the occasional fuzziness, it was as real as any of his visions. They stood at the cliff-edge of a giant depression, sparse desert grasses behind them. There would be no thick, sad voice this time.

"Sumo crater," Doj buzzed. Aderen saw smoke, and vekorna and humans running from a crashed shuttle.

Penagel was there, directly in front of him, but much younger. A blonde woman ran beside him, hair matted to her face. His mother. He almost reached out for her, heart aching. He also recognized Egalinsor and Nalimai, who ran as easily as the others, which meant this was before the accident.

The viewpoint dropped, and suddenly everyone was sliding down the edge of the crater wall, bumping and tumbling on the rough terrain. The group must have been in bad shape when they got to the bottom, but fear drove them to get up and run along the inner edge of the crater.

"I remember this clearly," Nalimai buzzed. "A kolb

terebar shuttle shot us down, but my memory was of fixing our shuttle and getting away after the kolbs left."

"The shuttle looks like it was destroyed, to me," buzzed Jye-Tan. Nalimai nodded.

They made it inside a large cave. Aderen turned with the viewpoint as he heard the spitting of laser fire, releasing mounds of earth and rocks that crashed down from above, collapsing the entrance.

His eyes adjusted quickly to the darkness, the cave emitting a faint glow much like the wanlight of Bol's dome. His father and the young Nalimai lit small lamps, pushing the darkness away.

Aderen watched from Jairon's point of view, his mother checking a bloody gash on his leg, without the emotions a real memory globe would add. Were they in love at this point in their journey? he wondered. Young Penagel was on his right with Kezim, examining the rockslide. The younger Egalinsor was sitting with Nalimai, checking for scrapes.

Above the excited human chatter, Jairon suddenly perked up and asked, "What's that?"

Aderen heard the sound of wings in the darkness beyond their faint illumination.

Vekorna rushed toward them, erect on two legs. "There is a tunnel, and something is coming." The speaker had to be Bolob. Aderen owed him his life, as did all Terrans.

Everyone moved to the side walls, and the viewpoint shifted toward the dark tunnel.

A roar of air passed into the cave, barreling over them. It tore at Kym's hair, and whipped Egalinsor's hood from his head. Aderen immediately identified it as a goses, thanks to his visions.

It was shaped like a flat muscle, widening in the middle,

thinning out near the edges, becoming feet in six points, on which it landed easily. Its yellow beak sat beneath two giant black hemispherical eyes, a white split in the center.

Penagel backed up instinctively, but the young Egalinsor approached, saying, "A goses."

Something black wriggled on the base of its long neck.

"We thought it was a rokel," the current Penagel buzzed. In the memory, Kezim made a similar comment.

"No, Kezim," said Bolob, walking up to the massive creature. "Look closely. Look at the color, and listen for its mental imprint."

"A siim?" Kezim asked, his mouth going wide.

Aderen expected that this was the moment Penagel, Egalinsor and Nalimai's mental blocks had shattered in the Memory Caves. He wondered if that's what happened to Sebenet when he met with Dairnehy. Like the siims, he'd never given Sebenet the chance to reconcile conflicting instructions, a puppet with free will except for that one string.

Where vekorna were blue and kolbs yellow, the siim was black, wearing red armor. Its sensor head was more spherical than that of the vekorna, like what he'd seen in his visions.

Despite himself, Aderen was fascinated. Penagel, Egalinsor and Nalimai had encountered siims and goses, and forgot all about it. How would his parents react if they could know?

"You are Bolob," said the siim.

"Yes," Bolob responded.

"You should not be here." The siim put one hand on the neck of the giant goses. "Yet the folems sent you. Interesting. I thought we were protected here against their pollen."

"It is meant to get everywhere," said another vekornan.

"That's Danosh," Penagel explained. The vekornan's memory blocks were likely still in place. Although he was aboard this extar, Aderen had no inclination to show him the truth.

Bolob stood in front of the goses and removed his faceplate, revealing the five-sided sensor head beneath. He extended several eyestalks, all drawn to the big black eyes.

Bolob raised his arms toward the massive creature, and said, "Thof."

"The last time you saw them, you were not able to touch the goses," said the siim. "This time you may."

Bolob stepped closer and removed his glove. He touched the goses for a few seconds, then withdrew.

Doj buzzed, "Bolob's memory of the time he helped the siims escape Metik had also been blocked, and was being restored here."

"You are not Flaorniti," said Bolob in his soft voice. "Is he here? Did he survive the explosion?"

"Flaorniti is long dead," said the siim, with a slight twitter, as if he was amused. "I am Megas. It has been three generations since the Kagmilatkra."

"The explosion that shook the world," whispered young Egalinsor.

"Yes, it did indeed shake the world. That was something we had not expected." But the goses had, Aderen knew from his visions. So had Persinjali.

"It threw the world into chaos!" another vekornan said forcefully.

"I do not think the world could become more chaotic than it already was. But the sympathy Bolob showed us developed into something more, and he brought peace to the world, for a time."

"Not peace," said Bolob.

"Unfortunately, it is not time for Rykol to know of our survival," said Megas. "You must be forced to forget us once again."

The memory faded as more goses arrived, and everyone went flying through the tunnel on their backs.

"This is as far as the memory goes," buzzed Egalinsor. "When we left the crater, none of us remembered our encounter with the siims and goses. But we do now."

Nalimai hugged him. "I remember their underground city, and their genetics machines."

Penagel nodded. "They were trying to save the goses."

"From what?" Pinoa asked.

"From extinction," said Egalinsor. "We helped stabilize a goses birth chamber, but there were other complications. They may all be dead by now."

Aderen hesitated. "Every time I've had a vision, it was accompanied by a voice in my head." Nalimai looked at him suspiciously. "I didn't know what motive somebody could have for sending me these visions. I think it was a goses. They want me to find them, maybe even to save them. That wasn't my mission, which has to come first. Find Mai. I sent her to speak with the loboms, hoping they can shed some light on this."

Their mission was a lot more difficult if he was adamant about not forcing a false memory of Terra on unmatured vekorna. They had to find another way to complete it.

"I need to think," he said. "The voice seemed lethargic, but the message was urgent. Maybe I can send Ketaris or Illian to search for the siims, but if we expose them while

Dairnehy has a large part of the fragment, it could put them in more danger."

They needed a new strategy. Rykol was too unstable for any solution to last without a little more interference.

"Whichever path we take, I can't do it alone," he said. "First, I need to find Kirina."

Egalinsor and Nalimai nodded. "I'll clear it with the folems. Bring our daughter home to us."

Learn more about Rykol and the history of my writing, including articles, maps and backstory by visiting the Rykolien Immigrants page at

World Anvil

Receive free updates directly to your inbox by signing up for my newsletter at

warrendunn.net

Interested in Ret's experience with the
kolbs on the Black Moon?

Check out the novella

CRYSTAL INSIGHTS

By Warren Dunn

which takes place concurrently with this
story.

Coming soon!

Look for the exciting continuation of the

Stellar Fragment Trilogy

with book 2:

SCATTERED DAYS

By Warren Dunn

About the Author

Warren Dunn has been reading, writing and watching science fiction for as long as he can remember. When he was thirteen years old he started creating stories about what would evolve into the  Rykolien Immigrants, and has been revising and expanding them ever since.

He has a Doctorate in Mechanical Engineering and works in the aerospace industry. Warren lives with his wife and two active boys. In addition to writing, he maintains a book and movie review website with a special emphasis on Star Wars, science fiction and fantasy books. He is also a registered author on goodreads, where he has accumulated a significant number of books on his list.

Warren can be reached at
warrendunn.net

Thanks for reading this book. If you enjoyed it, please use your influence on the internet and social media to pass the word along. Marking the book as read on goodreads will raise its visibility, which is essential for independent authors.